The
NATURE
of
REMAINS

GINGER EAGER

A Novel

New Issues Poetry & Prose

Western Michigan University
Kalamazoo, Michigan 49008

First Edition, 2020.

ISBN-13: 978-1-936970-64-3

Library of Congress Cataloging-in-Publication Data:
Eager, Ginger.
The Nature of Remains/Ginger Eager
Library of Congress Control Number: 2018914470

Editor: Nancy Eimers
Managing Editor: Kimberly Kolbe
Layout Editor: Danielle Isaiah
Art Direction: Nick Kuder
Cover Design: Graycen McCee
Production Manager: Paul Sizer
The Design Center, Gwen Frostic School of Art
College of Fine Arts
Western Michigan University

This book is the winner of the Association of Writers & Writing
Programs (AWP) Award for the Novel. AWP is a national, nonprofit
organization dedicated to serving American letters, writers, and
programs of writing.

Go to www.awpwriter.org for more information.

The
NATURE
of
REMAINS

GINGER EAGER

A Novel

NEW ISSUES

 WESTERN MICHIGAN UNIVERSITY

For Momba, Vickie, and Mama T

OROGENY

Georgia breaks in two along the fall line, a geological boundary that marks the shift from the packed red clay of the northern Piedmont to the friable soils of the southern Coastal Plain. Georgia's southern soils are the forgotten floors of past seas. They break easily for spade or shovel, and when cultivating them it is not unusual to unearth the tiny whorls of ancient fossilized sea creatures.

North of the fall line, in the Piedmont, fossils are uncommon. There the soil is the result of weathered crystalline rock. These decaying rocks are older than ocean sands, older than fossilized sea creatures, older than carbon-based life itself. The rocks of the Piedmont were formed during a long-ago mountain making, an orogeny so distant that the mountains themselves, the Appalachians, are now worn short and smooth. Millions of years of erosion have weathered away thousands of feet of stone. Soils as old as these are weary of change—they compact underfoot, resist both hand and plow. Too much has already been asked of them.

But the Piedmont's soils are not without magic. In both moonlight and sunlight, they glitter with the remains of deep earth's ruined crystals: her micas and pyrites, her pulverized quartzes. The hard red clay of north Georgia sparkles in the faintest light and, like the people it supports, hopes that this small display will be enough, hopes that no one will go digging, searching for more.

2009

1

Doreen Swilley walked into her kitchen and found her grown son, Jonathan, passed out at her table. From across the room she smelled him—stale beer, last night's whiskey. He'd left the door to the carport open. She slammed it hard enough to rattle the collectible plates hanging on the wall. He swore, snorted upright. His red curls were slicked flat across his forehead with sweat. "You owe me for the electric," said Doreen. "Air conditioner hasn't cycled off in hours." She went to the coffee pot and measured grounds into a paper filter.

Jonathan stretched his legs into the kitchen. "That pot's got a timer on it, Momma. You can set it before bed. Wake up to fresh hot."

"I know my own coffee pot." She'd asked for the damn thing last year for her birthday, and Jonathan and his family had given it to her. This year she'd asked for nothing, and nothing was what she got: a tuneless round of happy birthday and a check for twenty-five dollars. Jonathan hadn't even been there, just Lexie and the kids. She poured enough water into the reservoir for a full pot. She took the Tylenol from her windowsill, filled a glass with tap water, took these things to her son. "You plan to tell me what has you at my house when you should be heading to work?"

"Me and Lexie need some time apart. She's too haughty to exist beside." Jonathan shook four Tylenol into his palm, chewed them dry. "Sucks up all the air. Makes it so I can't barely breathe."

Marital trouble was what Doreen would have guessed. She'd cared for her grandchildren every Sunday since Lexie started nursing school three years ago, and since winter she'd been helping on Saturdays too, dropping in after breakfast and staying the day. She washed clothes and weeded flowerbeds, oversaw her grandchildren's homework. "You and Lexie can't make it through the work week alone? You need someone to move into your house full time?" She sat across from Jonathan.

"Lexie came after me last night. Hit me in front of the kids."

Doreen checked the soft tissue near Jonathan's eyes, around his lips. She scanned his wrists. She'd seen marks on him in the past months, but only a few and only from fingernails—those streaky scabs she recognized. She'd left them, long ago, on his father. On Lexie she'd spied finger shaped bruises along her upper arms, nothing worse. Jonathan's eyes were bloodshot from liquor, but he had no darkening, no swelling. If Lexie had struck him, it had been with an open palm. "You hit her back?"

"I got her to stop is all."

"That could mean anything."

Jonathan ran a fingernail along a scratch in the table, deepening it. "I need to stay gone for a while. Me and Lexie need time to cool down."

Doreen wanted to ask her son if he'd done his drinking before or after his fight with his wife. She wanted to ask him if it was at home that his wife slapped him, or while they were out in Flyshoals: Viti's Pizza, Mercer's Grocery. She wanted to know what her grandchildren had been witness to, and she wanted to know who else in town might have seen. But such questions would make him stop talking. "This is your home. Always will be. But that doesn't mean you should be here."

"Last time I left her, Lexie came by here to see me every day. We worked things out."

"Juliette was an infant then. Thomas wasn't even born. Lexie herself wasn't but nineteen."

"We're not so changed from then. Me and Lexie."

"Is that so?" Doreen stood to get their coffee. She wouldn't pretend to understand the vagaries of a long marriage. Her relationship with Jonathan's father had been a brief thing, four years and never legalized. Since then she'd been involved only with her boss, Emmanuel "Bird" Marxton. She knew from observing Bird's relationship with his wife that her affair with him was nothing like a marriage. As for Jonathan and Lexie, they shared a sibling-like familiarity mysterious to her. She poured two mugs and brought them to the table.

Jonathan slurped coffee over his tongue, gagged. "I'm gonna have to eat something. I went to Merle's after I left Lexie. Stayed 'til closing."

So the drinking came after the fighting. It was the progression Doreen had hoped for. She checked the time. Close to eight, but Bird only came in two or three days a week now and rarely before eleven. Fifteen years her senior, he'd been more or less retired for a decade. "I have time to make us something."

A familiar tension grew between them. Jonathan was nine the first time he got sent home for defending her honor on the playground, twelve the first time he told her the kids at school were right—she was a whore. Even now, after so much time had passed that everyone in Flyshoals, including Doreen and Bird, mostly overlooked their affair, Jonathan could still grow angry enough about it to pick a fresh fight.

But this morning he reached across the table and took her hand. "Pancakes?"

His calluses were rough against her palm. The strangeness of her boy having grown into a man caught her. Once he'd been a creature entirely in her care. "Get the Bisquick."

He stood to gather ingredients. When he was a child, she'd sometimes come into the kitchen on a weekend morning to find the eggs and the milk, the Bisquick and the butter, lined on the counter—his way of saying, "Please, Momma?" She caught him now in side view as he bent into the fridge. His ears had the same clamshell shape she'd traced with a fingernail when he was a newborn. She'd been so pleased that he'd gotten his father's ears. Her own stuck out. He'd gotten Billy's pale skin too, Billy's red hair. Her own hair was dark, her skin olive.

Jonathan motioned toward the counter where the ingredients were lined. He looked so much like Billy in that moment Doreen turned away. How had she not understood that she found her son beautiful only because he was hers? His father she remembered as an ugly man.

2

Doreen edited paperwork for a new life insurance policy, grateful for the attention the task demanded. When her mind wasn't busy, she thought only of Jonathan and Lexie and all she did not know of their night. Whatever happened was probably worse than Jonathan implied, but it hadn't been bad enough for Lexie to call.

The day was beautiful in a way that seemed impossible after her morning. Clear with a deep blue sky, clouds like a child's drawing. Her desk faced the front door as a receptionist's would, as it had since the day she started working for Bird. Across the front windows Marxton Casualty and Life was written in the curly font Bird's father had chosen when he opened the place after returning from World War II. Doreen thought Bird should change the name—he offered policies of all types—but Bird said that when people in Flyshoals thought insurance, they thought Marxton Casualty and Life. "That's because there are only two offices in town," she said. "Yours and Steve Wilkes'."

Bird honked as he parked in front of the office. She knew it was too bright for him to see her, but she raised a hand anyway, glad he'd come. He would be one more diversion from her circling worries. When he got out of his truck, she saw he wore shorts and a fishing shirt instead of khakis and a tie. He didn't mean to stay.

"Reenie!" he said as he entered. "You have the same idea as me?"

"What idea's that?"

"Hooky! Go change clothes. Let's go to my farm for the day. Go fishing."

It had been a long time since he'd come into the office in such a mood, ready to cancel plans and spend his hours with her. She took him in. What hair he had left was silver, and his cheekbones were no longer enough to save his face from time, but the shirt he wore was one he'd had since he was a much younger man. Doreen knew the slip of that cotton through her fingers; she'd fastened and unfastened those small white buttons. "I doubt the clothes I have here fit me anymore, Bird."

"Of course they fit."

"We haven't played hooky in at least six years."

He ran a hand through his hair. "That's my fault. Please, Reenie?"

His entreaty caught her. Bird wasn't one to beg. She glanced at his cheek, at the spot he'd had biopsied most recently. She didn't yet know the results of that test.

"You see if those clothes fit," he said. "I'll go down the street to Strickland's and get us some ham biscuits for lunch."

Doreen had to suck in her belly to button the shorts, but they would do for a few hours. She twisted shut the blinds, and hung a sign on the door, *Closed for the Day*. Back when there were still people alive to catch them, they'd met first in the national forest so she could hide her car. But all of those people were dead now—Bird's father, his uncle, the farm's caretaker. They only needed to give a nod to appearances in town. Bird would leave first, and a quarter hour later she would follow.

Doreen turned off the hardtop onto a stretch of unsigned dirt known locally as Lewis Loop. The farm Bird managed for hunting and fishing, his grandmother's childhood home, sat on this road. She passed the scrim of roadside trees that masked the staging area of the last logging operation, passed several rows of planted pines. Paused at a rusty stop sign riddled with bullet holes.

The road went left and right, formed a circle. Left was the quickest way to Bird's, but Doreen turned right. She wanted to see what had become of this land. She'd watched as the Forest Service bought the farms of the families who'd lived here, burned the homesteads to the ground, clearcut the hardwoods, replanted pulp pine. Wells hidden in the trees and jonquils that bloomed each spring were the only reminders of those homesites. She used to wonder why Bird's family had held on when everything around them was raw red clay and steaming windrows. They had the Marxton place in town after all, a huge, columned affair on the historic register.

Today though, as Doreen drove over the washboarded road, she understood. The timber company trees had grown tall, offering mottled shade and the cushiony quiet unique to pine forests. Four turkeys pecked on the roadside, and they raised their heads to watch her pass. The land had pulled through, changed but alive. Finally, it was something precious Bird possessed, an old farm in the middle of so much hushed green. Her own small piece of family land sat close to the highway, so instead of watching neighbors disappear over her lifetime, she'd watched them arrive. A trailer here, a cheap duplex there. Still, an inheritance was an inheritance; her own life would have been much harder had her grandmother not secured what she had, had her mother not managed to keep it. Doreen had raised Jonathan in the same house where she'd been raised.

She eased across the shallow creek and approached the McCormick place. This was the only other home standing in these woods. Old man McCormick had shot and killed his family on the upper landing of this house after the stock market crash of 1929 left him suddenly as poor as his neighbors. Nobody had touched the farm since then, not even the timber company.

Doreen rolled to a stop. The right chimney had collapsed since she'd last seen the place, ripping away portions of the outer wall and exposing murky innards. But fresh green vines snaked through the rubble, brightening the ruins. The homestead didn't look cursed, not today. When Doreen was a girl, she'd come here to drink whiskey and goad the ghosts. "Momma, Momma," she'd said, standing on the stairs with her friend, Janice. They believed that if they said it the right way, the way a lonely child might, then Mrs. McCormick would appear. They'd scared themselves into screeching, but they never saw Mrs. McCormick.

Doreen shivered against the story. She pressed the gas, went too fast down the rutted road. The pond at the back of Bird's property was in full sun by early afternoon; she preferred to fish while it lay in shade.

Bird sat on the back steps, coffee mug in hand. Doreen checked her phone a last time—no messages. Lexie would have gotten the children on their school buses by now and driven to Flyshoals Tech. If she still hadn't called, then she and Jonathan might work things out before the end of the day. Doreen could go home to find her son returned to his family. Doreen turned off her phone, dropped it in her purse.

Bird crossed the yard to greet her. He rubbed his little belly, and she rubbed his belly too as she slipped her arms around his waist. They held each other until she pulled back, brushed her fingers over his cheek. "It's healing well."

He kissed her fingertips. "Let's go before it gets too hot."

Soon they were crossing the backyard and following the faint path through the cornfield, past the rock outcropping that stood not quite as tall as Doreen. She touched it for luck as she always had, making a wish for Jonathan and Lexie, a wish for her grandchildren, a wish for Bird. At the pond's edge, Bird rolled the canoe to its side. Millipedes and cockroaches scattered. Doreen wiped away the spiderwebs with a stick.

He steadied the canoe so she could step in, and then he passed her the rods and bait, the paddles, their lunch. His gumboots disturbed the pond floor as he joined her, releasing the smell of established green colonies.

Together they paddled to the pond's still center.

Bird baited two rods, passed one to Doreen. She cast. Reedy native cane soughed in the breeze. Something bit; she set the hook. "Bream." When she reeled in, she was right.

"Want to keep it?"

"Not if we catch a bass." Doreen watched Bird's hands as he freed the shimmering fish from the hook and dropped it into a bucket of scooped pond water. At work, their rhythm was watchful and slow, dulled with silenced affection, but on this piece of land she could turn broadly toward him. She thought of horses, how the old ones grazed apple mast neck-linked. Almost forty years they'd been together. "I drove past the McCormick place on the way in. Chimney's collapsed."

Bird impaled a fresh cricket on Doreen's hook. "I've thought about buying it."

"You want a haunted house?"

"I lost my virginity there."

Doreen took her rod from Bird. "I thought I knew all your good stories," she teased.

"It's not a good story."

Bird waited, but Doreen didn't encourage him to continue. Memories were similar to family details in that some they shared and some they did not. If she'd not been told this one after so much time together, she didn't want it now. She cast, reeled in slowly.

"Your mother might have told you," Bird said. "About a girl named Marla?"

Doreen glanced over her shoulder, saw Bird's back in the shirt her fingers knew. "Marla went to my mother for an abortion."

"So you've known?"

"No. I'm guessing, Bird. It's not a hard thing to guess at. My mother was the only person in town who did abortions. But she was a woman of close confidence. She didn't talk about the women who came to see her nights."

"You were her daughter, Reenie. Surely she told you things."

Doreen thought of the time she'd been closest to her mother, the year before the woman died. Doreen was nineteen. She'd just left Billy and returned to Flyshoals with Jonathan. For a year, she and her mother and Jonathan had lived together in a way that was whole between them, a way that revealed to Doreen that the notions of family to which she'd clung—mother, father, baby—were skewed. Family could be a grandmother, a mother, a son. The abortions had been part of her mother's work, not part of their intimate life. They'd not discussed them anymore than they discussed the jams her mother made and sold, the cough syrups, the burn salves. "You're certainly not the only man in this county whose girlfriend saw my mother for that reason, Bird.

Don't worry about it."

"But did your mother tell you what happened after?"

"No." Doreen checked that her cricket was still kicking. After her mother's heart attack, people stopped Doreen in the grocery, in the post office. They whispered their secrets as if it were her responsibility as her mother's daughter to help them carry their griefs and fears. None of them asked her how it felt to be an orphan, a single parent. "Your history is your history, Bird."

The boat rocked gently beneath them as they fished.

The question Doreen brought to the pond grew more insistent until she could hold it back no longer. "Did you get the results of your biopsy?"

Bird issued a sound between a sigh and a moan. "I'm selling my client book, Reenie. I'm closing Marxton Casualty and Life."

The biopsy was malignant; the cancer had metastasized—there was no other way he would leave her without work in a town that was collapsing before the recession even hit. She turned on her seat and he turned too. They faced one other across the canoe. "Tell me what the doctor said. His exact words." She should be allowed to go along on doctor's visits, carry a legal pad, take notes.

"I got the all clear." Bird stuck a hand in the pond, wiped his chin. "Charlotte's the one dying."

Bird's wife.

Doreen watched pond water grow to drips in Bird's gray stubble. She felt the way the boat was small on the water, and the pond was small in the land, and she and Bird were but specks in the whole of creation.

"I thought I'd leave the business to Will like my father left it to me," he said, "but Will doesn't want it. He has his own job, his own life."

"You don't have to sell your business. I'll run things and you can be with Charlotte." Each time she'd brought up retirement, he'd said the same things: *I won't quit you if you don't quit me; You can run this place without me.* "I do your signature better than you."

Bird's shoulders curved toward one another, his torso sank into his waist. "Charlotte's making me sell, Reenie. She says she doesn't care who the business goes to so long as she sees you on the street before she's dead."

In Doreen's rare and loosely-woven fantasies of Charlotte's death, she'd not imagined the woman's vengeance or Bird's guilt. Bird told her that Charlotte tolerated their affair. Doreen thought she and Charlotte had found ways to play the roles that best suited them: wife, mistress. Charlotte couldn't be a divorcee; Doreen couldn't be a wife. Bird couldn't be monogamous. "There's something you're not telling me."

"Jesus, Reenie! What were you going to do if something happened to me? What if I was the one dying? Were you going to sue Charlotte to keep your job?"

Doreen grabbed the paddle and splashed Bird. "You're not dying. There's nothing wrong with you. And there are no jobs to be had right now. Own what you're doing, Bird."

He put his face in his hands. "I promise you'll be taken care of."

It was an awful thing to say. Doreen had worked harder for Bird than she needed to, learned more, so it couldn't be said she took advantage. She'd only accepted silly gifts, an ink pen with a rhinestone cap, a desk calendar of knock knock jokes. No jewelry. No trips. No roof for her house or brakes for her car. She'd thought he noticed these things. "Don't diminish all the years I've worked for you by turning me into your whore now."

Bird flinched. "Don't talk that way."

"Tell your wife no."

"I can't."

"You won't."

Bird ran his hands down his thighs. "The doctors say less than a year. I have to do what Charlotte asks. Just trust me when I say I have to. I really do. Help me with what I need to do, and I'll cover you while you're unemployed—Charlotte won't even know. And then after she passes. We can get married." He held his hands toward her. "Will you marry me, Reenie?"

Doreen turned in her seat and tried to pull the canoe toward shore. He'd brought her here for this conversation so that she couldn't get away from him. She was trapped in this boat, on this pond. "Help me row in."

"I asked you to marry me."

"And I'll tip the canoe over and swim to shore if you ask me a third time. If I wanted to marry you, I would've insisted upon it decades ago. How have you not understood that?"

"I thought you didn't bring it up because you knew I couldn't leave Charlotte."

"I couldn't live the way I have if I wanted to be your wife. What kind of person do you think I am, Bird? If you thought I wanted to marry you, you shouldn't have carried on with me. Not if you loved me." It wasn't a word they used often, but it had been said. "Help me get this boat to shore."

Behind her, Bird picked up his paddle and rowed.

Doreen was silent as they paddled in. At the bank, she scrambled from the canoe and hurried up the hill, leaving Bird to gather their supplies alone. He called for her as she entered the cornfield—"Reenie! Wait!"—so she went faster. She was in her car and pulling from the farm before Bird reached his backyard.

3

Lexie's car was in the drive. The woman wasn't supposed to be home—that was why Doreen had come to her house. Doreen's own house would still have Jonathan's stink and maybe Jonathan himself—it wasn't yet noon, and he'd been drunk enough when she left to warrant a half day's sick leave. She'd thought to hide out at Lexie's for a few hours, account for her presence by doing something helpful, clean the bathrooms, wash the sheets.

Doreen rang the bell instead of letting herself in with her key.

Thomas, answered. "Grandma!" He wore his school uniform, khaki pants and a blue collared shirt.

"Why aren't you at school?"

"Juliette's not ready to go."

"What's she doing?"

Thomas shrugged. "She's in the bathroom with Mom." He trotted into the living room and Doreen followed. She checked the state of the room, found the pictures straight on the shelf, the throw pillows aligned on the couch. Perhaps it wasn't because of what happened last night that everyone was home on a Friday. She sat down and Thomas leapt onto the cushion beside her.

"You've been back at school two weeks. Tell me the biggest thing that's happened so far," she said.

"Ben had a seizure during recess. Not the kind where you fall on the floor, but the kind where you walk around like a zombie." Thomas stuck his arms straight out and rocked to and fro.

It wasn't the story she'd hoped to hear, though it was a good sign that a friend's seizure overshadowed his parents' fight. A door opened in the back of the house. Thomas prattled on until his mother and sister came into the living room. "It looks okay now," he said.

Doreen went to her daughter-in-law, checking as she did so the soft tissue around Lexie's eyes, the edges of Lexie's crooked lips, the tender skin on her forearms. Lexie was a small woman with dark hair, skin like cream. The smallest of bruises peeked from the edge of her hairline. Other than this she appeared unmarked. She was dressed for the day in jeans and a pressed white blouse. Her hair was styled and she had on earrings, mascara.

Relieved, Doreen reached for her granddaughter. Juliette had Doreen's height, and at thirteen was eye level with her grandmother. At the edge of the girl's lip was an inch-long scab coated in make-up, a swelling foundation could not hide.

"Thomas hit me with a wiffle ball bat," said Juliette. She winced as she spoke.

"No, I didn't!" said Thomas.

Juliette looked at him pleadingly.

How had Jonathan explained it? *I got her to stop is all.* "Someone better tell me what happened here last night," said Doreen. She knew her voice was sharp. She intended for it throw

Lexie into apologies and self-recriminations. Into truth-telling.

"You took Johnny in," said Lexie. "Go home and ask him what he did."

Doreen scanned the room again, not a thing out of place. This house should be in shambles—the children unfed and in pajamas, Lexie worrying herself sick at the kitchen table. That nothing before her reflected the current state of the family struck Doreen as a betrayal. "He came to me. Asked for my help. That's more than you did."

"You're not my mother. I haven't had a mother in 20 years."

Doreen turned from Lexie and made her way to the couch. She needed to sit down. Lexie met Jonathan when she was fourteen and he was nineteen. Two years into their relationship, Lexie ran away from her father, and she'd had nobody to run to but Jonathan. Which was the same as running to Doreen—Jonathan lived at home. "You'll sleep in my bed beside me and follow my rules," Doreen had said when she opened the door to find Lexie clutching a trash bag filled with clothes. "This isn't a brothel."

Doreen made Lexie graduate from high school; Doreen taught her to balance a checkbook; Doreen walked her down the aisle. What was she to her if not a mother? Now Doreen looked across the living room and sought the outline of the girl she'd shared a bed with for years. No evidence of that child was visible in the woman who faced her.

Mothers keep the children when families fall apart. That much Doreen knew. The only person she was guaranteed in all of this was the man she'd fed pancakes to earlier. Juliette and Thomas stood behind Lexie, eyes downcast. If Lexie told them never to look on her again, they'd obey. "Let me take the kids to school for you," said Doreen. "I'll pick them up after too. Make us dinner tonight. Take them to church on Sunday. We can have a good weekend. Just the four of us."

"You've got him at your house."

"Please, Lexie." Doreen motioned toward Thomas, Juliette. "It's better for all of us if I know where he is."

"Come with me," Lexie said to her kids.

Doreen watched her family leave her. She imagined her daughter-in-law whispering instructions—who Thomas and Juliette could see, where they were allowed to go. Earlier this morning, Jonathan had wiped syrup from his mouth with a napkin. "Momma, I swear I didn't start any of this."

But it didn't matter who started a fight if the fight was inevitable and the outcome decided. Hadn't she sometimes thrown the first punch with Billy? Doreen remembered how it had felt to do that, to ball her fist and strike. It had felt like drawing a breath after being long underwater, a feeling almost holy with its predetermination. The sensation never lasted long. Even now, Doreen was less afraid in a dark and empty parking lot than she was in her own bed at night.

Lexie returned with Thomas and Juliette, each child clutching the bookbag Doreen had helped them pick out before the first day of school. "They're to come back here this afternoon. I don't want them at your house. I don't want them around Johnny at all."

Doreen stood, embarrassed by her tight shorts, her t-shirt. She wished she'd changed into her slacks and blouse before coming here. She was the only person dressed as if things were falling apart. "That's how it will be then."

Lexie led her children toward the front door. Doreen felt the boundary of her own skin like a wall she could not move beyond. There was no way to know what Lexie felt in this moment, what Thomas felt, what Juliette felt. No way to know what another person feared or needed, not even among family. Secrets could lay hidden like sinkholes, yawning open suddenly to engulf all that one knew of life.

_4_

Bird crept into his marital bed. He'd sat in the yard under the pecan trees with a bottle of bourbon until his bedroom lights flipped off. Charlotte no longer tolerated him sleeping on the sofa in his office as he used to do when they argued. She insisted he come to bed, no matter what. And he could only comply. Because what happened between them now wasn't an argument. It was blackmail.

"Did you tell her?" Charlotte's voice was hoarse in the dark. She'd been crying, Bird knew. She'd been crying since they sat across from the oncologist and received her diagnosis. The news had come three months after the birth of their first grandchild, a girl.

"I told her."

"How'd she take it?"

"Char."

"I wrote down everything you've ever told me. It's strung together in a way a child could understand. You know I was an

English major, Bird. There's a copy addressed to Doreen. One addressed to Will. One for Sheriff Johnson. He'll throw the letter away because he's your old friend, but he'll know what you did nevertheless. Other people will know too. I'm not telling you all the recipients, and there is no way you could guess. All I have to do is drop those envelopes in the mail, and your life is permanently altered. You might even go to prison. Tell me how Doreen Swilley took the news."

"It was awful."

Charlotte began to cry afresh. He rolled to his side and pulled her to him. She'd lost so much weight that in his arms she felt as small as she'd been when they'd met. He remembered her standing on the front porch of her sorority house wearing a dress like a wedding cake. It was the KA's Old South ball; he'd put on a Confederate uniform and gone to pick her up on horseback. "Remember when you couldn't ride my horse because of that dress you had on?"

Her crying slowed. "You were a pledge, but you'd been allowed a horse because you passed some sort of test. You were supposed to be in the mule cart. You showed up so proud on that horse, and then I couldn't ride it. I'd whipstitched a hula hoop into the hem of my skirt. It kept flipping up." She patted his hand, her rings tinkling on her emaciated fingers. "You kicked the other pledges out of the mule cart for me and paraded me through town. Ever the gentleman."

Enough moonlight filtered through the curtains to outline the room's heavy furniture, antiques from Charlotte's line. Bird thought of this room as Charlotte's, as if it were a place she invited him to visit, but not because of the furniture. He felt that way about the whole house, even though it was his great-grandfather who'd built the place. But Charlotte had managed its functions, the parties and the decorating, the housekeepers and yard help, the child-rearing, the service projects. Even his affair with Doreen she'd managed. *Keep it quiet, Bird. That's all I ask.* "She doesn't understand why you care now," he said. "When you didn't for so many years."

"When my mother died, everyone said, 'Oh that Dot, she was such a good woman. So kind and patient. Not a mean bone in her body. A pillar of the community. Birmingham wouldn't be the city it is without her.'" Charlotte's voice was plain in the darkness. "I thought you'd die first, Bird. I never doubted that God would grant me that." Her tears returned. "My granddaughter won't even know who I am. I'll die, and you'll marry Doreen, and my own granddaughter will call your mistress Mema."

Bird held her as tightly as he dared. She felt light as bone.

"Don't be mad at me," she said.

How could he be angry? He deserved what she threatened. He'd gone looking for those letters anyway though, had snooped through her lingerie drawers, through her desk, through her private bathroom closet where she hid enemas and hemorrhoid cream. "Char, what you're asking me to do with my business—it takes time. And your health. And the letters." He didn't know how to ask the question.

"Theo Waters has the letters."

Charlotte's family lawyer. Theo Waters hated Bird. It was Theo who'd advised Charlotte to keep her inheritance in her name after her parents died so that she could leave Bird if ever she wanted to. "Char."

"As long as you sell your business and fire Doreen, Theo will return those letters to you. Do something else, and he'll open the one addressed to him and mail the rest."

"Char."

"I don't want you to be unhappy. I know you can't stand to be alone. I already gave you my permission to marry that woman when I'm dead." She pulled the duvet over her shoulder. "But while I'm alive, I want everyone to see that I finally said enough."

"I'm so sorry for the way I've treated you. I wish I could roll back time."

"One more lie and I'll have Theo mail those letters whether you sell your business or not."

Bird shouldn't have told Charlotte about Marla. But she'd always been so kind and dear, holding him and shushing him when he wept. There had been too many nights like this between them, nights where they spooned in the dark and spoke into the hush, a lonely husband and wife trying to be happy in the midst of their little empire. Now her lawyer had her letters, and he couldn't escape his memories.

1958

5

Bird was a teenager then, still called Emmy.

He stood on the dirt road in front of his grandmother's farm. In the gloaming, everything was imbued with the grainy essence of itself—the trees, wood; the dirt, decomposed rock; the sky, uncountable atoms of gas. He traced where his blue veins emerged from the thicker flesh of his arm, watched as his heartbeat jumped in his wrist. In his heartbeat, in his veins, he felt his youth, his inability to save anyone or anything. His grandmother had been dead a month and his father and uncle planned to sell her farm to the National Forest Service. Today, on a quail hunt through her fields, he'd winged two birds. As he'd taken the soft brown bodies in his hands and snapped their necks, his father had said, "A man shouldn't shoot if he doesn't know how."

Emmy had left his father and his uncle on his Nana's back porch, making their plans. His Nana's house—her girlhood house—was nothing like the Marxton estate where she'd made a life with his grandfather. The Marxton house was silence and polish. But on Nana's girlhood land she'd taught him to play golf, wrapping her arms around his as he drove balls into the pond. On the day she felt he swung like a man, she'd taken him to the course to play the front nine. A child, a man. With her gone, he felt like neither. He felt instead like something inhuman and embarrassing, a medicine chest with its door ripped away, all those weaknesses exposed to the world.

Before him, the road was a bright line in the deepening evening. Nobody had stopped him when he stood from the porch and announced his intention to take a walk. Not his father, not his uncle, not even Herman, the farm's caretaker. Once, Herman had tended to Emmy as if he were his own child. Tonight though, the only sign Herman gave when Emmy announced his plan for a walk was a headshake so slight it seemed a tic. Since Nana's death, Herman had quit teasing Emmy about girls, quit asking him about school. He'd started saying yes sir and no sir to Emmy, and he'd begun to call him mister. Last night on the news, Emmy had watched the National Guard lead nine black students into a high school in Arkansas. He'd seen the angry white faces screaming at them, cursing them, and he'd wondered what Herman thought of those nine students. Emmy knew what his father thought, though usually his father left it to other men to say the word. He did not know if his father thought the same of Herman. Nana was gone and the whole world was changing. All Emmy had wanted was for someone to put an arm around him and tell him not to walk out into the cold night alone.

The road appeared to shorten as Emmy walked down it, as a fishing line appears to when it falls through water. Maybe, he thought, he was running away. Perhaps this is how such a thing happened, sadly and in piecemeal, a mile here, a mile there. He had two dollars in his wallet. A wind shushed dry leaves over the ground, and brought another sound besides: the faint resonance of a guitar and the lilt of a woman's voice. *I stop to see a weeping willow, Crying on his pillow, Maybe he's crying for me.* Emmy's aggrieved blood strummed along. *And as night skies turn gloomy, Night winds whisper to me, I'm lonesome as I can be.* The song was popular, much on the radio of late. He followed the sound down the road.

Soon he was standing in front of the McCormick place. Firelight shivered through two lower windows.

He'd never gone inside that house.

Nana had told him what happened.

"I was cooling off in the creek when I heard the first shot," she'd said. "In those days, gunshots meant you needed help. Dogs went rabid, horses broke their legs. I was crawling up the bank when the second shot came. Third, I went running. The fourth and fifth shots came as I ran. People say he lined them up and shot them, but what I remember is a pile, each child bleeding out onto their siblings, onto their mother. Mr. McCormick said to me, 'Go on home now, Jojo. This is none of your concern.' The last shot came as I left. He might've spared himself if I hadn't seen. When he saw me, he saw what I was seeing. He saw how bad a person can be."

Emmy shivered. He'd left without his coat, and he'd grown cold along with the night. Maybe this was part of running away too, a slow creep of worsening ills that could only be solved in unwanted ways. Inside the McCormick house was a fire.

The song's last notes sounded. Emmy crossed the yard, went up the porch. Eased the front door open. Inside the home's gloom, he paused. No voice called him forth or shouted him away. He passed through the foyer, entered the hallway, passed dark spaces that were empty rooms. He reached the place where firelight danced in the hall's darkness.

A man's voice, gentle and low: "Come on in."

Emmy stepped through the doorway. What caught him first was the smell. Woodfire heat amplified the tang of unwashed bodies and unwashed clothes. Odors rose from the floor where strewn blankets, discarded garments and spilled rucksacks formed a gray nest. The odors, the nest, the house itself—all of these things were stale and old, everything stale and old except the people in the room who, in their dishevelment, looked so different from anything Emmy knew it was as if he were seeing people for the first time.

There was an older man near the window, and beside the fire were a boy and a girl near Emmy's age. The girl's hair, white blonde, glowed in the firelight. The older man was a sickly color, gray in the beard, and he sat in the only chair, looking sideways out the tall window at the road, a pistol in his lap. "Took you long enough to come in. We got here first, but we don't own it." He slipped the pistol beneath the blanket covering his legs, a sign of peace. "We was having a song before bed."

"You traveling light," said the boy. He rested on his back, his head propped on the girl's thighs. His hair was the same color as the girl's, and his face looked like hers too. Emmy assumed them siblings, twins even. The boy spoke loudly, as if deafened by the guitar his sister held. She leaned against the hearth and the boy stretched long into the shadows, giving his pale face a disembodied look. "That is, if you traveling at all."

Emmy didn't hear a question in the boy's words, but the old man at the window gazed at him as if waiting for an answer. The boy lifted a Mason jar to his mouth. The girl strummed her guitar. The notes tumbled and tripped about the room. It wasn't a regular guitar the girl played, but a thing bewitched—it sounded like two guitars, three. "I've never heard a guitar like that," said Emmy.

"Called a resonator," she said. "Made for playing on stage."

"You play it well."

She set the guitar on the floor beside her, turned shy by praise. Around her neck hung a small leather bag, and she took it up with her right hand, rubbed it between her fingers. The boy shook the Mason jar toward Emmy.

Emmy stepped into the room, picked his way through the nest.

"There's nothing to step on in here," said the girl. "You can walk normal."

But Emmy imagined babies sleeping in the blankets, kittens, his grandmother's translucent teacups. The room was humid and dank. He accepted the Mason jar. Unscrewed the lid and took a drink. The liquor burned his throat and made him cough. What they drank was nothing like what he'd snuck from his father's liquor cabinet. This tasted harsh and homemade. Unbonded. Stolen, he thought, looking at the people gathered. Snatched from some moonshiner's stash.

The girl lifted her voice. *Through many dangers, toils and snares, We have already come, 'Twas grace that brought us safe thus far, And grace will lead us home.*

She sang without accompaniment, and her voice tilted the feeling in Emmy's chest toward the divine. It would be terrible to see God, he knew that. A glimpse would kill a proud man. The meek shall inherit the earth.

The boy joined in a soft falsetto. Emmy closed his eyes.

When the song died away, the boy said, "You'd best carry on now."

"We're going north," said the girl. "To Chicago. Cherlow says there's work enough there for everybody."

"North by way of South Carolina," said the boy. "Cherlow has to see his momma again. It's his car we're in."

Emmy turned to the old man at the window. "I don't want

to stay if they sell my Nana's farm."

"I reckon you'll find you another reason to stay around here," said the man. "Boy like you."

Emmy bristled at the man's certainty. He could stay or go, do anything he pleased. Emmy sat down where he stood; the gray nest received him.

"This here's my brother, Silas," said the girl. "My name's Marla."

The jar of moonshine was empty and the fire lived on in short blue flames. Silas had curled into himself to sleep, his head no longer guarding his sister's knees. The old man, Cherlow, slept upright in his chair, a second quilt warming his torso. Marla spoke into the cup of Emmy's ear. "We're relatives all, in a fashion. My brother's the only one shares my blood. Cherlow's been our neighbor since we was born. He's always had a say in our raising."

Emmy turned his head to speak into Marla's ear. "What if you don't find work in Chicago?"

Another trading of positions. "Same reason my momma'll have me back is why I left: babies. She needs help with the young'uns. Silas didn't have to do feedings or change diapers 'cause he's a boy. He's come along on account of he's such a loner. Says he needs to seek his own way to be a man. If we don't find work, we'll just hitch home."

Emmy took Marla's hand and helped her to standing. He collected quilts from the floor. Having rested there, he walked less lightly as he left the room. Marla reached into a rucksack and grabbed a flashlight. She clicked it on as they entered the chill murk of the house. Shadows leapt. Emmy guided them to the staircase.

Marla went behind Emmy and kept her light on his feet as

they ascended. Halfway up, he stopped. If he kept walking, her beam would find the stains. He thought this was what he wanted to show her, what he wanted finally to see for himself, but now the thought terrified him. It seemed unwise to encounter murder's marks while swaying drunk in the deep night. Marla lowered the beam to the stair she stood on. Looking down, Emmy saw her feet behind him, small in a bright round circle. She clicked off the light. He heard the shushing sound of her rubbing her leather necklace in the dark.

He turned. The shape closest to him was Marla. The darker shapes lining the stairwell behind and beside her he knew to be shadows, but he steadied himself with a hand on her shoulder anyway.

She touched his chest, and he caught her tangy odor. "Cherlow said why this house is abandoned. He fancies hisself a historian."

"Murder."

"It's not for good reasons houses get forgotten. Cherlow knows spots from here to Illinois."

"My grandmother heard the shots. She ran over and found them."

"This trip makes three times I left Atlanta. First time, me and Silas went to South Carolina with Cherlow to see his momma. Next time we went with Cherlow again, but to Florida, to catch a look at the sea. Every time we sleep in tainted houses. What you do is forget the parts what's bad. In South Carolina, there's soil white as talcum powder. The sea sounds like a busy street when you stand with your back to it, but it tastes like salt and looks like nothing you ever seen."

"They were heaped up on the landing."

Marla remained the darkest shape in the shadows as she stepped past Emmy and went to the second floor. She stood there until he felt ashamed and joined her. Then she took the quilts from him and fashioned them a nest.

The next morning, Marla's braid was loosed; her blonde hair covered them both. It was Emmy's first time greeting the day with a woman in his arms. Sobriety and the sun's thin first rays stilled his hands from asking for more of what she'd given him in the night: her pale limbs, her lips and hands, her hips rising to meet his.

"Them downstairs is awake," she said. "I reckon they think I stepped out for my toilet."

Emmy turned his head from the chatter and clattering that made its way up the stairs, and in so doing saw for the first time the stains on the wall. His body jerked. Marla startled to sitting, her attention focused down the stairwell. "The wall," he said.

She relaxed. "Floor too."

He made out, at the quilt's edge, a hint of the stain beneath him. He scooted off the quilt to sit on the top step.

"You have to hide up here until we leave," said Marla. "Watch through a window. Don't come out until you can't hear the car no more. It won't do for them to guess what happened." She stood and draped the quilts over an arm, picked up the flashlight. "Unless you want to come with us." She touched his forehead. "If what you say is true. That you got no reason left to stay. Cherlow'll take on a soul in need."

After undressing in the night, they'd redressed against the cold. Emmy noticed what Marla wore. A faded dress, cheap leather shoes, a paltry cardigan. No adornment but that length of leather with a little bag hanging off it, the thing tied around her neck like jewelry. Her long, long hair that had felt like opulence in the dark when he was free to touch it, muss it—so unlike the short, stiff styles of the few girls he'd wrestled against in back seats—

looked poor in the morning light. He thought of tent revivals, mill workers. Her bottom teeth closed outside her uppers. *You'll find another reason to stay around here. Boy like you.* "I'll think of you," Emmy said.

"You will." She watched him until he became self-conscious. He felt the itchy neckline of his wool sweater, the cling of his woolen undershirt, the full stretch of his tall winter socks. He pulled off his sweater, offered it to her.

"Them downstairs would notice."

He tugged it on again.

She took a folded slip of paper from her dress pocket. "Momma wrote this down for me, but I know my own home. Put the name as Marla if you write. It'll find me."

He grabbed her hand, kissed her wrist. Tasted the wood smoke there.

She turned, crept down the left side of the stairs, mindful of the tired center's creaks.

Soon, the noise from downstairs rose at her entrance, and Emmy tiptoed from the landing to the front room. The view of the yard and dirt road was clear. In a line of sun, he opened the paper Marla had given him. Fulton Bag and Cotton Mill. So he'd been right about her hair, her teeth. He balled the paper and dropped it to the floor.

It wasn't until later in the day, after he'd returned to Flyshoals and gone with his friend Clarence Hammond to buy a Coke float at Richard's Pharmacy, that he realized he'd been robbed. A fold of leather, two dollars and a Georgia driver's license, that was what Marla had of him. It seemed a fair trade. He was shed at last of the weight of a teenaged boy's virginity.

He didn't think he'd see Marla again.

2009

6

Doreen pulled across the gravel lot of Flyshoals First Baptist and parked beside her friend Janice's blue Monte Carlo SS. They'd talked on the phone, but today was the first time they'd seen one another since Doreen found her son in her kitchen. Janice sat with her car windows down, smoking a cigarette, and for a moment Doreen imagined crawling into her car and trembling on the floorboard like a wounded animal.

"Say hello to Miss Janice and then run inside." The children got out of their grandmother's car and Doreen climbed in beside Janice.

"Hey, Miss Janice," Thomas and Juliette sing-songed.

Janice pulled off her sunglasses and took Juliette's chin, turned the girl's head to better see her lip. "What happened?"

"Thomas hit me with a wiffle ball bat."

"Is that true, Thomas?"

"I don't know."

"It's a yes ma'am/no ma'am question."

"No ma'am."

"Juliette, if you're going to lie make sure the folks involved will cover for you." Janice ground out her cigarette in the car ashtray. "Your grandmother tells me everything. Y'all know that. Who's paying me a quarter this week?"

"Not me," said Thomas. "Psalm 139, verse 14: I praise you God, for I am fearfully and wonderfully made."

"Fearfully is right." Janice gave him a quarter from the handled to-go cup lodged in her air-con vent. "Juliette?"

"First Timothy, chapter four, verse 12: Don't let anyone look down on you because you are young, but set an example for the believers in speech, in love, in faith and in purity."

Janice gave her two quarters.

"Miss Janice!" said Thomas.

"Hers was twice yours. You want a longer one this week?"

"No ma'am."

"Get on to Sunday school then. Y'all have to give those quarters back if I hear you're late."

The children turned and started across the gravel lot, bickering between themselves as they went.

Janice grabbed Doreen in a hug, and Doreen relaxed into the claiming present in her friend's touch. She pressed her face into Janice's shoulder. Beneath the stench of cigarettes lurked the funk of old dog. "You stink like Dean's."

Dean was Janice's on-again/off-again lover. "Maybe when I can't hold my bladder he'll keep me in the bed, too." She released Doreen, picked up her cigarette packet, rattled it.

"No thanks." Doreen had quit when Lexie quit, hadn't wanted to be the only Swilley woman still smoking in front of the children. She leaned back in her seat to take in more of Janice. "You picked that dress out for church?" Janice was a 60s bombshell gone to folds, and the red wrap dress she wore showed every dimple.

Janice tugged the neckline lower. "Picked it with Pastor Hewell in mind."

Pastor Hewell was Flyshoals First Baptist's most recent pastor, and neither Janice nor Doreen liked him. Janice sought to rattle him, throw him off his sermon, chase him out of town faster. "How are things with Jonathan?" she said.

"He was in bed last night when I got home. We may as well not be talking for all the nothing we said this morning. 'You want a cup of coffee?' 'Weather sure is nice.'"

"He still hasn't told you what happened?"

"He hasn't claimed it at all. Not even to lie about it. I knew nothing about Juliette's lip until I saw it with my own eyes. I want to kill him. That's how mad I am."

"That's better than 'Jonathan said this, Jonathan said that.' I heard that shit for years."

A familiar and impotent fury rose in Doreen, one she knew there was no answer for. When she first returned to Flyshoals she'd gone out every night trying to quell it, sex one thing she'd been able to do, angrily and in bathrooms, angrily and in the backseats of cars. In the mornings she'd come into her mother's kitchen hungover, smelling of this man or that. "A gun would be quicker," her mother said after some weeks.

"Ma'am?"

"You can't kill Billy, so you're killing yourself." She pointed at Jonathan mushing banana into his mouth. "But that one there is who you picked."

There was nothing Doreen could say—the woman had offered her an out. Billy was a longhaul driver twice her age, and Doreen had been forbidden to see him. She'd done so anyway. When she came up pregnant, her mother said, "I'll make the tea tonight."

But Doreen wasn't going to spend a night moaning in labor only to birth a dead thing: a black fish egg, a bloodied peanut, a peeled rat. She ran off to Florida with Billy, Billy who promised her pies from the lemon tree that grew right in his front yard, Billy who promised her a fish caught fresh for dinner every night.

All of his promises lies. That was how she'd chosen Jonathan.

Doreen took a tissue from her purse and patted the sweat from her upper lip. "Lexie graduates from nursing school at the end of December. Jonathan can live with me until then. They can figure things out after that."

"Doesn't seem there's much to figure out."

"I don't want to hear it again," said Doreen. Janice wouldn't be so quick to say divorce if she had a son instead of a daughter. If Janice's only child, Tillie, ended her marriage, Janice wouldn't be the grandmother on the losing end.

A black minivan pulled in beside them and jerked to a stop. The Tarkentons, known for their tardiness and their two sets of twins. The mother got out of the passenger door and the father out of the driver's; both of them jerked open the doors behind them and began to unbuckle children. Doreen and Janice cranked up their windows.

In the parking lot, Janice locked arms with Doreen. They picked their way across the gravel in their low-heeled church shoes. The older Tarkenton twins, boys, ran past. Their mother hurried behind them, clasping their younger sisters by their wrists. The father, draped in diaper bags, brought up the rear.

"Free childcare," whispered Janice, but this morning Doreen couldn't laugh. She and Janice had started coming to church when Janice was divorcing her first husband, Tillie's father, and Doreen was learning how to be an orphan. She'd just put Jonathan in daycare and gone to work for Bird. She and Janice still joked that it was the hour and a half without their children that first brought them to God.

Pastor Hewell called, "Good morning, Tarkentons!"

"Pastor!" said Tim Tarkenton, raising a hand. Since Pastor Hewell arrived, there was a move to find more families like the Tarkentons. Young Christian breeders unafraid to praise online, that was what Pastor Hewell wanted. A light in the virtual wilderness, he said.

Doreen and Janice mounted the steps. Pastor Hewell greeted them with warmth, but not by name.

"Seventeen," said Janice as they entered the nave. She'd been keeping track of how many Sundays it would take the man to personally address them.

"He didn't even notice that dress." Doreen took the day's bulletin from Loretta Jones. Under the previous pastor, Loretta had been a deaconess, but when Pastor Hewell arrived he pulled the church in line with the Southern Baptist Convention: no female officers. No gay marriage either, he announced, though the only gay parishioner, Ferris Marks, was nearing eighty and the summer before had buried the man he'd lived with for as long as Doreen could remember. Ferris had left the church after Pastor Hewell's announcement, and nobody else had said a word.

Doreen and Janice slid into what Doreen thought of as their pew. Dust motes swirled in the colored light that came through the faux stained glass. Some years ago the church had collected money for real stained glass but fell short. Stickers were the compromise. The sticker above Doreen's head was of the Samaritan woman and Jesus at the well. Five different pastors Doreen had listened to beneath this particular image, and two others before the window had its sticker. One of those men, right before he left, told her that Flyshoals was a hard spot for ministry. But Doreen hadn't left. She'd sat here, beside Janice. They'd raised their children in this church, baptized them in it, married them off. *I've taken what you gave me, God, and made do,* prayed Doreen. *Gratitude is preached from that pulpit, and I've taken the command seriously.*

The opening hymn finished and Pastor Hewell stepped forth. The man's teeth alone could fund a stained glass window.

"Football," guessed Janice.

"Yesterday," said Pastor Hewell, "while I watched my son's Peewee League Football Game, the Lord set before me a test. It was the end of the third quarter, first and ten, and we were tied."

You dim the sun and part the seas, God. All I need is the smallest of signs. Lexie and Jonathan. Thomas and Juliette. Bird. My job. Tell me what to do about one of these things. I'll work hard, you know that. Most times I don't even pray for myself. Today I can't help but pray for me though, Lord. I'm lost.

"When that pile cleared, my son remained on the ground. What I wanted to do was run out of those stands and scoop my boy up, carry him home. But friends, I did not do that. And do you know why I did not? Because I understood, in that situation, that I was not my child's first father. His first father was on the sidelines, wearing a yellow coach's jersey, screaming, 'Get up, boy! Get up!' It was that coach's job to know better than me what my son could do, how high my child could rise."

"Does this remind y'all of another story about first fathers? About God? Genesis. Chapter 22, verse 1. God commands Abraham to take his only son, Isaac, and go to Mount Moriah. 'Take wood for an offering,' says God. 'Bind Isaac's hands and feet.' And what does Abraham say to this?"

Use my hands to fix things, Lord. All these years, all these blessings. How am I to care for them?

Pastor Hewell stared at his Bible and gave his message time to settle. "Abraham says, 'Yes sir, Lord God. My faith is strong.' Abraham says, 'I will do as you command me.'"

"When I hear someone say that what God asked Abraham to do that day was unChristian, I feel pity, for I know then that I am in the presence of someone who has yet to be reborn. A child is not God, my friends. A house is not God. A job is not God. We confuse the gifts of God with God. Abraham waited a hundred years for Isaac. He loved that boy with all his heart. He loved him so much there wasn't room left in Abraham's heart for God. Deuteronomy, chapter 6, verse 5: 'Love the Lord God with all your heart, with all your soul, and with all your strength.' God wants for there to be nothing before Him in our hearts. Nothing."

Please don't strip me of everything.

Whispered amens bounced through the church. It was terrible, what Pastor Hewell said.

In the wake of his words, Doreen lost her prayer.

Across the aisle, Pastor Hewell's wife, Bitsy, slowly raised her skinny white hands toward heaven. Bitsy's wrists were layered with bracelets, and it seemed this weight might keep her thin arms from reaching praise. But she kept pushing and pushing until her fingers pointed heavenward, and her face pointed heavenward, and tears slipped from the corners of her eyes.

Pastor Hewell smiled toward his wife.

What had Bitsy Hewell done as her son lay on that football field? Did Pastor Hewell have to hold her by the arm to keep her in the stands? Or did she bite her lip, dig her nails into her palm, draw her own blood as she restrained herself?

Doreen opened her Bible, found the day's passage. It was Sarah she looked for, Abraham's wife. What had Sarah said when God commanded Abraham to sacrifice Isaac? But Sarah wasn't in Genesis 22 at all. Genesis 23 opened with her death.

Doreen could pinch herself until she bled, but that wasn't proof she existed. She could reach to one side of her and pinch Janice, but Janice didn't exist either. She and Janice had been erased along with Sarah, along with Bitsy Hewell. Bird had done the same when he told her that he was selling his business but would keep her afloat until he could marry her. Jonathan had attempted something similar in his beating of his wife and daughter.

Doreen's mother had been a woman that people sought for their illnesses and their broken bones, for their broken hearts, but these same people often ignored her when she encountered them on the street. Her mother had spoken directly with God every day—Doreen knew; she'd heard the prayers. The woman never performed any sort of healing, not even an abortion, without asking God first. Yet she'd not been welcomed in any church. Doreen heard Sarah's words to Abraham: "You misunderstand God, you old fool. He entrusted you with Isaac and you are to prove yourself worthy. You are to protect the Lord's gifts, even against him. That is the test." It didn't matter that these words weren't printed in the King James version Doreen clutched. They'd come to her directly. If she were not in a place where women were erased, she could have stood up and said these words aloud and have them recognized as truth.

Doreen stepped into the aisle while Pastor Hewell nattered on about the ram. "Abraham was spared a ruinous task by the sweet, sweet grace of God!"

As if free will were a myth. Doreen walked down the aisle toward the doors. Obedience was the simplest of God's demands, a way to explain him to children. Two thousand years and still the fathers did not see.

She stepped through the church doors into the bright heat of the day. The door opened behind her; Janice came out. Without speaking they linked arms, went down the steps, turned toward the cemetery.

At the far side of the cemetery was a wrought iron bench that overlooked a dry field and a tin-roofed barbecue pit. Janice pulled out her cigarettes. Lit two, passed one.

Doreen took a drag and slumped against Janice's side. Where Doreen pressed against Janice she felt time's softness— there at the middle, at the hip. But alongside this softening was a hardness grown gradually over the years, a hardness Doreen hadn't noticed until now. It was there in the way Janice came to church in a too-tight dress stinking of her lover's dog; it was there in the way she chain-smoked anywhere she wanted. Janice's hardness was a kernel of certitude: this is what I am. Two days ago, Doreen would have said that she possessed the same certitude, but now, as she felt down into her chest, into her belly, she found only the cottony batting of sacrifice. Who was she if she was not Lexie's mother-in-law, or Thomas and Juliette's grandmother, or Jonathan's mother, or Bird's secretary and lover? She'd striven for independence, but everything she'd created depended on another. "I don't have anything of my own."

Janice shoved Doreen with her hip, forced her to sit upright. "Whatever pit you've fallen into you may as well climb on out of. There's no time for poor-me. Your family's a mess for one thing. And what are you going to do about your job?"

Janice was right. Doreen tossed her cigarette on the ground, rubbed it out with her toe. "I'll go to work until Bird quits paying me. Then I'll go over to that new Walmart, see if I can't get something in HR. I've been an executive secretary all my life. My resume's good."

"You've been more than a secretary." Janice leaned over and picked up Doreen's cigarette butt. "You can't leave these on the ground. Robins use them in their nests and get cancer." She grunted with the effort of sitting upright again. "You remember my niece Blake over in Athens?"

Blake was the child of Janice's hardest living sister, and throughout elementary school she'd been in special classes because of her lazy eye and erratic behavior. "I haven't seen her since she was a teenager."

"Well, she sells insurance now."

"Blake?"

"The child wasn't stupid, just bad in a classroom. She even took some college classes at UGA. That's my point. If Bird can do it and Blake can do it, you can too, Doreen. You're smarter than either of them. You buy Bird's business."

"Charlotte won't let me."

"God above forgive me, but Charlotte Marxton can't stop much anymore. Not for long anyway."

"Janice, I'm not even licensed."

"What do you have to do?" said Janice. "Take a test?"

"More than one."

"Well, what do you think's on those tests, Doreen? The same shit you've been doing for years."

"It's not the tests." She'd looked into getting licensed before Bird hit retirement age, thinking that then he wouldn't have to come in to work at all, not even to sign papers. It wasn't the exams that stopped her. She couldn't take the exams without proof of a high school degree. "I quit school in eleventh grade. Got pregnant and skipped town. You know that." Instead of getting licensed, she'd perfected Bird's signature.

"Get your GED."

"I'm not going to sit in night school and pay some twenty-year-old to drive in from Athens and talk to me like I'm stupid."

"That's not how it's done anymore." Janice put a hand on Doreen's arm. "You study online. Then you go take the tests. A girl I work with got hers in less than a month."

A doe and her fawn came into the field, and the women fell silent, watching them feed. The mother paused every few steps to watch and listen, her big ears twitching. After some time, the mother bolted, her fawn followed, and then from behind Doreen and Janice there came the sounds of church letting out. The women turned and watched congregants spill into the parking lot. "I'm not going back in there," said Doreen.

"Suits me fine."

"But I want to bring Thomas and Juliette."

"We'll drop them off at Sunday school and then we'll go to my house during the service. We can pick them up after."

Doreen laughed. They'd sometimes joked about doing the same when their own children were young. "I bet we can get away with it now, two old ladies."

Janice brushed a hand over her red dress. "Speak for yourself."

"Think God'll care?"

"Of course he cares," said Janice. "That's why we'll have our own church, you and me. 'Matthew 18:20: For where two or three are gathered in my name, there am I in the midst of them.'"

"You going to write sermons?"

"We'll be service-oriented. Good deeds. You can help me remodel my house."

"You're crazy." Doreen hung her purse on her arm, stood from the wrought iron bench. "I've got to get my grandkids."

Janice followed Doreen through the cemetery. "I'm serious about getting your GED and buying Bird's business. It's a whole new world, Doreen. And you and me, we're lucky enough to still be alive for it."

After church, Doreen drove toward Mercer's Grocery. Every Sunday Lexie worked a double and Doreen did her weekly shopping so she could go through Lexie's line and get an employee discount. In the backseat of the Honda, Thomas and Juliette argued over how to split the candy bar one of them had won in

Sunday school. Their bickering escalated to slaps, and Doreen reached behind her to pinch any flesh her hand found. "Stop fighting or I'll take that candy bar away."

"It's my candy bar," said Thomas.

"I don't want to hear another word about that candy bar," said Doreen.

The children slid to opposite sides of the car and sulked. When Doreen pulled into the lot, they jumped from the car. She reminded them to watch out for cars, but she needn't have—the lot was nearly empty. Mercer's wouldn't stay open much longer, not with a Walmart in town.

By the time Doreen entered the store, Thomas and Juliette were crowded into the cashier's cubicle alongside their mother. Doreen grabbed a cart and slipped into the produce section, made her way to a pyramid of peaches. She rolled a peach from the top, noted the prickliness. With time, those tiny hairs turned velveteen. These peaches were fresh. Marcel Mercer paid attention to such things. He'd been around long enough that Doreen remembered bringing him jams and eggs and homemade remedies back when she was a girl. She waved a stock boy over. "You have a peck left in back?

"Yes, ma'am."

"Bring one to the register for me if you will please."

"Yes, ma'am."

Each year Doreen put up peaches. They were her favorite as well as Jonathan's.

"Grandma!" Juliette came toward her shaking a package of chocolate chips. "I want to make cookies."

"Put them in the cart."

"I want to make mac and cheese," said Thomas, rattling a box of Kraft.

Doreen insisted that the children make real food if they

cooked with her on Sundays. No orange cheese in foil bags.

"This is better than yours," he said.

"Liar. He likes yours best, Grandma." Lexie had tried to cover Juliette's bruising for church, but the make-up had worn away, and a purple cloud was visible around the girl's lips.

Thomas dropped the mac and cheese in the cart.

"You can cook that by yourself," said Doreen. "I'll make mine and we'll have a taste test."

Thomas stepped onto the end of the buggy and hung his body over the side. Doreen pushed him though it made her hips ache. She wasn't sure how to be anymore, not with her grandchildren or her daughter-in-law, not with her lover. Not even with her son. She entered the grains aisle.

"Juliette doesn't want to see Dad," said Thomas.

"Why not?" Doreen took a soft sack of grits from the shelf, careful to keep her voice soft.

"Because he hit her."

Doreen said, "Why did your dad hit you?" Even before Juliette's face crumpled, she realized her words were wrong. Her question implied there was a reason good enough. "I'll get you a new shampoo," she said, a splurge. Juliette liked the ones that smelled so strongly of fruit nobody else in the family would use them. "Any bottle you want under three dollars."

The offer didn't perk the girl as Doreen had hoped, but she said thank you nonetheless, turned and started down the aisle alone. This was something else Doreen hadn't intended, Juliette walking away. "Bring it to the checkout."

Thomas grabbed the cart handle. He kicked the wheels as they went, making a racket, but Doreen didn't stop him. "Daddy hit her because she jumped on his back."

Doreen was careful not to look at Thomas. "Why'd she jump on his back?"

"To make him stop." He pushed the cart forward and back, forward and back, clanging the contents.

"To make him stop what?"

"You know."

"Hitting your mom?"

Thomas clanged the cart harder.

Doreen put a hand on her grandson's arm to still him. "You want a Matchbox car?"

"Yes, ma'am."

"Meet me at the checkout with it."

The boy shouted his thanks as he ran away.

Past the cleaning supplies, Doreen stopped and scanned the hardware selection. Nails and screws, WD-40, a few less common things: a plumbing snake, an eyeglass repair kit. Only two deadlocks hung on Mercer's display, and they didn't match: one was silver and one was brass. Doreen took them from their hooks and weighed them in her palm. She knew how to change a lock. She'd changed the ones on her mother's house after she left Billy and returned to Flyshoals, though she needn't have bothered. Billy didn't follow, didn't call or write, never even sent Jonathan a birthday card. He'd been content enough to lose forever the burden of girlfriend and child. Doreen knew Jonathan would not be the same. In that way, he was nothing like his father.

At the check-out, Juliette set the groceries on the rubber conveyor belt. Lexie beeped them over the red-eye and handed them to Thomas, who bagged. "Put the eggs by themselves," said Lexie.

Thomas rolled his eyes. "I know, Mom."

When the cart was empty, Doreen pushed it forward and

stood in front of her daughter-in-law. "How was the sermon?" said Lexie.

"Football again." Doreen took out her wallet. "I got a peck of peaches. Juliette, Thomas, go get Grandma's peaches."

After she'd sent her grandchildren away, Doreen took the deadbolts from where she'd hidden them in the side pocket of her purse, beside her Bible and away from curious eyes.

Lexie rang them, entered her employee number, subtotaled Doreen's purchases.

"You got a pair of scissors?" said Doreen.

Lexie passed her a boxcutter. "Seventy-five twenty-three."

Doreen took the bolts out of the bag. She sliced open the back of each lock. She pulled out the keys, offered them to Lexie. "You'll need these to come home tonight."

It took a moment, but Lexie opened her palm. Doreen set the keys in the center of her daughter-in-law's open hand.

"I didn't raise him to beat his family."

"I know. I was around for part of your raising."

Juliette and Thomas pushed the peaches up in a cart.

Doreen and Lexie held eyes. How many times had it come to this, making silent amends with her daughter-in-law over her grandchildren's heads, her son nowhere in sight?

Outside, the day's density dulled even the children. The blacktop was sticky from the heat. Doreen opened the trunk, and as Thomas and Juliette unloaded the cart for her, she prayed she was doing the right thing by locking her son out of his own home. It was impossible to know if she passed the tests God set for her. In church it had been clear that Abraham was to protect Isaac, but Doreen couldn't tell who to protect. She wanted to find a way to protect everyone, whether they deserved her protection or not. It struck her that failure might be what God really wanted for his people. All of those small, ceaseless, cracking-opens of the heart.

7

Doreen came home from her Sunday with her grandchildren and rode her brakes into her carport, parked beside Jonathan's truck. This carport had been where her mother's gardens were and her grandmother's before that. Doreen had paved those gardens, built a roof. She'd wanted a modern life, one with a salary and boughten bread, antibiotics for an earache. That was why she took secretarial courses in high school, and that was why she accepted the job Bird offered her when she went by his office to collect her mother's life insurance policy. Doreen was no fool. She knew why Bird hired her—they were sleeping together within the year. But she'd gotten what she wanted anyway. Her salary, her carport. Jonathan hadn't been called the witch's child.

Somehow none of that had been enough. Doreen took from the passenger seat the dinner she'd wrapped in foil for her son.

As she stepped from the car, she glanced across the street toward Luke's house. Luke was Jonathan's best friend. He'd grown up in that house, and after his mother died due to complications from sickle cell anemia, Doreen helped his father raise him. He'd moved back into the house with his family after his father went into the nursing home. Tonight, Luke's curtains were pulled and his wife's car sat in the drive.

It was in the woods that once covered Luke's lot that Doreen's mother had foraged the blue cohosh she brewed into a syrupy tea for the women who visited after dark. The plant had grown wild all around them, free for the taking. Her mother was no witch. Abortions were something women needed, and they brought in sustenance, even in January when gardens lay fallow and chickens didn't lay. Her mother pawned the jewelry women brought in exchange, spent the money, ate the cornmeal and beans.

On the other side of Doreen's kitchen door waited Jonathan. He'd been raised by a mother called whore, and she'd been raised by a mother called witch. She saw now, as she faced losing both her job and her family, that witch and whore were but two names for an independence that was hard-won and fragile and female. Two thousand years and still the fathers did not see. She shoved her door open. "Come eat. I brought you dinner."

Jonathan came into the kitchen, beer in hand, and sat at the kitchen table. Doreen set the foil-covered plate before him, handed him a fork and knife, a napkin. "Should be warm."

He pulled away the foil, took a bite of his son's boxed macaroni and cheese.

Doreen got one of Jonathan's beers from the fridge and joined him at the table.

"You remember that time you took everything out of my room?" he said. "My bed. My clothes. Made me sleep on the floor? How long did you do me that way? One week? Two?"

"You'd been brought home in a police cruiser. For stealing cassette tapes from the music store downtown. Thirteen years old.

I opened the door and you were standing there in handcuffs."

"*Since you think you're poor enough to steal*, that's what you said. You wouldn't even feed me."

"I left you a blanket and a pillow. Clothes for school." Janice had helped her move Jonathan's bedroom to the carport. "Only took you two days to find work mowing lawns and buy your own food. You've not been without work since." Doreen knew Jonathan was trying to guilt her out of being angry with him, but she didn't regret what she'd done. There'd been no father to ship him to, no grandparents who could take him in for the summer and break him with work. How many times had he been arrested? Five? Six? Every time for drinking and fighting though, not once for theft. He'd found trouble, but not the type to turn him worthless. "Only thing I did wrong was bring your stuff in from the carport. Maybe if I'd left it out there you wouldn't be sitting here now."

Jonathan set his fork down. "I'd change what I did if I could. That's what I'm trying to say. You might not regret any of the ways you parented me, but I got some regrets. What happened Thursday night—there are ways the body reacts. Instincts. Even one second of thinking and Juliette's lip wouldn't be busted."

He'd seemed almost grown to her when he stood on her porch in handcuffs, but he'd only been Juliette's age. What she said was true: she'd taught him to stand on his own. She knew she'd taught him something else besides. That love was earned daily; that loyalty could be destroyed in a breath. Now wasn't the time for apologies though. "Using other people's wrongs to justify your own is a coward's way."

His face hardened. "I plan to right my wrongs, not excuse them. My kids aren't coming from a broken family."

She'd chase him back if she wasn't careful. "Stay here with me until Lexie finishes school. It's only a few months. Thomas and

Juliette need a break from you and Lexie fighting." She softened her voice. "That's why Juliette jumped on you."

Such hope rose in his eyes. "You think so?"

Doreen knew she should confess to her son the doubts she held about him. "That's the only reason Thursday happened like it did."

"Thank you, Momma."

She drank from the beer she held. Tonight she couldn't do it, but there was time. Next week, next month. She would talk to him of his father. She would confess that she'd changed the deadbolts at his house. "Go ahead and finish your dinner. I've got chocolate chip cookies for dessert."

8

Lexie stood in the hallway and waited for Ms. Paulsen's class to empty. "Lexie," the woman said when Lexie entered. "It's good to see you."

Ms. Paulsen stood in front of a dry erase board covered in her sloppy handwriting. She wasn't the sort of teacher to come into class and click through a PowerPoint in the dark. She got in students' faces, insisted on revisions, gave pop quizzes. It was why students tried to take anatomy and physiology with someone else. It was also why Lexie trusted her. "Can I talk to you privately?"

Flyshoals Technical College faculty didn't have offices; the building was too small. Ms. Paulsen closed the door to her classroom, sat on the edge of a desk. "Shoot."

"I've got to get a job after graduation."

Ms. Paulsen waited.

"I need to leave Flyshoals."

"You'll have to leave if you want to find a job. I've told you that before. There's a nursing shortage but not in this town. You said your husband wasn't willing to relocate."

"He's not." *Don't go thinking I'll quit my job to follow you around*—that's what Jonathan had said to her. *You won't drag the kids behind you neither. They're staying here.* Lexie looked at Ms. Paulsen's hair, clipped short and wispy about her face. No make-up. Thick-soled clogs. Everything plain and practical. Ms. Paulsen had come to nursing through the military. She told her classes that she'd moved to Flyshoals because land was cheap, she wanted horses, and she'd grown up a couple of towns away. She spoke of a brother and some nieces, but no children of her own, no husband or ex-husbands. Lexie knew no other women in their forties with so few attachments. Ms. Paulsen understood how to keep her life her own in a way that Lexie did not. "I'm leaving town without him."

"You're getting a divorce."

"Without telling him I'm leaving."

"You're fleeing?"

Lexie considered the word. She'd been using "abandon." Lexie knew Doreen had changed the locks to make her feel safer, but the new locks only made her feel caged. Was it fleeing if what you ran from was love? "I have to give my children a better life."

"So what is it you're asking me?"

Lexie sat at a desk. "How to do it. How to leave."

Ms. Paulsen's voice was soft. "Why do you think I know how to do that?"

"Because you're here by yourself. Somewhere along the way, you had to leave someone behind. Didn't you?"

That evening, Lexie searched job boards for entry-level RN positions around Atlanta. That was the farthest she could imagine moving, though Ms. Paulsen had suggested Arizona, California. A plane ride was what she'd said Lexie should put between her and Jonathan. "I've never been on a plane," Lexie had said. The cities where she found jobs circled Atlanta like the rings of a bulls-eye. Canton. Cumming. Marietta. Smyrna. Decatur. The closest of these towns was over two hours away, and that felt very far indeed.

Lexie stood from the table, went down the hall, looked in on Thomas's sleeping form. He clutched a Nerf football, chosen to replace his teddy bear after he was teased at a sleepover. She'd been almost his age when her own mother died in a car wreck. Lexie pulled his door shut.

Juliette's door, across the hall, showed a strip of light beneath. Lexie tapped with a finger. No answer. She eased the door open. Juliette was asleep, the book she'd been reading for school open across her chest. *The Scarlet Letter.* Lexie dog-eared a page, set it on the bedside table. She'd been assigned the same book before she met Jonathan, before she ran away from home and Doreen took her in. Doreen, who had made her do homework nightly. Lexie remembered the warm bulk of Doreen's sleeping body, the scent of her face cream. When Lexie awakened crying, Doreen rubbed her back. "He's not here," she'd said, knowing without asking that Lexie's nightmares were of her father. "That bastard isn't here."

Lexie hadn't wanted to raise her children in a broken home, but it wasn't the loss of Jonathan that would break the house she kept. If she were to die suddenly, as her own mother had, Doreen was the one who would ensure a decent life for Thomas and Juliette. It was Doreen who kept Lexie's family together; Doreen who Lexie didn't want to leave. From Jonathan, Lexie fled; Doreen she abandoned.

She clicked off Juliette's light. Her daughter pulled the covers higher. In the hallway, Lexie leaned against the wall and wept.

9

Jonathan sat in the control tower watching a computer close-up of dry ready-mix leaving the load-out and sliding into Cecil's concrete truck. Cecil, never good at showing up on time, had been late today too. Due to his delay, another truck waited behind him. Here it was end of September, and this two-truck lineup was the busiest the plant had been since June. Only a year ago, trucks waited five deep this time of day because of demand, not tardiness.

The control tower was a utility shed on stilts, with windows on three sides. Through one window, Jonathan saw Cecil's truck idling under the load-out. Through the other windows was the plant itself, a gouged out place in the earth. A few gray silos were connected by pipes and belts. The silos, the pipes, the belts, Cecil's truck—everything was coated in the same thin gray dust.

At the far side of the lot, Manuel drove a loader to and fro, tidying a pile of crushed stone. He'd already loaded the hoppers for the next three batches of concrete. What Manuel did now was no different than a Quickie Mart clerk dusting the cracker display, something Jonathan had witnessed a few days ago: mean Wanda Jancey, three hundred pounds if an ounce, poking Lance crackers with a feather duster. Used to be Wanda only moved to tend the cigarette in her mouth.

Jonathan had set his Cokes and Bebos on the counter. "You're busy this morning."

Wanda fetched Jonathan his cigarettes. "Fine as my looks are, they won't keep me my job. That boy of yours liking Miss Stewart?" Wanda had a girl the same age as Thomas.

Jonathan didn't know the name of his son's teacher or who was in Thomas's class. "Well enough," he lied.

"Rayanne likes her too. I don't. Me and Rayanne made that damn sugar cube pyramid last night. Sugar's expensive when you have to buy it squished in blocks like that."

Had Thomas made a sugar cube pyramid? There was no way for Jonathan to know unless his mother told him. He paid for his day's supplies and left.

After talking to Wanda Jancey, Jonathan came to realize several things: Doreen hadn't told him who was in Thomas's class, or that there'd been a sugar cube pyramid assignment. He'd thought she told him what he needed to know when she told him his kids missed him, or that his gutters had gotten worse, or that Lexie wasn't so smart as she'd have them believe—she'd gotten a C on a quiz. But these things weren't the things he needed to know. So that night he'd stopped by his house for a visit. Should have been easy. His wife was gone; his mother had care of his kids. "Go home, Jonathan," she'd said when she answered the door.

"Lexie's not even home, Momma."

"She'll stop me from coming over here too if you're not careful." She fierce whispered at him like he was a cat she shooed. "Go on or we'll both lose contact with your kids."

From somewhere in the back of the house, Thomas called, "Who is it, Grandma?"

"Just the Mormons," his mother said and closed his door in his face.

He'd been cut out of his own family's life even as he lived under the same roof as one of them.

Jonathan watched Cecil leave the loadout and drive to the water station. The only truck in line pulled up, and Jonathan pressed buttons to ready the mix. Work boots resonated up the metal staircase. Jonathan recognized the plod of his boss, Powell McRae.

"Hey Johnny."

"Mr. McRae." Jonathan motioned toward the empty chair. Powell's midsection formed two neat rolls that circled him when he sat down. "Coffee?" said Jonathan.

Powell glanced at the coffee maker. "Two days? Three?"

"Not quite."

"No thanks." There was no joy in Powell's smile. He opened the manila folder he carried and laid out two spreadsheets rainbowed with highlighter markers. "Green is what we're doing now. Orange we've got backlogged. Yellow are bids."

Jonathan rolled his chair to Powell's side and looked at the spreadsheets. Mostly he saw yellow, but there was a lot of orange. "We have work coming up."

"Not enough to take us into winter."

"We're bound to get some of those bids."

"Some of those jobs are halfway to Atlanta. A good hour and a half one way. If we get those, it'll only keep us working. We won't make money."

Pouring concrete was a temperature-dependent process. If the day was too cold or too damp, the concrete wouldn't cure right. Too cold and too damp started happening regularly in November. Worse, pouring concrete was a low-margin business. Volume made money and McRae Readymix hadn't had the volume it needed in months. Jonathan didn't know how Powell managed his books, his finances. A few workless weeks may mean ruin. Already the dispatcher had been laid off, along with all of the maintenance crew save Jonathan.

"I'm down seventy-five percent from this time last year." Powell stacked the rainbowed sheets. "These days nothing's moving into Athens but spiders. I couldn't sell a driveway mix if I offered it two-for-one. I've gotta park five trucks."

Five trucks was over half the fleet.

"You pick first," said Powell.

Jonathan leaned back in his chair, his hands behind his head. Going first was easier. It was when you moved past the man or two you wouldn't mind losing that things got tough. "Cecil. He can't show up on time."

"Agreed."

Jonathan and Powell looked out the side window at Cecil's truck as he pulled from the watering station. His mixer spun, blending cement with rock, sand, and water, making concrete. Only a year ago, Powell had compared his mixer trucks to lottery machines. "There go our winning numbers," he'd said.

"Larry," said Jonathan.

"Larry's wife cleans my daughter's house. He can do most anything."

"Not since he hurt his back. Guy eats pain pills like Rolaids. Shouldn't even be driving his personal truck to work every morning."

"Fuck." Powell ran a hand over his mouth. "Table Larry. What about Walker?"

"Can't do shit but drive. His son's got some sort of bone defect."

"The hunched over looking one?"

"Yeah."

"You got anything to eat in here?"

"No sir."

"Make us some fresh coffee then. We've gotta have something."

Jonathan stood to make the coffee. Powell stared out the window at his readymix plant. Manuel tidied grains of sand, and the bay stood empty.

By noon, each man knew who he was responsible for firing over the next few days. Wadded tissues surrounded them. Jonathan slapped his thighs. "Time for lunch." He wanted away from Powell's lay-off list.

"Let me feed you," said Powell.

"I'd appreciate it," said Jonathan.

"Sandra's making us something."

A lunch invite usually meant Powell drove them to Strickland's, paid for lunch and sweet tea and two desserts apiece. But today he took out his phone and texted his wife.

Powell's house sat atop the hill behind the plant. Jonathan had never known Powell's wife, Sandra, a judge's daughter, to enter readymix property—she claimed the dust ruined her sinuses. Today, she drove her Cadillac down her driveway and idled at the gate until Manuel came for the cooler she held out the window. She waved in the direction of the control tower, put her Caddy in reverse, backed up her drive.

Manuel delivered the cooler with downcast eyes, as if delivering a casserole to a child's wake. His boots rang back down the steps quick and sharp.

"Half is yours," said Powell as he unpacked the cooler across the desk. He pushed two sandwiches toward Jonathan. "Ham and cheese. How's Lexie and the kids?" Most days, one of Powell's four grown daughters was coming or going from his house, a baby on her hip.

Jonathan considered lying, but he knew Powell would hear eventually. The man was like an uncle to him. "I'm living with my momma for a while."

Powell sighed. "That won't last long, I reckon. You get spoiled as a lap dog, being married. Get used to everything clean and nice. Don't know how you'd live without a cake under that glass dome thing."

"I reckon I'll stay gone awhile."

"Maybe since you're at your momma's. You've got her taking care of you."

It struck Jonathan that Powell was almost, but not quite, right. It wasn't that he was being cared for so much as he was being contained. Shelved. His mother fed him and did his laundry, visited his kids, remained a part of his family—and he was to wait while she and his wife decided between them his next step. "Come over and fix these gutters, Johnny," they might say one day. "Cut the grass." But they weren't telling him a goddamn thing that mattered. Not who his kid's teacher was; not how expensive cubed sugar got to be. They wouldn't even let him be daddy for an evening. "I'll bet you I stay gone. I'll bet you use of that fishing trailer you keep on Lake Hotchaburo."

"Place is a shithole."

Jonathan wiped his hands down his jeans and stuck out his right one. "When can I move in?"

"Leave here soon as you're finished eating. Get your ass in that stinking trailer of mine and get this thing over with." Powell shook the deal. "There's enough bad right now without losing your family, too."

Jonathan didn't want to lose his family. The problem was, they didn't realize that they felt the same way about him. It was time to disappear as best he could while living in Flyshoals. His good qualities were too easy to overlook when he was right there beside you on the couch, pining away for love.

10

Doreen pulled into her empty carport and assumed Jonathan was at work. She was glad he wasn't home—she'd been worried about him since he stopped by his house to visit his children and she refused to let him in. She'd brought the incident up, but he wouldn't talk about it, though he made his feelings clear in other ways: making only enough coffee in the morning for himself, not asking in the evenings if she'd like to change the TV channel. Tonight, in a sort of apology, she would make his favorite dinner. The surprise would be sweeter if he came home to the meal already prepared.

In the kitchen, she put water on to boil for the pasta, and she set the oven to preheat for the chicken. Then she went to change out of her work clothes.

It was when she entered her living room that she realized something was wrong. The afghan was folded over the back of the sofa, and the remote controls were lined beside the TV. There were no socks on the floor or ball caps on the sofa arms, no empty beer cans on the coffee table. "Jonathan?"

His bedroom door was closed. She opened it, flipped on the overhead light. The chifforobe's top was cleared of coins and receipts and the chair in the corner was bare of clothes. She opened his closet, found it empty too. He'd even taken the things that had hung there since high school.

Doreen ran into the kitchen, found her cellphone, called her son. He didn't answer. She called again. A third time. The fourth time he sent her directly to voicemail.

Where are you? she texted.

He didn't text back.

She called Lexie, who answered talking. "Speak of the devil! I was just picking up the phone to call you. What do you put in that cabbage dish you make? The one with rice and tomatoes?"

"Smoked paprika. Listen. Jonathan isn't here. He's gone. He's taken all his things. I've been calling him, but he won't answer. Won't text me either."

"You think he's coming home?"

"Maybe."

"When did he leave?"

"He was gone when I got here."

"Did y'all get in a fight? Why'd he leave?"

Doreen wasn't going to tell Lexie about Jonathan's attempt to visit his children. She'd done the right thing by not letting him in, so there was nothing to confess. "It's hard on him being away from his family. He cleaned the whole house before he left. Looks like a maid service came through."

Lexie didn't say anything for a moment. "He's not coming here, Doreen. Not if he cleaned your house."

"What do you mean by that?"

"Cleaning is the sort of thing Johnny does—I don't know—out of spite. He thinks it'll make you miss him. If he did that to you, then he's gone somewhere to make you mad. He's not leaving you to come back to me. He's leaving you to abandon you."

Doreen turned off the boiling water and the preheating oven. "He's helped me with all sorts of things since he's been here." She heard how feeble her words sounded. She'd known he was angry because he hadn't made her coffee or asked if she wanted to change the channel, and she missed those small kindnesses because they were the only kindnesses he'd shown. Mostly his arrival had meant extra cost and extra labor: food, laundry.

"Doreen, are you okay?"

"Where is he if he's not with you?"

"Luke's?"

Doreen looked out the kitchen window at Luke's house. Only Amanda's car was parked in the drive. Amanda disliked Jonathan, wouldn't let him in unless Luke was home. "Doesn't look like he's at Luke's."

If he wasn't with Lexie or Luke, Doreen didn't know where he could be. She'd lost track of him before, but only for a night or a weekend. She'd never not known where he was living. Doreen said her good-byes. She returned to the bedroom Jonathan had emptied. There were dark rectangles on the walls from posters he'd removed.

She dialed him a last time, ready, finally, for his voicemail. "I didn't know you could clean a house so well. And look at you— living on your own! I guess you've decided to grow up. Too bad you abandoned everyone who loves you in the process. I can't say I'm proud."

Doreen hung up wishing she'd thought of something meaner to say, something so biting that Jonathan, wherever he was, would feel as desolate as she.

11

Doreen sat at Lexie's kitchen table with the children's laptop. Since Jonathan disappeared, she and Lexie had operated in unspoken agreement: the children shouldn't be left alone. Tonight, Lexie was at the hospital until after midnight so Doreen was on watch.

She knew where he was living—Janice had told her after hearing it from Tillie. He'd moved into his boss's bachelor trailer out on Lake Hotchaburo. That made him the first member of her family to live in a trailer. Doreen had no intention of being the second.

She'd put Juliette and Thomas to bed, lined their bookbags in the hallway for tomorrow morning, packed their lunches and stuck them in the fridge. Now she opened their laptop, typed in their password. Navigated to the GED website.

Janice was right—there were online practice tests and study guides. But paying for those practice tests was as far as Doreen had gotten. She didn't have a computer at home, and her days at work were too busy to take the tests there.

She logged into the Mathematical Reasoning test. The other sections—Reasoning Through Language Arts, Social Studies, Science—didn't worry her much. She'd been a decent student, had completed all of her secretarial courses early, even took advanced English the first part of her junior year, right before she dropped out. But Algebra, Geometry—these classes she remembered as cryptic, unrelated to the math a person uses in real life. She knew how to balance a checkbook, double a pie, sew a skirt. She understood compound interest.

The instructions came up on the screen: she had an hour; she could use a calculator; she could flag answers she wanted to double-check. Doreen went into the hallway and dug through Juliette's book bag, found a calculator. She pulled a blank page from one of the girl's notebooks and borrowed a pencil too.

Back at the table, she hit continue.

The first problem had to do with counting on a number line and was easy enough. Some basic algebraic equations followed. Next came a question about the slope of a line on a graph, and Doreen felt confident in her guess. But then she was asked about the equation of a line passing through two sets of points. She couldn't remember having seen a problem like it before. Doreen rested her head on her hand. This was what she'd expected. When Lexie had decided to go to college, she'd had to take two full terms of remedial classes before she could even begin coursework. Remedial math. Remedial reading. Remedial writing. Doreen overheard her daughter-in-law working one night on a computer program meant to boost her reading skills. The computer's spoken commands were meant for children—*Spell redden. Spell fatten.*

Those plot points hung on the screen. Doreen guessed an answer, hit next. Guessed on the next question too.

The questions she didn't recognize outnumbered the ones she did.

She hadn't intended to be a woman approaching sixty without a high school degree. Her plan had been to finish high school in Florida after Jonathan was born. After moving back to Flyshoals, she'd thought to finish high school once Jonathan started kindergarten, but then her mother died and she'd found a job, and then her youth and middle years were past, her son grown, her grandchildren no longer babies.

Doreen entered the answer for the test's final word problem. The computer asked if she'd like to review any of her work. "No." She hit Score Exam.

The computer went through its paces. On the screen appeared a horizontal bar that went from red to yellow to green. The red was almost half of the bar and the green was the other half and the yellow a smidge in between. A score in the red meant the student would likely fail the Mathematical Reasoning portion of the GED; a score in the green meant the student would likely pass. Doreen's score fell in the narrow yellow strip between red and green. Too close to call, that's what the key read. Toward the bottom of the screen there was a note: she needed only 3 more correct answers to land in the green, to be a person who could anticipate a passing score.

Beneath her results was a study guide divided by topic.

Doreen went to the hallway and got Juliette's math text from her bookbag, brought it back to the kitchen table. *Linear equations,* she read on the computer screen. She flipped through the textbook's index, found the same term.

Her granddaughter could help her learn enough math to answer three more problems correctly. She could work with Juliette in the evenings while Lexie was at the hospital; she could work with Juliette on Sundays while Lexie was at Mercer's. No remedial classes. No computer commands meant for children.

When Lexie got home at midnight, Doreen greeted her with a beer. "Toast me."

"Why?"

"I signed up to take two GED section exams this Saturday at Flyshoals Tech."

"I didn't know you didn't have a high school degree."

"I don't make a habit of telling people. Even lied about it when Bird hired me." Doreen raised her beer. "Here's to lying no more."

Lexie tapped her can to Doreen's.

12

Halloween. Jonathan rode shotgun in the golf cart; his best friend Luke drove. Sandwiched between them were Luke's two boys, three-year-old Reese and four-year-old Ryland. Ryland was dressed as Superman and Reese had copied him. Both boys wore short capes that popped behind them in the wind. Amanda worked nights as a dispatcher at the police station and tonight she'd been called in unexpectedly. She'd dropped the boys off at Green Hills Country Club on her way to work. The boys had spent the final few hours of the day following their father around as he fertilized and watered.

But now the day was over. No golfers remained on the course. All of the grounds crew but Luke had gone home. Curtis, the golf pro, had gone home. Luke drove the cart straight down the fairway, heading for hole one. He drove fast, sitting on the edge of his seat. His bald head, a smooth browned nut, reflected what light was left in the evening sky. The cart hit a dip in the fairway, rattling the children. Each man grabbed the boy nearest him and held tight with an arm.

"Faster!" said Ryland.

"Let's go home," said Jonathan. "Give 'em some Benadryl. Put 'em to sleep."

Luke mounted the green and circled hole one. "Naw, man. They're kids. We've gotta wear 'em out." He left the green, took it straight and fast down the center of the fairway.

"One more time!" shouted Ryland.

Luke stopped the cart in front of the cinderblock box that passed for a clubhouse at Green Hills. Jonathan lifted each of the boys over his lap and set them on the ground. They ran to the door and the elder child knocked. The clubhouse girl opened the door. Luke had paid her ten dollars to stay late and help him out. "You again!" she said.

"Trick-o-treat!" Ryland stuck out his bag.

Reese copied his brother.

The clubhouse girl dropped a package of cheese crackers from the wire snack stand into each boy's bag. "Hershey's box is empty, Luke. This shit's gonna cost you a fortune."

"Naw. I'll put it back tomorrow."

"No, Daddy!" said Ryland.

"Just the crackers, son. What big boys keep are candy bars."

Ryland hid his bag behind his back. Reese copied him.

Luke clapped his hands. "Come on! One more time!"

"Jesus Christ." Jonathan reached into the cooler strapped to the back of the cart and took out another beer. The boys ran back to the golf cart; Jonathan lifted the boys one by one and returned each to the middle. Luke wrapped an arm around Ryland; Jonathan pulled Reese to his side.

"Maybe you'll get M&Ms this time," said Luke.

"M&Ms!" said Ryland.

"MMs!" said Reese.

"Benadryl," said Jonathan.

Hours later, Jonathan got his way. Reese and Ryland were asleep in Jonathan's borrowed trailer's only bed, younger one atop the big, sweet as littermates. Jonathan and Luke sat on the couch, watching a Freddy Krueger marathon on TV and drinking every time someone mentioned sleep.

The game had been Jonathan's idea, sleep being a topic on which he was bitter. He was doing so little of it. Five weeks he'd been gone from his wife and mother, and neither of the women who claimed to love him had shown up at his work, contrite and in need. Neither of them had shown up at his work in a fury. He'd moved to Powell's trailer to hasten his repatriation process, not to halt it.

"What you got to eat in this shit hole?" said Luke.

"Peanut butter. Go make yourself a sandwich."

"You're living in a bachelor pad. Where are the steaks, man? Bachelors don't eat nothing unless it's off the grill." Luke drank from the whiskey bottle.

"Nobody said sleep. Disqualified." Jonathan took the bottle and turned it up. "I'm no bachelor. Can't be a bachelor with two kids."

"What are you then? A divorcee?"

"Trial separation. We're trying out being separated."

Luke looked around the living room, into the kitchen. "It's working out good so far."

"Fuck you." Jonathan didn't need reminding that the trailer was a spongy-floored relic that stank of fish from years of catch cleaned directly into the kitchen sink.

Luke took the whiskey bottle back, nudged Jonathan's side.

He pointed out the open front door. The night was mild, the sky rich with glittering stars. The light from the trailer reached into the yard. At the light's edge, a brown and white bunny nibbled the long grass that grew beside the wooden patio.

Jonathan reached under the sofa, found his snubnosed .32. He fired a single shot through the open front door. The rabbit fell neatly to its side.

"Well, goddamn," said Luke. "Bet you woke the boys though."

The men waited. No wail came. "Benadryl," said Jonathan.

Luke took a red switchblade from his pocket. "Daddy won't eat peanut butter tonight." He walked out the front door of the trailer.

Jonathan said nothing. Something had gone wrong with the killing, though he couldn't say what. The boys were asleep. Luke had the rabbit in his hands. The sky was clear. But Jonathan felt lightning in the air. His hair stood on end with the threat of it, and there was an increasing scent of gunpowder.

Jonathan stepped onto the boards of the patio—they held. Nothing hot and errant fell from the sky.

"How you wanna cook this?" said Luke.

"You think it's okay to eat?" said Jonathan.

"Naw. I think we should sit on the couch and wait for something better to wander by. Maybe get us a veal cow."

"I've got charcoal." Jonathan went to his truck and rummaged around in the bed, found the charcoal. He took the cigarette from behind his ear. Coming in with the wind was a cloud or two, but high, thin, streaky ones. Lightning didn't seem possible.

He'd logged enough childhood hours at Flyshoals First Baptist to possess an image of a personal bolt sent by God though. This bolt was sneaking and vengeful. It crept through the woods on little feet and raised the minor symphony of twig snaps and limb cracks that he was indeed hearing. He strained his vision but could not see what passed in the woods. Little swift-footed lightnings.

Jonathan hurried to the porch, dumped the coals in the grill. They were self-lighting and flamed easily. He clamped the lid on.

Luke was in the kitchen, using toothpicks to wrap the rabbit in bacon like a present. "You had more than peanut butter. I found eggs for morning, too."

"Where's the rabbit feet?"

Luke nodded toward the trash.

"Why'd you throw out the goddamn feet?"

"Can't eat 'em."

"What's the point of killing a rabbit if you waste all the luck?"

Luke tossed the rabbit across the trailer. Jonathan caught it and fumbled about, trying to avoid the toothpicks. Luke stood grinning and bloody behind the kitchen counter, his bald head reflecting the fluorescent lights. He picked up a joint from the counter and stuck it in his mouth.

Jonathan took the kill outside. He rattled the grill to settle the coals and put the rabbit on an outside edge, away from the hot center. The smell of gunpowder lingered.

In the kitchen, Luke washed his hands and arms at the kitchen sink. The joint was a stub in his mouth. Jonathan took it from him.

Luke dried his hands on his jeans. "What do you want with those rabbit feet?"

Jonathan pulled on the joint; the paper burned down to his fingers. He flicked the roach into the sink. "I thought to keep one for myself and send the other to Lexie as a kindly gesture."

"From now on I'm gonna drink every time you're a

dumbass." Luke went back to his spot on the sofa and turned up the whiskey bottle.

Jonathan dug through the trash. He found the back feet, withered and tough looking with the bunny part gone. One had a bit of grass stuck in the paw. He rinsed them clean, set them to dry on a paper towel. Joined Luke on the sofa.

On the TV, Freddy Krueger, his body in flames, pressed against someone's mother. Luke turned the bottle up. "Nobody's asleep but it's still bad news." He passed the bottle. "It's only the left one that's lucky. That's the one you want."

"It's not me that needs help. Like I said, I aim to send one to Lexie. I got a paycheck coming to me. I got lights and water."

"You got a rabbit on the grill."

"I got a rabbit on the grill."

"You got a bottle of Jack Daniel's."

"I got a bottle of Jack Daniel's."

"You got a fish-smelling trailer and a jar of peanut butter."

Jonathan didn't agree to this item. "Everything Lexie's got is in my name. Car, house. Even her cell phone."

"She's got your kids, Johnny."

"Not for long. She can't afford to keep 'em. I cut bait. Canceled my direct deposit. Come tomorrow, I'll get paid but there won't be money waiting in the bank for her."

"Lexie tells Amanda you've been driving back and forth past your old house, spying. Amanda'd kill me if she knew I was with you now. I'll have to bribe the boys to keep 'em quiet."

"Me and Lexie are having a lover's spat. That's all."

"I thought it was a trial separation."

"Call it a trial spat."

"What the fuck do you do when you really fight?" Luke picked up the remote control and flipped through channels. Commercials, slasher movies, animated children's flicks. He stopped on *Jaws*. A woman floated on a raft close to shore while attack music played. "Watch this now. She don't hear that music playing. She thinks she's just getting her some sun." The woman on TV was taken down screaming. The sea stained red. "Trial spat." Luke turned the bottle up.

Jonathan went to the porch. There was the good smell of the rabbit cooking and, below that, the odor of expended fireworks. His scalp tingled. Powell's trailer sat perpendicular to the lake. The moon was nearly full, with its twin swimming beneath it. Revelers' sounds drifted over from the opposite shore, women shrieking, the low buzz of a chainsaw. Jonathan had no sense of how long the rabbit had been cooking. He tugged a leg and it loosened at the joint. "Dinner's ready."

Luke came outside and handed Jonathan a plate.

Jonathan took the rabbit from the grill. "Why don't you set us a table?"

Luke grabbed the two old rockers Powell had stacked in the corner of the patio. He slammed them down near one another, wiped away the spider webs with his hand. He went back inside, brought out the wobbly coffee table and set it between the rockers. Jonathan set the rabbit on the coffee table. Luke went inside for plates, went inside for forks, went inside for beers and the whiskey bottle and for knives and for a roll of paper towels. Then he sat down next to Jonathan. Inside, on the TV, somebody screamed.

"Go get my lucky feet," said Jonathan.

"Only one of 'em's lucky. I already told you."

"But bring 'em both."

"Why?"

"Because they're the only goddamn things you haven't brought outside yet."

Luke got the feet, brought them out on their paper towel and dropped them in Jonathan's lap. "Now say thank you, motherfucker."

84

Jonathan sawed at the rabbit until it was divided in two. He passed a plate to Luke and balanced his own plate on his lap atop the feet. Jonathan had cooked few things fresh since leaving Lexie, and the rabbit was moist from the bacon and smoky from the coals. It had the gamey twang of a life lived wild. He made pleased grunting noises as he chewed. The electrical threat hung in the air and might forevermore, but he had Luke beside him and food in his lap. There were the twin dancing moons, one on the wind, one in the water. "Look at those moons."

"I gotta wake up before they turn to suns," said Luke.

The men picked the bones clean and set their plates on the porch. Jonathan cupped a rabbit foot in each hand, rested his hands against his thighs, rubbed the furry toes and the dull claws. Mostly what he hoped for was the departure of his godawful scalp tingling, but mixed with this was the image of Lexie's legs as they'd once been of a summer, thin and tanned. She'd been as nimble as pinestraw, with two good tits on top. Jonathan pressed his thumbs deeply against the worn claws, willed magic into the bones.

He woke several hours later to the sound of Reese screaming from the bedroom. Luke jerked from his chair and stomped around the porch in the first-dawn dark, swearing and calling for his boys. He kicked his empty plate and it sailed out among the pines. Jonathan looked down at his own plate. The mess of rabbit bones that should've been there was gone. Local scavengers— raccoons, opossums, coyotes—something had come in the night and done away with all the parts the men could not digest. Even the lucky foot and its unlucky twin were missing, eaten right out of Jonathan's hands.

He checked his fingers, his toes—no bite marks. No charring either, no black smoking. The threat of the bolt had gone with the bones. No longer did his scalp tingle.

Luke went into the trailer, turned the television off on his way to his boys. Desperate soothing reached the porch: "Daddy's got to go to work. I'm taking you to Mommy at the police station. If you stop crying you can have a candy bar. Two candy bars. If you stop crying you can have all the candy bars you want for breakfast."

Jonathan steadied himself on his rocker as he stood. He was still drunk, but he had a few hours before work yet. He stumbled into his borrowed trailer to fill the small warm space left by Luke's boys. Maybe in the remains of another man's family he would at last find some rest.

13

Bird offered the little silver bowl of party nuts to Cece Hammond.

"Oh, no thank you," she said, straightening her yellow cardigan. She was as thin as Charlotte but there wasn't a thing wrong with her.

Bird offered the bowl to her husband, Clarence. He grabbed a handful, brushed off the salt that fell onto his massive belly. He and Bird were childhood friends; Charlotte and Cece had been sorority sisters. The couples were in the same supper club and had raised their children alongside one another, swapping carpool duties to the private school two counties away. As recently as last year, they'd holidayed together.

Bird returned the bowl to the coffee table. In the past six weeks, he and Charlotte had hosted more people for cocktails than they had in the past six years. Anyone living in town or close enough to visit wanted to drop by and offer condolences, which meant drinks, party nuts, conversations during which most anything other than Charlotte's diagnosis was discussed. "Another?" asked Bird, pointing at Cece's empty wine glass. Charlotte had always played hostess at their parties, but it was now understood that she was the guest of honor and Bird was to serve.

"Oh, why not?" said Cece.

Bird took the chardonnay from the wine bucket.

"Is Chuckie feeling better?" Charlotte asked, startling Bird. It had been some years since they'd openly discussed Chuckie Hammond with his parents, though behind Clarence and Cece's backs they'd discussed Chuckie often. Chuckie was Clarence and Cece's youngest son, and everyone knew he'd just come back from a third stint in rehab after overturning his car in a ditch during a blackout drunk and miraculously walking home unscathed. When the police knocked on Chuckie's door the next morning, they woke him up. He had no idea he'd done anything wrong. Clarence arranged things so Chuckie got a stint in a Colorado rehab in lieu of jail time in Georgia.

"Chuckie struggles so," said Cece. "He's our sensitive child."

"Our drunk, you mean," said Clarence.

Cece put her hand on Clarence's arm, but Clarence wouldn't be shushed. "This time he lost his job."

"He was in the company car when he had his accident," said Cece. "You know what sticklers insurance companies are these days." She looked pleadingly at Bird.

Bird murmured assent.

"He's coming back to Flyshoals," said Cece. "Athens is much too large for him. Too many temptations. He'll be better off here where people know him, know his family. He's not a bad boy."

Clarence turned to Bird. "We were married by the time we were Chuckie's age. You were working for your dad and I was working for mine. These women were setting up house. What's wrong with this generation?"

Bird heard Charlotte draw a sharp breath. He didn't want to get in the middle of the Hammonds' family drama, but he knew there'd be hell to pay later if he let Clarence compare Chuckie to Will. The boys—men now—were the same age, and once Bird thought they were similar in other ways too. For a long time it had seemed Will would never hold a job. He'd gone to school forever, two master's degrees and then a PhD. After each new degree he traveled for a year or so, claiming he knew too little of the broader world to plant himself. Charlotte had cried on Bird's chest about it, and Bird soothed her while quietly analyzing the ways that his son was a variation on his uncle, Nolin, a man who never settled down to a single woman, never worked a full week.

Then something clicked in place for Will. In the past five years, he'd taken a teaching job at the University of Georgia, married another professor, bought a house, had a baby. Charlotte would not have him compared to Chuckie over condolence cocktails, but neither could Bird deny Clarence's words outright— their great-grandfathers had been best men in each other's weddings. "Oh, things aren't so different now," said Bird. "You remember my uncle. Nolin catted around his whole life."

"That Nolin was handsome until the day he died," said Cece.

The conversation shifted to reminiscences, and Charlotte offered the little silver bowl of party nuts to Bird, a sign he'd done well.

After Cece and Clarence left, Charlotte and Bird moved to the couch, each with a fresh drink. She rested against the pillows and put her feet in his lap. He circled his thumb on her heels as she liked. "You could sell your book to Chuckie Hammond," she said.

"He'll need a job. Hammond Hardware doesn't make enough to cover the cost of keeping it open these days. Cece says Clarence is just too proud to let it go."

Bird rolled his head toward his wife without lifting it from the sofa. Nothing she said surprised him anymore. "If Chuckie Hammond takes over my business, all of my clients will go to Steve Wilkes."

"Steve Wilkes, Steve Wilkes. Every idea I have, you tell me that everyone will leave and go to Steve Wilkes. I'm sick of it, Bird."

"It's either him or me, Charlotte. We're the choices."

"I don't understand why he doesn't buy your book then. It makes the most sense."

Bird had explained, time and again, that with the options Charlotte gave him Steve Wilkes didn't have to buy anything. Steve Wilkes could just wait for Bird's clients to come to his door. Bird wasn't sure if his wife meant to ruin him, or if she had so little understanding of business she couldn't comprehend the situation. Certainly she'd not spent a minute in his office, hadn't wanted him to say more than "Fine" when he got home from work and she asked about his day. But she was smart—and cunning. He'd learned that much about her in the past several weeks. He found it hard to believe she didn't know what she was doing. "You're affecting Will's inheritance with this shit," he said, a new tactic.

Charlotte pulled her feet from his lap in protest. "Don't swear at me, Bird. I'm an excellent mother. Will gets everything in my name as soon as I die. I talked to Theo about it, and we made Will my primary beneficiary. He's protected no matter what you choose to do."

Bird didn't need Charlotte's inheritance to survive—she wasn't worth as much as him anyway—but it made him angry nonetheless. "How about I sell to Chuckie Hammond, effectively destroying my business and my career, and you let him keep

Doreen on?"

"If he keeps Doreen then nothing happens to your company. Your clients love her."

So she had been paying attention. "I can't keep Chuckie from re-hiring Doreen if that's what he wants to do."

"And in such a situation, it's Theo Waters' decision as to how to proceed. He knows, as you know, that this one thing is all I've ever asked of you."

But it wasn't an ask. Bird's marriage was a parasitic thing he no longer understood. He looked at his wife, aged twenty years since they sat together across from the oncologist. Did he love her? It wasn't a question that mattered. She would die, and he would not, and whether or not he was willing to go on living in the aftermath remained to be seen. It wasn't the grief of losing her that threatened him. Sometimes he even found himself wishing her dead. Shame was what waited, and it was shame that Bird was unwilling to survive. If Charlotte had Theo mail her letters, he planned to sit on the bank of his grandmother's pond and put his rifle in his mouth.

If she did not have Theo mail the letters—well then he didn't know what he'd do. If he couldn't convince Doreen to marry him, if she continued to reject him and he had to watch her suffer from afar, if he was left entirely alone—there were many reasons he might be finished with living beyond what Charlotte held over him. But so long as she didn't mail her letters, Bird could be the narrator of his own exit. He could write a careful suicide letter, craft a farewell that wouldn't ruin his family name. He would speak of the pain of losing Charlotte, the pain of a self-reflection begun too late. He would paint himself as a man who didn't appreciate the good, good wife he had until she was gone, while the deeper truths of his life—his feelings, his memories—would follow him to his grave.

1959

14

Emmy sat on his bed, his history text open before him. From the kitchen below came the sounds of his mother and Imogene, the maid, preparing dinner. Earlier these sounds had been accompanied by the low rumble of his father's voice, but that sound Emmy no longer heard, so he knew his father had retreated to the living room with the evening paper and three fingers of scotch.

Emmy rolled off his bed and went to the shelf that held his baseball cards, the one thing in his room that interested neither his mother nor Imogene, snoops both. He took off the lid and, using a ruler, slipped out the letter he'd folded and hidden along the edge of the box.

The letter had come last week to his parents' mailbox, and because he happened to be standing in the kitchen drinking a glass of water when Imogene came in the with the mail, it was delivered to him with only a raised eyebrow. His mother wouldn't have made it so easy. The writing on the envelope was old-fashioned and the envelope itself had a yellow tint, as if it had been waiting a long time to be put to use. He brushed a hand over the return address. Walthersville. First town to the east and an area he knew—he went duck hunting there with his father and uncle. He took the letter from the envelope and turned to better catch the spill of light from his bedside lamp.

January 15, 1959
Dear Emmy,

I'm the one stole your wallet at the McCormick place last fall. I write to say I'm sorry. I got your address off your driver's license. Circumstances being what they was then your wallet helped me some. But I ain't a thieving sort by nature and I've sworn not to go against who I am no more on account of Chicago turned out terrible for me and Silas. He's dead. I never thought to live without him. Most days I'm as sad as the day it happened. I write to ask forgiveness. A string of bad started up when I stole from you that I hope to end with this letter. I saved up your two dollars. You should find it in this same envelope. If you have a notion you can write me back at the address on the front. I'm returned to Georgia and married now. Cherlow had been one to take care of me and it seemed natural enough to marry him when Silas died. I couldn't stand being alone in Chicago. I'm the one gets the mail so you don't have to worry none about writing.

Sincerely,
Marla Hepple

His night with Marla stood out like something he'd dreamed. Once, he tried to share the details with Clarence Hammond, but stopped when he saw the expression on Clarence's face. The story made him sound like the sort of guy who claimed to have a girlfriend in another state. "I had you for a minute!" Emmy said, and Clarence laughed. But Emmy really had been seduced by a vagrant girl, an event that stood so strangely in his mind he sometimes thought of Marla as some sort of succubus, a mythical creature that had slinked over him after his grandmother's death.

From downstairs came the sounds of the front door opening and closing, his father greeting his uncle. Emmy returned the letter to the envelope, slipped it back into its hidey-hole. He returned the baseball cards to his shelf.

"Emmy!" his father called. "Nolin's here. Time for dinner."

Since Emmy's father and Nolin had told him that they planned to divest themselves of his grandmother's farm, Nolin had made greater efforts to befriend Emmy. While the sale crept through a governmental limbo, Nolin took Emmy there to hunt and to fish. He sneaked Emmy beer and girlie magazines, invited him to golf, even asked him over to play with his poker group one night. There weren't that many years between them—Nolin had been the only of the Marxton boys too young to draft during World War II. Emmy's own father walked with a limp from the time he served, and there was a middle brother lost forever at the bottom of the South Pacific.

Emmy pulled on the collared shirt his mother insisted upon at dinner. Two weeks ago, Nolin told Emmy's parents that he was with him for the night, and then let Emmy borrow his car to sneak pale, blonde cheerleader Sandra Wilmington all the way to Athens for a drive-in movie. At the movie, Sandra had let Emmy kiss her cheek and neck, had let him nibble her ear, had even let him slip a hand up her shirt and rub a single finger back and forth, back and forth, over the pointed foam cup of her bra while she stared straight ahead at the screen. After half an hour she said, "That's enough. I'm ready for popcorn."

Emmy wanted a date who wanted him back. A date who would spread quilts on the floor, and pull him down beside her, and unclasp her own underthings when his hands fumbled. He wanted Marla.

97

Dinner was nearing its end. "Pass the roast beef to your uncle," said Emmy's mother.

Emmy offered the china bowl, and Nolin held up a hand. "I've had sufficient," he said. "Thank you. That was delicious. You really outdid yourself this time."

"It was all Imogene. She's the real cook around here."

Emmy heaped another serving of beef onto his own plate.

"Governor Almond's going to have to reopen those schools," said Emmy's father, laying his knife and fork on his plate at four o'clock. Emmy had only been in eighth grade when the Governor of Virginia closed the public schools that were attempting to desegregate and then opened private schools for white students only. That meant that for three years he'd sat at his family dinner table and listened to his father hold forth about Governor Almond. "If they'd left well enough alone," his father said, "this wouldn't be happening. Separate but equal doesn't hurt anybody."

The kitchen door opened a few inches, and Imogene glanced at the table. Noticing that people were finished, she came to collect the dishes.

"I agree that black and white don't have to share a building," said Emmy's mother, passing her plate to Imogene. "But it's not right to leave that many children without education for so long. Some of those children are missing out on high school entirely."

Imogene collected Emmy's father's plate and Nolin's.

"Why don't you go up there and help the Quakers?" said Emmy's father. The Quakers had taken on the task of educating the children who'd been left without a school.

If his father started in on his mother about what he called her tenderheartedness toward the colored, she would go cold and stony and retreat to her bedroom as soon as the dinner clean-up was finished and Imogene had gone home. Then his father and Nolin would take the bourbon and escape to the two rusted metal chairs his father kept beneath the pecan trees, where they would drink until Nolin went home for the night. Emmy wouldn't stand a chance of getting his uncle alone. "I think it's terrible those kids can't go to school, Mother," he said.

Imogene took the plates into the kitchen.

Emmy's mother smiled at him. "You don't mind if we start dessert without you do you, Emmy? Imogene needs to get home to her family."

Emmy was usually the last one eating, and this usually bothered his mother. She liked for everyone to start together and finish together. Most nights she sat and watched him with a judge's scowl until he swallowed his last bite, but his comment of support had turned her towards him. "No ma'am. I don't mind at all."

Imogene returned to collect the serving dishes.

"Who wants dessert then?" said Emmy's mother. "Imogene made one of her apple pies."

"You know I'll never turn that down," said Emmy's father.

"I'll take a piece," said Nolin.

Imogene carried the serving dishes into the kitchen, and Emmy's mother went to help with the pie. After she and Imogene passed through the kitchen door, Emmy's father leaned toward Nolin. "Bourbon with dessert?"

"No need to ask."

"You sit here with Emmy while he finishes." Emmy's father left the dining room for his bar.

Emmy couldn't believe his luck. He was alone with Nolin. That such a window had opened with no effort on his part seemed a blessing on his desires. He leaned over the table and whispered. "You know how you told my parents I was with you and then let me borrow your car?"

"Yes."

"Will you do that for me again, please?"

"You like that Sandra, huh? She's a cute one."

"It's not Sandra."

Nolin swallowed the last of his wine. "You're too young to go steady anyway. Hell, I'm too young to go steady. Who is it?"

"Someone else." Emmy couldn't think of a good way to describe Marla to Nolin. "Someone Mother and Daddy can't know about."

"Why? What's wrong with her? Is she black?"

"No."

"Retarded?"

"No."

"Married?"

He wasn't going to tell Nolin that. "She's just poor is all. A sharecropper's daughter. I met her the night we were at Nana's farm. The night you and Daddy told me you were selling the place. Remember how I was gone all night?"

"You said you slept at McCormick house."

"I did. But I wasn't alone. There were some kids having a party there."

"I partied there myself a time or two."

"One of the kids was this girl. She wrote me a letter and said she wants to see me."

"So you got mad, ran away, and found a girlfriend in an abandoned house?"

Emmy felt the heat rise in his face. "Seems that way."

Nolin whistled soft and low. "My nephew the birddog. Flushing 'em from the bush. Where does this girlfriend of yours live?"

"Walthersville."

"That's closer than Athens. What're you gonna do, take her for a Coke float or something?"

"I guess so."

"Her parents know?"

"No."

"Keep it that way. Go for a picnic instead. Her parents

wouldn't want her with you anymore than your folks would want you with her."

"So you'll let me use your address to write to her?"

Emmy's father came into the dining room with a glass in each hand.

"I'd like an ice cube," said Nolin, winking at Emmy.

Emmy's father took the glasses into the kitchen.

"I'll cover for you, Birddog. Let me check my calendar and get back to you on a date."

Emmy shoved another bite of meat in his mouth as his mother came through the door holding two plates of apple pie with ice cream.

January 21, 1959

Dear Marla,

I forgive you for stealing my wallet. Circumstances explain behavior sometimes. The fact that you saved up the two dollars you took tells me who you are apart from circumstance.

I know the area where you're living. It's pretty out there. I go duck hunting there with my father and my uncle. My uncle told me I can borrow his car, so if you're interested, I could meet you sometime. We can talk face to face. I know you're married so we can't really go to town, but we could have a picnic. I can bring a blanket and some sandwiches.

If it's wrong of me to ask you this, I apologize. You can write and tell me no. Or you can not write back at all.

If you decide to write back, use the return address on this envelope instead of the address on my license please. The address on this envelope is my uncle's. If you write me at his house, nobody will know we're writing. My mother is a snoop and so is our maid. And, of course, you're a married woman now.

Affectionately,

Emmy Marxton

2009

15

"Doreen!" A young woman holding a striped golf umbrella and a massive orange purse fought her way through the front door. "God, this weather! I got your message! You know how Jeff is. Such an airhead." The woman sat in a chair across from Doreen and opened her purse.

Doreen passed her a pen. "Don't worry about it." Jeff and Joanne Smith seldom paid their premiums on time. As she did most months, Doreen called yesterday to let them know that if the money wasn't in before week's end their policy would no longer be in force.

Joanne ripped the check from her book. "How's Bird doing? So sad about Charlotte."

"He's home with her mostly."

"Is that the plan? To keep her at home?"

"I think that's what everyone wants."

Joanne snapped her purse closed. "He's lucky he has you

here to keep things going for him."

Doreen knew Joanne waited to see if she would get any information. Many of Bird's clients had asked, both directly and indirectly, what he planned to do with his business. "After all these years I can run the office as well as he can," said Doreen. "Nobody needs to worry."

"Well, you let Bird know the Smiths are praying for him. I put him and Charlotte on the prayer list."

"He'll be glad to hear that. Tell Jeff hello, and give that girl of yours a hug."

Joanne stood and took a mint from Doreen's candy dish. "She's not so huggable anymore. Twelve years old. I've got to go get her from school right now. Almost every week she gets sick. Headache, sore throat, you name it."

"You'll look back one day and laugh."

Joanne said her good-byes, and Doreen reached for her coffee cup, found it empty. There was still half a pot on the warmer.

While Doreen stirred her coffee, she looked at the photos on the wall behind the coffee station. Most of the pictures had been there since she began at Marxton Casualty and Life: Bird's father in front of the office on opening day; Bird's uncle beside the filing cabinet; Bird as a teenager typing at what later became Doreen's desk. There was a picture of Doreen too, the only photo in color, taken a few years after she began. Her hair was winged in the style of the times, her eyes heavily lined. She looked like a child in the picture, but she'd been competent at her work. Not that she'd recognized her competency. In some quiet corner of herself, she'd felt like a sham. Daughter of the abortionist and no high school degree. Now that she'd gotten her GED, the shame she'd carried for so long seemed silly. There had been no fundamental flaw within her. Last week she'd signed up for the insurance exams. When Bird stopped by the office, they carried on as if he were not threatening to overturn her livelihood. She hadn't told him what she was doing. She wasn't sure what a GED or licensure meant for her, didn't know how to play these new cards in her hand.

The door clanged; Doreen turned. Bird. He came to her and took her coffee mug, set it down, pulled her to him. Pushed his face past her hair to kiss her neck.

An adage of her mother's came to her: "A person's ways are like flames." In the past two months, Bird had revealed how his ways could burn her. But fire nourished too, warmed the body, filled the belly. She'd missed his touch. The blinds were up and so she stepped away from him. "Go wait for me."

He hurried down the hall. Two decades ago, she'd decorated the break room for them: a breakfast table with two chairs, a poster of a beach scene, an overstuffed sofa. She sent the phone to voicemail and hung the plastic clock on the front door showing that the office would reopen in forty-five minutes. She closed and locked the door, lowered the blinds over all of the windows. Went to meet her lover. Afterward, she could talk to him as her boss and find out why he was here and what this visit meant.

16

A couple months in Powell's trailer and beside Jonathan on the couch were two piles of cash: living and savings. The savings pile wasn't as tall as he'd like—Powell had him on furlough one day a week—but it was taller than it would be if he were giving his earnings to Lexie. On TV, a Muay Thai fighter kicked the shit out of his opponent. The rain on the trailer's tin roof intensified.

Commercial break. Jonathan wrapped the savings pile in plastic wrap. He couldn't trust the bank to keep his money safe. Flyshoals was small and if Lexie begged the right suit in the right way—if she flashed those legs, that marriage certificate: all would be for naught.

Good weather brought people to the fish camp, but bad weather emptied it. Jonathan could lose hours thinking of how far he'd need to walk in any direction before he found another living soul. There were homes on the lake outside of the fish camp, but those homes were also good weather destinations, empty now, and not owned by anyone in Flyshoals anyway. Beyond the lake were timber company pines. Beyond the timber company pines were a few farming operations, subsidized chicken mostly, some government hog, cheap syrup corn. So much space and him in the middle, a bored, beating heart.

He'd never lived alone. Without other people around, only work kept a man sane. Jonathan assigned himself tasks. Time to hide the money.

He shoved his living cash between two sofa cushions. The savings cash he stuck in a Tupperware bowl. He grabbed his raincoat and put on his steel-toed work boots, as if, on this Monday afternoon, he had something real to do.

Outside rain poured down, but an important thing he'd learned was to make a plan and keep it. Two nights ago he came home double-vision drunk, but still took up the ax and chopped the wood for his firepit.

The rain was too thick to see through. The advantage of this was that nobody would see his hiding place. In every situation, find the advantage. Another thing he'd learned living alone. The mind is neither friend nor foe until its owner makes it such.

Beneath the kitchen window was a loose board. Below this, a hole covered with a wood shingle. Jonathan added his savings to his hole, replaced the shingle. Replaced the porch board.

A day's work finished.

Motherfucker.

Still neither his mother nor his wife had shown up. He'd gotten a single voicemail from his mother after leaving her house. He'd gotten nothing from his wife. She hadn't even acknowledged that he'd canceled the direct deposit. Jonathan longed for rescue. Even asked God for it sometimes, a thing he'd not done since was a boy.

Jonathan saw through the rain, at the edge of the woods, a

spot of red.

The spot was round like a balloon, but it didn't bob. Somehow it hung in place only a few feet from the ground. Jonathan crossed his porch and stepped onto the grassy spot of winter rye he'd planted.

There, at the woods' edge, stood a boy holding a red umbrella. His camouflage raincoat, camouflage rainpants and camouflage rainboots dwarfed him.

Fatherly spirit awakened in Jonathan. The child looked younger than Thomas. "Don't be scared. I can help you." The boy wore ugly plastic glasses, the secondhand type one gets for free from the Shriners, and the lenses were fogged opaque. The child's hair was the same black as the frames. "What's your name?"

"Trayton. But everybody calls me Snooker. I'm waiting for it to stop raining so I can see to get home."

"I can take you home."

"You don't know where I live."

"You can tell me."

"You're a stranger." Snooker had streaks down both cheeks as if he'd been crying, but that could have been condensation from his glasses. He didn't look like a crier.

"How about I wait with you?"

Snooker raised his umbrella to cover Jonathan. It wasn't large enough to shield them both; a rivulet of water found its way past the neck of Jonathan's raincoat. He didn't complain though. Snooker was the brightest event his day had brought. He moved a half-inch left, sent the rivulet into his jeans instead.

When the rain paused, Snooker unzipped his coat and cleaned his glasses on his shirt. They fogged again when he returned them to his face. He took them off and waved them about, weary as a senior citizen.

"How old are you?" said Jonathan.

"Older than you think. I'm small for my age. But I don't care. When you're driving, every ounce counts."

"Driving?"

"Nascar." Snooker started walking.

Jonathan followed. "You wanna race Nascar?"

"I was almost sponsored by Red Bull last year."

"Almost." They walked past trailers modified with porches or additional rooms. Residents with more skill had lashed two trailers side by side or stacked them one atop the other. Some yards had whirligigs and strings of birdhouse gourds—feminine touches. Powell's place was off by itself and looked like hell.

"This is where I live." The trailer Snooker indicated was nice enough, and it had a new, black F-250 with a shiny trailer parked in the drive. Young Servants Racing was printed on the trailer's side in big yellow letters. Below this, in smaller script: Racing for the Dear Lord. "My dad's Faster Pastor. You probably heard of him."

Jonathan didn't have any idea what Snooker was talking about, but he followed the boy to the front door. The child pulled a key from this pocket, opened the door an inch, peeked inside.

"You can come back in," said a woman's voice. "Everybody's awake but Daddy."

Inside, the trailer was cozy with lamplight and the smell of roasting meat. A radio played Christian rock softly in the corner. At the stove, a plain, squat, white woman whisked milk into a pan. Lengths of flowery material wrapped around her upper body in a complicated way and held a baby on her back. The woman eyed Jonathan while she questioned her son. "You have a good time playing outside?"

"Yes ma'am. I met this neighbor." Jonathan and Snooker

dripped on the small square of linoleum inside the door.

"Nicole Hartley," said Snooker's mother. Her glasses were a similar awful plastic to her son's.

"Johnny Swilley."

"Nice to meet you, Johnny. Take off your wet things and give them to Snook. He'll hang 'em in the bathroom. Then close the door and come have a seat. Once I have this gravy settled I'll get you something to drink."

Jonathan and Snooker stripped off their rain gear. Under the outsized clothing the boy was even smaller than he'd seemed. Snooker took Jonathan's raincoat and his own damp things and disappeared into the back of the trailer.

Jonathan closed the door but remained on the linoleum. His clothes were soaked. Nicole eyed him. "There's nothing in this house to fit you." She spread a dishtowel over a chair. "Sit here and bring that space heater close."

Jonathan did as instructed. The warmth chilled him, set him to shivering and waiting to dry. Always something else to wait on. "I found your son lost in the woods by my house. He couldn't see through his glasses."

"Snooker's a homing pigeon. He was likely standing there hoping to meet you." She tapped her whisk, set it on a cow-shaped spoon rest. "We're not a drinking family, but I've got sweet tea, Coke and lemonade."

Pentecostal, thought Jonathan. Evangelical, Charismatic. All three the same so far as he was concerned. The trailer lost its charm. Jonathan's sinuses ached with chill and God's music and dull lamplight and the cloying maternality of Nicole Hartley. If she wrapped five more babies to her body she'd only look more herself. "No offense ma'am, but you don't even know who I am."

Nicole Hartley took a glass from a cabinet. "'Inasmuch as ye have done it unto one of the least of these my brethren, ye have done it unto me.'"

She scooped ice from the freezer with her hand. "Those words cover good things and bad." She took a 2-liter Coke from the fridge, filled the glass and set it in front of Jonathan. When he reached for the glass, she held it. "For all you know, I keep a pistol on my waist. Good behavior, that's what we'll show each other." She released the glass, turned away. "Staying for dinner?"

Noise in the hallway. "This is my dad," said Snooker. The man whose hand he held was not long from bed. Black hair sticking up, five o'clock shadow, groggy eyes. It was obvious where Snooker got his build.

Jonathan stood and stuck out his hand. "Johnny Swilley."

"Call me Faster." His grip was not the grip of a small man.

Faster sat down across from Jonathan, and Snooker joined them. Nicole brought two more Cokes to the table.

"I'm down by the lake," said Jonathan. "Last trailer on the left. Powell McGaha's place."

"Don't know him," said Faster. "We moved in last week. This place belongs to Nicole's stepdaddy."

"Nice thing to have in the family. So what sort of pastor are you?"

"If you mean which church do I lead, I haven't had one in a while. Last church I had was one me and Nicki ran together in a truckstop parking lot. Transdenominational. Get it?"

"Yeah."

"Didn't go over. Most people thought transgender. Truck stops don't attract the most open-minded congregations."

Nicole brought a handful of silverware and napkins to the table. "Lay these out, Snooker, and go find another chair."

"Yes ma'am."

Faster rocked his chair to its back legs, mashed at his hair. "The Lord has a plan for me other than church."

"Snooker?"

"You heard of him?"

"Only since I rescued him from the woods."

"He almost got picked up by Red Bull last year."

"So he said."

Nicole pulled plates from the cabinet, slapped out servings of mashed potatoes. "We moved into this place to save money."

"Two hundred dollars a pop," said Faster, "for tires alone. You can't resurface 'em but four times before they gotta be replaced. You can go through four sets in a weekend. There're other expenses too." Nicole slid a plate of food in front of Faster. "After dinner we'll go look at the car."

Snooker brought a stepstool into the kitchen, set it beside the kitchen table. "This was all I could find."

"That'll do for me," said his mother. "I can sit there and wear baby Roro." She set out the other plates, and then opened a paper napkin and spread it over the stepstool. "Grace." She bowed her head. "Would you like to say it, Jonathan?"

"Grace," said Jonathan.

Faster and Snooker giggled.

Nicole launched into a prayer about heathens, neighbors, chance, and salvation.

17

After making love with Bird in the breakroom, Doreen sat beside him on the sofa in her slacks, blouse untucked, legs curled beneath her.

"Hospice came in last week," he said.

She took his hand. "I'm sorry."

"Will and Leigh are driving back and forth from Athens, getting subs to teach their classes. Charlotte's so angry they don't want her left alone with me. She tells Will he shouldn't have anything to do with me. She says I shouldn't be around my granddaughter."

Doreen smoothed Bird's hair. "She could have left you a long time ago, and she didn't. Keep apologizing."

"You're the one I should apologize to."

"The only thing I stand to be angry about is this business. Clients are asking what you plan to do, Bird. I don't know what to tell them."

"Tell them nothing is changing."

"Is that the truth?"

"Reenie, if you don't tell them that they'll go over to Steve Wilkes, and I won't even have anything to sell. I have to find somebody to buy my book that I trust to run my business. Someone our clients trust."

"Someone licensed to sell insurance."

"That too."

"Someone who can afford to buy your business." Doreen had done her own research, and she had an idea of how Bird's business would be valued—maybe as high as seven hundred thousand dollars. "That rules out most of this town."

From the front office there came the sound of knocking on the door. Bird made to stand from the couch, but Doreen put a hand on his arm. "I put the clock up. We have ten minutes."

He settled again. "I'll have to finance it. I know that." He turned to look at her. "Have you thought about what I asked you before? The thing you told me not to ask."

Here in the breakroom, glowing from their lovemaking, she felt the ways Bird was dear to her. His proposal felt, for a moment, less like an insult. "I'll never marry you. Sell your book to me instead."

Confusion clouded Bird's features.

"I'll be licensed soon. I've signed up for the tests. Our clients know me, and I know them. My only worry was the loan, but if you're financing the sale." Again the knocking came from the front office, louder this time. Doreen checked her watch—five minutes. She stood and tucked in her blouse. "Tell Charlotte you're meeting her halfway. You'll retire and be with her, but you get to choose who you sell to." She took her suit coat from the back of the chair.

"Reenie, I can't sell a business my dad started to my mistress."

Doreen put a hand on the chair to steady herself. She'd not

expected such words. The image of a forest fire came to her, all of the woodland creatures fleeing the blaze. But she kept her face neutral and her voice calm. She stepped into her heels. "That is not how I'm seen in this office. I get Christmas cards from our clients. I know their dogs and their kids. I send them flowers when their parents die."

"You grew up the way you did—with the mother you had. What I'm saying is, you were raised not to care how this town judged you." The person knocking at the front door began a steady, ceaseless beat.

Doreen left the breakroom, flipping off the lights as she left, leaving Bird alone in the dark. She turned on lights as she passed through the office. Whoever it was didn't stop knocking, though they could see by the lights coming on inside that help approached. She pulled the cord to open the door blinds.

The person revealed foot to head was Charlotte. Not Charlotte as Doreen had known her though. The woman's once enviable thinness had worsened to emaciation. Pink scalp shone through her hair. Her coral lipstick glowed from her pallor. She tapped the metal cane she held against the window glass.

Doreen opened the door.

Charlotte used her cane to walk inside, her pace slow, her breathing labored. "I had Minnie drive me." Minnie, Charlotte's housekeeper, had a son the same age as Jonathan. Doreen had been room mother with Minnie when the boys were in third grade. She leaned out the office door, raised a hand toward Charlotte's BMW. Minnie didn't wave back. "You can say hello to Minnie when you get the toolbox from my front seat."

Between Charlotte and Doreen there had been a cold etiquette. Charlotte hadn't commanded Doreen, and Doreen hadn't been familiar with Charlotte. But now, as Charlotte limped toward a chair, she said, "Go get the toolbox, Doreen. I'm too weak to carry the damn thing myself."

Doreen thought on things that made her feel gentle toward Charlotte—the miscarriages the woman had suffered early in her marriage; the years Charlotte had nursed Bird's father, keeping him in her home even after he no longer recognized her as his daughter-in-law. Doreen went for the toolbox.

Outside, the sky was low and gray, the day cold. Doreen went to the passenger side of Charlotte's BMW, opened the door. "Do you know what's going on?"

Minnie's eyes were empathetic pools, but she kept her voice neutral. "Never has been any of my business."

Doreen took the toolbox from the floorboard of the car. She faced the red brick of Marxton Casualty and Life. To the left was a furniture store that had gone out of business a few months ago, the windows painted from the final sale: *Everything must go! All items 50-75% off!* To the right was a long empty space that had once been the music shop where Jonathan shoplifted cassettes. The closed blinds at Marxton Casualty and Life made it look abandoned too. Doreen opened the box to see what she delivered—tools only. Screwdrivers, hammers, a tape measure. No knife. No handgun.

Back in the office, she set the toolbox on her desk calendar.

"Go and get him," said Charlotte. "I saw his truck out front. I want the two of you to do something for me. Together."

Office talk was audible in the break room. Doreen knew Bird listened. "He went to Strickland's for lunch. He told me to lock up and go home." Bird could sneak out the back door and hurry down to the restaurant. "Go meet him. Surprise him. I'll help you down there."

"'Keep it quiet,' Bird, that's what I said. Men have affairs with their secretaries. 'Keep it quiet.' Then I would drive by and see the blinds closed in the middle of the day like an announcement."

"Let me walk you down to Strickland's, Charlotte."

"Thirty years and what did you get out of him? A few

closed-curtain fucks. I asked him what else he'd given you. He said nothing. Not even a piece of jewelry. How does it feel to be the sort of woman who gets thirty years of nothing out of a man and considers that enough?"

Charlotte was a wraith. Her silken shirt hung like borrowed clothes. She'd stopped her botox and filler regimes—her face was more pliable than it had been in years and all of her aging was bent toward fury. Doreen could have been the one to die first, or Bird. "I'm a woman who has cared for your husband. Just as you've cared for him."

Charlotte touched the toolbox. "We fought. That's why he came here today. Bird always has needed a babysitter. I suppose I should thank you."

Bird came into the office. He'd not bothered to finish dressing. In his undershirt and khakis, he kneeled beside his wife's chair. Charlotte fell into him, her cries raw and gasping. He slid an arm under her legs and stood, lifting both her and her cane. "It will never be any different," she said. "We'll never be anything but this."

Bird walked out the office door in his stocking feet, carrying his wife.

Between two slats of the window blinds, Doreen watched Bird ease Charlotte into the front seat of his truck. He buckled her seatbelt, pulled a handkerchief from his pocket and wiped her face. Minnie drove away. Doreen went to the break room and grabbed Bird's clothes and shoes. As she brought these into the office, he came through the door.

She shoved his things into his chest. "Go. She'll come in here again."

"What she said. It isn't true."

But after their exchange in the break room, Doreen could imagine Bird swearing to Charlotte that he'd never given her anything of worth, holding up as examples the desk calendar of

119

knock-knock jokes, the pen with the rhinestone cap. He wouldn't explain to his wife that Doreen refused nicer gifts. He couldn't even understand why she'd done that. Worth, to Bird, wasn't an internal state, but something determined by others. He wouldn't know how to defend her worth because he didn't see it himself. Somehow, Doreen hadn't understood until now that he was hollow. She resisted saying these things out loud. Not because the pain from Charlotte's accusations lay on his face, but because their conversation about the future of Marxton Casualty and Life wasn't over yet. "Sell me your book, Bird."

"Chuckie Hammond is going to buy it."

"Chuckie Hammond?"

"He's an idiot, but he's Clarence's son. Charlotte—she set it up."

Doreen nodded as if she understood. "Go to your wife."

The clanging door settled into its groove. Doreen stood in the shadow of Marxton Casualty and Life. She'd assumed a shuttered office said lunch. No: that was a delusion. She'd known damn well what an office closed at midday communicated to Flyshoals, and she hadn't cared. Is that why Charlotte was behaving the way she was now? Had she reached the end of her time and realized that she'd been lying to herself? Doreen summoned a feeling of kinship toward the woman: they both rushed to save themselves from traps they'd laid with their own hands.

From Charlotte's toolbox, Doreen got a Phillips head and a flathead screwdriver. In the hall closet where she kept her cleaning supplies, there was a collapsible stepstool. She carried the stool to the picture window in Bird's office and slipped off her heels. The blinds were hung originally by Bird's father, but the old screws left the plaster easily, as if even the objects in the room had long been praying for an increased transparency.

18

Because Jonathan was warm and heavy with Nicole's venison and potatoes, he did not laugh at the thing Faster backed onto the drive. It was a go-cart. Black and shiny and not quite so boxy as a regular go-kart, but a go-kart nonetheless. Jonathan didn't care for Nascar, but he'd held certain expectations of the racing trailer's contents. A fucking go-cart.

Eyes alight, Faster bent to a knee and stroked the body with a chamois. Snooker was inscrutable beneath a massive helmet.

The rain was gone, though the cold remained. "Mind if I smoke?" said Jonathan.

"Not if you share." Faster stood and stuck the chamois in a pocket.

The helmet shook no.

Faster peered in the tinted face screen. "It's hard for Daddy, but don't worry, I'm on a three-part stopping program. First, I quit buying 'em. Next I'll quit asking for 'em. Then I'll quit smoking 'em."

"Seems you've conquered step one." Jonathan passed a cigarette.

Faster pulled the helmet from Snooker's head. "Run on in there with your Momma while I do this." Snooker returned his glasses to his face. He'd already explained that he only wore his contacts on racing days on account of the expense. He walked across the yard toward the trailer door.

Faster bent for the light Jonathan flamed. "Kid's got asthma. Cigarette smoke don't help him none."

"Nor car exhaust, I'd reckon."

Faster pressed a leg against the go-kart as a man may do with a Grand Am. "You're one who says what he feels, straight out. Calls bullshit when you see it."

"I'll say that's a go-kart. Your son thinks he's racing Nascar."

"A man can't hop in a stock car and race like Earnhardt. That sort of racing takes years of build-up, all through boyhood. It's like football. You remember Fran Tarkenton?"

Jonathan cared for football only slightly more than he cared for Nascar. "I'm not one for group activities. Nascar. Football."

"A lone wolf. Whaddya like then? You like to fish?"

"Had a boat once."

"A boat's easy come, easy go. I lost a few myself. How about hunting? You hunt?"

"A little."

"Deer? Turkey? I know a helluva trick you do with a trotline and bait corn. One church I had, long time ago, I provided Thanksgiving turkeys for every family."

"Last thing I shot was a rabbit," said Jonathan.

"Rabbit's good eating. Nicki don't like the gamey twang but I tell her that's the part what puts hair on your chest." Faster stepped close. "Other thing I'm on a three-part quitting program from is drinking."

"Well, now. Drinking is something I like too."

Jonathan and Faster sat on the dock watching the sky and water turn rosy. It would be a clear night. Faster opened two more beers from the cooler. "Here's the thing: Nicki ain't my first wife. Snooker and Roro, they ain't my first kids. I got three more grown I don't see come Christmas." A cold breeze rectifying to the mind came off the water. "The two ex-wives I can do without, but those kids. One of my grown boys is a Marine. He's turned out as fine as a man can be and he's decided I'm not worth seeing."

"I'm not divorced. A separation is all this is. A trial separation."

"Your wife know that?"

"She'll figure it out once she gets to missing me."

"A woman only puts up with so many trials." Faster drained his beer and dropped the empty in the cooler. He pulled a pack of Juicy Fruit from his pocket. "Covers the smell." He waggled the pack toward Jonathan.

Jonathan waggled his can. "You going somewhere?"

"Work."

"You work nights? What are you, a security guard?"

"No sir." Faster made the short journey to his feet.

"Chicken plant?"

"Not this man."

"You're not a fucking cop are you?" Briefly, Jonathan imagined Faster at the police station laughing with Luke's wife, Amanda, the two of them mocking the pigheaded optimism of Johnathan Swilley, what with his trial separation and his borrowed bachelor hovel, his belief that things could work out.

"No, I'm a Renaissance man. Got my fingers in this pot, that pot."

Jonathan dropped his empty in the cooler and fished around for another. His beer was finished and he had hours before sleep. "What you are is a man who'll drink another man's beer and then take his leave." Jonathan jumped up and grabbed Faster by the collar, dragged him to the dock's edge. "You a strong swimmer?"

Faster put a hand on Jonathan's chest. "I invite you along. Night work gets lonely. And I'm the only one doing this work around here. There's too much profit for one."

Jonathan released Faster, brushed his shirtfront straight. "Seeing as how my social calendar is blank tonight, I thank you for the invite." Whatever he got into with the little preacher was sure to be better than sulking alone.

19

Lexie sat at Ms. Paulsen's kitchen table. Out the bay window the woman's horses, a pinto and a chestnut, grazed as the light shortened. From the waist up, Lexie was dressed in a shirt and suit coat. Waist down she was in scrubs, but the person on the other side of the computer could only see her top half. "We'll be in touch," said the woman on Lexie's screen, the lead nurse in a pediatrician's office in an Atlanta suburb called Snellville. "Please tell Janelle hello for me."

The interview wrapped up and Ms. Paulsen—Janelle, though Lexie could not bring herself to think of her that way—came into the kitchen. "From where I was it sounded like it went well."

Lexie drank from a glass of water. She'd asked Ms. Paulsen to eavesdrop and give her feedback. It was her fourth interview; she'd been turned down for three positions. "But what did I do wrong?"

"Why do you think you did something wrong?"

"I'm not getting any of the jobs I apply for."

"Give it time."

Last week, Ms. Paulsen had located Flyshoals Tech in the educational hierarchy for Lexie. It wasn't only that the nursing shortage hadn't reached Flyshoals. It was also that there wasn't a shortage for every type of nurse from every type of school. Lexie fought down Jonathan's voice in her head—*It's a racket they're running over there. Not selling you anything but debt.*

Ms. Paulsen took two mini cans Cokes from the fridge. "I know what I teach about soda, but sometimes a woman needs a Coke." She raised her eyebrows at Lexie.

"Yes, please."

Ms. Paulsen brought the cans to the table. "I signed up for the military in the cafeteria of my high school. It was a way to go to college. I wanted to be a doctor. Got sent to Desert Storm." She drank from her Coke. "I had some health problems after. So I became a nurse. And now I'm a professor. We don't plan most of what happens to us."

In the field, Ms. Paulsen's horses played, trotting alongside one another, tossing their manes. "I never thought on what I wanted to be," said Lexie.

"You were a child once. Children dream."

With some effort, Lexie remembered her mother. They'd sat together on the front porch, each coloring one half of a coloring book. *That's pretty, baby.* "An artist, maybe?" said Lexie, though what stood out about the memory wasn't the coloring, but the sense of being enveloped in something gentle and good and safe.

That was what she wanted. Safety. That was her dream for herself. It was what led her to Jonathan, and what led her away from him now. It was what she'd loved about Doreen. *He's not here,* Doreen had said, *That bastard isn't here.* Doreen had taught Lexie that safety was the result of a steady job and a balanced checkbook. But Lexie got those things for herself and they didn't make her safe. They didn't make her children safe either.

Lexie looked around Ms. Paulsen's kitchen. The glass front cabinets showed only a few plates; in the drainer a single mug dried. "I want to be single," said Lexie.

20

Doreen took the last window blind to the alley dumpster, Charlotte's imprint following along and haunting her as if she were already dead. Doreen had never struggled with guilt over her relationship with Bird, but now she couldn't shake Charlotte's presence. She wanted the woman gone. Bird had found someone to sell his book to, and Doreen wasn't going to be haunted forever by his dead wife. The Marxtons weren't a family that anyone could win in a fight against anyway. With his hollowness, Bird was a vessel that contained the whole town and kept it shaped as he liked, just as a pitcher keeps water from finding its level as a puddle on the table. Doreen went back inside, returned to her desk, and pulled up an example of proper resume format. It didn't take long to type one up—she'd only worked at Marxton Casualty and Life.

She pulled into the Walmart lot toward the end of the day. The

HR representatives and payroll managers, the employees with experience similar to hers, would be wrapping up their hours at their desks. She needed a few minutes with them before they went home. The parking lot was full of cars, more than she'd ever seen at Mercer's. She went through the front doors, caught the eye of a woman her age who was straightening shopping carts. Doreen didn't recognize the woman from around town. She'd heard the Walmart was pulling in people from up to an hour away. "I'm here to apply for a job," said Doreen.

The woman pointed toward the front of the store. Two gray-haired women worked a register together. One rang, one bagged. "Ask them to page Mr. Hale. He's the manager-on-duty. Tell him you want to join the Flyshoals' Retirement Community." The woman smiled without humor.

Mr. Hale glanced over Doreen's resume. They stood inside his office, beside a shiny poster of a snowy mountaintop. The space smelled of fresh paint. "You have to fill out the online application first. There's a computer near the entrance where you do it. Then I can put you to work on a register at once."

"So if I fill out the online application I have a job?"

"If you pass the background check. And the drug screening. This is a zero tolerance workplace. We do random urine tests."

"To run a cash register?"

Mr. Hale rubbed his bald head. He was a handsome man, but he'd aged early, was probably younger than Jonathan. "Will you have a problem meeting those requirements?"

"Of course not."

"You have to be able to lift at least sixty pounds. And stand on your feet all day. Can you lift and stand?"

"I can."

"You can lift *and* stand?"

Doreen wasn't going to be made to say it. "Believe it or not."

"A lot of women your age can't. You can work 34 hours a week but not a minute over. We're only hiring part time. No benefits."

Doreen tapped her resume in Mr. Hale's hand. She wanted full-time work with health insurance, didn't want to go uncovered until Medicare kicked in. "I've worked as an executive secretary for over thirty years at Marxton Casualty and Life. I have excellent recommendations. I understand business. Do you have any managerial positions? Something in payroll? HR? I fill all those roles at my current job."

"Those positions are filled by headquarters, and they require college degrees." Mr. Hale pointed his thumb over his shoulder. Behind his desk hung his framed diploma from the University of Georgia, over in Athens. The school where Bird's son taught. "Go up front and fill out the online application. That's the first step."

"Thank you for your time." Doreen stuck her hand out.

Mr. Hale's grasp was soft and his wrist weak and he failed to meet her eye. Doreen gripped his hand harder, gripped until he glanced up at her, surprised.

She left his office and walked out of the store without stopping. The man could thumb her eyes toward his degree a million more times and it wouldn't change the facts: she was too qualified to bag men's boxers and bars of soap. She couldn't afford to live on minimum wage. Not without Social Security. And she needed health insurance.

Charlotte's hobbled ghost faded to nothing while Doreen crossed the parking lot. Charlotte had never held a job in her life, and it was Doreen's efforts that had made that possible. Doreen was good at her work, but she knew Charlotte would have done as fine a job. Charlotte had never worked at Marxton Casualty and Life though and neither had Will, not even as a teenager. His father spent his teen years typing at what became Doreen's desk. It wasn't easy for a man to manage a small company in a way that didn't place demands on his entire family.

Doreen got in her car. She called Janice.

"I came home from work early today to get my living room ready for church," Janice said. "Got the furniture draped and the windows taped. I'm fixing to put plastic down on the floor." Doreen had already helped Janice paint her foyer, and over the last several Sundays they'd re-papered her bath. When Thomas or Juliette whined about going to Sunday School while Grandma skipped, Janice gave them extra scriptures and threatened to make them work. "The Church of the Good Deeds is shaping up."

"We've got a name now?"

"I'm thinking of recruiting members. Young guys who work shirtless and know something about roofing."

"God is going to strike you dead."

Janice laughed. "I know you didn't call to talk about church."

"I need you to set up a dinner at your house with me and Blake."

"Blake, my niece?"

"She's still selling insurance?"

"Far as I know."

"Good. You remember Rosie Washington?"

"The old dope grower? He died, didn't he?"

"He died. But do you remember in the 80s how Rosie got arrested and the government seized his farm?"

"Yeah."

"Remember how when the government went to auction off his farm, Rosie's family issued threats and made sure they were the

131

only ones there?"

"They bought the place back for two hundred dollars," said Janice. "Sold it to Rosie for a buck when he got out of jail."

"Well, Bird won't sell me his book." Doreen turned on her car so the heater would warm her. The day's clouds were mostly gone; it promised to be a clear night. "I need somebody to pull a Rosie Washington for me. I want to ask Blake to buy Bird's book, and then let me buy it off her."

Doreen heard the sound of Janice lighting a cigarette, inhaling her first drag. "Now there's the Doreen Swilley I know and love."

21

Jonathan had an idea where they were: edge of the county, not too far from the old McCormick place and that farm where his mother had long gone to ball Bird Marxton, asshole. Faster eased his shock-sprung station wagon down a dirt road. Bouncing on the bench seat was a picnic basket packed by Nicole. Hanging in the sky was an impressive slab of moon. The pine trees were shapely in the moonlight and every so often eyes glimmered from the roadside. Raccoon, deer, opossum. The car heater rasped against the plummeting mercury. "Nice night," said Jonathan.

"It's good to keep the spirits high. This is hard work. Not for everyone."

"Stealing trees?" Jonathan had once known a man who paid well for oak.

"No sir."

Faster flipped off his headlights, killed the engine, and coasted several yards before stopping. The men waited for their eyes to adjust to the dark. In front of them was a treeless space and at its center a swimming pool sized hole. Beside the hole a dirt mountain. "There's three holes almost that size out here and a lot of smaller ones, too," said Faster. "Don't fall in any of 'em."

"Why? What's in there?"

"Water. Mud. No ladder. You fall in there and I'll have to leave you here to scrabble and scrabble until you give in and drown."

"You left someone else in one of them holes?"

"It'd break my heart to do it. Only thing I've lost is a couple buckets and some rope, before I figured out the proper way to work this situation."

"What in the hell are we here to get anyway?"

"What you're looking at is the most valuable secret in this county: jewels."

"Diamonds?"

"Don't you know anything about geology? There's no diamonds around here. Library's free, son. There's no excuse for dumbassery. Brains is how a man makes his way of his own accord." Faster stepped out.

Jonathan followed suit. "So you're not gonna tell me what jewels we're here for?"

"The purple ones. This is one of the best places in the world for amethysts."

Jonathan doubted that the best of anything good or legal could be found in Flyshoals. "Well snap my picture. I'm standing on the very spot where the world's best amethysts are buried."

"No. There might be a better spot in the county. But without a backhoe, this is the best we've got, you and me."

For safety reasons, Faster refused to take Jonathan farther than the mud mountain. "Some holiday we'll sneak you out here in daylight, let you get the lay of the land. Tonight we work here. You can see that hole in the ground and this slag pile. That's enough."

The day's rain had turned the clay gluey. They wore ballcaps with flashlights taped top and sides and they attacked the slag pile with shovels, trowels and hands. "Pull out anything that looks different. Big. Small. Don't matter. If it catches your eye, pull it out."

Faster worked like a bassett hound, panting as he dug, baying when he stood, one hand pressed to his back. His pile was twice the size of Jonathan's. Jonathan worked because he couldn't stand to be beaten. He had no faith in the profitability of Faster's operation. In fact, he wondered if the entire exercise wasn't a practical joke.

"It's privately owned, but I don't see it as stealing since this is their refuse. We're taking what they don't want." Faster passed Jonathan a sandwich. They sat in the running car, heat on high, picnic basket between them. Roast venison on white bread, a family sized bag of Ruffles, a can of French onion dip. Two Cokes and the stars nearest celestial north circling in their steady way.

Jonathan pulled his sandwich from its bag. "If you have to do it at night, it's stealing."

"What we call stealing other countries call recycling."

"I agree there's ways to measure work besides legality. Dollar on the hour is a way to think on things. How much you make out here?"

"One night you make two hundred bucks. Another night you make two thousand. What you don't have is a boss. This is all choice, Johnny. The whole world is choice, when you get right down to it. Preordination's a lie told by the money changers in the temples. I choose to work. I choose to quit. Nicki chooses to make me a sandwich. She made you one, too. We're existing within the parameters of freedom here. How much is that worth per hour?"

Jonathan had worked for Powell McGaha since his twenties. All his adult life he'd had a steady paycheck and kept his family insured. And all that time, he'd heard men talk like Faster, most of them drunks on barstools begging drinks. Most of them towing behind a string of failed marriages, bastard children, worse. Just like Faster. One thing his mother had steeled him against was good-for-nothingness.

Faster stuck an arm in the picnic basket.

"Nothing else in there," said Jonathan. "I unpacked it all."

From the depths of the basket, Faster pulled two plastic-wrapped hunks. He passed one to Jonathan. "Let them eat cake."

Jonathan peeled the plastic from the cake and took a bite. It wasn't good pound cake, probably had margarine instead of butter. He knew these things because of Lexie. "A pound of butter, a pound of sugar, a pound of flour," she'd said when he complimented her cakes. "That's why it's called a pound cake." But for the past couple of years, if he wanted a slice of cake with lunch, he had to cut and bag it himself. Everything with Lexie had become a trade-off: your turn, my turn. *It's your fucking turn to pick up the kids. I'm not making money right now, but I'll make twice your salary in four years' time.* "What happened with your first two wives, Faster?"

The little man licked cake crumbs from his plastic wrap. "First one looked good and acted bad. I liked it when she acted bad with me, but if a woman'll act bad with you, she'll act bad with others, too. She got bad with my brother. After I found out about that I had to spend some time in one of them orange jumpsuits. While I was inside I got sober and found Jesus."

"Sober."

"And Jesus."

"Second wife?"

"She was like wine coolers when you're used to whiskey. An

overcorrection. I wasn't sorry to see her go, excepting she took the majority of my children. Only had one with the first, and I'm not even sure that one's mine."

"Marine's with the second?"

"Marine's with the second."

"That first wife. The bad one. She ever pack your lunch?"

"Wouldn't have done it if I'd asked her to." Faster drained his Coke. "But she looked like something you'd pay money to see."

Hours later, Faster said it was time to rinse. He had a trash pump he'd retrofitted for a garden hose. He set the thing up next to the hole in the ground, threw a length of hose in the hole, and turned on the pump. Water gushed. He rinsed his rocks. Jonathan watched as several rocks crumbled to nothing. He watched as rocks turned up dull and heavy, no more special than any other rock. He watched as one rinsed clean to reveal a cavity running through its center, a cavity filled with row after row of dark, sparkling teeth. "This one's a doozy. See that color? The darker the better." The amethysts looked black in the night.

"Come on man. Let me wash my rocks, too."

"Your heart ain't been in this yet. You can wait."

Jonathan sat in the mud beside Faster. Watching someone discover jewels had something in common with gambling and one-night stands. A man didn't know when he'd win big.

Faster sat close when it came Jonathan's turn. Jonathan rinsed clean a crystal as long as his thumb. "Tiny thing like that my dealer won't buy," said Faster. "What I'm doing with those is saving 'em at home in a box. Come spring, I'm gonna sell my scrap to the general public. At a gem show. Hippie types tape these rocks between their eyes to divine the future."

"Bullshit."

"I ain't saying I seen it personally."

Jonathan turned the hose on a hunk of clay the size of his head. It rinsed away to half before anything solid began to show. A cavity appeared. Crystals glimmered. "Dealer'll buy that," said Faster.

Jonathan turned his find in his hands. "When do we do that?"

"See my dealer? He rolls through about once a month. He's not a man to keep a schedule. I'll take your rocks to him, bring you your pay." Faster held out his hands for the stone.

"Now I see the swindle. Get me to dig, dig, dig for some pennies and how the fuck am I to know what they're worth? Either I take my rocks to your dealer or I find my own dealer."

"Let me ask you a serious question: what happened to make you such a suspicious sonofabitch?"

Jonathan returned to his rinsing. He watched a fist-sized ball of clay wash away to nothing.

"I asked you a question, son."

Jonathan disliked being called son, but in Faster's mouth the word was so tender it stung.

Water ran across the ground. The generator hummed, but its mechanical smell was lost in the metallic ubiquity of sodden Georgia clay. Jonathan didn't think of himself as suspicious. He thought of himself as cunning, wise.

"Miracles happen and happen," said Faster. "But if every time you find a miracle you beat it until it dies, you'll start thinking there aren't any miracles left at all."

The little man looked older now in the shadows cast by his flashlighted cap. Jonathan had thought he and Faster contemporaries, but Faster might be closer to his mother's age. "I don't know what the fuck you're talking about," Jonathan said.

"Here's something you should know about gem dealers: some of 'em'll get you arrested. You can't just dig anywhere there's dirt and find rocks like this. There are only a few places on this planet. Flyshoals is one such place, and even in Flyshoals they ain't easy to find. Right here, the ground is opened to us. Only place in the county that is. Now if you take rocks from this place to somebody who knows rocks, somebody who maybe is friends with the guy who owns this mine—maybe he and the owner have a special deal worked out—what do you think'll happen?"

Jonathan stood up. He was finished rinsing. Faster began dismantling the trash pump rig.

"Maybe I plan to dig somewhere else entirely," said Jonathan. He'd come along with Faster to quell boredom, but now it seemed there was something to prove.

"You own some land?"

Jonathan coiled the hose.

"Maybe you own some mineral rights somewhere?"

"How'd you find your gem dealer, then?"

"Providence, son. I already told you. You got to leave yourself open to God."

CRYSTALLIZATION

Below the Georgia Piedmont there was once an event so intense it melted rock. This melted rock sought release from such high temperatures and pressure. Following the rules for any liquid or gas, it pushed upwards through crevices and cracks. Along the way, the magma melted the stone with which it made contact and thus collected new elements unto itself.

When the magma could rise no higher, it began to cool and solidify. It had assembled too many new elements during its upward journey to harden again into the stone it once was. Some of the magma cooled into quartz veins, but the magma trapped in pockets of water or gas cooled into crystals. The color of these crystals was determined by the elements gathered on the melted stone's upward journey. Rose quartz, clear quartz, smoky gray quartz. Amethysts. Where there was space enough and time, these crystals grew until they could grow no more. They grew until they had acquired all of the faces and angles and points made possible by their particular chemical make-up. They grew until they reached their fully-realized form. Termination, this is called.

The elements that comprise the Earth's crust, making such things as amethysts possible, are the same elements that make humans possible. Oxygen, carbon, calcium, phosphorus. A handful of dirt is about 47 percent oxygen by mass. A human body is about 65 percent oxygen by mass. Scientists can take a handful of dirt and account for every atom present. The equation balances. But when a person dies and the chemical formula for death is run, there is $1/300^{th}$ of an ounce that cannot be accounted for. Some believe this loss is explained by escaping volatile compounds. It is true that many volatile compounds, such as oxygen, are held in place in the human body by biological processes, and thus some infinitesimal amount may be lost at the first, unmeasurable moment of death. Others argue that this unexplainable loss is the weight of the soul. $1/300^{th}$ of an ounce. Those who believe in the soul believe that since volatile compounds are held in place by biological processes, the weight of these compounds should balance throughout the equation: there should be nothing unaccounted for at death.

What cannot be argued is that if $1/300^{th}$ of an ounce represents the weight of the soul, then the human soul lives less in the flesh of the mind or the blood of the heart than it does the spaces of a cell, the soft empty curve of a lung. Perhaps, like a crystal, a human soul must find a hollow amidst life's heat and pressure if ever it is to grow into its fully-realized form. Perhaps, like a crystal, a human soul is best understood not in the context of a single human lifetime, but in vaster spans, something closer to geologic time: centuries of familial struggle, millenia of human suffering. An unbroken path of cause and effect. The problem, of course, is the mind: it cannot even remember the day the body was born. The day, not so long ago, that the feet took their first, small step. The mind makes the soul impossible to know.

2009

22

Bird was trapped in his bedroom.

Charlotte lay on hospice care in the white-columned Marxton estate she'd called home for the latter portion of her life. But as her drug regimen increased and opiates released her increasingly from pain to dream, she often thought she was dying in the house she'd first shared with Bird, a brick ranch they'd built on a few acres gifted to them by Bird's father. "Don't forget to turn on the well-house lights, Birdie. Those pipes are bound to freeze tonight." She pressed the bones of her hand against Bird's fleshy palm. Her hair on the pillow was a dry gray straw. From somewhere below them in the house came the sounds of their son cooing to their granddaughter, their granddaughter cooing in return.

"I've turned them on, Char." Bird had learned to agree, to allow his wife her dream. When he tried to correct her— "We don't live in that house anymore!"—her foggy trance cleared and there appeared in her eyes a struggling forth, a grasping. A terror. He didn't want her to be afraid.

She began to move the hand he held, and he released it. She reached out as if feeling for a fire. Bird pulled the kerosene heater closer to their bed. He'd sweated through his shirtsleeves, but still he tried to give her warmth: two heaters in this room and a fire she could not see in the downstairs grate. Charlotte dropped her hand, and Bird felt he'd accomplished something—she believed, for a moment, that she was warm. Such accomplishments were the measure of his days now. He'd learned to roll her brittle body to change her diaper, to arrange her hips and limbs against bedsores, to dampen her lips and tongue with pre-moistened swabs.

When Bird was a child, he once stood beside his father during a ceremony for World War I veterans at the VFW. "They're back in those foxholes today," his father had said as the honorees shuffled past. "You can see it on them." And Bird had looked at the hushed, stooped veterans—Mr. Briarley from church; Mr. Thames from the men's shop—and saw their haunting. That was the first time he understood that time was impotent against certain insults.

"Turn on the well-house lights, Birdie."

"I've done it, Char."

Already he was nostalgic for the start of her decline, when she'd only needed him to carry her up the stairs or guide her fork to her mouth. The stunted, breathy conversations they had then seemed memories from a time of reasonable human functioning. Worse, he knew that once she was gone—gone, gone beyond, gone completely beyond—he would, in grief, recall the haze of this deep morphine chatter as a final sweetness. He loved her more now than he ever had.

"Emmanuel."

Bird's nostalgia dissolved. When Charlotte called him by his full Christian name, he knew she'd awoken into the present, a time in which her fury burned. "Yes, my love?"

"I want to see that contract. Signed."

"Chuckie and I meet with the lawyer next week. I'll show you then."

Charlotte closed her eyes, and the set of her mouth again softened into the past.

Bird took Charlotte's cold hand in his.

"Turn on the well-house lights, Birdie."

"I've done it, Char."

"If I don't call Theo Waters, he'll mail those letters as soon as I die."

1959

23

Emmy drove again toward the pink house on the dirt road. The house wasn't on the hand drawn map Marla had mailed him. It was a mild day for early February, and the old woman on the porch inclined her head in greeting, as she'd done each time he passed. This time Emmy pulled into her drive. He was to have met Marla a quarter of an hour ago. The time he'd allotted himself to find a space and spread a picnic blanket he'd spent getting lost.

"You here to get a gourd?" the woman said as he mounted her steps. Birdhouse gourds were piled to both sides of her. She lifted one and clutched it between her knees, hand drilled a hole in the side using a tiny bit.

"No ma'am. I'm looking for Muskrat Road."

"These gourds here don't have holes. They're fifty cent." She pointed to the gourds to her left.

"That's more than a loaf of bread."

"These here are a dollar." She pointed to the gourds to her right.

"You're charging fifty cents to drill a hole?"

The woman lifted an intact gourd. "It's this you want, then?" She offered it and Emmy noticed her eyes, blue-blind with cataract.

"I don't want a gourd, ma'am. I only need directions."

The woman lowered the gourd to her lap. Her skin was such that Emmy couldn't tell her race. Either lightskinned dark or darkskinned pale. Her accent was indiscernible, but her nose looked Indian. With her blue-white eyes, she seemed a ghost. She clutched the gourd to her belly. "Nothing on Muskrat Road. No farms anymore. No tenants. It's all leased land. Crops belonging to no one."

"I'm going there to hunt for arrowheads." This was the story Marla had told Emmy to tell, should he need one.

"More of those in Flat Creek. That's yonder a ways."

Emmy pulled his wallet from his pocket. "I'll take a gourd with a hole."

The woman put down the gourd she held and picked up one from the other pile. "This here's a fine one." She opened her palm for Emmy's dollar. "Go back the way you first came, and turn left at the post oak. Not the post oak grown into Widow Carter's fence, but the next one. Looks like a hanging tree."

Emmy repeated to himself: *Second post oak, turn left. Second post oak, turn left.*

"When you get to the Gallant's farm, look for a turn off to the right that don't look like nothing more'n a deer path. It opens up fast to a decent road."

"How will I know the Gallant farm?"

"It ain't the Chilton place."

"How far until the Gallant farm? After I turn left?"

"You go on and on a little ways."

Emmy looked in his wallet. He had three more dollars. "I'd like another gourd, please, ma'am. With a hole."

By the time he found a copse of trees dividing two fallow fields on a road he assumed was Muskrat, night was full and he was more than an hour late. He was driving too fast and when he pressed the brakes, Nolin's car slid to the right. Emmy lifted his foot; the car eased out of its slide. He straightened himself on the roadside.

In Marla's letter, she'd told him to park and wait for her to come to him. He rolled the driver side window down to listen. The day's mildness had given way to chill. He grabbed a coat and a hat from the backseat. He hoped that Marla would have on enough clothes tonight, hoped her fortune had changed at least that much. He'd brought several blankets and an extra sweater just in case.

At first there was no sound in the winter night, but then, over the click of his cooling engine, he heard her guitar and her voice. *And as night skies turn gloomy, Night winds whisper to me, I'm lonesome as I can be.* It was the song that first drew him down the road to her.

The song grew nearer, and soon Emmy saw in his rearview a waifish shadow playing bardlike as it walked. Different parts of her flashed as she came—the metal plate of her instrument, the pale of her hair, a forward moving thigh in a light-colored dress. He was embarrassed for her to know he watched, so when she was close he put his head on his steering wheel. Her feet cracked a stick and the guitar was loud for a moment and then silent. He turned to where she stood at the open window.

Marla looked him over. "You're as I remember."

He couldn't tell if her memories were fond. She looked as he remembered too, the translucent skin and imperfect teeth, the long, pale hair so thin pieces lifted on an imperceptible breeze. She was thinner than he recalled, but she wore a canvas coat and heavy brogans. "Sorry I'm late," he said.

"I picked a place hard to find."

"I brought a blanket. And sandwiches."

She ran a finger along the door frame. "We could sit in this nice car awhile."

Emmy leaned across the car and opened the passenger door.

Marla put her guitar across the back seat before getting in. "Got you some gourds?"

"They're bird houses."

She picked one up, fingered the hole. "Awfully small for a bird." She returned the gourd to the floorboard. "Most folks use those to catch a haint. Mind if I borry one of these blankets?"

Borrow, thought Emmy. "I brought them for us."

Marla settled in the front seat beside Emmy. Beneath the blanket, she was so slight as to almost disappear.

He rolled his window up against the cold, and then reached across Marla to open the glove compartment. "I brought something to warm us."

"I'm not one to take a drink. Not since Silas. But I don't mind if you do."

The last time he'd seen her, the first and only time, they'd finished a jar of moonshine. That drink had contributed to his own boldness that night, and he assumed the same was true of her. He wanted her as he remembered her, frank and hungry, but he left the flask in the glove compartment.

"You're the one wanted to talk to face to face. Here I am. You gonna tell me what happened to your grandma's house?"

"You remember that?"

"It's why we met."

"My dad is selling it to the government for their national forest. They've bought most of the other farms in the area already. It'll take a few months to finalize everything, but soon it'll be gone."

Marla reached into her coat and pulled out her leather charm bag. "I know how you feel. With Silas gone the whole world feels changed."

"How did he die?"

At first, Emmy thought Marla wasn't going to answer his question, but then she began speaking all in a spill. "Silas hated bosses. That's why he went to Chicago, to be his own man. But it's the mob what runs all of Chicago. You have to pick someone besides yourself to be loyal to. Silas wouldn't do it. There was a strike at our packing plant; Silas crossed the line. Police say he got stabbed over a girl, but he didn't have no girl."

Didn't have a girl, thought Emmy.

"They got him right outside our house. I found him underneath the streetlight. Took him two days to pass. After he got killed I mostly didn't want to live either. Cherlow took care of me, same as he's done since I was a child. Seemed natural enough to marry him. Specially since it wasn't the first time he'd asked."

Emmy watched Marla in the moonlight. He wondered if she'd said her story aloud before. She still struck Emmy as impossibly true, impossibly honest, even though she'd stolen his wallet the first time they met, and she met him now on a forgotten road despite the gold band on her finger. "Does Cherlow know you're here with me?"

"He don't question much. He's an old man."

"He doesn't mind if you walk around by yourself at night?"

"We worked out a deal. I wouldn't have married him otherwise. I always have been one for night walks." She dropped the necklace back inside her coat and reached for Emmy's hand. Her fingers were dry and thin, calloused.

Emmy rubbed her hand in his, felt her fingers warm to life. He turned her hand over, kissed her palm.

"I missed you," she whispered.

"I missed you too," he said, and leaned in to kiss her mouth. As if they weren't more or less strangers. As if they'd been lovers for years.

2009

24

Jonathan and Luke sat on the top row of bleachers at the Stinkbug Dirt Track. Faster was running pit for Snooker, who was racing his go-kart against other boys in go-karts. It was off-season practice, but there was enough noise to awe Reese and Ryland into silence. Jonathan turned again to scan the parking lot with the binoculars hanging around his neck.

"Why you've got to control all there is to control is beyond me." Luke zipped his boys' coats against the day's chill. "Faster gives you better money than you should get for digging up rocks. Who gives a shit if there's a swindle?"

"Poop, daddy," said Ryland. "You got to say: who gives a poop."

Luke tousled Ryland's cinnamon hair. "'Come on out,' that's what Uncle Johnny told Daddy. 'See the races. The boys'll love it. I got beer and juice boxes.' Of course there's an ulterior motive."

"Reese! Ryland!" The boys turned to Jonathan. "You ever see anything cooler than this?"

"No sir," said Ryland. Reese shook his head no.

"That a beer in your hand, Luke?"

Luke raised his Solo cup. Alcohol was not allowed at the track, officially.

"That a juice box in your hand?" Jonathan said to Ryland.

"It's grape."

"So we're having the day I promised." Jonathan returned to scanning the parking lot. He'd been digging several nights a week with Faster, but he'd not shaken the suspicion that he was being used. "Here he comes." An older Toyota Tacoma eased into the lot and parked beside Faster's Young Servants Racing rig. Through his binoculars, Jonathan watched the driver emerge. A pasty white guy with a receding hairline, golf shirt, love handles, goatee. "That's him." He passed the binoculars to Luke.

"Dude's wearing a fanny pack," said Luke.

"Keeps a dead man's ear in that fanny pack. Faster says it's no bigger than a potato chip, said you can't even tell it's an ear for sure unless you look at it with a magnifying glass." Jonathan pulled his phone from his pocket, texted Faster to let him know his crystal dealer was in the lot.

"Why's he keep an ear in his purse?"

"Fuck if I know."

"Fuck's a bad word, Uncle Johnny," said Ryland.

"Amanda's got the kid trained to a quarter jar," said Luke. "Say fudge instead."

"According to Faster, that fudger is the biggest gem and crystal pirate on the East Coast. He's buying stones off anyone who'll sell 'em. We're not even a speck in his ointment, me and Faster. He's got Burmese emeralds coming to him right through the mail."

Luke still watched through the binoculars. "He looks like a state employee."

The steady drone of the circling go-karts altered. On the track, one kart spun in circles. Other karts drove into pits and into the center grass to avoid collision. The spinner slammed into a light post. A groan rose from the few people in the stands. Ryland grabbed Luke's leg.

"He's okay, buddy," said Luke, though the boy who'd crashed did not look okay, slumped as he was over the steering wheel. A man ran toward him.

Jonathan took the binoculars from Luke and turned back to the parking lot. The pirate had opened the bed of his truck and was arranging things for transaction: blanket, newspapers, scale, plastic Rubbermaid keepers. Faster had finally agreed to introduce Jonathan. Jonathan turned to the track—the preacher was in the pit, his body trained toward the course's grassy center where the wrecked boy's father twisted and tugged his child from the dented kart. Jonathan returned the binoculars to Luke. "All you gotta do is watch through these and make sure nothing bad happens."

On the track, the boy walked off the course. His father followed, pulling the go-kart with a hand. Every few steps he yanked it forward with such force it appeared he might throw it. A few folks clapped.

"Reese wants a juice box now, Uncle Johnny," said Ryland.

Jonathan opened the cooler at his feet, fished around in the ice, pulled out a juice. He passed it to Luke, who navigated the straw. "I'm a greenskeeper, Johnny. I spend my days growing grass. I don't know nothing about criminal activity."

"Keep an eye on the motherscratcher," said Jonathan. "That's all I'm asking."

"I know what word you thought, Uncle Johnny," said Ryland.

"You able to add up all those quarters yet?" said Jonathan.

"Yes sir."

"How many quarters in a dollar?"

"Four!"

"How many quarters I owe you already?"

"Two."

"How about instead of the two quarters I owe you, I give you four nickels?"

"Okay!" Ryland pulled on his juicebox in joy.

"You're a motherscratcher, Johnny," said Luke.

On the track, the race was getting underway again. Faster sent Snooker onto the course, watched him complete half a lap in his black go-kart. Then he turned and waved into the stands, pointed at the exit, hurried away.

Jonathan said, "You see me getting stuffed in a truck, come running."

Luke settled his ball cap farther back and pressed the binoculars to his face. "Reese! Ryland! Y'all turn around and help Daddy watch now."

Jonathan caught up with Faster in the parking lot. He slowed his pace and fell in step beside the little man.

"Enjoying the show?" said Faster.

"It's more like racing than I thought it would be."

They were within a few feet of the pirate's Toyota, and the man stepped forward and caught Faster's hand, pulled him in to slap his shoulder. "How you doing these days?"

"Doing good. Doing good. Yourself?"

"Can't complain."

Faster waved Jonathan forward. "This here is Mr. Tom. He's been known to take a shine to some of those rocks me and you find on the roadsides. Mr. Tom, this here is Johnny Swilley."

Tom and Jonathan shook.

"The man behind the myth," said Jonathan.

"You or me?" said Tom. Up close, Tom the pirate appeared even more benign than he did from a distance, his comb-over not quite enough to mask his spotty scalp.

"I'm not the one carries a dead man's ear in his purse," said Jonathan.

"That old thing?" Tom pulled his fanny pack to the front of his body. "Open your hand."

As Faster had said, the ear was no larger than a potato chip. Jonathan let it lay where Tom placed it. It felt the right temperature to still be attached to a head.

"You can't fully appreciate something like that without a hand lens." Tom slipped off the one around his neck.

With magnification, the ear was clearly an ear. There was a whorl leading down to the tiny void of the canal. Jonathan turned it over. Where it once attached to the body was shut with tiny, neat stitches. Jonathan felt like shrieking. Instead, he held his palm out so Tom could retrieve the ear.

Tom pressed the ear into Jonathan's palm with a finger. "You can tell the big story about a thing from the small."

"That's what I been telling him," said Faster. "Little crystals atop the ground mean big ones under." He went to his truck for the first box of rocks.

"So from this ear, you know all you need to about me." Tom plucked the ear from Jonathan's palm.

"Are you making a threat? Seems to me you could buy an ear like that."

"I know you can."

"You're admitting you bought that ear then."

"I've seen rhinoceros tusks for sale. Human organs. Screaming babies all in a row. If you want an ear like mine, I can get you one by next week."

Rhinoceros tusks, human organs, screaming babies—these things weren't for sale in Flyshoals. Jonathan had never caused trouble in a meaningful way. His life passed more or less quietly in this shrinking town. The most excitement he'd seen was the dissolution of his own marriage. It would be a new thing entirely to become a man with an ear in his pocket. Even he couldn't predict what Lexie—or anyone else—would say to such. "Mr. Tom? I'm interested in becoming a private contractor."

When Tom the pirate laughed, Jonathan could see all the way to his square, silvery molars.

Lexie stirred walnuts into the brownie mix. She remembered from 9th grade home ec this detail about Janice's niece, Blake Wilford—she preferred her brownies with nuts. Through all the years of high school, Lexie and Blake had been in the same slow-track classes. They hadn't been close, but they'd shared a wry camaraderie. This was the reason Doreen gave when she asked Lexie to come tonight to the dinner at Janice's: "Blake will be more comfortable if you're there."

Lexie poured the batter into the pan, slid the pan into the oven.

"Mom," said Juliette, "when you were my age were you allowed to go on dates?" She sat at the table outlining a paper for English class. Thomas was up the street, throwing the football with a neighbor boy.

Lexie rinsed the batter bowl though she wasn't sure she believed raw eggs deadly enough to avoid. "You've been pelting me with questions for an hour."

"I'm writing a paper comparing you and me."

Juliette's English teacher, Mrs. Jackson, had been around since Lexie was in high school. "Can't you think of a more interesting topic?" said Lexie. What Thomas and Juliette knew of Lexie's childhood wasn't much, and what they knew of their maternal grandparents was less. Lexie had told them the truth of her mother's death, but her father she'd claimed was dead too, though in fact she wasn't sure where he was. He left town shortly after she ran away.

"It's stupid you won't let me and Thomas stay home by ourselves anymore. We don't want to go to dinner at Ms. Janice's." All week Juliette had been hounding Lexie about this. She stood from the table, joined her mother at the sink. "It's because of Dad. I know that's why Grandma is over here all the time like we're babies."

"Grandma comes to make sure you eat a good dinner, do your homework, and go to bed on time."

Juliette took the batter bowl her mother had cleaned from the drainer and dried it with a dishtowel. "If Dad comes, I'll call you right away. Before I even answer the door." She put the bowl away in the cabinet. "I'll make him wait on the porch until you get home."

"You and your brother are coming with me tonight, and this has nothing to do with your father."

Juliette hung the dishtowel on its hook. "You say you'll tolerate most anything from us but a lie, but you're lying all the time. About Dad. And other stuff too. You even told me lies to write on my school paper."

"What did I tell you that was a lie?" Lexie put the challenge in her voice, knew it would keep Juliette from back talk. Still, the girl smirked. Lexie could only imagine what she might have heard.

"Go to your bedroom until I tell you to come out. I've had enough of your sass for one day."

Juliette sauntered from the kitchen, and Lexie fought against her urges. Of course Juliette sensed that something was wrong. Lexie hated to teach her daughter to ignore her intuition. She wanted to chase the girl down and pull her close, apologize for what she'd let their lives become. Assure her that they were on the same side, mother and daughter, woman and girl. She wanted to tell Juliette she was getting them out. She wanted to tell Juliette that her professor, Ms. Paulsen, had helped her get a second interview with a pediatrician's office. In an area with good schools, a mall, a movie theatre. Lexie wanted to say to Juliette, "Wait until you see what your mother has planned."

Not that Juliette and Thomas were likely to find what Lexie had planned all that wonderful. She didn't have much money. Since Jonathan canceled his direct deposit, she'd stopped paying the mortgage and the bills, sent the utilities a few dollars a month to keep things running. So she'd saved something, but not much. She'd pawned her decent jewelry and Jonathan's tools, the ostrich skin cowboy boots he bought her one Christmas. She'd been using her emergency credit card for groceries.

They might have to live in a hotel for a while, eat canned beans and ramen. But as Ms. Paulsen pointed out to her often, Lexie had run away once before, and she knew how it had to be done. Suddenly and completely. There were bound to be casualties. Doreen, Lexie knew, would be one. She hoped her children would not be.

26

In the center of the table was an empty casserole dish that had held Janice's eggplant parmesan, and beside this was the dish that had held Doreen's garlic rolls. From Janice's living room came the sound of the television—Thomas and Juliette had been sent to watch it so the women could talk seriously. Janice opened a second bottle of wine.

"Chuckie Hammond?" said Blake.

"That's what Bird told me," said Doreen.

"Thank you, Aunt Janice," said Blake, picking up her refilled wine glass. "I read about him in the Athens papers when he turned his car upside down in a ditch and walked home drunk."

"All he got for that was a stint in rehab," said Janice. "Third strike too."

"What the fuck is Bird thinking?" said Blake. As when she was younger, she swore too much and spoke too loudly. These traits had gotten her into trouble as a child, but now they made her formidable. "You know our field is built on reputation, Doreen. It's all chicanery, really. There has to be a reasonable expectation that Bird's clients will stay with the company and pay their premiums even after he's gone. If he hands everything over to a moron like Chuckie Hammond..."

"Everyone will jump ship and go to Steve Wilkes," said Doreen. "I know. His wife is making him do it. You know she's dying, right?"

"Bird doesn't give a shit what that woman thinks," said Blake. "Pardon me, Doreen, but I've known you were screwing Bird Marxton since I was, like, seven years old. Why does he care what his wife says all of a sudden?"

Doreen felt the heat rise in her face, but knew there was no reason for it. Of course Blake had known. So had Jonathan. Everyone in town knew. "I keep asking myself the same question."

"It can't be that she's withholding sex or threatening divorce," said Blake, "not if she's dying. Those things are off the table anyway. It has to be money. I hear her family's loaded. She's probably got her own lawyer. She's putting the screws to Bird now because she can. I bet she won't let him have her inheritance unless he does what she wants. Money's the only thing people like that care about." She drank from her wine. "How bad off is she?"

"Bird said hospice last time we talked," said Doreen.

"You don't have anything to worry about," said Blake. "If Chuckie wants to keep his business, he's going to have to hire you, and Bird knows it too. Wait until the wife kicks the bucket and then they'll both come begging.'"

"I won't work for Chuckie Hammond," said Doreen. It was the first time she'd said it aloud, and when Lexie and Janice looked at her with surprise, Doreen felt certain. "I won't. I'll starve first." She turned to Blake. "I want you to buy his book. You hire me to work for you. And in a year or two, I'll buy the book from you."

"No way," said Blake.

"Bird will sell to you," said Doreen. "Wear a short skirt and some lipstick. He's got a thing for women. He said himself that Chuckie is an idiot."

"Nope," said Blake. "My life is settled. I pay my bills, save for retirement, do what I want on the weekends. If I buy that book from Bird and he loses half his clients, I might owe him less at the one-year lookback, but I'll have a mess on my hands."

"The clients won't leave if I'm running the place," said Doreen.

"I don't know what people in this town might do, Doreen. People gossip about you sometimes, mostly because of your momma but I hear Bird mentioned too. Hell, a lot of people might stay with Chuckie Hammond just because they're friends with his daddy. You're taking on the way things are done."

There was a long silence around the table. Lexie picked up the wine bottle and topped off the glasses.

"Remember Mr. Stanley's class?" Blake said to Lexie.

"Senior math."

"'Hello losers. Hello scumbags.' That's what he said when he walked in the door. You told him to fuck off."

"I got a month of Saturday school for telling him that," said Lexie.

Doreen didn't remember Lexie getting a month of Saturday school, and they'd been sharing a bed when Lexie was a senior. "I didn't know about this."

"Johnny forged your signature for me. I told you I was going to work on the Saturdays."

"Because you knew you'd get in trouble."

"Because I didn't want to disappoint you."

Tears sprung to Doreen's eyes. The words were so unexpected. Bird didn't care if he disappointed her and neither did Jonathan.

Who had she tried not to disappoint? Bird and Jonathan, her grandchildren. She'd never thought about disappointing Lexie. She'd thought of Lexie as an extension of herself, someone to help her keep the family together. She'd assumed that Lexie wanted the same things she wanted. It hadn't occurred to her to consider what Lexie herself might want.

Doreen realized that Bird thought of her the same way. She saw herself for a moment as his wife, imagined standing in his house at an ironing board, starching and pressing his endless monogrammed shirts. Waxing his endless wood floors. Telling her grandchildren to lower their voices, stop running. Stop touching things, stop touching things, stop touching things because she didn't know which things could be broken and which were to be saved for generations. "How is your job hunt going, Lexie?" said Doreen.

Lexie shrugged, as she'd done each time Doreen asked this question. Doreen had taken this shrug to mean "not well." She'd even said, "You can still apply for a manager's position at Walmart." But now she thought of how she'd sweet-talked Bird even as she seethed inside because she wanted to continue the conversation about buying his book.

She didn't need Blake to buy Bird's book for her.

"I'm going to open up my own business next door to Bird's," said Doreen. "In that empty music shop. It won't cost much at all if I'm not buying his book."

"Bird never had you sign a non-compete?" said Blake.

There was a pause, and then all of the women burst into laughter.

"Do it," said Blake. "Leave and take his clients with you."

"It's a gamble, Doreen," said Janice. "What if they stick with Chuckie Hammond? What if they all go to Steve Wilkes?"

Doreen looked at Lexie. The woman had done nothing but

gamble since Doreen met her. "If it doesn't work, I'm looking for a job, same as I will be if I don't try."

"I'll give you a business loan," said Blake. "That's a risk I'm willing to take just to put this town to the fucking test." She looked behind her at the counter. "When are we going to eat those brownies Lexie made? I know she put nuts in them."

27

Dusk crept in from the west. Tom the pirate was gone, and Jonathan, returned to the stands, sat now in the front row beside Luke. Faster had all three boys in the pit, talking them through the changing of a tire. Snooker and Ryland leaned close, but Reese stood to the side with his hands covering his ears against the wrench's noise. "That preacher man's good with kids," said Luke.

"He's got enough of 'em."

"Your kids like him?"

"Haven't met him yet."

Reese came to the edge of the stands and held his arms up, his little lips quivering. Luke pulled the boy over the railing. "Too loud, buddy?"

The child nodded.

"That kid ever gonna talk?"

"He's got Ryland to talk for him. Doctor says it's normal."

In the pit, Faster helped Snooker into the kart. Ryland passed

Snooker's helmet. Snooker zoomed from the starting line.

Luke bounced Reese on his knee. "That boy of Faster's won all but one of the races out here today."

"Costs a fudging fortune. The karts. The tires. I don't know what all else."

"Faster told me he digs to fund his kid's racing," said Luke. "Said he doesn't really need a job otherwise. Lives rent free in his wife's stepfather's place and has a kitty from the man's death besides."

"Must be nice," said Jonathan. "Living rent free."

"How is Powell's lake house these days?"

Jonathan rocked to a hip and pulled from his pocket the wad of bills that was his payment. "Eight hundred dollars. Three nights of digging, no more than four hours a night."

"Sixty-six dollars an hour."

"More. I'm not finished being paid. Faster's got a table at the North Carolina Gem Show. We'll sell our leftovers there. He booked a room at Harrah's Hotel & Casino. Slots, blackjack, poker, roulette. He invited me along since his wife thinks gambling's a sin."

Luke continued to bounce Reese. "I've got a good back, and I'm not afraid of the dark. But do I meet a semi-retired pastor with a Nascar-racing kid and a business plan? No, I fudging don't."

"All you get is a cop for a wife."

"She's a dispatcher."

"I seen her directing traffic."

On the track, Snooker flew in circles. Jonathan said, "I got a way to bring you in."

"Going thirds won't even cut your profit. I'll get the ones y'all miss anyway."

"This isn't a plan for three. This is a plan for two."

Luke stopped his bouncing. "There's not enough money in

the world for me to kill that little preacher, Johnny."

"Jesus Christ, Luke. I'm not talking about killing anybody. I'm talking about something Faster don't want to do hisself. Claims it's too risky." Jonathan lifted a short cardboard tube from between his feet. "I got this thing off Tom the pirate." He pulled the plastic cap off the tube, stuck a finger inside and pulled out a map. It was hand drawn and hand colored, with a key in one corner and a compass rose in another, a joke in one small blank space: *Here there be Dragons*. Tiny cross-hatches ran in lines, denoting crystal veins. There were miniature trees and a little farmstead and wee highway markers. "Tom drew it himself." One corner was dominated by an exploded cross-section detailing what Tom believed existed underground.

"Holy shit," said Luke.

Reese put a hand over his father's mouth.

"I had to put down a damage deposit," said Jonathan.

"Why don't he just photocopy it?"

"I said that. He goes, 'Why not scribble it on a napkin? Why not make an app?' Dude's crotchety. This is a map I rented for you and me, but we need a backhoe."

"I don't have a backhoe."

"You drive one every day."

"Not stealing the country club's backhoe, Johnny."

"Borrow."

"You say borrow, my boss says steal. No matter who's talking I'm out of a job."

"We dig at night, pay for our own gas. You have keys to every lock at Green Hills. That backhoe will be back come dawn, in time for work. Nobody notices dings and scratches on a backhoe. You don't have to steal a thing. And nobody's gonna die."

28

Doreen's doorbell rang as she sat down to a dinner of scrambled eggs and toast. She'd worked late, dealing with a car wreck that hadn't called the police or gotten the other party's insurance card. She sighed, rose to answer the door.

"Bird!" He'd only been in her house a handful of times, and he'd never stopped by unannounced. "I must have missed your call."

"I didn't call." Bird held aloft a brown paper bag. "Am I disturbing you?"

"No. How's Charlotte?" This, Doreen thought, was the reason for his visit. His wife's passing.

"She's still with us." Bird pulled a bottle of champagne from the bag.

Doreen had expected whiskey or Scotch, some earthy sorrow drowner. There were only two pieces of celebratory news she knew of that he could share with her: either he was keeping his business or selling it to her. "Bring it in the kitchen. I was sitting down to dinner. Hungry?"

"Minnie fed me earlier."

In the kitchen, Bird took the towel from the sink and draped it over the bottle, popped the cork. He found two jelly jars, poured them each full. "Cheers." He handed Doreen a glass.

She didn't care for champagne. It tasted bland but carbonated, similar to that flavored soda water Lexie had been trying to get her to drink instead of Coke. "So tell me your good news." She wasn't going to throw her arms around his neck until he'd given her good reason. Even after so much time together, they were strangers to one another when they stood in her kitchen.

"Everything's finalized. I've signed the contract with Chuckie Hammond." He put a hand on her arm so she would let him finish. "And that means the first part of all of this is behind us. I know you won't marry me, and I know you won't take my money, but I've been thinking about it, and I can find you a new job somewhere else in town. There are people here who owe me favors." He lifted his glass of champagne. "So here's to moving on with our lives."

Doreen set her champagne on the table without taking a sip. "You've come to fire me."

"Reenie, did you hear what I said? Let it be a new beginning for both of us."

"I don't owe your wife any favors. And I don't owe you any either."

She snatched the paperwork she'd been going through from the table and shoved it into Bird's arms. "This is my notice. I'm quitting immediately. I'll come by tomorrow and collect my things."

Bird dropped the paperwork on the floor. The sheets skidded this way and that. "Goddammit, Doreen! There's nothing wrong here except where you're making problems! I'll help you find a new job. We don't have to get married."

Doreen pushed past Bird and went into her living room. She opened the front door. "It speaks to your character when you treat me like shit. But it speaks to my character when you treat me like I'm stupid. Get out."

"Reenie."

"Take your champagne with you."

Bird ran a hand through his hair, looked around Doreen's kitchen. "There's no good answer. Don't you see that? I have to consider Charlotte too. I can't make a right choice."

"That's true. Cowards can't make right choices."

Bird set down his jelly jar, picked up the bottle of champagne and went to the door. He reached a hand toward Doreen and she slapped him away. "Consider this my notice as your mistress too. We're finished in all the ways we've ever been connected." She'd expected the words to make her cry, but instead something in her solidified. She recalled the day she sat beside Janice in the cemetery, the day she'd felt inside herself only the cottony batting of sacrifice. "Get out."

Bird stepped out of Doreen's house, the open champagne bottle held like a bat in his right hand.

She didn't step onto the porch to give him a last gracious wave as he pulled away. She slammed the door and went into her kitchen for her cellphone. She needed to hammer out the terms of that loan from Blake. She had a business to start.

1959

29

Emmy sat at the kitchen table struggling through an algebraic equation while his mother mashed potatoes in the heavy green ceramic bowl. It was Sunday, Imogene's day off, so there were only Emmy and his mother in the kitchen. The late May sun through the window caught the edge of the cut glass trifle bowl on the counter and threw rainbows across the cabinets.

When the phone rang with their family's tone, Emmy didn't move. He was engaged with his math. But his mother didn't pause in her mashing. "Emmy, answer the phone."

"Yes ma'am."

"Emmanuel Abraham Marxton V, please," said the operator.

"Pardon?" Emmy thought the operator must have meant to ask for his father, the fourth. There was no reason for Emmy to receive a long distance call.

The operator repeated his name.

"Speaking."

"Your party, ma'am," and then there was the sound of the operator leaving the line.

"Emmy?"

He recognized Marla's voice immediately. They'd met and made love in the copse between the cotton fields a week ago, and he was to meet her there again in three weeks; they'd already planned it. Behind him, his mother slowed in her mashing as she eavesdropped. Emmy strained for the sound of a neighbor on the party line. "May I ask who's calling, please?" said Emmy.

"It's Marla." She waited for him to drop the formality, speak to her intimately.

"Yes?"

"You have to meet me tomorrow. In the morning. 9 am. Usual place, but then we'll walk back to my house. Cherlow's going to town for the day."

Tomorrow was a school day. Marla would be in school as well had she not quit in seventh grade. Nolin would be driving his car to work. If only Emmy's mother were not so close, he could explain to Marla the impossibility of her request. "I'm sorry, I can't do that. I won't have the time." He stretched the cord toward the hall, moved as far away from his mother as possible. She had stopped her mashing entirely.

"You'd best come."

"Perhaps you can find someone else to help you."

"I'm pregnant." Marla breathed on the line, waiting for an answer. "It's yours." She hung up.

Emmy didn't speak until the dial tone returned, startling him to action. "Okay, thank you. Good-bye." He returned to the kitchen and settled the phone in its cradle.

"Who was that?"

Emmy placed one foot in front of the other until he'd returned to his seat. He put his hand on the chair and drew it backward. "A teacher from school. She's looking for someone to tutor one of her students. But I don't think I have time."

"What an honor to have been asked. Perhaps you should reconsider. Which teacher?"

Panic clenched his gut. His mother might call the school. This was the first of many lies he suddenly anticipated telling, and already he was doing it wrong. "Miss Slokely," he said, picking the teacher his mother was least likely to speak with in passing. Miss Slokely was in her twenties, single and beautiful, with a wardrobe it was rumored her salary could not purchase.

His mother went back to the potatoes. "You do have so many responsibilities."

The first hurdle was scaled; she would not call his teacher. Emmy's mind emptied. Marla pregnant was too much to consider now, in this kitchen with his algebra homework spread before him and his mother mashing potatoes in her flat, certain way. He put his chin in his hand and watched the cut crystal rainbows move slowly across the cabinets in the kitchen of the house his great-grandfather built. It was remarkable how much they looked like flames. Cold, cold flames.

2009

30

Charlotte died on the first of December. Doreen stood alone in front of St. Luke's Episcopal Church, avoiding the eyes of the last few mourners who hurried inside for the service. The day was a withered one, gray and dry. Against this, the holy white clapboard glowed. She'd intentionally arrived late. As Bird's former secretary, it could be argued that she had an obligation to attend. As his mistress, it could be seen as disrespectful. What Doreen told no one was that she came to the funeral mostly in thanks: she had signed a contract with Blake for a small loan, and she'd signed a contract with Todd Phelps to rent the empty space next to Bird's office. She was stepping into a version of her life that she'd never dreamed, and it was all because of Charlotte. "You ready for this?" Doreen asked Charlotte silently.

Janice's boyfriend, Dean, pulled to the curb and Janice and Lexie got out. "I'll get you after if you need a ride," he called as they closed their doors.

Doreen hadn't asked Lexie to come. She avoided discussing Bird with Lexie as she avoided discussing him with Jonathan. Yet here Lexie was at Charlotte's funeral. She wore the black, tie-waisted dress, long out of style, that Doreen had bought her for her high school graduation. She took Doreen's forearm. "Ready?" she said.

"Oh, she's ready," said Janice as she hugged Doreen. "But I'm not. We should skip this damn funeral and go to Merle's, get a beer."

"Just sit with me for the service," said Doreen. "We're not following the hearse graveside."

Inside the sanctuary, ushers no longer waited and standing room only remained. The three women stepped behind the last pew. They nodded and smiled toward the people they knew. Nobody seemed surprised by Doreen's presence; the attendees most likely to feel outrage or shock were crowded into the front pews, the family pews.

The choir began. In her heels, Doreen could see all the way to the closed dark wood casket. Bird's gray head was bent forward; to his right, Will's head mimicked his father's. Will rubbed a hand over his father's back. Despite her threats, Charlotte had not, in the end, convinced Will to abandon his father.

The priest stepped to the pulpit as the choir finished. He began speaking of the children's book, *The Velveteen Rabbit*, and the steadfast love of the bunny. Doreen couldn't figure out if the bunny was God or if the bunny was man—who was supposed to be made real by whose love? Doreen stopped listening, unwilling to do the work demanded by the Episcopalians with their cryptic sermons, every message cloaked in robes and incense, general faith in God's good will. Doreen considered it the Christianity of those mostly able to make such things true for themselves. But Lexie seemed moved by the words. She took her mother-in-law's hand.

Lexie's palm was warm and clammy, unquestionably alive, and with this touch Doreen felt the particular tenderness of funerals seep into her. She became aware of her damageable human body, aching in the hips, and of how this body was only the casing for whatever it was that made her herself. She felt radiating from those around her the uncomfortable warmth of so many closely-packed, damageable, human bodies, soul-casings all. Charlotte's body lay at the front of the church, ready to go in the ground, but Charlotte herself was with God now, the vulnerability of her physical form conquered by Christ's body on the cross. His body the answer for all of the souls in all of the bodies. *Sacrifice yourself like this for one another,* he said with his body. *This is how to save the world.* But who could do it?

Inside Doreen's body she felt a desert space. It was a desert that was meant to contain a jungle, a garden, a house—whole worlds both tamed and wild. But somewhere along the way, that fecund landscape had been reduced to searing heat and blowing sand. Doreen had stood in that desert space before. She'd been trapped in it right after she left Billy, lost in it all those nights she went on the prowl in Flyshoals. When she was in the desert, her hands might touch and feel, her mouth might soothe and smile, but in her body she felt nothing except her heart's dumb, steady, beat, beat, beat. Beating sterile the place where she should be nurturing flowers.

Doreen didn't want anyone she loved to suffer even an acre of desert heart. But this want had come too late. She could sense the barren spot in Jonathan. He could claim love while making a fist. Doreen couldn't save him, even though she understood him.

Her daughter-in-law, her grandchildren—they could get away from Jonathan, away from her, away from Flyshoals. Doreen knew that she should say these words to Lexie, but she couldn't. The desert inside her heart wouldn't let her. It was a ravenous place, selfish and terrified, and it said her grandchildren and daughter-in-law belonged beside her. To her. Doreen knew that wasn't true, but she couldn't feel it wasn't true. "Stay for me?" she whispered to Lexie.

Lexie nodded yes.

Janice made to leave with Doreen. "You stay too," said Doreen.

Janice rolled her eyes but didn't move.

Doreen exited the funeral as silently as she could. Outside, the parking lot was full and the streets were lined with cars, but there were no people. No movement. Even the clouds hung still. There was not a single person to see Doreen weep, and so she did.

Doreen sat on her couch eating a child's lunch, a peanut butter and jelly sandwich with a glass of milk. On television, a daytime soap played. She didn't know the characters, didn't know the plot. She worked days and had no understanding of daytime TV.

Her life, her life. For most of it she'd lived in this house. Did the few years in Florida with Jonathan's father even count? Though she tried, she couldn't seem to string her years together into a storyline. Rather, she carried a series of episodes, as if her life was not something she'd lived but something she'd glanced at sidelong as she hurried past. She could see in the kitchen the table where she told her mother that she was pregnant and her mother offered a syrupy tea she refused.

Why could Doreen recall nothing else from that day? Like so many other days she and her mother had talked and touched, eaten dinner together, slept down the hall from one another. Why hadn't she held onto those moments, the plain and decent ones, the ones uncomplicated by hard feelings?

On the television, people wore rhinestones and sequins in someone's living room.

When Doreen's mother died, Doreen sent Jonathan to Miss Caldwell for childcare while she went to work for Bird. The woman lived in a shotgun shack that dogs had the run of. Along one side of the center hall were cribs; along the other side playpens. Jonathan got a playpen. He was allowed out when Miss Caldwell took him out, but if he crawled out he got spanked. Doreen put his favorite book, *The Runaway Bunny*, in his playpen. She bought him diecast cars and a Viewfinder with discs. Every day, she called from work and had Miss Caldwell hold the phone to his ear so she could tell him she loved him.

Doreen resented every penny she dropped into that woman's cracked palm.

Jonathan had never said anything about Miss Caldwell's. Doreen never spoke of it either. It terrified her to think of what he remembered.

History couldn't be corrected. It couldn't be strung into a storyline. It couldn't even be properly possessed. Was this tale she lived hers? There were darker, vaguer fragments. Driving away after a fight with Jonathan's father, Jonathan small in the seat beside her, chanting the only prayer he knew: *Now I lay me down to sleep*.

On the television, a woman waved a gun in a mansion library. Behind her was a Christmas tree.

The holiday was three weeks away. There was a graduation ceremony in the new year, and then Lexie was finished. Doreen planned a small party. After that she didn't know what would happen.

Perhaps the desert Doreen felt in herself was genetic, one of those strange traits like the sickle cell anemia that killed Luke's mother, an ancient mutation that protected a person from one type of death while ensuring another. At times in her life she'd longed for the exit tap of a pistol against her soft palate, but such fantasies had never plagued her long. Maybe this emptiness spared her suicide. The desert of her heart gave her a safe space in which to hide from the worst of her thoughts.

The doorbell rang. Earlier, Doreen had changed from her funeral suit into pajamas because the pajamas were there, on the closet floor. Watching soap operas mid-afternoon in pajamas and wallowing. She huddled on the couch, hoping the visitor was a Jehovah's Witness or a Seventh Day Adventist, some sort of missionary who would go away. The bell rang again.

Doreen didn't move.

A key in the lock: Lexie or Janice, then.

"I brought lunch." Jonathan held up a pizza.

His red curls had grown into a puffy mess and she could tell from the dust on his jeans that he'd been at work that morning. The time he'd been gone evaporated. He may as well have left her house that morning.

He closed the door and took off his dirty boots, set them on the towel she left there for shoes. Joined her on the couch. He set the pizza on the coffee table. "You don't have to eat any if you don't want," he said, nodding toward her sandwich. "Shit must be dire if you're watching the soaps."

"Did Powell kick you out of his trailer?"

"Luke told you where I was living."

"No. Just because we're neighbors doesn't mean we talk much."

Jonathan fished something from a pocket. "Luke tell you about this, too?" He set a rock on Doreen's sandwich plate. Most of the rock was plain and gray, but on the left side there was a skin of tiny, sugar-coated pyramids. Rising out of the pyramids was a single needle-like crystal, dark as a blackberry.

Doreen picked the rock up, held it on the flat of her palm. "My uncle found something like this once in his field. He turned it over harrowing. Wouldn't let anyone touch it."

"That one's yours. You can keep it."

Doreen imagined the rock on her desk in her new office space, in front of her picture of Thomas and Juliette. Oh that, she would say to those who noticed, Jonathan gave it to me. "Bird's wife died."

"I heard."

"I thought that might be why you stopped by."

"If I wanted to offer condolences, I'd go see Bird. He's the one lost a wife." Doreen tilted the crystal and watched the colors flash in the television light. "Are you planning on staying?"

Jonathan wiped his fingers and set his greasy napkin in the open pizza box. "You know I think Bird's a sonofabitch to have used you the way he has all these years, and you know I think you're a fool for letting him do it. I don't want to rehash all that. I thought you might want someone to sit beside you today is all. I've been lonely, and I thought you might be lonely too."

Doreen ran a hand over her son's back. His shoulder muscles were dense and hard. How long had it been since he'd been touched gently by anyone? He didn't even have a child to hug him. "Do you remember when I first started working with Bird, and I had to send you to Miss Caldwell's?"

"No."

"Right after Grandma died? I put a copy of *The Runaway Bunny* in your playpen. I got you a Viewfinder with animal discs because you liked animals." She wanted to make it a good memory for him. Save him. Save herself.

"I don't remember it, Momma."

They both had deserts inside of them, but Doreen felt

complete with Jonathan beside her. There was no remedying the heartbreak of that truth. "What about your dad? Do you remember him?"

Jonathan muted the television. "You raised me. He didn't. You're my mom and dad both."

"I felt the same way about my mom."

"Tell me what you think of that rock in your hand."

"It's pretty."

"Worth a pretty penny, too. That purple part is an amethyst, like they use to make jewelry. See how dark it is? The darker the color, the better."

Doreen poked the pointed end of the crystal.

Jonathan leaned close. "That's how they look when they grow all the way and don't break."

"I didn't know rocks grew."

"They grow underground. These grew a long time ago, but now you can dig 'em up."

"What's the stuff that looks like sand?" Doreen brushed the smaller crystals out of which the amethyst grew.

"It's quartz, same as the amethyst. Drusy's the word for it. It grew different is all."

"Not as pretty."

"People who buy rocks like it. Flyshoals is one of the only places in the world with amethyst rocks that nice."

Jonathan smelled of soil and sweat, as he had when he was a teenager cutting yards. "How do you know so much?" said Doreen.

"Library's full of books, all of 'em free. I don't want you marrying Bird Marxton."

Doreen dropped the rock and it clattered against her plate. She picked it up, blew away the crumbs. "Nothing broke."

"I know he's fired you and gave his company to that

Hammond kid. But that rock you're holding? Me and Luke have found enough like it or better to open our own jewelry store. I'm telling you that so you won't marry Bird. You don't have to. What you're holding in your hand could change things for our family."

"Money, that's what you mean." Doreen set her plate on the table. It made her angry that her own son assumed she needed to be saved, the son she'd kept and raised and fought for. He should know her capabilities. But she wasn't going to tell him what she had planned. Not now when he'd let himself into her house unannounced and full of assumptions. "This crystal isn't going to eat dinner with me at night. It's not going to raise your kids."

"If you need somebody to watch you eat, get a dog."

"I won't have you talk to me like a dog."

"If a man can't turn to his mother for help where can he go? I let things get bad with Lexie. What would keep things bad is if I went right back to her with nothing changed. She's changed, and I've got to change, too. It's not about money, Momma. But pride—a man can't stand as he should in front of a woman if he has no pride. I want to stand tall in front of Lexie and in front of you too."

"Your wife finishes school in three weeks."

"So she'll be ready for something new."

Did Jonathan anticipate Lexie leaving Flyshoals? Surely he knew there were no jobs for her in town. Did he think he'd go with her? Did he think he'd keep her from going? Doreen had no idea what sorts of ideas her son might have. He'd come into her house decided about so many things he was blinded to what was right before him. "Why are you here?"

"Clear off that table." Jonathan pulled on his boots, walked out the front door.

Doreen carried her plate and glass and the pizza box to the kitchen. Jonathan returned to the house with two large shopping bags, stepped again out of his boots. He unpacked the bags across the coffee table. Presents, boxed and wrapped. "Give these to my family. Tell them Santa exists. Tell 'em he visited you in the night, and his name is Johnny fucking Swilley." He handed her a little box wrapped in shimmery paper. "This one here's for you."

Doreen looked at the gift's label, handwritten on a scrap and taped crookedly to the top: *Merry Christmas, Momma. Love, Johnny.*

"Bribery. That's what this is." She gave the present back to her son. "I offered to help Lexie buy Santa for the kids, and she took me up on it."

"Are you saying you won't give these to my family?"

"I'm saying your wife only accepts help if she can't refuse it. She took me up on Santa money because she didn't want to disappoint her children. If she's letting me help, she's struggling. I don't know what the arrangement is between you two these days, but there's better ways to spend your cash than showboating. You could start by making sure your kids have what they need."

Jonathan set the present on top of the others. She expected him to yell, but his voice was quiet. "Tell me what to do."

"Something decent, son. Something helpful and honest. Try to see what Lexie needs instead of deciding what you want to give her."

He grabbed her arms and pulled her to him, kissed the top of her head. "I'm sorry I didn't call you after I walked out." He went to her front door and stepped into his boots. "Maybe what those presents right there say is I'm sorry. An apology is a decent thing to do." He blew her a kiss, and then he was gone.

Doreen looked at the gifts littering her coffee table. *I'm sorry.* Was that what these presents said? She picked up her gift, slipped a finger under the paper. Inside was a jewelry box. Inside that a gold chain with a gold charm: *Mom* it read, a little diamond on one curve of the 'o'. She'd never been given a diamond, and she didn't want one now. The presents in the rest of the boxes she was sure would be the same, items she and Lexie and the children had never been expecting to call their own.

Doreen recalled a joke Thomas told her last week: "One fish asks its friend, 'How's the water?' and the friend goes, 'What's water?' Get it, Grandma? The fish doesn't know he's in water because all he's ever been is wet!"

Doreen returned to her slipcovered couch. She'd never expected much from men, and then she'd been given a son. He'd behaved as she'd expected him to, and she'd done what she thought she must: run behind him, clean up his messes, make his apologies.

Doreen took the heart charm between two fingers and pinched—it bent in half. She wished she'd been able to love him better when he was a child. Wasn't every mother's wish the same?

31

A few weeks after handing over his business to Chuckie Hammond
and witnessing the death of his wife, Bird couldn't properly leave
his bed. The funeral was over and the mourners had all gone
home. The casseroles and hams and cakes he'd thrown in the
garbage. He'd looked up the home addresses of the hospice nurses
on the Georgia state licensure site and he'd sent them flowers. His
son and daughter-in-law had divided with him the responsibility
of the thank you letters, and then they'd taken his grandchild and
returned to Athens.

Theo Waters had mailed all but one of Charlotte's letters to
Bird. The one letter Theo reserved he said he would mail only if
Chuckie Hammond hired Doreen. Bird didn't know the addressee
for the single letter Theo kept. He might be able to guess if he
flipped through the stack, but he couldn't bring himself to remove
the rubberband. The bundle sat on Bird's bedside table as it had
since the day it arrived. Each morning Bird lifted the bundle—the

letter on top, the only one whose address he could read, was addressed to him—and then sat it down again. Today he'd spent the day in bed right beside the letters, but still he'd done nothing more than lift the stack once that morning and then return it to its place.

The day was gone for all intents and purposes. Bird reclined against his pillows watching *The Shawshank Redemption*. A bit of lettuce clung to his t-shirt and two fingers of bourbon sloshed in his coffee mug. The lettuce fell from his shirt to his sheets; he picked it up and ate it. It didn't matter, there was nobody to witness his sorriness.

On the TV, Andy Dufresne bargained beers for his fellow inmates, and then sat in the shade without drinking one himself. Bird was sure as hell no Andy Dufresne. He threw the sheets from his body, got out of bed. It was late enough that the hallway should have been dark, but years ago Charlotte had stuck solar powered nightlights in each socket, so the floor was puddled blue like a moonlit river bottom. The light flowed to the polished steps and then flowed down.

Bird wasn't going to walk in Charlotte's river. He turned left, opened the door to the steep servant's steps. The wall switch was sticky with neglect, but when he flipped it an overhead fluorescent buzzed to life, illuminating what three generations of Marxton women had stored on the staircase. Rolls of wrapping paper, piles of towels, a broken vacuum cleaner, stacks of baby clothes, quilts, college yearbooks, extra serving pieces. He'd hidden on these steps to spy on his parents as a child, and sometimes Imogene, on her way up or down, had discovered him. He stepped around the first pile of hoardings. All of this was now his to sort out. His father moved into the house when his grandfather died, and Bird moved in when his father died, but Will had made it clear he wouldn't return to Flyshoals. The house would be sold when Bird died. He navigated his way down. A box of recycled Christmas bows caught on his sweatpants as he passed, but he forged ahead, strewing holiday cheer.

At the base of the steps he opened the door and shuffled across the hall to his study. "Wouldn't you rather do that in your study?" Charlotte used to say to him, quietly, fingertips on his shoulder, as he sat at the kitchen table paying bills or tinkering with a crossword. He never did. He hated being alone.

He flipped the wall switch and several lamps clicked on. Charlotte had read books about things like lighting, had taken seriously the care of candlewicks. This room was a stage set for a man Bird was not. He shuffled to his wooden desk, pulled out his matching chair. He opened a file drawer and took out the folder labeled Remains.

Inside were Marla's letters. Charlotte had read them, he knew. Probably more than once. It used to make him feel better to know that what he had of Marla was in this unlocked drawer, easily accessible. It had made him feel that Charlotte was complicit in his wrongs. It had almost made him feel forgiven.

He set Marla's letters to the side.

Doreen was opening her own business next door to his. Well, not his anymore, but Chuckie Hammond's. She hadn't even bothered to tell him personally. He'd found out through Chuckie: "Your former secretary came to see me today. Said she's setting up shop where the music store used to be. She shook my hand and said, 'Good luck, kid.'"

Bird had laughed in Chuckie face. That night Clarence Hammond called Bird to have a serious talk about "our little venture." Bird didn't know if Clarence's "our" referred to Clarence and Chuckie, or to Clarence and Bird, or to all three of them. And he didn't care. It was out of his control. His clients would do what they wanted. Just like Theo Waters would do what he wanted with the single letter he'd kept once he heard that Doreen had gone rogue.

Bird took Marla's leather charm necklace from the file folder. It had belonged to her grandfather. He'd lived with her family when she was young, and she'd been the one to nurse him to his death. In return, he'd left her his worldly possessions: this necklace from a man he'd fought beside in World War I and a guitar he'd won at a poker table. Bird didn't know what had become of the guitar. Marla hadn't had it with her the last time he saw her. He rubbed the necklace between his fingers. Its contents clicked in the way he remembered. Marla had furrowed her pale forehead when she'd rubbed this necklace, convinced it brought her good fortune.

Bird slipped the necklace over his head and took out the only thing remaining in the folder. He unfolded the paper over the felted writing surface of his desk. Along the lines where the map was creased the coloring had worn away, but Bird didn't need color to know his grandmother's farm. His farm. The last time he and Doreen went fishing there, she'd led the way to the pond. Her legs had been thick and strong in her tight shorts, and she'd touched the boulder in the cornfield for luck.

Bird flipped the map over and picked up a pen:

December 17, 2009

When I, William Emmanuel Marxton V, am dead and buried, the piece of land and all of its holdings located at 1974 Lewis Loop Road, Flyshoals, Georgia, is to go to Doreen Swilley to do with as she sees fit.

He signed his name. The contract wasn't legal—Bird knew that. But it didn't matter. He only needed Will to carry out his wishes once he died. He scratched out the date and wrote a new one above it: November 27, 2009. Then, below his signature, he added: Witnessed by Charlotte Chandler Marxton, on this day, the 27th of November, 2009. Bird forged Charlotte's signature, as he had so many times in his marriage.

Will would honor his mother.

Bird rubbed the necklace, gazed at the map. These two things told no story in and of themselves. Even if someone read Marla's letters, they would only have proof of a brief teenage tryst. But wasn't that the nature of remains? A settler's chimney happened upon in some piney woods, a single twist of hair in some unknown relative's tarnished locket. Such things opened a well of nostalgia in the heart, even though all humans were subject to time, to mortality. Why could the soul be played like a lute by objects that were essentially empty of meaning?

1959

32

Emmy put a hand on Marla's back and led her into the abortionist's gardens as if he knew the way. Two big brown dogs ran from the side woods, and Marla froze. Emmy urged her forward: "She said not to worry about the dogs." The dogs stormed them, licked their hands, circled and leapt and barked as they made their way toward the side door. A tethered goat joined in the dogs' announcement, bleating and stomping his feet, straining at the rope that held him. The side door opened and a tall, black-haired woman stepped onto the stoop. "Cocoa, Millie, hush! Be gone!" The dogs ran back into the woods; the goat kept straining and bleating.

"Those dogs wouldn't hurt a fly," said the woman, "but that goat's another story." She took Marla by the elbow, led her into the kitchen.

Emmy followed along behind.

The abortionist led Marla to the kitchen table and seated

her across from a girl child, a toddler. In front of the child was a plate of mashed yams and pole beans, a few pieces of hard cheese. The girl looked from Marla to Emmy with a flat gaze. "This is Doreen," said her mother, walking around the table to cup the back of the child's head. "Please call me Lucille. You're here to terminate a pregnancy?"

"Yes ma'am." Marla sat on the edge of her chair. She pulled her lucky necklace from inside her shirt, rubbed it so the contents made their soft clicking noise.

Lucille sat next to Marla. Still she had not looked at Emmy. Emmy pulled out a seat for himself, embarrassed by the scraping noise his chair made across the floor. He sensed that he was to be invisible.

"Momma, cookie please?" said the child. In the center of the table sat a plate of sugar cookies.

"Finish your cheese first."

The girl looked at Emmy as she shoved a whole piece of cheese in her mouth.

Lucille pulled the cookie plate toward Marla. "Please, have one. How far along are you?"

"I don't rightly know, ma'am. Ten weeks. Eleven. I been putting in the kitchen garden and thought that's why I missed the first time."

"Hard work makes you miss periods?"

"Yes ma'am."

Lucille rolled the flesh of Marla's lower arm between her fingers.

"Skinny's a family trait, ma'am."

"Thin women can have problems with bleeding. Too much. Too little. You're far along."

Emmy kept his eyes on his hands. Once, when he was taking out the trash, he'd seen one of mother's soiled pads, a thick, rectangular diaper dark with blood. The memory soured his stomach.

One piece of cheese finished, the girl child shoved the second into her mouth, working for her cookie, this abortionist's daughter. Emmy felt a strange curiosity about her—she was what he was here to avoid, a person this size who would grow bigger, big enough to track him down and call him daddy.

"I put the herbs on to steep earlier," said Lucille. "You can drink the tea whenever you're ready. I ask that you stay here until morning so I can keep an eye on things."

"You don't go inside?"

"I work with God, not against him. We'll use what he gave us." The child's cheese was finished. "Good job, Reenie." Lucille handed her a cookie.

"What's the cost?" said Emmy. Nolin had given him two hundred, and he'd taken another fifty from his savings account.

"I won't take your money." Lucille turned to Marla. "But you and I should have an exchange. Anything you can afford to offer is fine. It can be as simple as a feather. Something meaningful to you."

"Does it hurt?"

"You'll go through labor."

"And when it's born, will it be. Dead?"

"It won't be able to live outside of the body. You may or may not be far enough along to identify it as a baby. It may or may not be alive. I'll be with you. You can hold it while it dies."

Emmy felt the world growing cottony and dim. He put his head on the table to keep from falling from his chair as everything faded to black.

When he awoke, he was alone in the kitchen. The table had been cleared. He got up, walked into the living room. Marla sat on the sofa clutching a Mason jar filled with a dark tea. "Miss Lucille is putting Doreen to bed."

Emmy joined Marla, but he sat at the sofa's far end, suddenly frightened by her. She had a husband at home who spoke to strangers as a farmer does a foal. Her life wouldn't change if she had the baby—she would only ever be a sharecropper, baby or no. But Marla didn't seem to understand her own poverty, how it would be with her forever, how this choice she was making wouldn't improve things for her. "How does it taste?"

She offered him the jar.

"It could do something to me."

"That's why you drink it."

"I mean something bad. It's made for women."

"You don't think what it does to women is bad?"

Lucille returned to the room carrying two quilts and two pillows. She set these on the table beside the sofa. "Y'all make yourselves at home in here." On top of the quilts were a belt and a maxi-pad. "Go ahead and put these on. First you'll cramp, and then you'll bleed. Wake me when the cramping starts. You should try to sleep until then too."

"Yes ma'am."

Lucille brushed Marla's hair back from her face, tucked it behind her ears. Tears ran down Marla's face, but she made no noise of grief.

"Wake me when the cramping starts," repeated Lucille.

"Yes, ma'am."

Lucille turned her crow-dark eyes on Emmy. He wanted to offer her something in exchange, just as she'd asked for from Marla. Something to keep him from feeling so bad about this. He wanted to feel like this was an experience he'd bought and could discard. "Thank you," he said.

Lucille wouldn't even accept that. The child, Doreen, called from the back of the house. "Water please, Momma!"

"Sleep while you can." Lucille went down the hall to care for her daughter.

Marla handed Emmy a quilt and a pillow. He stretched out on the floor, certain he wouldn't sleep, while she went down the hall to the bathroom.

He awoke to a tapping on his shoulder. Staring into his face was the child. Her pajamas were too big for her, the right foot dragging behind her like a broken leg. Early, weak light filtered through the thin living room curtains. The couch where Marla had slept was empty. "Is it over?"

The toddler put a hand on either of his cheeks and pushed them straight back, then pulled them forward, straight back, then forward. She laughed so hard she stumbled over her dragging pajama foot and tumbled to the floor.

He had asked a baby about an abortion. Christ. The house was too quiet. He stood and looked into the kitchen—empty. The short hallway had only three doors, two open, one closed. "Marla?"

One of the doors opened and Lucille stepped into the hall. She came to Emmy and put a hand on each of his shoulders. "It didn't work."

She tightened her grip as he weakened from her words. "We can try again," he said. "I don't have to have her at the bus station until after lunch. She's going to Waycross to stay with her cousin for a few days after this."

"God said no. If she drinks more it could retard the baby. You're going to be a daddy." She stepped past Emmy in the narrow hallway and picked up her daughter who stood behind him, one finger in her mouth.

Emmy went into the room Lucille had exited. In one corner were a dollhouse and blocks. The curtains were pink gingham. Marla lay on her side on a short twin bed, her back to the door.

Emmy touched her shoulder.

"It didn't hurt. I didn't bleed at all." She rolled over, grabbed his hands. "We can run away. Raise this baby anywhere we want. We'll come back one day, you and me. When he's older." Marla put Emmy's hands on her belly. "Then he can meet his family."

If Emmy emptied his bank account and took to the road with Marla, his parents would scratch his name from the family Bible. He had enough money to support them for a short while, but then his own future would collapse to match Marla's and the child's. Sharecropping. Factory work. Tenements and rented shacks. He didn't know how to live that way. "You have Cherlow."

She pressed his hands deep into her stomach. Emmy imagined the baby swirling away from the pressure as a goldfish in a bag might. "You won't trap me forever with an old man on a borrowed farm."

Emmy yanked his hands free. "You can't make me do anything." The crack in his voice embarrassed him. "You're married. Nobody will believe this baby is mine."

"Lucille knows you came here with me. Claimed it."

"Lucille can't say anything. It's illegal, what she does. Everyone pretends not to know. She has a child of her own to raise. You'll ruin her life and her daughter's life if you expose her."

"Take me home. I want to see Cherlow."

"What will you tell him? About who the daddy is?"

"I'll tell him it's you."

"You can't be sure. If we're honest." Nolin had advised Emmy to say this only if nothing else worked. Marla had wanted Emmy to wear a condom, but the times he didn't have one she

210

hadn't refused. A woman wouldn't be more careful with her husband.

"There are normal married things Cherlow can't do. I told you that. That's why he never married before. That's why he's silent when I wander nights."

She sat up, her back against the headboard. She looked young enough to have a room with a dollhouse and pink gingham curtains, and beside her Emmy felt young enough for a child's room too. "Those of us what worked at Fulton Bag and Cotton Mill understand such. Comes from the spray they put on the cotton plants. It damages the sex parts first. Women grow rocks in their titties. Men end up like Cherlow. Girls miscarry." Her eyes were blank. "Not me though. Part of our arrangement was that I never shame him."

Emmy remembered Cherlow sitting guard with a pistol in his lap. "Go to your cousin's house in Waycross. Keep up our alibi. I have another idea." He began to gather her belongings. "We're not going to run away together. I'm going to help you get rid of this baby. And then we're finished."

He expected his words to upset her, but relief flooded her face. "We have to find someone who goes inside. I know of a man in Atlanta, but we can't see him, not if I'm going to stay with Cherlow."

Emmy handed Marla her shoes. "I'll find us someone."

The bedroom door creaked open and the girl child, Doreen, toddled in. She dropped to her knees in front of her dollhouse and picked up a handmade cloth doll with long black hair. "Momma," she said.

In the kitchen, Lucille stood at the stove flipping pancakes. "Breakfast." She motioned toward the table where four places were set.

Marla moved toward the table, but Emmy grabbed her arm. "We'd like to go, if you don't mind, ma'am."

"It's a few hours before you catch your bus. No need to wait at the station." She waved a hand toward the open windows. "It's a beautiful day." The light in the kitchen was brilliant, the air alive with birdsong.

The child wandered into the kitchen and pulled her chair back, climbed onto it. She sat on her knees to reach her plate. "Momma, pancakes, please?"

"Go inside just this once," said Marla. "Please. I know you know how."

Lucille set down her spatula and went to Marla, took her hands. "It's too dangerous. You need a doctor for that."

"You have to know a doctor who'll do it for me. Someone." Marla slipped the leather necklace from her neck. She turned Lucille's right hand palm up and pressed the necklace into it. "Please."

Lucille turned her palm over, returning the necklace. "You don't owe me anything."

"You said there had to be an exchange!"

"I wasn't able to help you."

"You won't tell me who can help, and now you won't do the trade. It's like you don't want it to work. Like you're working some other root on me, something bad!" Marla threw the necklace at Lucille's feet. "Don't you put no eye on me, you witch."

Lucille picked the necklace up and held it for a moment. She slipped it over her head. "I don't work magic. I work with plants. I work with God. The only thing I'll do is pray for you, child."

Marla wrapped her thin arms around herself. "Keep your prayers to yourself."

Emmy put an arm across Marla's shoulder and urged her with touch toward the kitchen door. She allowed him to guide her and for this much Emmy was grateful: he'd found a way out of the witch's kitchen.

A quarter of an hour later, Emmy pulled into Nolin's garage. "This is my uncle's house. We can wait here until your bus comes." He wished Nolin weren't going to meet Marla and hear her speak and see her crooked teeth, but there was nowhere else for them to go. Sitting in the bus station was out of the question. They couldn't be seen together. The thought of leaving her unattended made him uneasy too. He didn't trust that she wouldn't run to Cherlow. He had to keep her beside him for the next two hours and he also needed to come up with a new plan in that time. Only Nolin knew the bind he was in. Only Nolin might know another way to help him out of it.

Marla hadn't spoken on the ride over. "I'm not going inside," she said. "You brung me to your uncle's house what told you about that root woman."

"You can wait in the car for two hours then."

"I'll get my bag and walk to the station." She leaned her head against the window. "All this started when I stole your wallet. I want to go home."

Emmy pushed Marla's hair behind her ear. It scared him to see the way she suffered. "What if I ask Nolin to stay in his bedroom while we're here. Then would you come inside? If you don't have to meet him?"

She turned her blue eyes on him. "I better not even see his shadow."

Emmy went in expecting to find Nolin at the kitchen table. But the table was empty and the newspaper was still rolled from the paperboy. "Hello?"

No answer.

"Nolin?"

Emmy tossed the keys on the counter and walked through the house to Nolin's bedroom. The bed was made and a smell of aftershave came from the bathroom. Emmy hurried to the hall closet where Nolin kept his golf clubs: gone.

His uncle wouldn't be back until after lunch, and by then Marla would be on her way to Waycross. This meant Nolin didn't have to meet her. But it also meant he couldn't ask Nolin if he knew of another abortionist. He wasn't going to call the country club and pull his uncle off the course. Emmy would have to lie to Marla, give her a fake name, a fake appointment time. He could sort out the real details later.

In the garage, he opened Marla's door and took her hand. "Nolin isn't even here. Won't be back until we're gone."

There were circles under her eyes and she smelled sour, as if she needed to bathe.

"You can get cleaned up while I make us toast and coffee."

"You got a tub with hot water?"

"Yes."

"I can use it?"

"Of course."

She allowed him to help her from the car then.

Marla followed Emmy to the guest bathroom. He took a clean towel and washcloth from the cupboard and laid these on the counter by the sink. She stood beside the towel rack and looked at herself in the mirror. Against the bathroom's bright turquoise tile she looked old-fashioned and out of place, like one of those pictures from the Great Depression that he'd studied in school.

"I'll call my uncle while you're in the tub," said Emmy. "Get the name and phone number of a doctor. When you get back from

Waycross, we'll go."

"I don't trust your uncle no more. We got to do it ourselves. Before we run out of time. I know how." She stepped to him, pressed her sour mouth to his. He tasted last night's bitter herbs on her lips. Emmy jerked from her, gagged.

Marla changed then. Turned calm, distant. Became again the hardscrabble girl he knew, the one who drank moonshine and slept with boys she'd only just met, the one who stole wallets and went to Chicago. "Teach me how to run the bath," she said.

He sat on the edge of the tub, turned the taps. "Come and feel it. How do you like it?"

She stuck her hand in the stream. "How hot can it get?"

Emmy showed her the hot tap and moved so she could run her bath herself.

She held her hand in the flow, turning her wrist so the water coursed this way and that into the tub. "I never have been the first one in the tub. Always I have to go after someone."

"There's soap and shampoo too." Emmy pointed them out, showcasing the amenities, glad he could give her something, however small. "On the back of the bathroom door there's a robe." Marla began stripping off her clothes, an act that to Emmy felt too private to witness, though he'd seen her naked many times. He hurried to the door as Marla stepped out of her dress. He would never again have sex without a condom, not even if the girl he was with begged. Especially if she begged.

It had been over an hour and a half that Marla was in the bathroom—the wonder of hot water, Emmy assumed. He'd heard the tap turn on several times, replenishing the heat. Not long ago the tub had drained and the toilet had flushed a few times. He didn't mind that she was lingering, hoped she would bathe until it was time to leave. He had a piece of paper ready for her with a fake name and a fake appointment—the less time they had to speak of this paper, the less time she had to find him out.

It seemed to him, after thinking on it over coffee, that even if he could not find someone to help them, Marla would be happier once the baby came along. The baby would give her someone else to love, and wasn't that why she'd had an affair in the first place? She'd been so lonely since her brother's murder. Cherlow too. He was so lonely he settled for half a marriage to a woman he'd more or less raised. How could he not welcome a child? There was such truth in this thinking that Emmy felt Marla would surely see it herself. It was a realization she might reach on her own while she spent time with her cousin's children in Waycross. She needed to finish her bath and dress—they should leave for the station soon. He poured her a cup of coffee, added milk and sugar, took it down the hall to the bathroom.

"Marla?" He knocked. "I brought you coffee." There were some slight shuffling noises, and the sound of water dripping down the tub drain, but she didn't answer.

"We need to leave soon."

This time there weren't the shuffling noises. "Answer me, please." What if she locked herself in the bathroom until after the bus departed, or insisted on returning to Cherlow? He tried the knob: unlocked. A good sign. "Are you dressed? Can I come in?"

No answer.

He could walk in, but she might be on the toilet. She might be naked, bent over the sink. "Talk to me. You're not the only one in this situation."

Emmy looked down Nolin's short hall. The only decoration was a mounted bass. "I'm coming in." He turned the doorknob and eased it open a few inches, waited for but heard no protest.

He peeked inside. The toilet bowl was red with bright

blood. His joy outpaced the cottony sensation that threatened to overwhelm him as it had at the abortionist's table. "Marla? Is it working?" He pushed the door wider. There were a few drops of blood on the turquoise tiles. The small trashcan was filled with soiled paper.

He stepped into the bathroom and set Marla's coffee on the counter. The tub was behind the door, and when Emmy turned he saw that Marla lay on her side in the drained tub, wearing the robe from the bathroom door. Her back was to him. The robe was bunched around her waist, and her lower body she'd wrapped in towels from the cupboard. A bright red dot showed where the towel covered her buttocks. He knelt on the bathmat beside her.

"It's working," she said faintly.

Emmy gathered her clean, damp hair in his hands and smoothed it into a loose twist. "Does it hurt?" Lucille had said she would go through labor. But Marla didn't look like the women he'd seen in Westerns, sweaty and screaming by a basin of steaming water. Her eyes were closed, her face bloodless. Her arms were crossed over her chest. He put his hand over hers and her fingers felt as cool and sleek as stone. He took her hand, rubbed, but couldn't find even her calluses, those signs of the life she lived. "Let me put you in the guest bed. I'll squeeze in beside you. You'll be warmer that way."

"I'll ruin the sheets." Her shivering was a steady, dull tremor. "I'll ruin the mattress. I only have one Kotex."

Should they worry about the mattress? The sheets? Emmy didn't know. He'd never been responsible for another person in this way. Nolin was his only source of wisdom, and Nolin wasn't home. Emmy left the bathroom, grabbed a blanket and pillow from the guest bed, returned with them. He put a pillow beneath Marla's head. The blanket he folded and tucked around her waist to shoulders, pressing the edges under her tiny body.

He sat back on his heels. Even as he watched, the red spot on her backside grew larger. At the drugstore, he'd seen the container on the counter where women deposited their money before discreetly taking their paper-wrapped box of Kotex. That was something he could do for her. Anyone who saw would assume he shopped for his mother. How long did it take to finish labor's bleeding? She needed to leave for the bus station in less than an hour. If he brought her a Kotex, could she ride the bus? Did they need a new alibi?

He lifted the edge of the towel covering her. She placed a hand on his but lacked the strength to push him away. Beneath the towel, she'd abandoned her panties and wore only the elastic belt for her sanitary napkin. Her napkin was soaked to a solid maroon and two trails of blood ran along either side of her right thigh. On one side a pool formed. On the other side, blood ran steadily past her legs and dripped down the drain.

Emmy put a hand to her forehead: cold. He took the blanket from her shoulders, unfolded it, and covered her from neck to toes, staining be damned. He rubbed her arms through the blanket, trying to force warmth and life back into her. "Is this how it's supposed to be?"

He could call Lucille and ask, but her phone number was on a scrap of paper hidden at home in his baseball cards. He wrapped a hand over Marla's forehead. "Do you remember Lucille's phone number?" Marla panted quickly and softly through her mouth like a rabbit he'd once rescued from the mouth of a dog.

"Is this normal? Is this what happens after?"

Marla fluttered her eyelids open and her eyes rolled. "Don't tell Cherlow."

There shouldn't be anything to tell Cherlow. Emmy slipped an arm under Marla's shoulders, and an arm under her hips. He lifted her from the tub. Something clattered onto the porcelain.

A length of twisted metal, one end curved like a hook. Not yet understanding he turned, holding her, her body seeming to weigh less than the towels and blankets she was wrapped in. Her overnight bag was open and her things were scattered around the bathroom, a toothbrush on the counter, a bleached sock beside the tub. The sock was worn to transparency in the heel but was as brilliantly white as the day it was purchased, and as Emmy looked at this small, carefully tended sock, he understood: Marla had done this to herself. She'd used the metal hanger that the robe had hung on. He sank to the tub's edge to keep from dropping her. She moaned.

Emmy kissed her cheek, turned his face toward her mouth. Her breath was so light he wasn't sure if he felt or imagined it. He reached into the blankets, found her wrist. It seemed he would hurt her, so hard did he have to press to locate the dull thump. "Stay awake, Marla." He rattled his arm supporting her head. "Stay awake. Goddammit! We can move anywhere you want. Do you hear me?"

Emmy hurried from the bathroom, turning her shrouded body so that he did not knock her head or her feet against the doorframe. He ran down the hall, into the kitchen, into the garage, to his uncle's car. With some effort, he slid her into the backseat. "I'm sorry," he said. "I'm so sorry. We're going to get help." He arranged the blankets around her in the backseat. "I know you're cold. As soon as I start the car it will get warm. I'm going to get the keys right now. I don't know where to go. Think of where to go! Stay awake, Marla. Hold on."

Emmy found the keys and then, without locking the house door behind him, got behind the steering wheel of his uncle's car. He noticed the lawnmower in the corner, grass browning on its shell, and a cracked dartboard propped against the wall. The garage was in shadow but the day was an illuminated rectangle behind him. He started the car, turned on the heat. "Where do we go, Marla?" He could drive to the hospital; he could drive to Lucille's. He pressed his hands to the heating vent. "Can you feel the warm air back there?"

"Will you answer me, please? Can you feel the warm air?"

"Do I go to Lucille's or do I go to the hospital? I don't know where to go."

In the backseat, Marla took a deep breath.

Emmy slapped the steering wheel. "This is your fault, dammit. Your fault!" He backed out of the garage and prayed clumsy, obvious prayers. He righted himself in the drive and pulled to the street. Sun poured down like a benediction. A child rode by on a red bicycle. God did not tell Emmy what to do.

In the backseat, Marla drew another breath. If she exhaled, he missed it. He pulled into the street and turned left toward the hospital.

He would need a story when he arrived. He didn't know if it was illegal for Marla to have done what she did to herself. He didn't know if what she'd tried last night at Lucille's was illegal, especially if it didn't work. He didn't know if a woman dying from two botched abortions was allowed to receive medical care. And he didn't know if he was legally responsible for any of it.

At the end of the block, Emmy stopped at the sign and raised his hand to an old man sitting in his yard on a woven lawn chair, taking in the sun.

In the backseat, Marla exhaled. She exhaled until Emmy was forced to turn. He focused on the unformed shape of her shrouded body because he could not bring himself to look at her face.

When she stopped exhaling, Emmy understood that the moment was irrevocable. Nothing blew but the heating vents, yet he felt he sat in a hurricane. Outside the car, the old man tilted his face to the sky.

Marla's wrist fell from the blankets. Her eyes flipped open. The hurricane wildness in the car increased.

Some essential part of Emmy slipped free from his skin and glided to the car's empty passenger seat. This part of Emmy could bear to look on Marla. This part of Emmy saw that Marla did not look dead, but peaceful. Her lips were barely parted. Her face had more color than it had a moment ago. This part of Emmy understood, finally, that Marla was beautiful, even with her hair, her teeth, her grammar. But when this part of Emmy, this part that felt such fearlessness and compassion, turned to himself, and saw the way he would not look on Marla's face, not even as he clutched her pulseless wrist—when this disconnected part of Emmy saw what he was, he turned vaporous.

Vaporous Emmy, who was slipped free from his skin, eased between the window and the window frame and dissipated forever into the brilliant blue and yellow sky.

With vaporous Emmy's departure, a woman whose job it was to pick grit and twigs from raw cotton in an Atlanta gin paused in her work with a thought of her daughter. She'd not seen the girl in more than a year, and that struck her as wrong. But the gin's delivery vacuum did not pause, and the carding machine thundered on, so the woman only put a hand briefly to her womb and then returned to her work.

With vaporous Emmy's departure, a soft-voiced old man whoaed his mule in a red clay field outside of Athens. Man and beast had both aged out of such work, though neither could afford to quit. But harder than such work was loneliness, the old man thought. It was good he'd married. Soon, his wife would return from her cousin's, and he wanted her to see this field complete. A gift. With this bit of labor, she would not have to help. He slapped the mule with its reins.

With vaporous Emmy's departure, an eighteen-year-old in

Birmingham, Alabama ignored her history teacher's lecture and drew a heart around the name of her latest crush. Come fall she would finally be in college, and then her life would begin.

With vaporous Emmy's departure, a girl in Flyshoals crawled from the bed where she was supposed to be napping and ran to find her mother. The girl's mother was at the kitchen stove, stirring the thick purple jam she made each year from spring's violets. "You have a bad dream?" said the girl's mother. In answer, the girl lay on the rag rug beneath the kitchen table to finish her nap, as she had done so many times before.

With vaporous Emmy's departure, lumpen-flesh Emmy tucked Marla's arm beneath his uncle's blanket. He pulled the blanket over her face. It was a gorgeous spring day and the outside world suspected nothing, not from a handsome young white boy in a well-kept car. Emmy waved again to the old man taking in the sun, and he turned his uncle's car left. He circumnavigated the block, passing the child on the red bicycle. He returned to Nolin's garage.

If the world were not as Emmy knew it to be, he could take Marla's body to her husband. Cherlow deserved to know what his young bride had done. But there was no way to predict what the old man would do in his grief. Would he suffer stoically, biblically, as the salt of the earth were said to do? Or would he grow angry and make demands, cast accusations? He could shoot Emmy, three lives wasted then, the baby's, Marla's and his own. He could turn the gun on himself, make the total four. It was better for Cherlow not to know. There wouldn't be much effort put into looking for a girl like Marla, a white trash sharecropper girl from out of town, a girl known to wander alone in the night, playing a guitar. Asking for trouble. It had only been a matter of time until she went missing, truth be told.

Emmy saw what he was doing, saw how he turned things in

his favor, saw that while he was smart enough to notice problems in the world, he was unwilling to change even one of them. Meanwhile, all around him, people were galvanized by causes. Last week there'd been a sit-in at Strickland's downtown. Blacks wanted to eat with whites and some whites, like his mother, agreed with this. Those schools in Virginia had been reopened. Lucille demanded something of him when she refused to take his money. But what? What had she wanted from him? He was just a seventeen-year-old boy—why was it his job to rewrite the world's stories?

Emmy turned the rearview mirror toward himself and straightened his mussed hair. He ran a finger under each eye, smoothing the guilt and fear away. Practicing his new face. The nickname Nolin had given him was apt. Like a bird dog, Emmy sniffed the air and retreated if he smelled danger, charged only when his own power was mirrored back to him. He smiled at himself and saw the lie there, but knew that nobody else would.

He straightened the rearview. In his uncle's garage, the lawnmower sat as it had minutes earlier and the dartboard leaned yet against the wall. Bird, as he would forever after think of himself, as he would forever after be known—this name his only outward penitence—got out of the car and went inside to sit at the kitchen table and wait for his uncle to get home. Nolin would know what to do with Marla's body. The man had no choice but to help him.

2009

33

Doreen stood in the space where her son was once arrested for shoplifting. She wore coveralls and unwrapped a paint head for a long-handled roller. Janice was across from her on a ladder, using a small brush to dab paint along the 90-degree angle where two walls met so that the corners would match the rolled spaces. "Make sure you get the fuzz off," Janice said to Doreen.

Doreen whisked a piece of masking tape about the head. "How many walls have I painted with you? Your whole damn house."

"This is different. We're painting your office. Get the fuzz off."

Doreen stuck the defuzzed roller on the handle, loaded it with paint, and ran it up and down the wall. She liked the way the paint pulled away from the nap, giving the wall a subtle sponged look. She liked the sound of painting too, a soft whooshing as of a distant creek. There was a calm that settled over her while working with Janice that was similar to the calm she'd once found in church. "Swilley Insurance," she said slowly. "I've got someone coming over from Athens day after tomorrow to paint the words on the front window. Same font as Bird's." She planned to open during the first week of the new year. It was the week before Christmas, and Janice had taken vacation hours to help her prepare.

Bird had sent Doreen the same letter he'd sent his clients. In it, he said that he trusted Chuckie Hammond implicitly. Doreen had borrowed his wording on the letter she sent to all of Bird's clients and also to two hundred other addresses in Flyshoals and the surrounding areas: "I know many of you personally, and I trust you implicitly. You can have the same level of trust in me." Already she'd gotten phone calls and emails and texts.

Janice came down from the ladder to admire her work. "You've made it look easy," she said.

"Painting's not hard."

Janice held her tiny paintbrush and faced the wall. "I mean you've made it look easy to get your own in the world."

Doreen didn't turn to Janice. All the years of their friendship they'd urged one another to be the strongest versions of themselves. Their successes had been the type that demanded further shows of strength—not compliments, not recognition. Not moments of calm. It was the difference between reaching yet another fork in the trail and finally reaching a vista. "All you have to do is get pregnant at seventeen and drop out of school," said Doreen.

Now Janice turned, grinning. "Spend most of your working life as a secretary."

"And thirty years of closed-curtain fucks. That's what Charlotte told me I'd gotten from Bird when she stopped by here right at the end. Right before she died."

"You never told me that." Janice set her brush down in her paint tray. "Well, it does us no good to wish ill of the dead." She pulled her cigarettes from her coveralls pocket. "Come outside with me while I have a smoke."

Doreen got her coat from the rack. "Flooring's looking tired," she said. "Todd Phelps told me I can do anything I want so long as I leave the walls intact." Todd Phelps had moved to Atlanta so long ago Doreen didn't remember what he looked like. When she called to ask if she could lease the space, he seemed surprised that she'd not just squatted. "I've been on YouTube. I can tile the floor if you'll help me."

"I'll help you."

Outside, Janice and Doreen sat side by side on the bench that Doreen had bought. The only other bench was in front of Strickland's Restaurant. Once there had been chairs and benches all along the sidewalks in Flyshoals, lots of places to sit and chat, but now there were so few shops, so few people. Still, each light post for the length of town was hung with a plastic Christmas wreath. Doreen snapped her coat against the cold. It was close to freezing, and the weather was not predicted to warm until the new year.

Janice blew a stream of smoke. "Have you decided what to do about Jonathan?"

"I'm not handing out his Christmas presents if that's what you mean. And I'm not inviting him to Lexie's graduation party either." Lexie had gotten her final grades—she'd done it; she would get her nursing pin at the graduation ceremony on January ninth.

"He might show up. On Christmas. Or at her party."

"I guess he has a right. She's his wife and those are his kids. But he won't help his case any dropping in unannounced. He's done nothing but stand in her way. I think things between them are too far gone to fix."

Janice stubbed out her cigarette on the bench arm. "I found those napkins Juliette wanted. Party City online. Con-gradulations. I went ahead and got the matching cake plates too."

"Tell me what I owe you."

Janice pointed down the road. Bird's truck headed toward them. "Think he's coming to see you?"

"No reason for him too." Unlike Jonathan and Lexie, she and Bird could split apart without complication. Nothing legal bound them; they had no shared property, no children. They'd not spoken since Bird came to her house to tell her that he'd signed a contract with Chuckie Hammond. They never had to speak again.

But Bird pulled to the curb and idled parallel to the sidewalk. He rolled down his window. "I hear there's a new business opening up here soon."

"Want me to tell him to get lost?" said Janice.

"I might as well see what he wants." Doreen wished for a moment that she was wearing something other than coveralls and an old winter coat. Something she knew Bird liked. It made her feel silly to think these things, but thoughts were private. Had Bird mourned her? She'd shed some tears over him. Not for him alone—every time her tears were mixed with tears for other things too, but she had thought of Bird while she cried. She walked to his truck. In the front seat was a suitcase and in the backseat were presents.

"I'm heading to Athens for Christmas. I'm staying with Will and Leigh. Her parents are coming too."

"Sounds nice."

"I've only spent Christmas in the house where I live now. When I was a kid we went there and my Nana cooked, and then after she died my Dad moved into the place and my mom cooked, and then after he died, Charlotte and I moved in and she cooked."

"I'll be at Lexie's."

"I know. That's what you do every year."

It was new, this recognition of her personal life.

Bird reached across the truck and took her fingertips. "Maybe we could go to dinner. After the holidays."

Something inside of her responded. It wasn't something she could put a name to. Not love. Not even desire. Curiosity maybe. Who were she and Bird on the other side of all that had happened? "Maybe if you ask me."

"Doreen Swilley, will you go to dinner with me? After the holidays?"

She couldn't help it, she found herself checking the spot on his cheek where he'd had his biopsy in the fall. There wasn't even a scar. "Call me when you're back in town." She pulled her fingers from his hand, turned from his truck. Heard him pull away from the curb behind her.

Janice had slipped back inside. Doreen stood alone in front of her office. Through the front window, she saw that Janice had picked up the roller. Next door, Marxton Casualty and Life was open for business. Nobody sat at what was once Doreen's desk; she wasn't even sure if Chuckie Hammond had hired anyone yet.

Doreen went back inside. "Do you think I'd be crazy to go to dinner with Bird?"

Janice pulled the paint down the wall. "I think all the things you were crazy to do with Bird you've quit doing. As for dinner, don't ask me. I'm a woman who sleeps with a man that lets an incontinent dog share his bed."

34

Lexie stood at her kitchen window scanning the road in front of her house. She should have realized Juliette was lying when she walked out the door that morning claiming she was going to cross-country practice. Cross-country season was over—Lexie had even driven Juliette and her friend, Susie Hines, to Walthersville for the final meet. But Lexie had been too wrapped in her own thoughts to think things through, and now it was five-thirty—almost dark—and not only was her daughter not home, she wasn't answering calls or texts. Lexie shifted her cellphone to her other ear. "At least they got their lie straight," Beth Hines said. Both mothers had been told the girls were going after practice to an end-of-season cross-country party at Viti's Pizza and would be home by four.

"Can you think of anyone they'd be with?" said Lexie. She thought *boys* and *older*.

"Sometimes they go off with Beth's brother, Ross. But he's helping his granddad cut firewood today. I already called my dad and checked that Ross is there."

"How old is Ross?"

"He's a senior."

Lexie hadn't heard anything about Ross. What was it Juliette had asked while she worked on her paper? *Mom, when you were my age were you allowed to go on dates?* "Do the girls run around with him a lot? Ross?"

"He takes them to get ice cream sometimes."

Lexie realized that she knew very little about the Hines family. Susie and Juliette became friends this year, during cross-country, and Lexie had spoken to Beth only in passing. "Could they be with one of Ross's friends?"

"Susie knows there'll be hell to pay if they are. A brother's one thing, a senior boy's another."

The answer soothed Lexie. At least Beth Hines wasn't encouraging her middle school-aged daughter to run around with boys old enough to legally count as men. There were women who did that.

Silence on the line.

Three years ago, Lexie would've rattled off a list of places her daughter might be, children she might be with. Today she couldn't. She knew she no longer listened to Juliette as closely as she once had. "I've told you about her a thousand times!" Juliette shouted when Lexie couldn't remember if a particular girl was a friend, an enemy, or both. Lexie had missed most of Juliette's cross-country meets this year, and the few she'd made she watched alone, choosing a far section of the bleachers instead of the starting line seats where the mothers gathered in a gossipy clutch. She'd been so grateful for those quiet moments in the stands that even now she couldn't regret them. Beth Hines had sat off by herself too.

"I think the girls got close because of their home situations," Beth said. "Susie's daddy and I split last year. Juliette says you're going through the same."

Lexie hadn't said the word divorce, not to the children, not to Doreen. If she said it, anyone could repeat the word to

Jonathan. "My daughter shouldn't be talking about things she's too young to understand."

"It's hard on the kids when parents have problems. Ross doesn't even live with me anymore. He picked his daddy."

Lexie felt herself soften toward Beth. She longed to talk, and not as she did with Ms. Paulsen, not about logistics and timelines, but about feelings. This, though, was the very thing Ms. Paulsen warned her against. *No confidantes. Be your own friend.* Lexie had even quit talking to Luke's wife, Amanda, and they'd been close since they were teens. "I need to let you go so I can call my mother-in-law," said Lexie. "She's with the kids a lot. She might have some idea where the girls are." Lexie hung up before Beth could push for more.

"Mom, did you find her?" Thomas yelled from the living room.

She'd told Thomas an hour ago to watch a movie, and while she heard battle sounds coming from whatever he'd picked, he kept the volume low enough to eavesdrop. "Stop listening in!"

Soon it would be fully dark outside. What Lexie had told Beth Hines was true: Doreen may have an idea where the girls were, who they were with. But the problem Lexie faced with Beth Hines would be amplified with Doreen. Lexie had once made a habit of speaking with her mother-in-law, and there was so much she wanted to say now.

Her worry over Juliette highlighted how alone she'd become.

In moments like this, she missed Jonathan.

She knew how to keep peace with him, she'd done it for years. She'd cooked and cleaned and cared for the kids, fucked him twice a week so he would not turn sullen and short-tempered. Thomas and Juliette had been happy enough then. And it hadn't been unhappiness, exactly, that led her to Flyshoals Technical College. Longing was a better word for what she'd felt.

Lexie picked up her phone, found Jonathan's contact info.

He would come if she called. She could apologize and set about making things as they once were. She could go to the Walmart and get a job not unlike what she'd had at Mercer's. She could go back to cooking and cleaning and caring for kids, measuring her life in a series of bi-weekly fucks. What good was there in a move to a better school system, a better chance at college, if Juliette blew it all on the first boy who came along and showed her some kindness?

"Mom?" Thomas stood in the doorway. "Did you find Juliette?"

This time Lexie didn't fuss at him for eavesdropping. "Not yet. But I will. Go on back to your show."

Thomas wandered away. Lexie recognized the trick her mind was playing. She wasn't confused about what was best for Juliette, for Thomas. She knew she needed to leave. She doubted herself because it was in her nature to do so. She doubted herself because, like a beaten dog that rolls belly-up when kicked, there were ways she had been broken.

After her father had been out of her life for several years, she'd grown nostalgic for the way he'd once taught her basic car care. It had been so disorienting to think kindly on him, she'd almost made efforts to find him. She'd wanted to apologize for the times she'd screamed at him, for the fights she'd picked. Often he'd called her ungrateful, and she felt that she was—he'd fed her after all; he'd clothed her. But then one night, she sat by herself in the bathtub and made herself think not of how he'd taught her to change the oil in her car, but of how he'd spoken to her when he was drunk, how he'd come into her room at night. She understood then that, because of the way her life had gone, she could not trust her own mind.

Lexie clicked out of her phone contacts. Juliette could be anywhere, involved in anything, and the last thing Lexie needed was Jonathan's help. If he tracked Juliette down, his answer would be fists and hateful words. Those were the only ways he knew to communicate when things didn't go his way.

On the street, a tall, equine figure ran fast down the center of the road. Lexie didn't need to make cross-country meets to know that gait. She'd watched it grow tall and taller still as it crossed her backyard, to and fro, as it ran down the hallway into her arms. She hurried to the front door, threw it open, stepped onto the porch. Behind her, the television's volume went even lower. Lexie pulled the door shut.

"I'm sorry, Mom." Juliette took the steps two at a time. She stood a head taller than Lexie.

Lexie noticed details she'd missed that morning—Juliette's hair was blown straight and silky; she wore mascara, lip gloss. Tricks of womanhood she'd learned on her own while Lexie demanded other adult skills from her: vacuuming, mopping, laundry. "Where in the hell have you been?"

Juliette's eyes fell to pleading. "Tonya took me and Susie to the mall in Athens. That's the truth. But we got lost on the way home. That's why we're late."

Lexie believed her, and in her relief, her anger flared. Her instinct was to cuss Juliette, slap her, snatch her into the house by an arm. But she resisted. Tonya was a high school girl who helped coach the middle school cross-country team. She was a polite, straight-laced child, determined to get a college scholarship somewhere, anywhere. "Does Tonya know you lied to me?"

"No ma'am. She wouldn't have let me go with her. She thinks you knew where we went."

"Why did you lie then?"

"Because you told me not to get in the car with anyone under the age of thirty. You would've said no if I asked."

She was right. This was a good thing that had happened, Tonya getting lost, Juliette getting caught. The girl was growing up, and Lexie was going to have to be more careful about saying no. If she didn't give Juliette some freedom, next time it may not be Tonya she snuck off with. "You're almost in high school. That means the rules have to change. I don't know how yet, but if you talk to me instead of lying to me, we'll figure it out." Lexie's own words surprised her; her calm surprised her.

"You're not mad?"

"I'm furious."

"You're not acting like it."

"You're grounded for a week, but not for going off with Tonya. She's a good kid. And there's nothing wrong with a mall. You're grounded for lying to me and for sneaking out."

Juliette grabbed Lexie in a hug. "Thank you."

Lexie was stunned to feel how the girl trembled. Juliette had been afraid. Afraid of her. "Come on inside," said Lexie.

As soon as Juliette entered the house, Thomas pegged her with questions about where she had been, and she volleyed back, arguing it was none of his business. Lexie left her children bickering in the living room. She went into the kitchen and leaned against the counter. She too trembled. On the porch, she'd felt how there was a space between her thoughts and her actions. It was a small space, but enough to stand in, and in it she was empowered to choose her own behavior. Which meant she had greater control than she'd thought possible over the events that unfolded in her life. There was a way to stand inside herself and watch the rise and fall of her own emotions, vet her words before they left her mouth, keep her hands soft and at her sides. Nobody had ever told her this was possible. She'd had to stumble across the knowledge on her own, and she hoped to remember how it felt in her body.

35

Being a man of dual existences was taking its toll on Jonathan. Though he and Luke were making good cash with their crystal piracy, they'd both kept their day jobs. This digging they did, this night work, was extra. While a life held hours that could be pinched for labor, there were no extra hours to steal toward sleep. Jonathan reached in his pocket for the pills he took to erase weariness. The guy he bought them from swore they were Adderall, but they never looked two the same. What mattered was that they worked. Jonathan passed some to Luke. "Yours."

Luke tossed them in his mouth and chewed.

They drove down a road deep in the country, so far from any city or house lights that the sky was sugared with stars. In the beams from Jonathan's flashlight cap, the colors shone on the map spread across the seat. This was the second map they'd rented off Tom, and tonight was their first night to use it. They'd made three thousand dollars apiece at the first location and left that spot not because it ran out of crystals but because they fretted discovery.

"New place is less than a mile ahead, up on the left."

"You flagged it already?"

"Yesterday." Jonathan's furlough day. It had kept him busy to come out here and stick orange flags in the places where Tom's map showed crosshatches. He'd brought tools to pull back the surface of the earth, but he hadn't needed them. "Crystals were sticking right out of the ground. Little ones laying around for the taking."

"That's not what I'm asking about. I want to know if this rig can make it in and out of there." Luke drove the battered golf course truck, and behind him he towed the course's backhoe on its trailer. The men made a tremendous racket as they passed through vegetation that was developed from undergrowth to canopy, that sat dense on both sides of the road. Limbs scraped the truck like claws.

"You're too far in to drive out in reverse. Might as well keep going forward."

"You're going to chew me a path through the goddamn woods like a beaver if this rig gets stuck."

Jonathan kept uncertainty from his voice. "You can turn around in the field." He'd flagged in the daylight. Night changed dimensions, distances. He looked at the map again, touched the lines of hatchmarks that crossed the field like veins. "Low-hanging fruit, that's what this spot is."

They passed an old mailbox, belonging to no one, which was the landmark Tom gave. Jonathan flipped off the flashlights taped to his cap to better find the field through the window. "Less than half a mile now." With his flashlights off, the cab was very dark.

Luke drove so slowly the speedometer didn't bother to register it. Still the truck made noise. Jonathan flipped on the radio, but the sound was lost. Luke turned it off.

Because the half moon was obscured by cloud, the field appeared suddenly, a massive black openness to their left ringed by the deeper darkness of the woods. Luke eased into the space and turned slowly, the truck dipping and jerking and jarring. He inched forward until the trailer was clear of the road and then he slowly circled around. He opened his door, glanced down. "I'm still on the street."

"You worried about blocking traffic?"

"None of your fucking lip." Luke hopped out. "This is the last night I'm doing this shit."

"Broken record, you are." Jonathan got out of the truck too. "Every night is your last."

It was three days before Christmas, the wrong season for tree frogs or cicadas. No crickets. The engine ticked as it cooled and there was the low hiss of Jonathan's cigarette paper burning down. Far away, an owl called. The silence felt massive after the clamor of the journey.

"What worries me," said Luke, "is that someone's going to come poking around. This sort of quiet ain't used to being busted open in the night."

"Nobody's bothered us yet."

"Last time we were in plain sight. You don't look like you're doing anything illegal when you're in plain sight." The other map had led them to a place close enough to the interstate to be partially illuminated by pole lights. Every trucker driving late sounded air brakes as he rubbernecked.

Jonathan ashed his cigarette. "I got my gun in the truck."

"So if Farmer Fred comes poking 'round, you'll shoot him?"

"No."

"We should have our story straight. That's all I'm saying."

Jonathan's story was one he'd borrowed from a tent-squatter's tale he saw on TV. "We're in national forest, so technically, this is our land. We pay taxes on it. We should be able to do what we want on our own land. Including dig it up."

"You really believe this shit is legal?"

"It's a gray area."

"I'm putting sleeping pills in Amanda's beer at night so I can do this."

"She's got a prescription for those pills. It's not illegal for her to take 'em."

"She thinks I'm taking the missing ones."

"Then she's the one committing the crime. Not supposed to share doctor drugs. She won't tell. She's a cop."

Luke went to one side of the trailer and began to unfasten the restraints. "My wife's not a fucking cop."

Luke scooped the first few dippers of earth and dumped them in a line. He and Jonathan began to kick and dig and scrape. They'd not found a way to transport water to wash clean what they found, so they had to box anything that looked interesting and rinse it later at Jonathan's borrowed trailer. "Caught a glimmer," said Luke. He hefted a soil-covered chunk the size of his head, staggered with it to the empty trailer, crashed it down.

He and Jonathan leaned close, shining their lights. Luke spit on the rock, wiped it clean some. There was a hollow in the center, either crevice or bowl, and the shape was lined in crystals. The dipper tooth had scraped away the outside of the rock, exposing a swath of amethyst. "It's crystals growing inside a crystal," said Luke, his voice hushed. "Is that even possible?"

"Why do you care? You're quitting." Jonathan turned his beams toward the field. The light from his flashlights petered out before it reached the treeline, even before it reached the end of the orange flags.

"One more bucket of dirt," said Luke, "One more bucket, then I'm done." He headed for the digger.

"Goddamn broken record."

36

Before dawn on Christmas morning, Doreen stood in Lexie's kitchen, putting the cinnamon rolls she'd made yesterday into the oven to warm. After opening presents they would eat the rolls for breakfast, and then Doreen and Lexie would prepare the Christmas meal.

"Hurry up, Grandma!" said Thomas. He danced from foot to foot in the hallway, waiting to be allowed to run into the living room and see what Santa had brought him, no less excited this morning than he'd been two years ago when he thought Santa real. Beside him, Juliette's eyes were alight as well, though she claimed to need coffee. Doreen poured coffee into three mugs, added sugar and cream. She'd been concerned about what this morning would feel like without Jonathan, but in many ways it felt like all of the others since Juliette was born, except that this year it was Lexie who stood in the living room with a hand on the light switch waiting for Doreen to deliver the cup of coffee that meant

Christmas morning could begin.

Doreen delivered the coffee. Lexie flipped on the room's overhead light.

Thomas ran to the end of the sofa where his presents were arranged and snatched up the thing he'd asked for: a Nerf Gatlin gun. He began to fight with the packaging.

"Hand it here." Doreen took scissors from the pocket of her robe. While she freed his toy, Thomas leapt around the living room and mimed shooting invaders.

Juliette had only one present from Santa. She held up the leather boots that both Lexie and Doreen knew she'd wanted but hadn't dared ask for because of the cost. "You didn't have to do this," Juliette said to Lexie.

"Grandma helped."

Juliette beamed towards Doreen. She sat on the edge of the sofa to pull on her new shoes.

Doreen handed Thomas his gun, and then joined Lexie on the loveseat. Behind them was the Christmas tree the children had decorated. Beneath the tree were the presents the four of them had bought or made for one another. The presents Jonathan had brought to Doreen's she'd left at home, hidden in the top of her closet. She wouldn't let him ruin what she and Lexie had created here with extravagances he'd purchased at the expense of his family. Thomas examined the other gifts Santa had brought him. Some jeans, a new sweatshirt, a new race track for his Matchbox cars. "I got more than you," he sang to Juliette.

"I don't care," said Juliette, smiling again toward her mother and grandmother, letting them know that she appreciated what the boots represented, that she was one of the women in the room.

"Someone needs to hand out the presents under the tree," said Doreen.

"Me!" Thomas crawled under the tree and came out with a

present under each arm and an envelope in his hands. One present was for Lexie, one for Doreen. He read the front of the envelope and then turned it so his mother and grandmother could read it as well: My family. "Who's this for?"

"Give it here," said Doreen. On the front of the envelope, she'd mimicked Jonathan's squat, fortress-like handwriting, but she wasn't sure that her forgery could pass Lexie's inspection. "I don't know what that is. Your daddy asked me to bring it." She opened the envelope with a finger and took out the letter she'd typed up yesterday.

Dear Lexie, Thomas and Juliette,

I wish I could be with you today. Take the money in this envelope and go to the movies tonight on me. Remember how much fun it was when we did that on Christmas last year? I keep thinking on that day and wishing we could do it over again.

I love you.

Daddy

Doreen pulled out the fifty-dollar bill she'd put in the envelope and waved it in the air.

Thomas whooped and jumped. The closest movie theatre was in Athens, and the children begged to go far more than they were taken. "Is Dad coming too?"

"No." Doreen turned to Lexie and Juliette, scared of what she might find in their faces. She was surprised to see softness.

She'd texted Jonathan yesterday and told him that she would help him on Christmas and that she would let him know how it went on the twenty-sixth. She knew he'd assume she meant that she'd deliver his gifts. *Enjoy the day on your own as best you can,* she'd written, a polite way of saying don't come around.

Tomorrow, she would tell him what she'd done, and she

would tell him how well his family had received it. She would tell him that she'd changed the locks on his house. She would tell him that she'd put him, one last time, in a good position with the people he claimed to love, and that now it was up to him to make the next right step. His life was his own to salvage. His family didn't have to know that it was Doreen who'd helped him exhibit the decent possibilities of his own heart. He could keep that a secret. After all, he hadn't forgotten his children on Christmas. He hadn't done the right thing, but he'd done something.

37

Christmas day. Jonathan finished off a pot of coffee while Faster snapped together pieces of molded plastic. Faster's youngest had gotten a play tower that had some assembly required. The tower was the type where the baby stands in the middle and presses buttons for noise and for lights. Faster hit a button and *Old MacDonald* played. He took a swallow off the vodka bottle beside him. "What I told Nicki is that I came down here to ask you to help me put this together so that you could feel like a father." He offered the bottle to Jonathan.

Jonathan waved the bottle away. "I don't drink white liquor." He swallowed the last of his coffee.

"White liquor is gentler on the mind and gentler on the breath."

Jonathan leaned to press a button on the play tower. *Mary Had a Little Lamb*. It was a cute toy. His mother texted him yesterday and said she'd decided to help him. That meant his own kids must have opened their presents by now. A real pellet gun for Thomas, jewels for all the ladies. Even Juliette he'd given diamond studs. The only other time he had given a woman a gemstone was when Lexie got pregnant and he'd married her, but as he'd learned with his crystal digging, that engagement ring was only a flake off something real. He planned to replace it once things were better between them. "Faster, let me say something to you and have you hear it."

"Ready, my friend."

"You're a goddamn drunk."

Faster gazed at the toy he'd assembled as if Jonathan hadn't spoken at all.

"You've been a helpful man to me. I don't want you to look back one day and say, 'Well that good-for-nothing Johnny Swilley, I did and did for him and he never gave me a damn thing.' I know you love that squatty-bodied woman you call wife. She won't long tolerate the level of drinking you've reached."

"I appreciate that, Johnny." Faster tilted the vodka again. "You know how highly I think of you. I'll contemplate your words. But right now, that squatty-bodied woman is making us a Christmas meal, and it would be unChristian to keep her waiting." Faster hooked the play tower with an elbow and, bottle in hand, walked out the front door of Jonathan's trailer, the tower flashing and playing *Farmer in the Dell*.

Once on the porch, Faster returned the vodka to its hiding place, an empty toolbox sitting under the kitchen window. Jonathan's phone buzzed in his pocket: Powell again. That made the third time today his boss had called, so Jonathan knew it wasn't Christmas greetings. He'd listen to the man's messages, but not until after his phone rang with the call he wanted, the one of glee from his wife and kids. Unless this was the first year Thomas slept late on Christmas, they'd had their presents since dawn. *Ring*

Around the Rosie played as Faster walked up the road. Jonathan hurried to catch up.

It was a miserable day, gray and overcast, not predicted to warm much above freezing. "I been watching that bottle," said Jonathan. "You're drinking it without me, too."

"No sir."

"Was a different brand last week."

"Like a tack, you are. Can't pull a thing over on you." Faster clapped Jonathan's shoulder.

Part of the problem with the little man was that drink didn't damage his charm.

Christmas lunch was deer tamales. "It's a Mexican tradition," Faster said, as Nicole delivered the plates. "My dad was Mexican, and Nicole's real father went to Mexico after he died and helped build a church."

"He helped build a church and then he died." Nicole set a plate in front of Jonathan. Everything on it appeared to be doused in ketchup. "In Mexico they eat tamales on Christmas Eve. Not Christmas Day. You're the one should know this, Faster."

"My old man left when I was three."

Snooker pushed his glasses up his nose. "I don't think there are deer in Mexico, Dad."

Faster clapped his hands. "Alright then. Alright! Deer meat tamales on Christmas Day is a Faster Pastor family tradition, starting now."

Nicole took her seat on the stepstool. Baby Roro napped in a crib beside the sofa. She'd yet to see her new play tower. Nicole took Snooker's and Faster's hands. Jonathan linked hands to finish the circle.

"Dear Lord," said Nicole, "Thank you for another

opportunity to do your work on this, your fresh green Earth. On this particular day, accept our thanks for your Son and our Lord, Jesus Christ, who taught us to love our neighbors as ourselves, and to turn the other cheek, and not to comment on the mote in a neighbor's eye when, lo!, we have a beam in our own. Bless this food to our bodies so that we might better serve Thee. In Christ's name. Amen."

Faster squeezed Jonathan's hand. "I've got an addendum here, Jesus. Please be with our friend and neighbor Johnny Swilley as he tries to repair the holy sanctity of the marriage with which you blessed him. We're rootin' him on, Jesus, so please help us, too. Lord knows it's hard for everyone involved. Amen."

The eating of the newly traditional tamales began.

Snooker sat at the table in the racing suit that was his Christmas gift. It was dark green and fit close. There were leathery patches on the arms. He held an arm out toward Jonathan. "What you think of this, Mr. Johnny? Pretty nice?"

"You look like a Ninja Turtle."

"What's a Ninja Turtle?"

"You gotta get this kid a TV," said Jonathan.

"Anything we could learn from TV we learn from the library," said Nicole. "I homeschool Snooker, and I'll do the same with Baby Roro. At the library we can choose our influences instead of being open to the influences of the world."

"It's true," said Faster, "no need to pay for satellite. They got most every DVD you could hope to watch at the library. You can borrow 'em and play them at home and it's no different than picking to watch that show on TV."

"You don't need a TV then," said Jonathan. "You need a Ninja Turtle DVD."

Faster and Jonathan laughed, but Nicole did not. She said, "Will you see your own children today, Johnny?"

Faster shook hot sauce over his plate. "What we need to do when we're finished eating is go down to the dock and feed the fish some bread. Saint Francis, he took a bag of seed and fed the birds every Christmas."

"I won't see my children today, Nicki, thanks for asking. How about that Marine son of your husband's? He planning on stopping by? I don't believe you've met him have you?"

Faster slapped the hot sauce down. "What Johnny's trying to say is that there are lots of good men who will not be blessed enough to spend today with their entire God-given family."

Nicole forked a bite of tamale. "Johnny Swilley, I know you're as good as running a one patron honky-tonk out of that nasty trailer."

"Guilty. I'm bartender and patron both. Gets expensive, being the only one drinking." Jonathan understood Nicole's needling, searching. She didn't know how concerned to be about her husband—Faster drunk was similar enough to Faster sober you couldn't be sure of his habits unless you caught him with bottle in hand.

The silent tension at the table stretched on. Jonathan's phone buzzed in his pocket. Powell again. This call made four. "You're gonna have to excuse me. I need to take this call." Powell's interruption of Christmas dinner was the first thing Jonathan had been grateful for since he rolled out of bed that morning.

38

Bird sat in Will's house in Athens, an old home that had at one point been some other family's ancestral center before those elders died and those children moved away and Will and Leigh came along like cowbirds laying their eggs in a robin's nest and claimed the structure as their own. Will and Leigh's hand-cut Christmas tree twinkled in the corner, the fire they'd built burned in the grate, their family pictures hung on the living room walls, their tow-headed child lay on her stomach on the floor, giggling along with her maternal grandparents.

Leigh's mother, a Swedish immigrant, and Leigh's father, a ruddy-nosed chemical engineer from Iowa, bent their heads down to the height of the baby's and sang yet another song in Swedish. As they sang, Leigh's mother waggled a troll doll in the baby's face. From what Bird could tell, all Swedish children's songs were about trolls.

"Dad, do you want more glogg?"

Bird looked at the empty glass in his hand. The glogg went down more easily than one would think, given its name. "Yes, please."

Will patted his arm. Bird did not doubt that Will missed his mother this holiday season, but on the whole his son seemed delighted to celebrate Christmas in his own house, engulfed in the strangeness his wife and her half-Swedish parents brought to the day. Straw goats stood in front of the Christmas tree—guarding it, Leigh said—and earlier, during Christmas dinner, there'd been no escaping the fish. Even the dish Bird took for scalloped potatoes had anchovies hidden beneath the cheese. They'd opened all of their presents last night too, another Swedish tradition, so today there was nothing to do but sit around in the itching scarves Leigh's mother had knitted and listen as she sang her songs about trolls.

Bird snuck his phone from his pocket, checked the screen. He'd texted Doreen that morning, wished her a Merry Christmas. She'd texted him back the same. He'd then sent her a picture he staged of the troll doll on the back of the straw Christmas goat. She'd responded a few hours later with a close-up of her greasy fingers holding the larger half of the turkey's wishbone. It was as intimately as they'd communicated since Charlotte went on hospice care.

Bird didn't care if Doreen ruined his business. In fact, he sort of hoped she did. A strange glee had taken hold in his soul since Charlotte's death. His parents were dead; his wife was dead; his son was the sort of man to take his father aside and say, "Mom's gone and I'm not moving back to Flyshoals, Dad. Do anything you want." A few weeks ago, Bird had been planning his suicide, and now here he sat, the lone survivor of some inexplicable battle. For the first time in his entire life, there was nobody alive to make him tow the line.

Not even Theo Waters.

Last week the man had emailed to say that he had it on good faith that Doreen was opening her own business. "So long as I don't hear that you helped her in any way, your deceased wife's letter stays safe with me," he wrote. There was a threat in Theo's words, but it wasn't a threat Bird had to fear—Doreen had refused every offer of help from him. She'd liberated herself of any obligation to Bird and in doing so had liberated Bird of his final obligations to anybody.

He loved the woman, he really did.

Bird texted Doreen: Are we on for dinner in January?

Why not? she texted back.

"Dad, your drink."

Bird took the glogg from his son. He sat in a moment of his life that he couldn't explain. Last night, after everyone else had gone to sleep, he'd come downstairs and burned the packet of letters that Theo Waters had sent to him. He'd burned them without ever reading one, and he felt good about that decision too. Reading Charlotte's words would have only made him angry at her again, and he preferred feeling toward her as he did now, grateful and adoring. She'd given him a decent life while she was alive, and with her passing she'd made things even better.

1959

39

Within a month of Marla's death, Emmy's father gave him a second glass of wine, unwatered, at Sunday dinner, and Emmy understood that something ill would soon befall him, the dinner itself being Sunday standard: everyday china, unpolished silver, yesterday's candles. Today was Imogene's day off. There had been a pot roast and canned pears dolloped with mayonnaise, French cut green beans. The family lingered over chess pie while Emmy's father poured the wine.

His mother let him take a sip, and then set her fork on her plate at four o'clock. "I've spoken to Principal Ewell and he assures me you're doing quite well in your classes." His mother had no reason to mention the principal of Flyshoals High. But Emmy knew how his mother smashed her true meaning against the backs of her words—what this meant was that she didn't think he was doing well. Not at all.

He investigated the texture of his piecrust with his fork tines while his mother waited for someone else to mitigate the tension she'd delivered to the dining table. Emmy didn't think she knew what had happened, but he couldn't be sure. His father might have told her.

"What your mother's saying is that we can't sit here and watch you flounder for another year."

"My grades are good," said Emmy, though he knew it wasn't academics to which his father referred. In the past few months, he'd quit the golf team. He turned down every invitation he got from friends. He'd misfiled documents and lost phone messages and forgot to insert the carbon paper when he typed copies at work. He spent too much time alone in his room, and, worst of all for his mother, slept until noon every Saturday.

"Principal Ewell thinks you're bored," said his mother.

Emmy's father said, "He's seen it before in—what was that word he used?"

"Precocious."

"In precocious boys. But there are opportunities for young men such as yourself."

"And what kind of young man am I, Dad?" To Emmy, this seemed the question he'd been trying to answer ever since he, his father, and his uncle, buried Marla's body in his grandmother's cornfield.

"Certainly not the young man we thought you were." Emmy's mother seized her wine glass and gulped the remaining tablespoon of cabernet. "Given who you've become, we're prepared to make you an offer."

Against all etiquette, Emmy's father rested his elbows on the table. "Your mother wants you to leave Flyshoals."

Emmy's mother slapped her napkin onto her dessert plate. "You will not vilify me, Eames. I leave all further decisions in this matter to the two of you." She left the table and could soon be heard clattering dishes about in the kitchen.

258

Emmy's father bent his impolite elbows and rested his head in his hands.

"Mom knows?"

Emmy's father lifted his head. "No, your mother—she knows you had an affair with a married woman from out of town. That's all she knows, and it was Nolin who told her that when she asked him why he kept calling you Birddog. Listen, it's time for you to go to college. If you take a math class this summer you can skip your senior year. I talked to the Dean of Admissions over at Georgia. He's an old friend. He'll get you in. You'll start fall of '59 with the rest of the freshmen. You can live in a dorm, go through rush. You can count on a bid from KA. I was a KA. Your grandfather was a KA. You can put all of this behind you."

"I loved her, Dad." This was something Emmy had come to believe since watching her die in the backseat of a car.

"You're a good kid. It's terrible what happened. Tragic. But you've got to carry on with your life. There's no way to bring her back. One day, you'll forget this even happened."

2009

40

Jonathan stood in the big window of the control tower, looking out on a downed plant. The cement had set in the silo. There was no way to make concrete or load trucks. Though it was a holiday and the place was supposed to be closed, knowing what had happened made the plant look doomed. The loader sat quiet in the lot. The empty plastic chairs in the smokers' corner had been blown over by the wind.

"It's been so cold," said Powell. "I came down this morning to check on things, make sure everything was dispensing right. We're supposed to start shipping a thousand yards of DOT approved concrete into Athens day after tomorrow."

"It's too cold to pour. Won't set right."

"You think I give a shit about that, Johnny? My job is the product, not the weather."

"Ship from your other plant."

"Can't. Not without relocating stockpiles. That's a cost. And to ship from there adds onto haul times—another cost. My bid was barebones. No wiggle room. Got any other ideas?"

"Only what I told you when you called. Water got in the system. I don't know how. Damp air compressor maybe. The cement set in the tower because it got wet."

"I'm not asking you how it happened. I'm asking you how to fix it."

"You've got to get you one of those bust-it-loose companies in here. They'll lower robots in with a boom truck."

"You're the maintenance manager. You're telling me to hire somebody else to fix it?"

"I'm telling you it's more than I'm able to fix."

The small electric heater at their feet was set to high and blowing hard but warmed nothing above their ankles. "Follow me," said Powell.

The men clomped down the ringing metal steps.

At the base of the steps lay a black garbage bag. Powell opened it, took out a length of rope and a harness. He handed these things to Jonathan.

"You're not dropping me in that silo."

"I can't afford a bust-it-loose company." Powell picked up the sledgehammer leaning against the steps and a backpack filled with supplies. "We can't afford a bust-it-loose company."

Jonathan wanted to shout and cuss, have some asshole fired. But Powell had laid off everybody that worked on site besides him, meaning Jonathan was the only asshole left. He followed Powell toward the master control room.

Gravel crunched beneath their work boots. Neither man spoke. In the control room, Powell flipped the breaker and padlocked it with his special padlock, the one he'd set the code for. He stepped back and waited for Jonathan to do the same. "Worried about OSHA?" said Jonathan.

"OSHA lets me drop you in. They just don't let me drop you

in with the power on."

Jonathan padlocked the main breaker too. The men fell back into their line for the walk to the silo.

At the cement silo, they looked up and up. It stood three stories tall. A network of metal ladders and metal catwalks led to the top. Jonathan had crawled all over the thing as recently as last week, but Powell hadn't been up those ladders in years. The ladders were narrow and ensconced in safety cages. "I don't think you can make it up there, boss. We've got to call in help."

"I'll call them, and you pay them. You should have some money saved by now, living all this time rent free."

Powell had never before used the trailer as collateral.

Jonathan mounted the ladder nearest them. "At the first catwalk, I'll throw down the rope. You tie off that sledgehammer and that backpack and I'll haul 'em up. Then you try to crawl your fat ass up."

Jonathan started climbing. His hands and back and thighs hurt from the crystal-hunting he'd done a few nights ago. Today was supposed to be a holiday. Christmas, for Christ's sake. The metal rungs were hoary with frost and his hands grew damp with exertion. Each new grip did more damage to his palms. He had some pills in his pocket to chew when more seemed impossible, but that moment couldn't be now, not when he was just getting started.

At the first catwalk, he pressed his palms to his jeans until the stinging subsided. He threw down the rope. Powell tied off the bag. Jonathan hauled it up. They repeated the process with the sledgehammer. It was Powell's turn to climb.

Jonathan squatted and watched through the grate. The ladder was long, and Powell's sides brushed the safety cage as he rocked and strained for each new hold. He hadn't climbed more than a few rungs before he began to pant.

Jonathan turned away, embarrassed. The panting and

huffing grew closer, and when it was very close, Jonathan became aware of another sound, a faint squeak. He looked again through the grate. The squeak came from somewhere deep in Powell's body. He sounded on every exhale. The man's face was eggplant dark. Jonathan leaned over and pulled Powell up as best he could.

The men collapsed on the catwalk. "Only two more stories," said Powell between wheezes.

For Jonathan, the second ladder was much like the first. Hard on the thighs, hard on the back. Hardest on the palms because the rungs were cold. At the top, he did the rope work with the bag and the sledgehammer. Threw the rope down a third time. "Tie yourself off now. Around here." Jonathan motioned to his armpits. "Tug when you're ready." He settled his weight in his thighs and leaned back. Pulling Powell up was a further hell on his palms. When the man gained the catwalk, Jonathan collapsed first, and then Powell joined him. "Thank you for riding Swilley Elevator Service," said Jonathan.

Powell's squeak was pronounced. "Hardest fucking ride I've ever taken."

Jonathan peered into Powell's eggplant face. "You can't have a heart attack up here. Think how much it would cost to rent a boom truck to lift you down." He went to the third and final ladder. Climbed up, shoulders and thighs quaking. The day's work hadn't even begun. He threw down the rope to haul the bag, the sledgehammer, the boss.

At the top of the final catwalk, Powell didn't bother to stand, but crawled the few feet to the silo and fell against it. Jonathan sat beside him. Powell's face dripped. His internal squeak was steady as a pulse. He smelled fruity, like an apple. Jonathan recalled Lexie telling him that fruitiness was a sign of some common but deadly health disorder. She'd learned that in nursing school. "You need to go to the doctor," said Jonathan. "You smell like fruit salad."

"You smell like fish and mildew."

"That's how your trailer smells."

"Least my stink is my own."

Had there been a fourth ladder, Jonathan wouldn't have helped Powell up it.

The view from the top of the silo differed from the control tower view in that Powell's house was visible on the hill behind the plant. Even from this distance, two female figures—one large, one small—were discernible on the porch. As the men watched, a third female figure opened the front door and then all three disappeared into the house. "Sandra told me she likes the changes I've made at the plant," said Powell. "Said it's been so quiet a deer came to the kitchen window yesterday." He tried to draw a deep breath and the dog-toy thing in his chest sounded, gagging him. Jonathan put a hand on the big man's shoulder and squeezed.

A short access ladder led to the cap platform. Jonathan climbed the ladder and unbolted the waterproof cap, but when he planted his feet and tried to wrench open the cap, it wouldn't budge. "You'll have to help me."

Powell's physical state was unimproved but he got to his feet anyway, climbed up beside Jonathan. The space was small; their bodies pressed together. They wrenched the cap free.

Jonathan returned to the catwalk, looked inside Powell's bag: duct tape, two buckets, a hardhat with a light, a claw hammer, a bottle of aspirin, two liters of Coke. Dust masks. "Motherfucking work gloves," said Jonathan, taking them out. "Next time let's put them on before we start working." He crawled back up the ladder with a flashlight. There was no way to avoid Powell's damp, rotting apple side. Jonathan shined a beam into the hole. He couldn't make out the bottom, and this far up the sides looked clear. Dust floated like mist.

There hadn't been a respirator in the bag. Jonathan considered climbing back down the ladders, walking across the grounds to the control tower, getting a respirator, climbing back up the ladders.

The sky hung low enough to touch. There would be rain soon, and when it rained, they would have to close the silo's cap to keep more water from entering the system. Powell squeaked. "You bring lunch?" said Jonathan.

"No."

Jonathan hedged his bets: early rain, Powell's hunger. "Up and at 'em, Rottweiler. You're the one's gotta throw me down that hole."

Jonathan was harnessed and roped, dust-masked and safety-glassed, with his buckets and supplies dangling like a cartless merchant's. He balanced at the silo's opening.

Powell grasped the rope. Jonathan had tied a portion of it to the catwalk railing so that, hopefully, even if the man dropped him he would not hit bottom.

Powell squatted, rope in his hands. "Ready?"

"Going. Now!" Jonathan released his one-handed grip and delivered his full weight to Powell, who did something wrong.

Freefall. Jonathan dropped the sledgehammer and screamed. He had time to consider pissing himself and time to decide against it. There was time for him to guess at how Powell had screwed up, to guess at whether this mistake could be corrected before he hit bottom.

The rope jerked to a stop.

Jonathan dangled. He swallowed hard and didn't vomit.

"Whoops." Powell's voice was cottony and distant.

"Son of a bitch," whispered Jonathan.

"Yell when you're ready to go again."

Jonathan hung in the silo while the reverberations of his fear dissipated. In the silo, there seemed to be infinite space for dissipation. He hung alone in almost nothing. No rain, no planes, no cars, no dogs. Only a gentle woo-wooing sound as the wind edged against the opening. The space was dark except for the small places his flashlight touched. Seeping through the cardboard smell of his dust mask was an abandoned odor, like empty parking decks in the rain. Nobody who thought of him—not his mother or Lexie, not his children or Luke—would think of him dangling here, like this, no part of his body touching a supportive surface. Powell could close the cap and Jonathan would never be found. He was as close to gone as a breathing man could get.

He rested his forehead against the rope. In a less sleep-deprived state, he never would've let water get in the system. It was the overall most important and obvious fucking rule of cement: don't add water. He'd had to beg his mother to take Christmas presents to his kids. He'd wanted to buy a football jersey for Thomas, but didn't know what size the boy wore. Hadn't ever known what size the boy wore. Didn't even realize he hadn't known this. Gray in the beard and his great plan for the future lay in selling rocks to a man who wore a fanny pack. "Drop me!"

Powell released him another ten feet, but this time Jonathan didn't scream.

The beam on his hardhat illuminated the silo's bottom, a space about the size of the kitchen he'd shared with Lexie. His sledgehammer sat in a web of cracks. He followed the gray mass over the whole of the floor, up the walls. At the height of about two feet, the gray grew lighter where the clean wall began.

Powell had figured out how to handle the rope and lowered him now by inches. In fits and jerks, Jonathan approached the bottom and then landed, the rope pooling around his feet.

So he'd not tied off enough to keep from crashing to his death.

Powell blocked the light at the opening. "Tug the rope when you're ready to send up your first bucket!" The light returned, and

Jonathan heard the heavy sound of Powell sitting down.

A layer of dust puffed around Jonathan's feet as he walked. Beneath the dust was the hardened mess he had to knock free. It wasn't concrete like a sidewalk, but hardened cement. Rock glue, dried solid. Bleak as the surface of the moon. He stuck his safety glasses on his face, his earplugs in his ears. Dug in his pocket, found a pill, chewed it. He pulled the sledgehammer back and made a first experimental smash into the solid mass underfoot.

The aftershock sent him to his knees. An eight or nine inch crack ran between his legs. Jonathan stood, lifted the sledgehammer, struck the crack again. Even with ear plugs, it seemed unlikely his hearing would survive this venture. Old dental work might need repairing. He was a vigilante astronaut on the dark side of the moon, stranded and hell-bent on destruction.

Five hours later, Jonathan had sent up enough buckets to build an uninspired sea wall. Lunch had been Coke and aspirin. His backbone was a burning seam that divided him into laboring halves: stronger right, weaker left. The early damage done to his palms had worsened despite the gloves. Dust lodged so thickly in his sinuses he swallowed postnasal mud. A ceaseless exploding sounded in his head. He'd crushed and snorted two of the pills from his pocket. The floor was less than half clear.

Jonathan sat on the sloping floor of the silo, head on his knees, and waited for Powell to return the rope and buckets to him. He'd been waiting long enough that it seemed possible Powell was dead.

This wasn't an unwelcomed thought. If Powell was dead, Jonathan could sleep. He let his eyes close. Incredible, how one's whole body could register the heart's beating. All it took was pain.

In his dream, he slept pain-free in a warm forest, curled

on a bed of soft pine needles. Beside him was a magical cave about which he was too exhausted to care. Lexie stood inside the cave's mouth, wearing nothing but a miner's light. Her pale body shimmered like crystal against the damp stone walls. "Come on baby. Get up." She talked gentle and slurry, as when she'd had too many Miller Lites.

"I'll wait here for you," he said.

"But there's treasure, baby."

Jonathan snuggled into his pine needles.

Lexie snatched handfuls of his bedding away. Hadn't she always been a bitch in just this way? He didn't move. She hooked her arms under his shoulders and, with surprising ease, dragged him into the cave's mouth. "You have to get up. You have to care about the treasure." Tunnels branched away from her in several directions.

God, but she was beautiful. Her hair was as it had been when they first met, hanging over her shoulders to her waist, so thick it hid her small breasts. He wanted her to push her hair back, lift her shoulders, turn in a circle—show him, show him—but he could say nothing. Nothing to her body, nothing to her beauty. Nothing to her hope for treasure.

"I'm done waiting on you." She slid down a tunnel. He watched her light recede, heard her happy shouts. It wasn't hard to let her go. He even felt relief that she was gone, no longer urging him into caves and down tunnels.

In his dream, he slept a second, dreamless sleep.

When the rope brushed his face he startled awake, cussing and scrambling, unsure where he was. It seemed a grave but for the errant light zigzagging over the walls. Awareness returned, and Jonathan grabbed the rope, jerked it. Powell waved from the silo's mouth. He had to listen very closely to hear Powell over the roar in his head. "Come back up! Rain!"

Jonathan experienced, briefly, tears of gratitude. He stepped into the harness, pulled the rope through, secured it, gave a tug. He didn't even bother with the buckets, the empty Coke bottle, the sledgehammer.

The ride up was excellent in that all the effort of it fell to someone else. Jonathan ascended a few inches and then dangled. A few more inches and then a dangle. He turned off the light on his hardhat and hung in limbo, the only light the stormy gray at the opening, the only sound his own explosive deafness.

When he reached the lip of the opening, Jonathan was too weakened to perform the chin up necessary to free himself. Powell reached in and grabbed him by the belt, pulled him from the hole. The men stumbled down the ladder to the uppermost platform. They sat against the silo as they had at the start of the day. Nothing had changed. It was cold, gray, humid. Powell squeaked. "I thought you'd died down there."

Jonathan remembered his dream. Lexie naked in a miner's light, urging him on. She looked as beautiful as she'd ever been standing in that cave, but he'd felt relief when she was gone. The memory of that relief terrified him now, in his waking state. "I fell asleep."

"You look like you died. You look like a ghost."

Jonathan looked at his torso, arms, legs. He was a single, solid color. Beside him, Powell was gray too, though not nearly so uniformly. Powell's face shone luridly through the dust. Thunder rumbled.

Jonathan stumbled to his feet and threw himself up the ladder. "Help me close the lid. We can't let it rain in there. It's too much. Too hard."

"I'm calling in a company tomorrow."

Jonathan found momentary strength in anger's adrenalin and slammed the cap shut by himself. He collapsed over the rounded top. "Fuck you."

"I'm not calling them in because of your work, Johnny. I've never met a man who can do what you do. I'm calling them because I can't do this again. I've turned into a sorry sack of shit. If I come up here tomorrow, I'll die."

"How will you pay them?" Jonathan wanted to hate Powell more. He wanted to learn about money in reserve. Money withheld. Secret wealth.

"Old man Thompson called while you were down there. He wants gravel for his driveway. Truckload of 57s. I told him I'd take it to him today. Like a Christmas present. I can use what he pays us today to pay the company tomorrow."

A wind carrying raindrops gusted over them.

Powell said, "I need you to run those 57s to old man Thompson."

Jonathan stood over Powell. He removed his work gloves and dropped them in Powell's lap. He unclipped his key ring from his belt. He had various keys on this ring: his truck key, his old house key, his key to Powell's trailer, all of his keys to the plant. The trailer key he removed and held up for Powell to see. "Bet's over. You win." He needed for Powell to stop punishing him. "I'll go clear my things out this evening and leave your key under the mat."

"Put it back on your ring, Johnny. Keep the trailer. I'll sign the thing over to you. That's not what this is about. You've got to run that rock to old man Thompson so I can pay somebody to bust this thing out. We got a thousand yards of concrete to ship day after tomorrow."

Jonathan had no energy left for fighting, and he had no energy left for Powell. He could no longer be the one who kept them afloat. Jonathan took his truck key and his old house key off the ring, put them in his pocket along with the trailer key. All of his plant keys he dropped in Powell's lap. The keys slid between the man's parted thighs and jangled against the catwalk, but did not slip through the gridding. "I'll leave my padlock beside the breaker and the trailer key under the mat."

Despite the cold wind, Powell's face grew no less red. His chew toy heart sounded as before. Jonathan knew that what Powell said was true: the man would die if he came up here again.

Powell said, "You can lower me in that hole tomorrow if you'll stay."

Jonathan grabbed the railing for support. His knees wanted to bend to Powell. His arms wanted to embrace the fat sonofabitch. He'd worked alongside him so long. Everything he knew of himself as a smart man, a capable man, a man of salt and sweat and success, he'd learned at Powell's side. But those same lessons, that same pride, was why he had to quit now. "I'll run the rock. I'll do that one last thing for you. Then I quit."

"What are you going to do? There's no work to be had."

Powell wasn't wrong. The crystal hunting was lucrative, but Jonathan knew it would only last until the night Tom's map led them to dirt, and then Luke would quit, taking his backhoe with him. That night wasn't coming soon though, maybe not for a year or more, and Jonathan had set by enough cash to buy some time. Enough to go home head-up. Jonathan looked to Powell's big white house, that abode of female languor. The woman he'd married was nothing like Sandra McGaha. There was that, too. "Lexie'll make us decent money soon," said Jonathan. He went to the ladder and started slowly down, leaving Powell to find his own way off the silo. He'd run the stone for the man, but then he was clearing out of that godforsaken trailer and going home to his family. The war was over. He surrendered. He was ready to be on the same team, him and Lexie. Swilleys-versus-the goddamn world.

41

Jonathan drove slowly by his house. His mother's car was in the drive, but Lexie's was gone. The only lights on were waiting ones, the porch, the hall. He carried on down the street to park in the scrubby space between the last house on the block and the start of the trees. His family may not come inside if they returned home and saw his truck.

Jonathan got out with his duffle on his back. The rain had mostly passed. The remaining clouds were storm chasers that gave the moonlight a dull disco strobe. Jonathan limped toward home. Most of the houses he passed were quiet. Only at the top of the street was there any sign of a Christmas party. There, a bonfire burned in an oil drum.

Jonathan reached his drive. The yard was full of sticks and rotting leaves, untrimmed shrubs. If he got a rake and started now, he could make a change Lexie would notice before she entered the house, but the thought made his back seize. His body couldn't deliver what his mind desired. He'd had nothing to eat since breakfast but pills. His body demanded food, a shower, some sleep. He shifted the duffle but his back did not unlock. What if Lexie found him like this, ugly-dirty and frozen with pain in the drive? He forced a shuffle toward the porch, his nervous system raw and unrecognizable. If Lexie were to appear and speak one gentle word to him, he'd curl around her ankles, finished.

He mounted his steps slowly, house keys in hand. At his own good front door, the one he'd once set up on sawhorses to sand and to stain, he began to weep. His weren't the wracked sobs of a beaten boy running home, but the tired, slow drip of a failed man. Each tear took a long time to form and a longer time to fall. He leaned against the door trim. He'd shed more tears today than he had since he left diapers—inside the silo, on top of the silo, on his own front porch. His back released as he released his grief. He cried until the night's chill reached him, and then he wiped his eyes and unlocked the door knob with his key.

He moved his key to the deadbolt. His key stayed fast and straight. Jonathan tried to twist his key left. He tried to twist his key right. He wiped his arm over his eyes, opened and closed his weakened hands. Again, the key moved neither left nor right. He bent for a closer look. The brass deadbolt was shining as if polished, and on the left side was a pale half-moon where the lock didn't line up as it once had with the paint.

Jonathan removed his keys from the lock. He turned too quickly and again his back seized. Hobbled, he dropped his duffle over the porch railing into the bushes and limped down the steps and around the side of his house. All he needed was to eat, bathe, sleep. Whatever this was that had happened to his front door he could work out tomorrow with Lexie. After he was fed and cleaned and rested.

He went through the fence to the backyard, to the laundry room door. The security light clicked on as he pulled at the screen.

The screen door was locked, but only with a simple clasp meant to keep the kids in when they were young. He hit the door on the crack that had developed over the years and the latch popped loose.

Jonathan put his key in the doorknob—the lock tumbled open. He put his key in the deadbolt—it accepted his key but went no further. This deadbolt was not only shiny and misaligned with the paint, it was silver. Their hardware was brass. Jonathan turned his key harder, until it bent slightly in the lock. He left his keys hanging there, stepped away from the door, let the screen slap shut.

Change the locks is what he would've advised Lexie had a stranger shown up throwing punches, but there were no strangers in his house, none in this yard. Only a husband, a father. A man who gave diamonds for Christmas and worked himself to cripplehood and hoarded all his pay for his family. All that money in his duffle, ready to hand over.

The opposite of tears took hold in his eyes, an aridity he refused to blink away. A tiny blood vessel burst and sent a thin red filament creeping across the white of his eye, toward the green of his iris. Through his angry eyes, Jonathan watched black clouds fly across the sky.

In the backyard was the shed he'd built to house his lawnmower and the kids' bikes. There was the fence he built once Thomas was born. There was the back of his house, his gutter that sagged away from the eaves. A hillock of pine needles sat in the gutter's dip. "You won't even fix the goddamn gutter!" Lexie had screamed at him one night as they fought in the kitchen, pretending the kids couldn't hear.

Jonathan's pain drained out through his feet. His back, his hands, his shoulders and eyes and guts—these had not failed him. He marched across the yard to the sagging gutter, grabbed ahold and yanked. The metal flattened toward him and the pine straw hillock plopped to the earth. Jonathan wiped his hands down his jeans, leaving behind blood. He secured a second grip on his gutter. Nails screamed shallowly against wood, metal creaked and whined. He pulled until the section ripped free. He panted in his yard, holding six feet of rust-spotted metal. Cursing and stomping, he fought the length of gutter until it was folded in two.

Jonathan held his gutter and looked at the back of his house. Among the things he'd been fond of when he bought the place were the outsized old windows that gave every room a hothouse feel. "This here's a winter tomato you're growing," he'd said when Lexie's belly, filled with Juliette, grew so large her skin stretched thin and glowed a dusky red. His words mocked him now. He stood in his yard holding a length of tangled gutter and looking through the hothouse window into the room where he'd spoken of tomatoes.

How in the fuck had all this happened? And: Goddamn, but there were a ceaseless number of reasons to be angry. The red line reached his iris.

Jonathan lifted his gutter and smashed his window. The screen folded at its edges but did not rip, so he tore it from the window and tossed it into the yard. The wooden slats of the window cracked, but did not break, so he hit at them until they did.

Jonathan threw the gutter aside. He used his thighs as support for the first big step up and bent his body slightly to make it through. He stood in the silence of his bedroom. His house smelled of the soup Lexie made with the holiday turkey carcass, a soup she let simmer in the crockpot for twenty-four hours. Broth like liquid gelatin, green peas, rice and bits of carrot, shreds of turkey. No fucking deer. No enchiladas.

He was home.

Jonathan went to his side of the bed and turned on his lamp. His half of the bed was made, Lexie's side unmade, as if she slept each night waiting for him to return. He sat down. From his lower dresser drawer poked a sock. On top of his dresser, a soft coating of dust sweetened his coins and crumpled receipts, a book of matches. She'd changed nothing.

He lay down and rolled to her side. Her pillow smelled of shampoo and the perfume he'd given her last Valentine's Day. The pillow she clutched between her legs as she slept was hidden in the sheets and he dragged it out, held it to his face and sniffed along its surface until he found the small place where it smelled of cat piss and cumin.

His bleeding hands stained everything he touched.

Cold wind gusted into the room through the missing window, lifting a receipt from the top of his dresser and rustling the pages of a magazine on Lexie's bedside table. She would freeze in here tonight, and be unsafe. Anybody could come through her window. Anybody could come into this house.

Jonathan stood from his bed. He returned to the window, renegotiated, stepped into his yard. It was easier to get out of the house than it was to get in, easier to step down than to step up. He crossed the yard to his shed, ran the padlock through its code, swung open the door.

Most of his tools were missing. The sawhorse remained, and the lawnmower, a pile of tarps, but all of his power saws were gone, along with the sander, the leaf blower, his paintbrushes, half of his fucking extension cords.

His goddamn wife had locked him out of his own house and pawned his tools.

Jonathan returned to the busted out window and stepped again into his bedroom. Glass crunched underfoot as he went toward the hall. The smell of turkey soup grew stronger when he turned from the small hall that led to his bedroom into the larger hall that bisected the rest of the house. His stomach grumbled. He passed the children's bedrooms, went into the kitchen. Christ, but his head hurt. The deepest cut on his left hand throbbed. He held it under cold water, watched blood run into the sink. Grabbed a dish towel, tied it around his paw. Dishes waited clean and dry in the drainer. He grabbed a serving bowl. Threw the crockpot lid against the wall. Scooped turkey soup out with the bowl.

The soup wasn't what it would be tomorrow, but it tasted better than anything he'd eaten since leaving home. He spit a bone onto the floor. Broth dripped down his chest, his thighs. He pulled each kitchen drawer from its slot, upended it, kicked through the silverware and napkins, the plastic jar openers and leftover takeout plastic, looking for a key to his own door. Jonathan tilted the bowl to his mouth and drained the contents. He waded through his kitchen's innards to scoop another bowl of soup.

Dripping fresh broth, he went into the living room. No key beneath the TV he toppled. No key under the figurines he swept from the shelf. Nothing beneath the Christmas tree he shoved to the floor. There was wrapping paper on the sofa and loveseat, presents in piles, but nothing he'd bought. No wonder nobody had called him. He threw the soup bowl against the wall. No key in the stain this left behind. No key in the shattered ceramic. He turned over the loveseat from behind.

How the fuck was a man supposed to right his wrongs? He was a capable motherfucker. He'd broken a window he could seal in less than an hour, shattered glass he could replace by tomorrow evening. But his means of rectitude had been sold out from under him. The presents he'd bought nobody received. He couldn't even walk through the front door into his own house unless he found an extra key.

In the hall, he emptied the drawer from the small hallway table. No key in this mess. He grabbed the table, leaned his weight onto it, moved it back and forth across the floor. No key in the gouges.

He paused at Juliette's room. On her dresser was the tiny jewelry box he'd given her when she turned ten—double digits. He went into her room, opened the box, pushed through the contents with his finger. No key. He closed the box, straightened it where it sat on her dresser. Returned to the hall. Walked past Thomas's room entirely.

In the small hall that led to his own bedroom, Jonathan turned right toward the laundry room. He felt along the top of the door. A key. A key! He slumped against the dryer. When he could, he straightened and stuck the key in the lock.

It was the old key.

Jonathan opened a bottle of bleach and poured it into the laundry hamper, ruining all the clothes there. Let his bitch wife replace those.

He returned to his bedroom. Cold came steadily through the window, forcing the warm air out the door, into the hall. Soon, cold would overtake the house.

Sounds from the Christmas party up the street reached him. How long had he been here? One hour? Two? It felt like minutes. He didn't know where Lexie was, or if the kids were with her, or his mother. The four of them could come home right now and find him like this, standing in the ruin of his own creation.

None of the things he'd done made him feel better.

What would he say to his family now?

There was nothing he could say. It wasn't his place to say. It was women's work to explain human inconsistencies, human frailties. Love. If he were gone, Lexie would make everything he'd done okay for Thomas and Juliette. She'd have to. As their mother. As his wife. Even on the night they fought in the kitchen and she screamed at him about the goddamn gutter, she'd made it better for the children the next day, explaining to them over breakfast how hard it was to be a grown-up, while he sat silent with his coffee thinking *Preach*.

He had to get out before his family returned home.

Jonathan saw for the first time the blood he'd gotten on his sheets. He pulled them from the bed, took them into the bathroom, dumped them in the tub. Turned on the cold water. Another thing he'd learned from women: soak blood stains in cold.

There was no time to shower. He went to the sink. In the mirror, his face looked as he'd expected it would, tired and pale, dark circles beneath bloodshot eyes. There was no reason for him to look like anything other than shit. He opened the medicine chest, found some old Percocet. Chewed three, pocketed the rest.

He looked around the bathroom for signs of infidelity. His extra toothbrush was still in the cup. Only one towel hung on the rack. Lexie's birth control pills were on the counter. He yanked the foil packet from the plastic container and popped each pill into the toilet.

He turned off the tub and returned to the sink, washed his hands and arms and face. He bent his head to the warm sink water and did what he could with his hair. He dried off with the hand towel. Dirty water was splashed about and he wiped this up. He used his extra toothbrush, returned it to the cup.

In the mirror, his face was cleaner, but he'd never seen it look so goddamn sad. His face went beyond normal sad into the realm of circus clowns. Performance sad, that's what he'd become. Lexie's make-up bag sat open on the countertop. Out poked two lipsticks and Jonathan opened one—a bright, glittering pink. He smelled it. He licked it. The taste was different without Lexie's lips beneath, but recognizable all the same, makeup for his woman, makeup for a clown. He opened the other lipstick, a bright red, a clown red. With a lipstick in each hand, he looked at his wretched face in the bathroom mirror. Jonathan took the uncapped lipsticks into his bedroom.

I love you, he wrote in red on one of the bedroom walls. He

made the letters huge, filled in the space between the closet door and his dresser, used the length of the lipstick. I'm sorry, he wrote on the facing wall. There was less wall space there and the pink was difficult to see in lamplight, so he wrote it a second time, then a third. He tossed the empty lipsticks into the corner of the room.

Jonathan exited his home the same way he'd entered. Light blazed from his house. The gutter was ruined. The window was a hole. He pressed the palms of his hands to his eyes. How right the cold wind felt on his sad clown face. How right the cold wind felt cutting through his sweatshirt. His truck keys were in the side door, his duffle waited behind the front shrubs.

Lights shined up the driveway, illuminating him.

Lexie.

She blasted the car horn.

Fear erased the pain from Jonathan's body more thoroughly than anger had. He ran, crossing the yard, scaling the fence he'd built, cutting through the back neighbor's garden plot. He kept running when he reached the empty highway, ran right along the double yellow lines like the last soul fleeing the apocalypse.

42

Doreen knew as soon as she saw the house that something was wrong. Every light inside was ablaze, but she'd turned off all but the hall light when they left for the movies. Jonathan didn't have a key, and his truck wasn't in the drive. Still, Doreen knew: her son had come home. Doreen had offered to drive them back from Athens and beside her, in the passenger seat, Lexie was turned to face the children. She laughed as Thomas imitated a moment from the movie. But she would face forward in a moment, and she too would see the house, and then, Doreen knew, their lives would change. Again.

Doreen pulled into the drive. In her headlights, Jonathan stood crooked and hunched in his own backyard. He was so filthy Doreen's first thought was that he'd been dragged by something. He was injured, in pain. He lifted his hands to cover his face, palms open toward the car. He was hurt. This, thought Doreen, was why he'd come home. Her boy.

"I should've known it," said Lexie. She shoved a hand past

Doreen and blew the horn.

Jonathan straightened into the man they knew then, tall and broad, filthy from work. He bared his teeth toward the car, took off across the yard.

Lexie leapt out to give chase.

"Get back in the car!" Doreen shouted, but Lexie didn't turn. Doreen ran after her daughter-in-law. She heard the slam of Thomas and Juliette's car doors behind her.

Doreen's grandchildren ran past her. Jonathan scaled the fence and dropped to the other side. Lexie scaled the fence, hung at the top, dropped back into the damp green yard. Grabbed her children as they reached her.

Doreen turned to look at the back of the house. Here, too, every light burned. The light reached long into the yard through the space where there was no longer a window. Sitting in this extended reach of light was a twisted length of gutter.

"He sent us to the movies so he could fix the gutters," said Thomas.

"He smashed out the window, stupid," said Juliette.

"He broke into the house," said Lexie.

Doreen looked on the wreckage and understood. "Your daddy came by to see you on Christmas. But I'd changed the locks on him. He lost his temper. Broke a window. That's all this is."

"He sent us to the movies to get us out of the way," said Lexie.

"No," said Doreen. "I'm the one who put that money in the envelope for the movies. I wrote that letter and put his name on it. I didn't want y'all to think he'd forgotten you on Christmas."

For a long time nobody spoke. Then Lexie said, "You got us out of the house so Jonathan could break in."

"No. That's not what I did."

"Why don't you tell me what the fuck you did do then?" said Lexie.

"Mom," said Juliette.

Thomas started to cry.

"He brought presents, Lexie. For me to bring to y'all. But they were—they weren't the right kind of presents. He tried to do something decent, and he couldn't manage it, and I tried to help him." She held up a hand. "Just like I always do. I know."

"He got us presents, Mom," said Thomas.

Lexie grabbed Thomas by the arm and yanked him across the yard toward the window. "You want to see what your father brought you?"

"You're hurting me!" He tried to squirm from her grip.

"Don't hurt Thomas because you're mad at me," said Doreen.

"Let's see what his father did," said Lexie. "Then we'll talk about presents."

Juliette ran past them all to look in the window. "Mom. Don't make Thomas look."

Lexie stopped. She let go of Thomas. "Go wait at your grandmother's car."

Doreen expected him to run to the window anyway, but he ran across the yard toward the driveway, his willingness to be spared this highlighting how little he'd been spared in other ways.

Lexie and Doreen joined Juliette.

I LOVE YOU

I'M SORRY

I'M SORRY

I'M SORRY

A scrap of memory returned to Doreen: driving down a Florida road, windows down to catch the thick night air. She pressed a dishtowel to her nose to staunch the blood, and sitting beside her on the bucket seat was Jonathan, eyes groggy with sleep. He patted her leg as he prayed, *Now I lay me down to sleep. I pray the Lord my soul to keep.* She'd driven and driven, all the way to the Everglades. Near dawn, they stopped at a diner not far from the Seminole Reservation. Pancakes, scrambled eggs, sausage. Cheap presents from the gift shop. An effort to disguise the trip as something fun.

By evening she was back at Billy's. He blocked the door against her. "Scream it so the neighbors can hear," he said.

"I love you!" she shouted. Jonathan, on her hip, crying. "I'm so sorry!"

Empty language that promised violence, that's what she thought of sorry, that's what she thought of love.

Doreen wanted to tell Lexie this, but even with Janice, who had her own such stories, Doreen spoke in euphemism—*he got me back that time; he didn't let me forget.* Janice spoke the same way. Maybe all women who knew these truths did. Doreen took her daughter-in-law's hand. "Let me take the kids to Janice's. I'll come back and help you clean this up."

"Were the money and the note really from you?"

Looking on the wreckage of the bedroom, Doreen wished she'd kept that to herself. Those details changed things so little. Whether Jonathan had planned this or done it in a fit of rage, the effect on his family was the same. Only a judge would care if this was premeditated. "I was trying to do right by everyone."

"I'd appreciate it if you took the kids away from this," said Lexie, "but I'd like for you to stay away too."

43

Lexie sat on her bare mattress and looked at the room her husband had vandalized. Last week, she'd sat in the emergency room with a veteran awaiting transport to a psychiatric ward after a suicide attempt. "What I should've done is gone back," he said. "At least what happens there is real."

She understood. Her husband, her father. Her real life had been violence or the threat of violence. Her real life was Jonathan destroying her house, and her pretend life was the Christmas that came before, both children happy, everyone laughing. At Flyshoals Tech, she was careful with her speech—especially around the women from town, the ones who knew her history, the ones who knew her as Joey Hart's daughter, Jonathan Swilley's wife. "I wouldn't call it a separation," she said. "We married young. We're taking some time. That's all. It's friendly. Mutual." In the lie she'd woven, Jonathan was the sort of man who could have such a conversation with his wife. His wife who was capable and independent, near the top of her class.

In two weeks she would graduate, and all of those people for whom she'd woven such lies would be gone, while her domestic truth—this shattered window, that graffitied wall—would remain. If this ruined house was her reality, then few people in the world knew her: Jonathan, Doreen, Thomas, Juliette—all family. Doreen's friend, Janice. Luke's wife, Amanda.

As a child she'd sat in class and wondered if she was the girl drawing blocky houses with smoke curling from the chimney, or if she was the girl her father said she was at home. By the time she was thirteen, she erased her own confusion by becoming the same person outside the home that she felt herself to be within it.

She couldn't do that now. She had two children to raise. She had to find a way to become her pretend self.

The room was freezing. Lexie stood to go to the kitchen, where she could make coffee. She needed to work quickly if she was to have the glass cleaned up and the window boarded, the messages washed from the walls, by the time the children came home tomorrow.

When Lexie stepped into the hallway, she saw, at the end of the hall, blue liquid seeping from the laundry room.

When she stepped from the small hall into the larger hall, she saw the gouged floor, the smashed bowl.

She began to feel fear. Not that Jonathan would return tonight. He had to rouse his ire between attacks, talk himself into righteousness and vindictiveness. What she saw was that he was a man who struck blind; he didn't know going in what he was willing to do. Somehow Lexie had believed, for years, that she knew his limits.

She went into the kitchen, kicked through the contents of her drawers on the way to her coffee pot. Jonathan's desperation had become more than she could predict. One day an attack of his may prove so unpredictable—to him and to her—that they would not both survive it.

She needed help to clean all of this by morning. Doreen had offered, but Doreen's efforts to help were why this had happened in the first place. She wasn't going to call Ms. Paulsen, the woman who was writing her job recommendations. The only other woman Lexie could think to call was Amanda Baxter.

Lexie had been careful around Amanda since Jonathan moved out, worried that she might repeat something to Luke, who would repeat it to Jonathan, who would act on what he'd heard. But she also knew that Amanda hadn't liked Jonathan since he left her when Juliette was born. The wall phone was still attached to the wall. Lexie knew Amanda's home number by heart. It was the same as it had been when Lexie was living in Doreen's house, and Amanda was freshly married to Luke. In those days, Lexie had thought of Amanda as her best friend.

44

Jonathan had walked the five miles down the highway to Merle's Bar before, but never on a night so cold. Worse, his coat was in his duffle, which was still behind the bushes in his front yard. His hat and gloves were in his duffle too. The cold made the raw places on his palms ache more. He moved as his back would allow, meaning he stumbled along, half-running, half-falling down the roadside embankment when cars passed. The Percocets he'd chewed in his bathroom hit his mind more than his body. Incredible was the moon in its bright waxy steadiness. Incredible was the light of the distant stars. Miraculous, really, because without all this illumination he would've been blind as well as frozen during this pained stumble toward drink, seeing as how his flashlight was also back at Lexie's, in his duffle. Everything he owned was in that duffle. All he had was his cellphone, his wallet with his single credit card, and a few hundred bucks stuck in his front pocket.

The breeze kicked up anew and Jonathan shoved his hands under his armpits, trying to spare the bloodiest places further exposure. An empty Wonderbread bag, its clear plastic shimmering in the moonlight, rolled gently past him. Jonathan looked at that bag and considered covering his raw hands with it.

Buck up, he told himself. No need to start collecting roadside trash yet. To prove this to himself, he kicked an aluminum can into the trees. Aluminum prices had gone up quite a bit since the housing market crashed.

When Jonathan reached Merle's, the neon sign out front was turned off and in the parking lot there were only two cars besides Merle's Caddy. Jonathan went around to the back. He crossed the enormous porch—big enough to double as a dance floor come summer—and beat a long time on the back door. Eventually, a little plate in the door snapped open and Merle peered out. "Well, I'll be goddamned," he said. The door opened and Merle stood there with his arms spread wide and his white belly hanging out from under his tank top, waiting for a hug like an old woman.

Jonathan embraced the man. Merle stank of beer and fry grease. Jonathan knew he smelled no better himself.

"Been a long time," said Merle. "I would've sworn you dead."

"Not dead. But sure enough in Hell."

"Get the door." Merle turned and stumped back into his bar. His right foot was fake, on account, he claimed, of breaking the real one off in someone's ass.

The men exited the short hallway and entered the bar itself. Cigarette smoke made its own atmosphere at about head level. At a table in the corner, a man and a woman leaned close and petted heavy. In the middle of the room, four women sat at a table covered with empties.

"Look what I brought you," said Merle as he stumped by

the women.

"Johnny fucking Swilley!" said one. It was Wanda Jancey from the Quickie Mart. A cigarette hung from her mouth. "This one's married, Merle. Got kids, too. Can't you find us one that ain't already swallowed the hook?"

While the women raised glasses to this, Jonathan took a seat at the bar.

Merle passed him a beer.

"Let me have a shot of Wild Turkey, too. Double."

Jonathan chased the liquor with his beer. Merle pulled himself a beer and dragged his stool to sit opposite Jonathan.

"Hey Swilley," said Wanda, "If you'll pretend you're a single man, you can sit on my face. What I don't need are no more kids or exes!"

"I hear she can grip it like a vise," said Merle. "For what it's worth to you."

"What are they drinking?"

"Bud Lite."

"Send 'em something girly on me. Pink. Double the liquor. Triple it. Shut them the fuck up."

"You gonna get them a cab home, too?"

"Flyshoals don't have cabs."

"Friar Johnson's out of work so he's transporting drunks. Ten bucks a head for a ride in the back of his truck."

"You ever done a ménage à trois, Johnny Swilley?" said Wanda.

One of the other women said, "It ain't a ménage à trois if it's four women!"

"What the fuck is it then?" said Wanda.

"An orgy!" The table of women hooted and stomped.

"Lonely moms," said Merle. "All four of them without their kids on Christmas."

"I'll get their cab. Give 'em some liquor, give me some liquor, get some liquor for yourself and call Friar Johnson."

"You know what they say about men who turn it down," said Wanda.

"He's buying y'all a round of drinks," said Merle. "Says it's the best a married man can do for lookers such as yourselves." He slid Jonathan another double, another beer.

"That's what we wanted all along, baby," said Wanda. "Don't fret."

"Prick teases," said her friend. "That's what we are."

"You would have been disappointed," said a third. "Been so long for me there's cobwebs down there."

"It's better just to get drunk beside us and dream big," said the fourth.

Merle stumped to the women's table with a pitcher of something pink and cherry studded, a stack of plastic cups. Wanda served her friends and then herself, led the table in a toast to Jonathan.

45

Lexie collected silverware and cooking utensils while Amanda Baxter surveyed the house with her Glock. "You call the police?" she said when she made it back to the kitchen.

"It's not illegal to break into your own house."

"Like hell it isn't. Stop cleaning. Leave everything like he left it. This is enough to get you an ex parte and then you can work on a restraining order."

Lexie dumped what she'd gathered into the sink. She'd known this would be Amanda's first response. The woman was a police dispatcher. "The only thing a restraining order does is help the police know who killed you." Lexie went to the fridge and got two beers. She took these to the kitchen table, righted two chairs, sat in one.

Amanda picked her way through the mess. "You'll want a restraining order if he fights for custody during the divorce. Don't tell me you want this jackass around your kids."

"Divorce proceedings will trap me in Flyshoals." Lexie

drank from her beer. "Johnny alone I can handle, Amanda. But I'm not pulling anyone else into the ring. No lawyers. No cops. Nobody telling me what I can say to him and when. Nobody telling me what I'm allowed to do."

"You have a plan."

"All I want you to do is help me clean the house up before my children get home. And tell Luke something that won't make Johnny suspicious. Say I wish I'd never torn my family apart."

Amanda ran a hand through her short blonde hair, mussing it further into a cockscomb. "I don't even talk to Luke like that. What I to say to Luke about Johnny is, 'Birds of a goddamn feather.' I don't want him around the man." She took her jacket and shoulder holster off, hung both on her seat. "I thought you might be planning something when you fell out of touch with me after Johnny moved out."

Lexie noticed that Amanda's shoes weren't tied; she was in pajama bottoms. She'd run out the door at Lexie's call. "I can't trust anybody. Not even my kids."

"You're right. You can't." Amanda went to the drawer where Lexie kept the kitchen rags, took one out. "Tell me where to start."

A car pulled into the driveway, its headlights illuminating the kitchen through the blinds. Lexie looked out the window. "Doreen."

"What the hell is she doing here?"

"She thinks it's her right to be here. Because it's her son that did it, I guess. And I'm hers too."

"I hope you know not to trust her either."

46

It was nearing dawn when Doreen turned to the words lipsticked on the walls. Lexie was taking the sheets from the tub to the washing machine, and Amanda was hauling another bag of trash out to the bin. Doreen dunked her sponge in a bucket of soapy water and scrubbed at her son's declaration of love. The words disappeared into a pink cloud studded with mica. "Shit." She slapped the sponge against the wall. Once she and Janice finished painting the walls of Marxton Casualty and Life, they could come here, repaint Lexie's house.

"He poured bleach in the clothes hamper," Lexie said as she returned to the room. "Ruined everything in the basket."

Doreen had said *I'll help you fix that* so many times she didn't bother to say it again. "Why don't you and the kids move in with me, Lexie? Leave him to deal with this. We can start packing instead of cleaning."

"You have a two-bedroom house, Doreen. What do you want me to do, sleep in the bed beside you again?"

Doreen turned back to the words on the wall.

The front door opened and closed. "Just me," Amanda called. Each time she entered the house she announced herself in this way. Doreen fought the urge to tell Amanda Baxter to shut up. Jonathan had some awful qualities, but he wasn't the type of man to show up at four in the morning and kill everyone as they slept. Or as they scrubbed away the words he'd painted on his own damn walls.

Amanda dropped Jonathan's duffle on the bed. "Found this in the bushes."

Doreen had noticed the duffle when she first arrived, and she'd left the bag where it was. She'd planned to take it with her when she left, get it back to Jonathan through Luke. She knew that seeing the bag would make Lexie angrier. And she knew that losing the bag would hasten Jonathan's return. But all of this was better left unsaid.

"He's planning on coming back," said Amanda.

"No," said Doreen. "We surprised him. He ran away so fast he left it." She thought of how her son had looked in the moment before Lexie blew the horn, how he'd looked the moment after. Like two different men.

Lexie loosened the cord on the duffle, upended the contents. A smell of fish and mold whooshed from the bag, and a thin gray dust lifted into the air and hung a moment before slowly settling. "Smells like he's not bathing or washing his clothes."

Doreen went to the bedside.

Lexie grabbed a stained t-shirt, balled it, threw into the duffle. She grabbed a pair of jeans and shoved these in the duffle too. She picked up another t-shirt. Beneath it was Jonathan's pistol.

The women stood for a moment, looking at the gun. The pistol had been Doreen's—she'd bought it after leaving Billy. It sat unloaded in a drawer through all of Jonathan's childhood, and at some point he asked her for it, and she gave it to him. She was used to seeing the gun in his glove compartment, around his house. She was used to men having guns—even Bird kept one in his truck. Her initial surprise at seeing this one had been only the mild shock that always accompanied the discovery of a pistol, a little jolt such as one has when a snake slithers away.

Amanda picked the gun up, flipped open the cylinder. "Loaded. Asshole." She shook out the bullets, checked the chamber, set the ammo on the nightstand, flipped the cylinder closed. Offered the pistol to Lexie butt-first.

Lexie didn't take it. "I've lived around guns all my life, but I've never had much to do with them."

"I'll take you to the range later, but here's what you need to know for now." Amanda demonstrated the safety switch beside the trigger. "When you see that orange color, you can't shoot."

Lexie took the pistol, held it straight down at her side.

The tarp the women had stapled over the window shuddered in the wind. Jonathan could step back into the house tonight. He'd made it so a key was no longer an issue.

What was her son capable of? What was her daughter-in-law capable of? Doreen saw that none of them should have that gun, but there was no getting rid of it. A pistol couldn't be rinsed down the drain like a house chemical, or flushed like prescription pills. "Why don't we let Janice keep the gun until all of this blows over?" said Doreen.

"Ms. Doreen, I mean no disrespect, but I'm not going to take a gun away from a woman whose husband just did this to his own house."

Lexie still held the pistol at her side. Doreen picked up a t-shirt, started to fold it, felt Lexie and Amanda's eyes on her. She did then as they'd done with her son's clothes, balled the t-shirt and threw it into the duffle. "You keep the gun."

Lexie set the pistol on her bedside table.

Amanda set aside a jar of peanut butter, a shaker of salt. "You may as well keep the food after what he did to your kitchen." She pulled out two Tupperware containers, tossed one beside the peanut butter, opened the other. Inside was a plastic wrapped block. She unwrapped it, revealed a stack of bills. She flipped through the money: twenties, fifties, hundreds. "Jesus Christ." Amanda sat on the edge of the bed. "I knew Luke was lying to me. He's been contributing a lot more lately. Claims it's his small engine repair business, but he's done that for years and it's never helped much. He's up to something with Johnny."

Doreen knew. *Me and Luke have found enough like it or better to open our own gem mine.*

"Johnny's not up to anything," said Lexie. She took the money from Amanda and put it back in the Tupperware container. "That's the money from his paychecks. He canceled his direct deposit after he left."

Doreen felt relief—until she realized what Lexie's words meant. "How are you paying the mortgage?"

Lexie said nothing.

"They'll take the house from you if you don't pay."

"They won't take it from me. It's not my house."

All of the help Lexie had asked for from Doreen, all of the help she'd accepted, and she'd been secretly letting Jonathan's house move toward foreclosure. Doreen slapped her across the face.

Lexie's head jerked to the side. Her left hand she lifted to where she'd been hit. With her right hand, she returned the blow.

Doreen bent at the waist, both hands to her cheek. It had been so long since she'd been slapped. She'd forgotten how badly it hurt.

Amanda ran to get between them, but the fight was over.

Doreen put her hands on her thighs, pushed herself upright. She was taller and broader than both Lexie and Amanda, but she felt small and weak. "I don't want you to be Jonathan's wife anymore. I don't want him around his kids. I want you to keep that money and even that gun, and I don't care if you keep his clothes too. But I don't want him to lose everything he's ever worked for." Doreen walked toward the bedroom door. "He has to live his life, Lexie. After you destroy him. He has to find some new way to be." She went down the hall then, out the front door.

47

When Merle pushed Jonathan out the door, the sun was reddening the eastern horizon. The two men stood in the gravel parking lot. Even the cigarette butts on the ground were rimmed with hoarfrost. An hour or so earlier, Jonathan had lifted Wanda and each of her friends into the back of Friar Johnson's truck. Merle pointed at his Caddy. "Let me give you a ride home."

Jonathan couldn't think of where Merle could take him. "I'd rather walk. Clear my mind some. It ain't far." Jonathan started across the parking lot, grateful, at least, that the alcohol gave him a reason to stumble other than the pain in his body. "Merle, I need to see more of you."

"I second the notion, brother." Merle got in his big Caddy, roared it to life and screeched onto the highway going the opposite direction.

When Merle's engine was out of earshot, Jonathan stretched out on the roadside, closed his eyes. Sleep was so close. Liquor could be blanket and roof both, but for some vague idea that niggled. Exposure, frost bite, hypothermia, death. Hadn't he once seen a picture of a fat Russian in a striped bathing suit, swimming past a polar bear? That man could sleep on this roadside. Mind over matter. Jonathan imagined himself in the bathing suit, barrel-bellied and full of vodka, but the image wouldn't hold. Already his eyeballs felt frozen. Finer men than himself had died of exposure. There was nothing to do but keep going. He rocked his head to and fro on the sharp rocks, jabbing himself awake.

He sat up, tried to think sober. Considered his circumstances and his options.

Lexie, obviously, was out of the question.

His mother? When last he saw her, he'd given her a table full of gifts. But she'd not seen fit to deliver those gifts to his wife and his kids. There was more there than he could understand. And he didn't want to hear what she'd say about his little stunt in his house. The graffiti and what not.

Jonathan pulled his phone from his pocket. Dialed.

Luke answered as if he'd been waiting. "This is the last time I want you to call me on this number. If Amanda has proof I've been talking to you, she'll go out of her fucking mind."

"Amanda's never liked me. Come on out to Merle's. Bring a bottle. We'll sit on the porch and watch the sunrise."

"Don't you listen to your messages? You went crazy last night, man. Amanda's at your house with her Glock."

Jonathan shivered on the gravel. The temperature was dropping as it did at dawn. "I'm gonna die of exposure if you don't come pick me up."

"Go inside the goddamn bar, Johnny!"

"Bar's closed. Merle went home."

"You got kicked out of Merle's? Well it's your own fault if you freeze to death then. You've only known the good life, man. You act like Lexie wanting to triple the family income is an insult.

You act like your mother wanting to care for your kids is an insult. All your fucking life, you act like people helping you is an insult, and still good shit happens to you. You walk out on your kids and a gemstone scheme falls right in your lap. You got more money in your pocket than you've ever had in your life, and you're still doing shit so fucked up my wife has to leave my bed to go help your wife straighten it out. Maybe God is finally paying attention, Johnny. Maybe freezing to death is what you get for being an asshole since the day you were born."

Jonathan forced himself to standing, through alcohol and fatigue and bodily pain. "I lost my job today. Lexie changed the locks on me. I lost all my cash and my truck too. Powell took his trailer back. You don't know shit about my life."

"I know if your mother hadn't looked out for me after my mother died I might not've graduated high school. I know if your mother hadn't hauled my ass out to Green Hills after graduation, I might not have a job. The woman even goes to visit my dad in the nursing home like he's her own fucking relative."

"That's your life, not mine."

Luke hung up on him.

Jonathan threw his phone. He regretted the loss before it left his hand. He fell as he stumbled after it, rolled down the small incline, hit his head. He sat at the bottom in the wet grass and trash, dazed. The phone was a few feet from him and he crawled to it. It still worked. The cut on his hand had reopened in the fall. Blood dripped on his jeans and on his phone as he searched his contacts.

Jonathan knew one man who was honest about the fragility of human existence, one man who understood that there was no solid ground to stand on—wives left you, mothers and friends turned their backs, children forgot your face, employers lathered you near to death. Faster answered. "I need for you to come pick me up," said Jonathan. "There's been a terrible accident. I caused a terrible accident."

"Are you injured, son?"

"No."

"Is your wife injured?"

"No."

"Your children? Your mother?"

"Nobody's injured."

"Then whatever it is that's happened can be overcome."

"You ought to open a 1-800 number."

Jonathan heard Nicki mumble in the background.

"Just a parishioner," said Faster. "You go on back to sleep."

Nicki's voice was no longer a mumble. "You're not a pastor! You don't have parishioners!"

"What are we all to one another but parishioners?"

Jonathan nodded from his place in the ditch.

"Another drunk," said Nicki. "That's what you are to one another. Tell that good-for-nothing lowlife he'd best learn to call when the sun's up."

Jonathan felt a lift of his spirit that Nicki was willing to let him call at all. That made his relationship with her better than with the other women in his life. He looked east. The sun delivered all sorts of messenger rays. "Tell her to listen for the rooster."

"Nicki's a grumpalump first thing in the morning. Where are you, son? I'm pulling on my pants as we speak."

48

Less than twenty-four hours after slapping her daughter-in-law and being slapped in return, Doreen sat once again at Lexie's kitchen table. She'd brought Thomas and Juliette home from Janice's. She and Jonathan could go weeks, months, without speaking, but she and Lexie were too entwined to go a day. Doreen listened as Lexie stood in the living room and answered her children's questions as best she could.

"Why did Dad break the stuff on the shelves?" said Thomas.

"I don't know," said Lexie.

"Why did he break the TV?" said Juliette.

"I don't know," said Lexie.

"Is he mad at us?" said Thomas.

"He's not mad at you and your sister," said Lexie.

"Is he mad at you?"

"He's mad at me."

"Is he mad at Grandma?"

"I don't know."

Eventually, Lexie settled the children in the living room with her laptop and a DVD. She joined Doreen in the kitchen.

"Dean said he'd come by today around four to board up that window for you," said Doreen.

"I called the husband of a gal I go to school with."

Doreen almost protested, but she reminded herself, as she had been doing all day, not to position herself between her son and daughter-in-law. "I'll call Dean. Let him know he needn't come."

Lexie pushed back from the table. "You want a glass of sweet tea?"

Doreen grabbed her daughter-in-law's arm. "Last night shouldn't have gone the way it did. Not any part of it. Not what Jonathan did. Not what happened between you and me."

"We both did things we shouldn't have."

Doreen pulled from her pocket a check she'd written. Fifteen thousand dollars. It was more than half of her loan from Blake and all she felt she could give without ruining her own future. "That money's to go to Jonathan's back mortgage first, and then you keep what's left over. You two can work out in court what to do with what he left in the bushes. I'm not getting in the middle of that. I'm done getting in the middle, Lexie. This money is me fixing my child's future without damaging yours, and then walking away. This is me making things as good as they can be right now so that I can bow out. I wish you and Jonathan both the best of luck, and I'm here to help with my grandkids. That's all I can say."

Lexie was quiet for so long, Doreen feared she would reject the gift. Finally though, she folded the check and stuck it in the front pocket of her jeans. Her face didn't look soft, as Doreen had hoped it would. Doreen pushed away the anger that rose up in her chest. She knew gifts were to be given without strings, without even the expectation of gratitude.

"I have something for you too." Lexie left the kitchen. She

returned a few minutes later with two manila envelopes stuffed full. These she sat in front of Doreen.

Doreen reached into one, pulled out a letter to Santa from Juliette, the script huge and loopy, year one cursive. She remembered sitting at the table while Juliette wrote the letter. It had been Christmas Eve, and Jonathan and Lexie were at the table too, proud of their daughter's accomplishments. Thomas was asleep down the hall in his crib. Doreen peeked in the other envelope, spied a thumbprint mouse with Thomas's name written across the bottom. "These are things for a mother to keep," she said, her voice breaking. She shoved the envelopes across the table.

Lexie pushed the envelopes back. "I'll ask you to return them to me one day. It may take me twenty years, but there will come a day that I pay you back and ask you to give those envelopes back to me. Consider them a promise. Keep them safe."

Doreen saw the stubborn set of Lexie's forehead, and she knew she would only be allowed to leave this table with either her own check or Lexie's memories. Why had she spent so many years of her life carrying the burden of other people's outcomes: their successes and their failures, their joys and their sadnesses? She'd done it with Jonathan and she'd done it with Lexie. She'd thought she was sacrificing for others by behaving this way, but really she'd been blinded by pride. She wasn't God. At some point, adults were responsible for who they became. Doreen held the envelopes against her chest.

49

Lexie feared madness would overtake her before she could graduate and escape with her children from Flyshoals. She had more than enough money now. Her guilt at stealing from Doreen made it hard for her to eat, but it wasn't guilt that threatened her sanity. She could speak to her guilt: what she planned to do she did for Thomas and Juliette, and one day Doreen would thank her. Doreen would thank her because, Lexie knew, the woman loved her grandchildren.

No, what Lexie feared in herself was her own fear. *I know him better than he knows himself,* she used to say, but that wasn't true.

Lexie tried to stand in the small, quiet space inside of herself, the place she'd discovered the day that Juliette lied to her about going to the mall. If she could get into that space, Lexie knew she could choose how she responded to her fear. She would be able to step outside of it and examine it, hold it in her palm. But she couldn't find that quiet space. The fear yanked her from sleep during the first dark hours of the day. She jolted awake fully alive, every sense heightened. The smallest sound from the most distant part of the house met her ear with its story intact—a man's footsteps in the foundation plantings. A knife slicing open the kitchen window screen.

Lexie would then ease to the edge of her bed and slowly work her nightstand drawer open, a millimeter to the left, a millimeter to the right—no squeaking, no scraping—until she created a space wide enough for her hand. A space wide enough for the pistol.

She held the pistol the way Amanda had taught her: double-grasp, butt supported; arms straight and down; safety off. Finger trigger ready. Lexie tried, even as she crept, to talk herself out of her behavior. She tried to find the quiet space. She told herself she was hearing things. Imagining things. Making up stories. Overreacting. It was the icemaker. The sounds of an old house settling.

She told herself she was losing her mind.

None of the things she said changed her behavior. Because what she feared more than creeping about in the dark with a pistol was failing to protect her children. And what the creeping felt like, every time, was certainty. Even when she did not find Jonathan standing in their kitchen with his deer knife in his hand, she felt certain. Wrong, but certain. Certain, but alone. Certain and wrong and alone.

50

Jonathan stood in front of the hotel mirror and gelled his hair into spikes as the girl who'd cut it had done. The hairstyle was new, as were his navy sports coat and his pressed cotton shirt, his khaki slacks, the silly loafers on his feet, the bottled woods smell that wafted from him when he turned to check his profile in the hotel mirror. He'd laid a small fortune on his credit card to look like a banker. "What you gotta do," Faster said, "is spiff up and go to her right after she graduates. She'll be feeling good. Tell her you're proud of her. Tell her you can't live without her. Tell her in front of your kids and your mother and anyone else you can get to listen. You need witnesses, son. You got to prove to the jury you're not a mad man. Go in expecting the best." The hotel room Jonathan had laid on his card had a Jacuzzi tub and a king-sized bed and a No Smoking sign on the door—seeing as how Lexie had quit the habit.

The other thing Faster had said to him after picking him up outside Merle's was this: "Recall God ain't afraid to make even his chosen people wander thirsty and starving through the desert for forty years. That means we shouldn't take personally what he'll do to unchosen assholes like you and me." Then he'd driven him to a campground and handed him a pup tent and a sleeping bag. "Nicki's got that line you don't cross," he'd said as Jonathan got out of the truck. "It's one of the things I love about her." In the overhead light of the cab, Faster's black eye was visible. "I'll bring you a sandwich when I can."

Which meant that Jonathan had no choice but to sweet talk his wife into taking him back tonight. All he'd ever meant to do was make her beg him home, and now here he was, the one reduced to begging. No money, no job, no house. Jonathan crossed the parking lot and got behind the wheel of his truck. He jostled the screwdriver he'd rigged in place of a key. Sometimes his life was so un-fucking-believable he couldn't believe it came for free. Surely someone somewhere had to be selling tickets.

Through the window of his mother's house, he eyeballed the celebrations. On the right side of the living room was a folding table set with snacks. Dean, Janice's more-or-less boyfriend, hovered there over a bowl of chips. To the left of the front door, in the vicinity of the couch, three women Jonathan didn't know talked in a clump. Two of them wore those neck sashes that marked them as graduates—friends of Lexie's he assumed—and one was in a plain gray suit. Both of the women wearing neck sashes had babies, one an infant, one a toddler. Standing with them was Janice's daughter, Tillie, whose own baby bounced on her front in a cloth carrier. Near the kitchen door, Lexie talked to Janice and Luke's wife, Amanda. Jonathan had steeled himself against the moment when he first saw his wife, but it overtook him like a sorrow. Lexie had her hair twisted up and her make-up on thick and she wore a pair of sky-high heels. He should've known the moment a woman who could look like that agreed to a date with a guy who looked like him that things wouldn't end well. He squatted so his head wouldn't be visible through the door's glass and rang the bell.

Janice threw the door wide in greeting, her arms ready to embrace.

Jonathan moved to hug her, but she slapped him away and shoved him onto the porch. "You're not on the guest list." She stepped out and closed the door behind her.

Jonathan held aloft the mixed bouquet he'd gotten at the Walmart. "Just want to give these to Lexie."

"What are you doing in those clothes? Nobody's died."

"Me and Lexie have got to talk sometime. We have kids together. At least there are witnesses here."

"You can pay somebody to witness. They're called mediators. Don't barge in here tonight and ruin her graduation party."

"I can't pay anybody to do anything. Can't even feed myself. I've lost my job. And maybe you haven't heard, but Lexie has all my money. I left it in the bushes. After I did that thing to my house. Even if I can't see her, I need a loan from her. Tell her she can pay me to go away."

"You've got on those fancy clothes and you're coming around saying you got no money?"

Jonathan realized his miscalculation. "Did Lexie tell you she don't want to see me? Could be she'd be happy to have an apology. Take these to her and if she says scram, I'll go away, promise."

Janice snatched the flowers from his hand. "I'm locking this door behind me. Don't break another window."

Jonathan watched Janice go to Lexie and Amanda and hand his wife the flowers, say something with a sour look on her face. Lexie's head whipped to the door. So did Amanda's. So did the woman's in the gray suit.

Jonathan waved.

Janice pushed Lexie and Amanda into the kitchen where he couldn't see them.

Jonathan decided against going around the side of the house and surprising them through the kitchen door. That was the sort of behavior he had to guard against in himself. What he anticipated was Janice being sent to the porch with some small sum of cash, which, given his current predicament, he'd count as a success. But instead Lexie herself came out of the kitchen and headed his way. She held his flowers and had a pleasant enough look on her face. "Johnny," she said as she opened the door. "What a surprise."

Jonathan stepped slowly into his childhood home. The party fell silent. Every adult in the room seemed to know him as the man who had graffitied his own walls. Which was an awful thing to have done, but not illegal. It was his house. "I'm not a criminal," he said.

"Elinor," said Lexie, pointing out the woman with a baby on her hip. "Ruthann. You know Tillie. That's Ms. Paulsen."

Ms. Paulsen, Ruthann, Elinor. Names he'd never heard. "Nice to meet y'all."

"Johnny!" Luke came into the living room from the hallway. "I heard it go quiet and figured you'd shown up." He came to Jonathan, shook his hand, pulled him forward to slap his back.

"It's been too long," said Jonathan, though he and Luke had dug for crystals three nights before.

"Your boy is back in your momma's room watching a movie with my kids and Tillie's." He guided Jonathan deeper into the living room. "You remember Dean, Ms. Janice's boyfriend?"

"Good to see you again, Johnny," said Dean.

"Lexie introduced you to her friends, so now you know everyone. Your momma and Juliette went to the store for ice cream. They forgot it earlier."

Jonathan turned to his wife. The flowers she held dripped

onto the carpet. Nobody here seemed inclined to save him. Jonathan went to a knee as he'd not done when he asked Lexie to marry him. "I didn't support you like I should've and by God, you went and did it anyway. I'm proud of you. I miss you, baby. You're starting something new, and I hope you and me can start new, too."

"Johnny," said Lexie.

"Dad!" Thomas barreled across the living room and leapt onto Jonathan. Jonathan rolled backward with him in his arms. "It's my dad! Come on! Get him! Get him!" There were cries and running and then all of the other little boys barreled into the living room and piled on top of Jonathan too.

"Help me, Lexie! Help!" Jonathan said from the bottom of the pile. "They've got me!" He hoped she'd laugh at the roughhousing, shake her head at him for being just another kid. But through the flailing arms and legs, Jonathan saw his wife leave the living room. Tillie and Lexie's school friends pulled their circle in closer.

Luke grabbed Reese and held him around the waist, hooked one of Janice's grandsons in his other arm. "Lay off Mr. Johnny. He don't need to get beat up no more." The boys stopped their punching and shouting, stood grinning and tousle-headed.

"That's my dad," Thomas repeated.

"Go finish your movie," said Luke. "Me and Mr. Johnny need to talk."

Thomas wouldn't leave. Jonathan grabbed the boy and held him, felt how much taller he'd grown, felt the way his body curved into the hug. "I'm not going anywhere. I'm home to stay, buddy." In Jonathan's arms, Thomas quivered against tears. Jonathan stood his son on his feet, shook his shoulders. "Straighten up now. Go watch that movie."

"Your daddy will be with me in the kitchen drinking beer," said Luke.

Doreen came in the kitchen door and slapped the ice cream down on the counter. "So that was your truck."

Jonathan was entrenched at the kitchen table, Luke to his left and Dean to his right, empty bottles scattered in front of them. "Hey baby," Jonathan said to Juliette.

Juliette busied herself putting the few groceries away.

Jonathan kept from squirming while his mother took in his shirt, his tie, the coat on the back of the chair. This was her house, and she could kick him out of it. "Nobody died," she said. She turned to wash her hands at the sink. "Juliette, go back there and tell your brother we're about to bring the cake out."

Jonathan relaxed some, the hurdle of his mother cleared. "My own daughter won't even give me a hug?" He held out an arm.

Juliette came to his side but did not touch him. He pulled her close. She stood stiff and straight, her mouth a line. "You sure have gotten grown-y. You give hugs like your momma."

He released her, and she stalked from the kitchen. "Girls are tough," he said.

His mother opened a box of candles and began to stick them into an iced sheet cake.

"I don't know who let you in here, but if you cause a scene tonight, I'll call the police my damn self."

"Lexie's the one who let me in. I got on a knee and apologized. Thomas ran out to say hello. A lot's happened."

His mother paused in her candling, and Jonathan knew his words had struck home. "Get the ice cream and the scoop. The cake server. Follow me to the living room." When she was angry all the way through, she didn't let him help. Jonathan knocked back his beer, hurried to the utensil drawer.

"Ruin this," she whispered as they walked into the living room, "and you won't get another chance. I don't know why

316

you're getting one now."

Jonathan didn't believe it himself. He suspected a ruse. But at least it was a ruse his mother didn't seem to be in on.

Doreen set the cake on the table she'd set up in the living room. "I don't know what you're supposed to do at a college graduation party. But I know these women worked hard, and they deserve a wish. Come on up here."

Lexie and her friends joined Doreen in front of the cake. Elinor bent so her baby could see. The horde of boys pressed close, ready to blow out the candles. "This isn't for you," said Doreen, shooing them away. "You can only blow out these candles if you're a college graduate." She lit the candles. "On three."

Jonathan watched while his wife closed her eyes and blew hard. He had no idea whether or not he wanted her wish to come true. Before the clapping was finished, he started scooping ice cream onto plates that he passed to his mother for cake, as if this was a party he'd planned, as if he'd been one of the hosts all along.

Hours later, Jonathan sat at the kitchen table playing hand after hand of spiritless poker with his mother and his wife. Thomas slept in Jonathan's childhood bedroom; Juliette slept on the couch. Everyone else had left shortly after the cake, and Dean had dragged Janice home two hours ago. Jonathan realized that his mother would play cards until dawn if that's what it took to keep him from being alone with his wife. He pushed in a Cheeto for an ante. "You can't sit between us forever, Momma."

"Go on home to Powell's trailer, Jonathan. We've all had enough for one night."

"Powell kicked me out."

Doreen folded her hand. "You have some place you're staying. A homeless man can't do that to his hair."

317

Lexie began to clear the table. "Go on to bed, Doreen. I'll leave the kids here, take Johnny home with me. He's right. You can't sit between us forever. We have to talk sometime."

Jonathan scanned his wife for signs of a lie. The best he'd hoped for these past hours was an invitation to sleep on the floor of his mother's house. Now here was Lexie, jumping over the fight completely, landing on the conclusion he'd not even let himself hope for. "Don't do anything you don't want to. I'm not here looking for hand-outs."

Lexie stared at him in such a way he could almost hear her calculating.

"Seeing as how you're the only one can open the door to get us back in the house," he said.

His mother slapped the table. "I'm the one who changed your locks. I did it the day after you punched your daughter in the face."

Jonathan turned from his mother's gaze. He'd assumed all along that it was Lexie who changed the locks, and he'd finally decided while living in the campground that lock-changing was something he could forgive her for. But his mother.

"Are we going home?" Juliette leaned against the doorway, her voice thick with sleep.

"No, baby," said Lexie. "Go on back to the couch. You and Thomas are staying here with Grandma. I'm going home with Daddy. I'll pick y'all up tomorrow."

Jonathan didn't miss the look that passed between his wife and daughter.

His mother pushed herself up from the table. "Come on, Juliette. Let me tuck you into my bed. I'll take the couch."

"I'm fine on the couch, Grandma."

"This is my house. I decide." Doreen went down the hall toward her bedroom, and after a moment, Juliette followed her.

Jonathan ran his hands down his thighs to dry his palms. Never in front of Lexie had he felt so nervous. The weight of what they shared together settled on him. "I don't think our house is the best place for us to work things out." She couldn't have repaired all he'd damaged. How could she forgive him while what he'd done stared them in the face? "I got a hotel room. Non-smoking. With a Jacuzzi tub."

"We'll go there then."

The woman all but shrugged. This wasn't the Lexie he knew. "What is it you're planning?"

She came around the table to him, took his head, pulled it to her chest. She tugged on his curls in the way he liked. He smelled her clothes detergent, and below that the faint scent of her perfume, and below that her smell, cumin and caramel. He moaned into her breasts, put his arms around her waist.

"Maybe we work things out and maybe we don't," she said. "But tonight, let's not talk about it. I've been so lonely."

He pulled his head back and found tears in her eyes. Lexie only cried when she was angry, but anger wasn't what he saw in her face. She looked as he felt, wounded and ashamed. He wiped the dampness from her right cheek.

"I replaced those birth control pills you ruined," she said.

Jonathan dropped his hands from her body. "Birth control wasn't something I thought you'd be needing."

"It's for a night like this I stayed on them. A night just like this."

If he'd told her what to say, those were the words he would've picked. He let her pull him to standing, remembering how she'd cradled Juliette as a newborn, how she'd modeled the father he needed to become. "I'm following your lead, baby."

51

Five days of lies too numerous to count passed before Lexie was alone in her house with her children. She watched through the kitchen window as Jonathan's truck turned from their road, on his way to Athens to get what he needed to repair the damage he'd done. "Thomas! Juliette!" It was 7 am, and the children were getting ready for school. But today there would be no school. Lexie didn't trust that Jonathan wouldn't grow suspicious, return hours ahead of schedule. In minutes maybe. He could abandon the trip entirely. This was the first time he'd let her out of his sight since they'd left her graduation party at Doreen's.

Thomas and Juliette came into the kitchen. "What's wrong?" said Juliette.

Lexie pulled two brown paper shopping bags from the dusty stash she kept between the fridge and the wall. "Pretend there's a fire. Grab what's vital. We're leaving in half an hour."

Juliette took her bag and ran from the kitchen.

"You can't make me!" said Thomas. "I'm staying here with Daddy!"

Lexie slapped him across the face. Then he did as he was told.

52

The night after Lexie disappeared with the children, Jonathan and Doreen fought hard about the details of her escape.

Left behind were a cellphone wiped clean, a house going back to the bank, an empty bank account. Taken were the children, Jonathan's money, Doreen's money. Cash impossible to reclaim.

As dawn pinked the horizon, Jonathan slammed his mother's front door behind him a final time, his duffle of clean clothes on his back, his trash bag of undelivered Christmas presents in his arms.

Doreen was relieved to see him go. He'd been right in his accusations—she had given Lexie the means to leave. And no, she hadn't really believed Lexie would use that money to save his house from the bank. Some truths aren't meant to be shared though, especially between mother and child.

Waiting months followed.

Through local gossip, Doreen developed an idea of where Jonathan was. Of how he survived.

Swilley Insurance developed a small client base.

She had experimental dates with Bird: his house, her house. A single long weekend on the Gulf Coast, the ocean close enough for them to hear in bed.

On Sundays, she met Janice for prayer and painting, prayer and wallpapering. They tiled the floors of Swilley Insurance.

At first, the only information online about Lexie was old information—her college graduation announcement, a list of parent volunteers for Juliette's fourth grade play. But Doreen continued to check the Georgia state licensure site, the same site where her own licensure could be verified, and eventually she found her daughter-in-law. Lexie had passed her NCLEX; she had a home address. Google Earth revealed a deep suburban lot and a ranch style house, dated but well-kept.

Sometimes when Doreen couldn't sleep, she pulled the photo of Lexie's house up on her computer screen and sat before it while sifting through the manila envelopes of thumbprint mice and report cards, letters to Santa, silken infants' curls. One day Lexie would return for these mementoes. One day she would invite Doreen back into her life.

1959

53

Even thoughts of his innocent little girlfriend, Charlotte, who last night at the bar had tucked a pair of her clean panties into his pocket, weren't enough to distract young Bird from the hell that he was, thus far, surviving. He lay on the floorboard behind the passenger seat. Another KA pledge was curled beside him, and wedged between them was a squealing piglet.

Something poked the center of Bird's back. "Don't look up, Birddog," said Chet, the brother in the passenger seat. "If I see your eyes we'll pull over again. Reach a hand out and take what you're given."

What Bird brought to eye level was a half bottle of bourbon.

"That goddamn bottle should be empty by the time this car stops."

"Sir, yes sir!" Bird opened the bottle and bubbled it a few times.

"Give some to the pig, too. See if you can't shut it up."

Bird looked at the pig, only a few inches from his face. It was a young one, not quite as long as Bird's forearm. A rope around its neck ran to the front seat. The rope was so taut the pig's tiny cloven front hooves only brushed the floorboard. The pig screamed and clambered, but the rope kept it from grounding itself. Bird hurt for the creature but he knew that if he pled on its behalf Chet would release it to run again around the backseat. Bird already had gashes on his back and forearms from the shoat's hooves. He poured bourbon on the pig's head, hoping that if it smelled like alcohol, Chet would assume it had been given a drink. The pig squealed.

Chet popped Bird in the head. "Stop fingering the pig!"

Bird passed the bottle to his pledge brother, Duke. The bottle was taken from his hand.

The car hit a pothole and Bird's head struck the floorboard. He was too drunk to control his neck well, especially while folded into the floorboard of a car. Nobody rode on the backseat, but Bird knew better than to reposition. "Pledges and swine ride on the floor." That's what Chet had said.

The pig loosed its bowels inches from Bird's face.

Bird swallowed the vomit that rose in his throat. He would be punished for the pig's sins, he knew—he didn't want to be punished for his own as well.

"Is that shit?" Chet looked over the seat. "The pig shit on the floor! Scums, what did you do to my pig to make it shit the floor?"

"Sir, nothing, sir!" Duke was a pale, skinny kid from Mississippi. Like Bird, he was a fourth generation Kappa Alpha legacy. Great-grandfather, grandfather, father, not to mention various uncles and cousins.

"You think you're important enough to lie?" Chet, as the fraternity president and only other fourth generation legacy in the Gamma chapter of the Kappa Alpha Order, had taken it upon himself to personally haze Bird and Duke. The Kappa Alpha Order considered General Robert E. Lee its spiritual father and revered the ways of the old south: chivalry and courtship, gentlemanly manners. "That pig shit because you gave it liquor!" A fist struck the back of Bird's head. "Were you trying to get that pig drunk so you could have your way with it? Are you a swine fucker? Did you give that pig liquor, you ignorant farmhand?"

"Sir, no sir!"

"Didn't I tell you to give that pig liquor? You recalcitrant piece of single-minded scum! What will great granddaddy up in heaven think when he sees that three generations down the line, the Marxton men have lost what it takes to be a KA?"

As instructed to do each time the fraternal order was invoked, Bird and Duke burst into song: *In eighteen hundred and sixty-five at Washington and Lee, There was a band of soldier boys as brave as they could be!*

"Louder!"

They followed Lee and Jackson from the mountains to the bay, And they said we'll get together and we'll call ourselves KA!

The car slowed to a stop. "Y'all get out. Bring that drunk pig with you."

Once its rope went slack, the shoat collapsed into its waste.

Bird eased himself to the backseat. It was dusk and they were parked on a grassy floodplain beside a wide river. Other cars parked around them. From the back of each car emerged two or three pledges; each group held a leashed piglet. A small fire burned on the river's edge and a few brothers huddled close to it, warming themselves.

Duke joined Bird on the backseat. He bent his head between his legs and held the liquor bottle loosely between his knees. The shoat whimpered and Duke, not in jest, copied it. "Don't puke in the car," said Bird.

Duke sloshed the bottle he held. "We got to finish this."

Bird took the bottle from Duke. He lifted the panting pig from the floorboard, held it out his open door. Bird rinsed the beast clean with the liquor and then gave the pig to Duke. Bird's bare chest was slick with sweat and the phlegm of his future brothers; he stepped out of the car and rinsed himself with liquor, too. Duke rubbed his cheek against the pig's scalp. "I can't do it. I can't."

"It's hard at the beginning and it's hard at the end. The middle is all wine and women." This is what Nolin had told Bird about pledgeship anyway. Since accepting his bid, he'd not slept for more than two hours at a stretch. He was unsure when last he showered or ate something not forced on him: sticks of butter, lard cream cones. He emptied the last of the liquor on the ground. "Come on. Get out."

Duke obeyed. He was bare-chested too. Their hair was slick with mayonnaise. They stumbled to the place where their hoped-for friends circled the fire. A whitewashed wooden cross caught faint starlight through the trees. On either side of the sandy beach were two long wooden pews. They were at a church's baptismal site. Through his drunkenness, Bird felt new fear bloom. Sacred sites didn't tolerate disrespect. Lord Carnarvon, pillager of Tut's tomb, died from an infected mosquito bite. Bird learned that in history class. Lord Carnarvon's dog died too.

"For the Kappa Alpha man, the heart is always turned south." Chet stared into the fire as he spoke. "The mind is always turned south. The soul? The soul resides in the south. Tonight, gentlemen, we test your very souls. Your job is to find your way back to your soul. All you must do, gentlemen, is travel due south. Who can point due south?"

A heavy boy from coastal Georgia pointed to a certain star in the sky. "North." He turned to face the river. "South."

"Anyone not at the house by sunrise should consider themselves unworthy for KA. Anyone who returns without their traveling companion should consider themselves unworthy.

Anyone who returns without their pig should consider themselves unworthy. First pair back gets to ride horses to the Old South ball. The rest of you are in the mule cart. Best of luck, gentlemen." Chet walked toward his car. All who were inducted followed him.

"Bird," said Duke. "I think our pig's dead."

Bird took the pig and turned it to and fro. The pink head and legs fell limply. Its eyes were open. Duke didn't wipe at his tears. Bird needed to get back to the house with Duke and pig in tow. His parents had banished him to this particular hell. Where would he be hidden away if he failed at this as well? This was, he knew, his father's final offer.

Bird held the dead pig over his shoulders by its front legs. "He didn't say we had to bring it home alive, Duke. Stop crying and tie it to my back."

Duke guided the leash over Bird's chest.

If Bird survived this, then in three nights, on Saturday, he would don his rented Confederate uniform and go to pick up Charlotte from the wide front porch of the Chi O house. She would wear a hoop skit, and he would bow and kiss her hand, and together with their brothers and sisters they would parade through the streets of Athens, Georgia in their Confederate regalia, *look away, look away Dixieland, the South shall rise again.* Charlotte was a girl who'd been born to her silver pattern; she'd picked out the song for her first married dance at age twelve; she believed in Jesus and the sanctity of the wedding night. *If you keep me alive,* Bird promised God, *I'll ask her to marry me.* Wasn't this what God had wanted from him all along? To live as his father and his grandfather and his great-grandfather had lived before him? Not to cavort with sharecropper girls he met in abandoned houses.

Before him, the river seemed a warm and lazy oil-stream, but Bird knew it had currents and chill invisible. "Wrap that pig tight," Bird said. "Swimming never has been a strength of mine."

WEATHERING

Minerals are stable at the temperature and pressure in which they form. Olivine, for example, forms deep in the earth under crushing pressure and searing heat. Dunite, a rock composed of olivine, is a brilliant green color, gritty as granulated sugar, beautiful to see and to touch. Dunite is rarely found on the earth's surface though. Life in the cool, light air is hard on dunite. Impossible even. Freed from the terrible heat and pressure under which it forms, dunite can disintegrate rapidly. A piece placed on a windowsill may disintegrate in visible time, the chunk surrounded each morning by a few more salt-like grains until one day it sits in pieces, as if split by a ghost.

But ghosts are a fictive device. What cleaves that chunk of dunite is time. Not only the time that it rests on the windowsill visibly disappearing from the naked eye, but also the whole of time before it came to the surface of the earth. If the magma that formed deep in the earth and then pushed up through a crack to cool into dunite had risen a kilometer higher, it would have cooled at a lower temperature and a lower pressure. It might have formed a gabbro. A gabbro is not so green and grainy and beautiful as a dunite, but it will last a long time on a kitchen windowsill. It will certainly outlast the person who places it there.

This is not to say that the chunk of dunite is weak. Maybe the rest of the body it came from has crumbled to dust. Perhaps in that dunite's disintegration and cleaving what one witnesses are the death throes of the strongest survivor. Death throes are living too, until something truly is no longer.

2010

54

Jonathan bathed in a pool in the creek. He'd raked this depression clear of leaf decay and crawdaddy nests; he'd killed the moccasin that claimed the red clay bank. A fallen branch served as soap tray and clothes hook both. Jonathan grabbed the soap, rubbed it over his head. A water strider kicked by, tickling the hairs on his chest, but Jesus bugs didn't bother him none. Nor did the toe-nibbling minnows.

What bothered him, plagued him in fact, was something Faster had said to him not too long ago. "God wants to get to know you, son. That's all this is." Faster had said this as the two of them stood on the dirt road squinting at the McCormick ruin where Jonathan now made his squat. "When all a man's got left is what's between him and God, it strips him clean."

Jonathan scooped cool water in his hands and splashed his face, rinsed the soap from his hair. He didn't feel stripped clean; he felt enraged. He'd lost his wife and his kids, his house, his job, his truck, his mother. Even Faster he saw only when Tom the pirate was in town and they met to exchange crystals for cash. He depended on Luke to bring him food and water, whiskey and weed, to pick him up once a week to drive into the countryside and dig for amethysts. Another water strider kicked by and he snatched it from the surface, crushed it in his fist.

The hovel where he lived now was mostly collapsed, but his room had been reinforced by previous wanderers and vagrants. Plywood held up the walls. Stained towels covered the glassless windows. The ceiling plaster was mostly gone, but the massive beams held strong, each one once a whole tree. At night Jonathan gazed at those beams and considered how a body could dangle there. Six months—that was what he'd sworn to God: "You and me are supposed to be a team. I'm doing my part, the sweating and the suffering. Now you'd best do yours." Jonathan could talk to God like this now that nothing stood between them. Now that God was his intimate.

He unfurled his fist and let the carapace of the Jesus bug drift downstream.

55

One Saturday in late August, Doreen stood next in line at the new Walmart. Mercer's was no longer. The cashier was younger than Lexie, with dyed black hair and pitted white skin, toothpick arms. She took the WIC check from the woman in front of Doreen. This woman wore cut-off shorts that revealed a blurry thigh tattoo and around her wrist was a tether. At the end of the tether a little boy strained to touch the Hershey bars. "I saw him last week at Merle's," said the cashier. "He's still free."

Trash, thought Doreen.

"I don't know. We had it between us in high school, but that was twenty years ago." The woman with the tethered boy stepped forward.

Doreen put down the divider, added her cart's contents to the conveyor belt. The cashier double bagged two gallons of milk. "He'll be grateful," she said to her friend. "Glad you got your own. Own house. Own job." She rang up a box of cereal.

The tethered baby grabbed a candy bar and raised it in

glee. His mother yanked him to his bottom and slapped his hand, returned the candy to the shelf. He wailed. "You knew better than that." The little boy's mother raised her voice to be heard over her his wailing. "Take off that ground beef. It's getting high."

The baby quieted, and Doreen saw he'd stuck his wrist in his mouth.

His mother fiddled with her SNAPS card. Doreen hadn't seen both forms of assistance used at once, though Lexie had told her it was common enough. Decent people starved to death before taking government money. *Trash*. The woman with the tethered boy said, "I can't see going after a grown man living feral on the county edge."

"All I know," said the cashier, "is that Johnny Swilley? He still looks fine."

"Excuse me," Doreen said to the man in line behind her as she pushed past him, leaving her items on the belt, her cart in the lane.

56

The undercarriage of Doreen's Honda scraped as she eased into the front yard of the McCormick homestead. *Living feral on the county edge.* She parked, opened her door to a standing heat. Humidity bleached the sky white. She stepped out and the dry grass reached past her ankles. Doreen bent into the car and retrieved the small sack of shelf foods she'd found in her cabinets at home. A narrow footpath traced the way to the front door.

Clanging her bag to announce herself to snakes, she made slow progress toward the house. She paused at the steps to check her ankles for ticks, and then gentled herself up the decaying steps. From the front porch, she could see the field to the left of the house, turned up here and there by something she couldn't identify, boars maybe. Doreen beat on the front door.

She got no answer, but the silence was a waiting one, breathless. Doreen sensed Jonathan there on the other side of the door, holding still. She knocked again. She slammed her bag against the door, worrying as she did so that the cans would dent, the gift deliver botulism, death. "Jonathan Swilley, I know you're in there, son."

The front door cracked. She saw Jonathan's lips. "You don't want to come in here, Momma. There's nothing worth seeing."

"I've come to see you and there you stand. Let me in." His lips disappeared but there was no sound of his body leaving. Doreen held her ground. After some time, his fingers wrapped the door's edge. He pulled but the door didn't move much. "I go in and out through the side window," he said.

Doreen threw her weight against the door, shoved until there was a space wide enough for her step through. She stepped into the darkened hall and stood facing him.

"Come on in," he said.

She thrust the grocery bag toward him. "Brought you some Dinty Moore and Campbell's. Some peaches I put up last summer."

He took the bag, hung it over the useless knob. "Take that with you when you go. I live here so as not to be beholden." He turned into the house shadows. "Watch the floor and keep to the left. The right side's not sure."

Doreen followed close behind him, passing by the rubble of the stairway. They walked on floorboards laced with the white filament of rot, passed a hole big enough for a man to crawl through. At the end of the hall, Jonathan turned left into a room where the floor and walls were reinforced with plywood. Towels were hammered over the windows, and a whirring electric fan was plugged into an orange drop cord. More cords ran lengthwise and long and flashed like snakes in the television light. A muted television played in the corner. "Electricity?" said Doreen.

"From the street. Somebody before me stole it." Jonathan flopped onto a dirty brown loveseat. A girly magazine on the cushion beside him was open to the centerfold: naked, spread-eagled, shaved bare. Jonathan flipped the magazine closed and shoved it under the sofa cushion.

Doreen stared at the sofa cushion until Jonathan snatched the magazine out and threw it across the room.

She sat opposite Jonathan, but against the loveseat's other arm, committing as little of herself as possible. There was a fight on the television, the sound muted. Jonathan lifted the remote and changed it to a soap opera.

"Looks like you got all the channels," said Doreen.

"Satellite." He puffed up a little with this good thing.

"Who'd you steal that from?"

"If you came out here to ride my ass you can go home."

Doreen looked at the flashing orange cords and the fan. The room was stifling. She'd not come out here to harass him. "I have a new job."

"I heard."

"Started my own business." They stared at the silent TV. "Jonathan? Come on home with me. Sleep in your bedroom. Rest up. I can teach you how to do what I do, hire you once you catch on. You'll inherit the business after I'm gone. It's a good job, an easy job. You're inside at a desk all day."

Jonathan pointed to a stack of shoeboxes in the corner. "Crystals. Nicer than what I showed you at Christmas. Some of 'em I dug up by hand right outside that window. What you see here is me relaxing in my time off."

Doreen flicked an earwig from the sofa arm to the floor. "Stinking. Unbathed. Digging rocks for food."

Jonathan stood. Stretched. "What I got more of than you is time," he said. "Stay here long as you want. Move in for a while. But your job won't wait for you. That house of yours won't wait. You'll leave me be sooner or later." He left the living room and disappeared down the hall.

Doreen listened and tried to discern where he went, but there was no sound from the hall. The emotion in her body pushed into her throat, choking her. She couldn't release it. It began at the level of her belly as a broken, wailing grief, but by the time the grief reached her throat, it was anger. When it came to her child, grief and rage and love became one emotion, confused everything.

She went into the hall. Jonathan was a murky figure standing distant in the light from the forced-open front door. He appeared to wait for her.

She'd forgotten which side of the hall he deemed unsound. He didn't offer guidance and she refused to ask. She moved forward two feet. Three. Her foot went through the floor, and she pitched sideways, caught herself against the wall. Jonathan did not move. Doreen braced her free foot, braced her hands, twisted and turned her ankle trying to work herself loose.

"Jesus Christ, Momma. Why don't you go home?"

"Can't with a house on my foot." She dipped and tugged. Sweat dampened her face.

Jonathan came down the hall and stood behind her, hooked his elbows beneath her armpits. "Put your weight on me."

He was close enough to smell—stolen electricity and no running water. But he held her with such tenderness her shoulders slackened into his touch. Her head turned toward his chest. She heard his heart repeating, insisting, throwing blood all throughout his body. His body that she'd refused to chase out of her with herbs, his body that she'd known before it was even a part of the world. She forgot to twist and turn her ankle, forgot she was trapped. "I miss them too," she said.

Jonathan spooned Doreen with his torso and hips. He bent to press his unshaven face to hers. "But I bet you know where they are. Tell me, is my family in Georgia?"

She'd assumed that he'd found the same information as she,

had seen the same picture of the ranch house. She'd assumed that self-respect kept him from hunting them down. What kind of man showed up to his family in the shape he was in now? But she heard the fury and scheming in his voice and realized she was wrong. The knowledge she carried of their whereabouts terrified her. He might find some way to pluck it from her mind. She fought to rip her foot free. Her sneaker came off and fell into the unknown space beneath the house.

Jonathan's body was gone.

Doreen landed hard. Her teeth cut her tongue; her neck whipped; her hips slammed pain up her spine. She squeaked but did not cry out.

"Oh shit, Momma." Jonathan squatted before her. "I'm not very strong right now. Living this way." He peered into her face. "You okay?"

His cheekbones, his chin—these were sharp. But a softness had appeared with his hurting of her. Around the eyes, there at the lips. Doreen could see his softness. He hadn't wanted to hurt her, not really, but he didn't know this until after he'd done it. Only through remorse could he feel his own softness. "There's no fight between us," she said. "Nothing to win. You and me, we were both left."

"You should've gone with 'em. You should all be gone for good. That's what I wish for."

Doreen swung a hand to slap her son's face, but stopped. Her palm quivered near his cheek. He raised a hand to match hers.

"Hit me," she said.

"Kill me," he answered.

Doreen eased her hand from the air.

Jonathan rocked back on his heels. "It's just a rotten floorboard." He seized the plank and pulled until the wood snapped in two. He tossed aside the piece he held and then stood and offered his mother his hands.

"Don't drop me." She clutched his wrists.

He hefted her up and released her once she steadied. They looked down at her unshod foot, the line of bright blood on her white sock. They glanced into the place where her shoe had fallen. Doreen imagined them patting around in the cobwebby dark together, looking for one small thing of value. She turned away, sidestepped the hole.

This time, Jonathan guided her down the hall. At the front door, he slipped her shelf foods from the handle. "Take these."

"I won't eat them. They'll go to waste."

"I'll carry 'em out for you."

Doreen limped first onto the porch; Jonathan came out after. They shielded their eyes against the sun's glare. She looked at the dry red places overturned in the field. His work. No handouts, not even from her.

Jonathan put a hand on her back, pressed her forward. She went to the steps, and then down. He followed. They stopped on the last step. In front of them began the grass and the narrow footpath. Doreen put an arm around his waist. "Help me to my car. Don't make me get a bur in my foot."

Jonathan squatted and stood, lifting Doreen slightly. They hobbled three-legged into the yard, their awkward, twinned gait crushing the footpath wider as they crossed.

57

Some few hours after helping his mother to her car, Jonathan stood beneath a planted pine and watched Luke bend at the waist to vomit beside his truck. They were in the clearing behind the scrim of buffer trees off Lewis Loop, which is where they met up on digging nights so that Luke wouldn't have to drive the backhoe on its trailer down one more narrow, washboarded road. It was dark enough for the late summer night's full cacophony of frogs and cicadas. Jonathan lit a cigarette. "We should get going soon."

"I think I'm dying." Luke dry heaved. His face was ashen. "Lyme disease or Ebola or something. I didn't feel anything but tired when I left the house, but I feel that all the time."

Jonathan waved a hand toward the moon above them, close to full. "You can't be sick tonight." Moonlight was the best light for digging. The celestial shine caught crystal glimmers better than any manmade beam. "I can't afford to skip a week."

"It's not working, Johnny, you having nothing but the digging. You got to find something else."

Jonathan thought of his mother's offer of a bed, a shower, a new career. Luke would encourage him to take it, so he didn't tell him about it. "There's shit a man's got to have before he can even look for a job." Jonathan held his hand out for Luke's keys. "I'll dig by myself tonight. You can sleep in the passenger seat of the truck."

"Fuck no."

"You think I don't know how to handle a backhoe?"

"You're not messing with my real job, Johnny. Amanda's suspicious. She's asking questions. Who knows what she's heard."

"You drugged her tonight for no good reason, then."

Luke dry heaved again.

"At least let me take the CAT down to my house and turn over some dirt in that field where I been digging. Something I can go through later. You've seen what I've been finding by hand, who knows what's deeper under. I'll ride you down there and you can stretch out on my sofa while I'm working. Turn my fan so it blows right on your face. Rest your head on my pillow, watch my TV. I'll cut you in half on anything I find."

"You won't even cut me in a quarter."

"It's not about money, Luke. It's about giving me something to do with my days. If you teach a man to fish and all that."

Luke jerked at the restraints that held the backhoe on the trailer, loosening them. "One hour."

"No puking inside my house. You puke on my sofa, I'll make you lick it clean."

Well over an hour later, Jonathan flipped off the flashlights taped to his ballcap and sat in his field on the country club's idling backhoe, smoking a joint. He'd turned over half of the field by his house, and he'd driven back and forth through his front yard crushing the grass and weeds and brambles that previously he'd tunneled through like a rat. A bushhog would have cleaned things up better, but the property was improved, almost pretty beneath a moon that looked like it could tip out of the sky and crush him. The moon's light made the trees look painted onto the landscape, and in its shine Jonathan could read the single word some other indigent had spraypainted on the side of the McCormick house: *fuck*.

I'm sorry, I'm sorry, I'm sorry, thought Jonathan. *I love you.*

He shifted the machine forward and pulled it parallel to his window. "Luke! Luke!"

A hand pushed aside the sheet.

"Night's finished!"

Luke crawled out of the window, dropped to the concrete blocks stacked there as an entry aide, stepped to the ground. He paused with a hand to his head before walking an unstraight path to the backhoe.

Jonathan pulled him up. Luke half crouched behind the seat, held onto the ROPS for support. "Puke on the couch?" said Jonathan

"Naw, man. No guarantee I won't puke down your back on the way out though."

Jonathan shifted into gear and trundled across the yard. They bumped over all that Jonathan had flattened. The safer route was left—they didn't have to drive by the Marxton place then—but the quicker route was right. Jonathan didn't want to get puked on. He turned right onto the dirt road. The moon blinked through the dark of the trees.

Luke shouted over the engine, "Something ran over my legs while I was on your couch. It's not healthy, the way you're living. You gotta get your ass on assistance. Situations like this is why it exists."

Jonathan shifted into third. He hated the things in his house too, the spiders, the snakes, the goddamn rats. But each time he thought of welfare, he either sent his eyes up to that body-supporting beam, or he sent his mind out to his wife, tucked away somewhere in fine financial standing, in possession of a roof, a refrigerator, municipal water, and his kids. One of these things he deserved. Which one was something as yet unresolved between him and God.

The Marxton security light danced like a will-o-the-wisp through the dark. Luke said, "Last week Bird Marxton ate waffles with my boys. Amanda was working third shift, so I took the boys over to your momma's on my way to work. Bird's the one greeted me at the door."

The Marxton place was on their right now, all that the McCormick place was not. Roofed, painted, paned, of a piece. The field of bait corn was a verdant sea. "She's a grown woman," said Jonathan.

"Ryland said he called 'em champ. 'You want another waffle, champ?'"

Jonathan wrenched the wheel to the right and bumped into Bird Marxton's yard. He drove into the green sea and laid down a path.

"Amanda won't let the boys go over there anymore," said Luke. "She says the last person our kids need to be friendly with is Bird Marxton."

At the end of the field, Jonathan turned and took another pass through the thriving corn. It was illegal to bait the damn doves anyway. Build them a McDonald's and then kill them when they came to eat.

Luke said, "I think he's a right sonofabitch myself."

Later, Jonathan would wonder what took Bird so long to appear. Surely he'd heard the backhoe driving down the road on the way to the McCormick place, heard it working through the night. Seen it, maybe, through a window, even before it turned into his field. But it wasn't until Jonathan and Luke reached the end of the second row that Bird ran into the yard in pajama bottoms and a bathrobe, his gray hair mussed from bed. He leapt about where his yard met the corn.

"Is he wearing a robe?" said Luke.

"Guess he put it on to chase us out of the field," said Jonathan.

"Do another row."

Jonathan turned in the yard while Bird Marxton ran alongside them, shouting and beating on the backhoe's metal flanks. The only words Jonathan could make out were his own name. "Johnny Swilley! Johnny Swilley!"

Jonathan said to Luke, "He don't seem to remember you, champ." He drove onward, knocking down a fresh row of corn.

Luke pointed. "Rock."

The rock wasn't quite large enough to stick above the corn, but it was big enough to cause a problem if they hit it. Jonathan swerved around it.

Luke looked behind them. "He's limping away. We better go, Johnny."

Jonathan turned again at the end of the field. "I'm crushing it all." He trundled forward in high gear. It was a small stand of corn and he'd flattened half the crop.

A different man ran out the back door and into the yard.

"Is that Will Marxton?" said Luke.

"Looks like."

Will Marxton didn't give chase, but stood on the yard's edge and waved his arms in big, desperate movements as a cheerleader might.

"He don't have half the balls his daddy does." Jonathan drove straight for Will, who started running and didn't stop until he'd scrambled onto the porch. Jonathan took some pleasure in this. He'd never had a shot at Will before, not once in all their boyhood, and Lord knows he'd had reason what with the things Will's daddy did to his mother. But Will had spent his life in private school so as to be protected from the general likes of the county. Jonathan idled near the porch while Luke issued jeers. Will continued his cheer moves and begged them to go away.

Jonathan turned again toward the corn. As he entered that wall of green, a blast rang out. Shot twanged the backhoe, pinged their exposed necks and the tender backs of their arms. Jonathan slapped at the places he'd been hit.

"They're trying to kill us." Luke crouched in the small space where the seat swiveled.

"It's just doveshot."

Luke assessed the situation. "Will's trying to make his daddy stop. They're fighting over the gun. Now's a good time to leave, Johnny."

Jonathan drove toward the centerfield rock. Bird fired a second round and then a third.

"He's got the plug pulled, Johnny. We don't know how many rounds he's got or what he's packing after the shot. Might have a slug lined up next." Luke curled into his few inches of floorboard.

Jonathan scrunched in his seat and lowered the bucket. He dug in so deep he had to fight the machine to lift the bucket into the air. The bucket held soil, that centerfield rock, and a slim green line of corn that fluttered like a girl's eyelashes over the bucket's edge. The rock slipped from the top of the bucket and slammed onto the ground, crushing more corn. Jonathan kept the bucket high, held onto the Marxton soil, turned the backhoe right to cut across the field. Bird ran toward them with his shotgun at his shoulder, stumbling fast through the crushed corn, Will slipping and jumping after him. Bird skipped sideways so that he had a clear side shot.

He paused, fired.

The shot was at closer range over open space. Luke had tucked himself to the right of Jonathan, but Jonathan took the hit directly. He screeched, let go of the wheel to slap at his arm, his thigh, his cheek.

"Just doveshot, right Johnny?"

"Fuck you." Jonathan grabbed the wheel again, went as fast as he dared.

Bird ran away from them and crashed through the woods toward the road.

"Wiley sonofabitch," said Luke. "He's trying to cut us off. You're gonna have to go the other way."

But Jonathan turned onto the road to face Bird. The man stood in the middle of the road before them, shotgun at shoulder level.

"Fucking Swilley," said Luke. "I'm getting off this thing."

Jonathan grabbed Luke's wrist in his hand and sped forward, soil spilling from his raised loader bucket.

"They'll put us away if we kill him!" Luke fought to get his wrist free. "Don't hit him, Johnny!"

Jonathan didn't even have the chance to try. Suddenly Bird was flying through the air. He landed near the far ditch, side tackled by his own son. The shotgun had flown from his hands. Will scrambled up, grabbed the weapon, ran for the house.

Jonathan passed Bird, raining him with soil. He let go of Luke's wrist. Luke held onto the ROPS and leaned out to dry heave.

An unnatural howling pierced the backhoe's racket. Jonathan quickened his pace. The sound continued.

"You better have a look," said Luke.

Jonathan turned. Ten yards back, Bird Marxton stood weaponless, his chest spread to the sky, his throat exposed to the man-crushing moon. With his whole being he sounded an ungodly ululation.

Jonathan turned forward again, silenced, trembling. Behind him, Luke was the same.

Jonathan sucked at the place on his arm where he'd been hit at close range. He spit over the side of the backhoe.

"No question but that's unsanitary." Luke's voice was shaky. "You gotta dig the pellets out. Careful like. With tweezers and alcohol."

58

By the time Luke and Jonathan secured the ratchet straps that held the backhoe, dawn threatened in the east. The stolen soil sat in a pile between the buffer hardwoods and the timber company's planted pines.

"I'll take you to your momma's," said Luke. "You're safest there."

"My money's back in that house," said Jonathan. "The crystals I've dug. My clothes. Everything I own, what little that may be."

"Come back for it tomorrow. Or next week sometime. Let your momma bring you back here. Bird won't do nothing to her."

Jonathan considered being taken into the McCormick house by his mother. "I'm not using my mother as a shield."

"Grounds crew shows up in half an hour." Luke kept a hand on his truck for support as he made his way to the driver's door. "I don't have time to beg you. I'm looking at being found out. Bird's a member in good standing at Green Hills."

Jonathan raised a hand. "I'll see you around then."

"Get in the goddamn truck, Johnny."

"Get to work before you get in trouble."

Luke stepped into the cab. "Last chance."

Jonathan took the cigarette from behind his ear.

Luke started the truck, drove away so slowly Jonathan knew he was hoping he'd chase him down. Jonathan stood and smoked and watched until he could no longer hear the tickle of Luke's engine, until he knew Luke could no longer spy him in the rearview. He didn't know what might happen today with Bird Marxton. He wanted to make sure that Luke's last sighting was of him cool and unworried, smoking a cigarette in the rising dawn.

The first morning bird peeped from the trees. *Last man standing ain't always the nicest,* thought Jonathan, a line from a song and little comfort since Bird was still living. Jonathan turned and kicked Marxton's fucking clayball, started to break it up, see what he could find.

The first thing he found was her left hand.

Jonathan recognized it immediately as a hand, a bunch of finger bones laid out just like finger bones, the chips slipping whitely down to his feet. Dead soldier, he thought at first, a Yankee killed and hid away by Marxton women. Original Marxton, he thought next, the first one to cross the sea and claim a spot, that simple stone grave marker honored all through the generations in story and in agriculture, not moved from the field even when early Marxton bellies hungered for grain. Booty, he thought, and plunder. Historical bits and pieces to sell to Tom the pirate. Civil War relics. Some pilgrim's rough leather shoe.

The sun was only half above the horizon. Jonathan flipped on his headlights. He collected the bones he'd found and lay them out in the flat of the small clearing. Then he bent to his most careful scraping and brushing in the Marxton clayball, a slow moving of dirt, teaspoon by teaspoon. In this way, he unearthed the wrist bones. The long, slim arm bones. The collarbone. Each new discovery he lay in the clearing as a scientist does a dinosaur.

He found scraps and twists of material, all of it too thin and finely woven for a soldier or a pilgrim, all of it stained the same color as the earth.

The sun rose in the sky. August's heat descended.

When he was finished, what he'd found was a pitiful thing. He'd done his best with the bones, even the spongy, porous ones and the white flecks skinnier than a snake's spine. It was the hair that told him he'd found a woman. Even in death her hair was a thing of wonder, at least a yard of it colored dirt-red, same as the remnants of the shroud that once wrapped her. Jonathan took off his t-shirt and draped it over his find. The shirt collapsed into her hollows, nothing but cotton slump where breasts and hips and a good soft belly used to be. Jonathan knew, just as he knew that little crystals atop the ground meant big ones under, that these remains were the reason for Bird's caterwauling. Jonathan had gotten everything but her legs. The legs, he figured, were still in the cornfield.

The sun bore down through breaks in the pine boughs. Jonathn sat beside the girl, lit a cigarette. For all of his remembered life, his mother had been involved with Bird Marxton. He'd always known who the man was. When Jonathan first met Lexie, she'd said, "Johnny fucking Swilley," and he'd said, "Lexie fucking Hart"—they'd never met but they sure as hell weren't strangers. Luke had said earlier that Amanda was hearing rumors of their night work. Each time Jonathan went on the run, his mother only had to open her ears to find him. This was the sort of town he'd thought he lived in. This was the way he'd believed the world to be.

Yet Jonathan had never heard mention of this secret he'd unearthed. This secret that belonged to the man his mother loved.

He couldn't imagine that his mother knew of this. Whatever her faults, she wasn't a woman who would stay with a man who hid a woman's body in the ground. Unless the story she'd been told of it was woven so tightly, so cleverly, that she was left no gap to imagine the remains Jonathan smoked beside now. No gap to think on what a human body reduced to without embalming chemicals and a casket. Almost nothing, that was the answer. This woman was nearly gone.

Jonathan realized that the world was so vast there could only be a pretending at human transparency. Only lies of understanding.

What could be known of any single person on this planet— truly known—was infinitesimal. Jonathan himself was minute. Less than a puff of air. He would disappear.

Everyone, inevitably, disappears.

Disappearance is what he'd thought he threatened God with at night when he lay looking at the ceiling beams, but that was a threat he issued against himself. There was no white robed babysitter. No heaven or hell. No perfect playground waiting on the other side of a cloud, filled with family and friends.

What waited was his own blinkout. This blinkout might be the single irreducible truth of human existence. Jonathan began gathering the girl's bones into his t-shirt. Her decayed shroud he left in its miserable pile on the ground. His cigarette burned down and he ground it out, lit another. Took the skull in his hand and wrapped all that hair around and around it like padding.

Here he was holding proof of the great blinkout, life's only transparency, yet he found it impossible to comprehend. Mortality could be glimpsed but in dots and flashes, was too much to hold for longer than a breath. A clear, bright, high, steady terror—that's how it felt. A screaming mirror that gave birth to universes. Even if the only reason to stay alive was to avoid this horror, that was reason enough. Jonathan pulled his cigarette to the filter.

He tied all the bones into a misshapen hobo's sack. Nothing mattered, not for this girl, not for him. Yet he couldn't leave her here, exposed in a clearing. In discovering her, he'd pulled her back from eternity's maw in some small way; he was all she had now.

And she'd delivered him unto himself.

There was nothing special about Flyshoals, nothing special about the life he'd created, nothing special about the life he'd lost. Nothing special about any life, really. The thing to do was to stop his hiding and hoarding, his boasting and pretending, stop imagining himself capable of being tomorrow someone he plainly was not today. All of that was over. He'd find Lexie. That was what he'd try first. She might have him back, or she might not. His children might love him, or they might not. He might spend his life living with his mother and working alongside her, or he might not. His heart might melt in his chest from the pain of his own existence. But if he didn't get out of these woods, what this bag of bones had of life would be all that he had too. A secrecy, a hiding, a decay. What a waste of so brief a miracle, to live as if already dead.

59

Jonathan hid in the trees for a long time, cradling the girl's bones and watching the McCormick house. He was unsure how long he'd spent in digging and arranging, in thinking on what these bones meant, but he knew it was long enough for Bird Marxton to have walked down the dirt road and found a place to ambush him.

Jonathan needed his money, but not for the reasons he'd previously thought. Not for self-worth. He needed his money because he owed it to his wife and children to let them decide, first, if they wanted to try a life with this new him. This post-bones him. This him capable of so much gratitude. And he couldn't find Lexie on his own; he'd tried to look her up on Luke's phone. He would have to pay a private eye. But if he found her and she told him no, he would leave her in peace, no questions asked. He'd terrorized his family. That shit had to stop.

Jonathan touched his cheek where it was scabbed from dove load. Bird had shot at him in a robe, while Will danced like a spirit girl. Out of a whole cornfield, he'd scooped up the few square feet housing a human skeleton.

Fuck it.

He left the woods and started toward his house, walking through the grass that he'd laid down the night before. As he grew closer, he heard Bird and Will talking inside, their voices in a normal range. "You're keeping us here so long," said Bird, "we won't get to fish today at all."

"Dad, there are more important things than fishing. Stop fiddling with the remote. We're not here to watch Johnny's TV."

"Look at this place. His mother would be horrified if she knew he was living this way."

"I'm sure he's doing the best he can. Most people do. Nobody would choose to live like this."

Of course he'd chosen this, thought Jonathan. It wasn't what he'd planned for, but how many people's lives go according to plan? He stepped onto his concrete blocks, moved aside the towel and tossed the bones in their t-shirt hobo sack into the middle of the room. They clacked like bamboo when they landed.

Bird leapt from the loveseat, shrieked once. Will remained seated, but found Jonathan's face at the window. "There's nothing to be afraid of, Johnny. We wanted to make sure you're not hurt. Dad's come to apologize." Will's eyes were as scared as a doe's.

Jonathan crawled through the window. The room was sweltering; they'd not even turned on the fucking fan. He pulled off his ball cap with the flashlights taped to the sides, tossed it onto the sofa arm next to Will. Bird stared at the bundle in the center of the floor.

Jonathan went to the bundle. Straddled it.

"Dad?" said Will.

Jonathan held up a hand. "Let me go first. I'm sorry I crushed your corn last night. Sorry I dug your field up too. I had no idea what I was getting myself into, that's for goddamn sure."

Jonathan hadn't spoken to Bird since he was a teenager. "You're probably the only person on earth who knows how sorry I am about last night, Bird. In fact, I hope to God you're the only person on earth who knows how sorry I am." He tapped the bones with one foot for emphasis. "I hope my mother has no idea."

Bird's eyes weakened. All the privilege leaked from his face. Standing now before Jonathan, he could have been any passing vagrant. "Not even your own mother could imagine how sorry you must feel right now, Johnny. I promise you that."

Jonathan had to wipe his eyes. He hadn't realized how afraid he'd been that his mother knew. That she'd known for years.

"It happened so fast," said Bird. He spoke to the small and lumpy bundle. "The years went by—they seemed slow while I was living them, but it's fast thinking back on them. I planned to get her one day. I meant to do right by her. It was an accident, Johnny. What happened was an accident that I've had to live with my whole life. Nobody was at fault."

Will leaned forward and rested his elbows on his knees, his face in his hands. "You should have left us, Dad. Mom told me about your affair with Doreen Swilley before I was old enough to know what an affair was. I grew up knowing it was a different family you wanted. Him for a son. Her for a wife."

Jonathan locked eyes with Bird as he worked to understand why Will said what he did. He slowly realized that Will thought Bird spoke of his mother when he said that nobody had been at fault, that he'd meant to get her one day. "It's not my mother we're talking about, buddy," Jonathan said, surprised to hear his own voice go thin and mean. He'd not thought himself capable of sounding that way after his realization by the bones. "Let me fill you in on a few truths about your daddy." Jonathan picked up the bundle.

"I found Lexie," said Bird.

Jonathan pulled the bundle to his chest.

"We can trade." Bird took a piece of paper from his pocket. "This is her address."

"Bullshit."

Bird took his phone from his pocket and tapped on the screen. He passed the device to Jonathan. There was Lexie's name and a street address. According to the screen, she lived in some town called Snellville. She was still in Georgia.

"Who is Lexie?" said Will.

"My wife," said Jonathan.

Bird said, "Let me work this out with Johnny, Will. This doesn't involve you." Bird went to Jonathan's side. "That's the state licensure site you're looking at. You can look up anybody who has a license with the state. I sent flowers to all of Charlotte's nurses after she died, that's how I know about it."

Jonathan had his electrician's license, but he hadn't realized he was listed on a website like this, for all to see. "I Googled her. She never came up."

"You have to go to the site directly. As a safety measure."

Jonathan compared the slip of paper to the screen. The information was the same. He handed Bird the phone and the bundle of bones.

Bird stuck the phone in his pocket. The bones he held with one hand at some distance from his body.

"What's in that package, Dad?" said Will. "Somebody needs to explain what's happening."

Jonathan didn't want to spoil things now that he had Lexie's address. He crossed to his stacked shoeboxes, took the top one. "What's in there are the rocks I stole from your daddy last night. Here's one for you, from my own field." He took the box to Will, dropped it in his lap. "I was supposed to pay your daddy to dig his land and I didn't. I been stealing from him. That's why he shot at me. Sorry about that Bird."

"Don't let it worry you, Johnny."

Will lifted the lid. He took out the rock and let it sit in his palm, sparkling. "I guess you felt like he owed you something, Johnny. Some inheritance. Growing up, did he bring you fishing out here? Buy you Christmas presents? I'd like to know what your life has been like now that I'm a grown man. Now that Mom is dead."

The three men formed a loose triangle. Jonathan looked at Lexie's address written in Bird's old-fashioned script, thought of his mother working for Bird all of those years with no knowledge of the body in his cornfield. He thought of the body in the cornfield rotting away to something that could be tied up in a t-shirt. The man wasn't a father to anyone. But if Jonathan told Will what Bird actually was—a liar, a murderer—his own progress home would be halted. "Damn straight," said Jonathan. "Your father's been like my own father to me. Hunting, fishing. Last thing I'll ask of you—Dad—is a ride to the bus station."

Will looked so pitiful that Jonathan almost took back his words. Hadn't Will saved his life last night? He'd never done anything to Jonathan personally except be himself. But instead of making amends with Will, Jonathan grinned at Bird. "Cat got your tongue, Dad? Want me to speak for you?"

"I'll give you a ride, Johnny."

Jonathan went to the corner of the room and lifted away a piece of wallboard. He pulled out his plastic wrapped stacks of money, stuck them in a plastic grocery sack. He picked up a t-shirt from the floor, smelled it, pulled it on. "Gentlemen? Shall we go?" He went to the window and yanked off the towel.

Will left the crystal sitting on the sofa. "I don't think anyone should pick up a gun against another person, Dad." He half-crawled out the window and paused as he felt around with his feet for the step. "I brought him here to apologize to you, Johnny." Will found his footing, dropped out of sight. He called up from the ground outside. "Last night, you almost killed a man you've loved like a son." Will's voice caught on the word son, but he forged on. "Leigh and I will not keep a weapon in our home. And we aren't comfortable leaving our daughter in the care of a man who keeps weapons in his. Especially one who handles them like you do."

Jonathan was close enough to Bird to see the papery texture of the man's neck. Bird had located the skull in the mess Jonathan had given him, and he held it with two hands, as if tender cheeks were still attached. The rest of the bones hung weighty at the bottom of the sack. "I was so scared when it happened." His voice was low enough to stay inside the McCormick ruin. "She had a small life, Johnny. I'm one of only five or six people who missed her. You can't imagine nowadays how small a life could be back then."

Jonathan matched his voice to Bird's. "Five or six people means four or five of them spent their lives not knowing what happened to her. Thinking terrible things. It was you made them feel that, old man. For their whole fucking lives."

Bird pressed Marla's skull in its stained cloth against his own face.

"I got everything but her legs. Her legs are still in your bait field." Jonathan crawled out the window.

60

Bird sat in his truck in the parking lot of the tiny Flyshoals bus depot, watching the bus that held Jonathan idle in the bay. It was to depart for Athens in seven minutes. Bird needed to see that bus pull away, needed to know for sure that Jonathan did not get off and circle back toward town with some scheme. Will waited at the farm—Bird had asked him to stay behind, claiming he needed time alone with Jonathan. Had he allowed Will to ride along, Jonathan may have revealed what was hidden in the sack, and Will would have insisted, with his typical self-righteous earnestness, that his father go directly to the police and confess.

Bird reached to the passenger seat, picked up Marla, set her in his lap. He was going to do the right thing, eventually. He'd started writing his own letter, his own version of events. One day, Bird would die and Will would go through Bird's house, and he'd open a file folder labeled "Remains," and he'd find his father's full confession. He could then pursue justice in any way he wanted.

As for Marla's actual remains—Bird wasn't sure what to do

with those. He hated to put what he had of her back in the field. He also knew he would never loosen the t-shirt that held her. And he would never go after her legs. He rubbed the curved tip of a bone through the cloth.

It was a wrong thing he'd done, handing Lexie's address over to Jonathan. He knew the girl had fled her husband for good reason—Doreen herself had hinted as much. Bird hadn't even told Doreen where her daughter-in-law was, and he'd known for a long time. He checked the licensing site after the girl left, and at first he didn't find her there. This had worried him, and he'd kept checking back. He took her eventual appearance as a sign that her life was working out well. It was from this moral high ground that he'd not told Doreen—he'd told himself he was protecting Lexie somehow. Protecting her as he had failed to protect so many other women. Marla, Charlotte, Doreen.

The bus to Athens pulled from the bay

Bird kept a hand on Marla's skull while he rang Doreen at work.

"Swilley Insurance," she answered.

"Reenie. I've done a bad thing. A really bad thing." Bird thought as he spoke, concocting a story. The only thing Doreen needed to understand immediately was that her son was heading toward her daughter-in-law. And maybe she needed to know that it was Bird who had set him on that path. Jonathan would tell Doreen that much himself after all, as soon as she tracked him down and got him back under control.

1976

61

From the hall of his office, Bird watched the Swilley girl, the abortionist's daughter, grown now into a young woman. She sat on the couch in the waiting area, reading a book to the boy child at her side. She wore a medicine bag necklace that looked like the very one Marla had thrown at her mother's feet. "Once there was a little bunny who wanted to," she read.

"Run away!" said the boy.

Bird knew from his secretary, Mrs. Oakes, that the girl had a right to be there: she'd come to collect her mother's life insurance policy. It was a policy her mother had bought through his father, a policy that predated Bird's affair with Marla. But the Swilley girl wore Marla's necklace, and Bird carried the memory of her mother's broad hands strengthening him to stand as she told him that her medicine hadn't worked. Blackmail was what came to mind. This girl's mother may have told her on her deathbed to wear the necklace when she came to see him. But blackmail for what? What could she want?

"So he said to his mother," read the Swilley girl.

"I run away!" said the boy.

Bird reminded himself that this girl's mother, Lucille Swilley, could not possibly have known what happened to Marla after they left her house. Nobody knew, except for him, his father and his uncle. And Herman, the home's caretaker. Herman knew something. They'd sent Herman to town on an errand while they did what had to be done, but of course he'd come back to a flattened stand of corn and a plot of disrupted earth with a boulder in its center. He seemed to accept their lie, that this was the newest way to attract deer, but when Herman passed away a few years later, he refused to allow Bird, Nolin, or Bird's father to come into his hospital room and tell him good-bye.

"If you," read the girl.

"Run away!" said the boy.

No news of Marla's disappearance ever reached Flyshoals— Bird knew, he'd scoured the local paper for months afterwards. She'd been new to Walthersville and poor, married to an old man, given to wandering nights. What was known was that she'd taken a bus from Walthersville to Flyshoals and then failed to meet her cousin in Waycross. Even standing here now, watching the abortionist's daughter read to her son, it sounded to Emmy like Marla had escaped with a young lover. He hoped that was what Cherlow believed. It was such a better story than the truth.

"I will run after you. For you are my little bunny," read the Swilley girl. She pulled the boy to her and kissed the top of his head.

Bird felt Mrs. Oakes watching him from behind her wooden desk. His father hired Mrs. Oakes after Bird left for college, and left her with him once he retired. Bird suspected the woman of reporting to his father, letting the old man know his every misstep. "Miss Swilley," said Bird.

The girl on the couch stood, pulling the boy to stand alongside her. She didn't look nearly so young standing. Her eyes were level with Bird's, and he considered himself a tall man. She didn't smile at him as women usually did, but watched him with curiosity and caution, as an animal might.

Bird stuck out his hand, "Bird Marxton. Your son knows that book well."

"Doreen Swilley." She turned the book to show the cover. *The Runaway Bunny.* "My mother got it for him when we moved home. I've read it so many times he has it memorized."

"You have to keep an eye on the smart ones."

"My mother said the same."

Bird motioned toward his office. "Shall we? Mrs. Oakes will be happy to watch your son while we talk."

Mrs. Oakes was heading toward the sofa with a lollipop in hand, her fusty shoes squeaking as she walked.

"Please, call me Bird," Bird said as they settled into his office. He sat in the chair behind his desk, and the Swilley girl—she seemed a full woman to him now—sat opposite him.

"Call me Doreen."

The blinds were open, letting in the afternoon sun. A woman in a pink bell-bottomed pantsuit hurried along the sidewalk. Doreen picked up the bag around her neck and rubbed it, making the clicking noise he remembered all too clearly. Bird said, "I met you once. Long ago. Do you remember?"

"No sir."

"Of course not." Bird opened the manila folder on his desk. "You couldn't have been much older than your son is now." He pulled out a piece of paper and put an X beside a blank line, slid the paper across the desk to Doreen. "I didn't realize your mother was a client of ours. She worked with my father. It was a long time ago that she and I knew one another."

"My mother knew a lot of people." Doreen signed and returned the paper. "But she rarely spoke of them. She never mentioned you."

Bird had the next paper ready. "How old is your son?"

"Three." She signed again.

"And your husband? What does he do?"

"You know my name is Swilley, same as my mother's." Through the office door, Bird heard the child laughing with Mrs. Oakes. "Jonathan is a Swilley too." She returned the paper.

A stupid misstep. The necklace had him flustered. He'd seen similar necklaces a lot on women in the past six years or so, knew it to be a style, but sitting in front of Doreen Swilley while such a necklace hung around her neck was more than coincidence, he was certain. "You're young to be motherless. That's what I should have said. Young to be here collecting a life insurance policy. My own mother passed a few years back. It's not something you ever get over. I'm sorry for your loss."

"Thank you."

They sat for a moment in the shared silence of acknowledged grief.

Bird had a final paper to be signed, but he didn't push it across the desk yet. Instead, he stood and closed the blinds on his windows, turned his office shadowy and cool, made it a secret place. Bird returned to his chair. "I apologize if this is forward. May I see your necklace?"

Doreen looked confused, but she slipped the necklace off anyway, passed it across the desk. Bird opened the pouch, stuck a finger inside. He pulled out a little stone and a twist of metal. So these were the things that made that clacking noise. All these years he'd wondered.

"I got it when I lived in Florida," said Doreen. "I drove all the way to the very tip of the state one night, and I stopped near an

Indian reservation. Seminole. I bought it in a gift shop down there. It's not real. The same place sold plastic arrowheads. But the paper that came with it said it would bring me luck."

Bird thought she must be lying. He returned the stone and the twist of metal to the pouch, cinched it closed. "It looks exactly like a necklace that belonged to someone I used to know. Someone who also knew your mother."

Doreen closed her eyes for a moment. "Mr. Marxton."

"Bird."

"Bird. Some of my mother's work required great delicacy. Secrecy, even. I swear I know nothing about you. I also want you to know that I don't do the same work my mother did. I'm looking for work as a secretary. That's what I trained to do in high school."

So that was why she'd come here wearing this necklace—she wanted a job. Lucille Swilley hadn't acknowledged him the few times he'd passed her in town, but that didn't change Bird's feeling that she somehow knew what had befallen Marla. He rubbed the necklace in his fingers, heard the sound, felt again as if he were standing on the dark McCormick stairs with Marla behind him, her feet illuminated in a tiny round flashlight spot. "You can type?"

"Sixty words a minute."

"You know shorthand?"

"I completed all of my secretarial courses before. Before I had my son."

"You have your high school degree?"

"Of course."

Bird opened the pen drawer on his desk and dropped the necklace inside. "You let me keep this necklace, and I'll retire Mrs. Oakes and hire you. I was planning on letting her go anyway. You can start in a month." He slid the final piece of paper across the desk.

Doreen paused briefly before signing the paper. She stood

and stuck out her hand. "A month."

Bird sealed the deal.

She smiled then, the first time she'd directed such a look at him. He liked her face, liked how changed it was by every emotion she felt. "I guess that necklace did bring me some luck." She laughed, and Bird laughed with her. "I really can't thank you enough, Mr. Marxton. Bird. Now if you'll excuse me, I better get back to my son."

2010

62

"Jonathan's going to get there before us," said Doreen. She sat in the passenger seat while Janice drove. They'd left within forty-five minutes of Bird's call, but she felt as if days had passed.

"That bus stops in every little town." Janice blew smoke out the window. "Bird didn't have anything else to give you? Lexie's phone number? Where she works?"

"He only had what was on the website. What I already knew."

"You didn't tell me you knew that."

"Why would I tell you? She didn't want to be found." Doreen cracked her car window against Janice's cigarette smoke. When Bird had called, he'd told her that he and Will had gone hunting, and that they'd wandered beyond the boundaries of their own property until they found themselves on McCormick land. "I'd not seen the inside of the house since I was a teenager, so Will and I went in. We didn't know Jonathan was living there, Reenie. I thought he'd left town. We went into the room he's living in, and I guess we startled him. He got aggressive, demanded money. Shook Will by his collar. I didn't have my wallet on me. So I took out my cellphone and gave Johnny the only thing I had that I could think he might want."

Doreen could believe that Bird and Will went inside the McCormick house, and she could believe that Jonathan rattled Will by the collar. But she knew damn well that Jonathan hadn't demanded cash from Bird Marxton. Yesterday she'd offered her son shelter and career, and he'd turned her away. He'd even refused her tinned soup.

Bird's lie was a problem for another day. Right now Doreen was focused on reaching her daughter-in-law's house before her son got there. Doreen wanted to be the one to open the door when Jonathan knocked. She'd not forgotten the way he'd dropped her in the hallway of the McCormick ruin, hadn't forgotten that it wasn't until after he'd hurt her that he realized he didn't want to hurt her at all. The order on such things was backward in his mind. Today, Doreen planned to be the changed lock that stood between her son and her grandchildren. Whatever it was that she rushed toward was a long time coming.

63

Jonathan reached Athens and instead of buying another bus ticket, he hired a taxi. It didn't matter, really, if he showed up with no money in his palm. Lexie was either going to sense the ways he'd changed and ask him back or she was not. How he looked, how he smelled, what he had—these things weren't a part of it and never had been. He understood that now. There were depths to her that he hadn't appreciated. Somehow, he'd married a woman alive to the world. The dreadlocked taxi driver who carted Jonathan to Snellville had talismans hanging from his rearview mirror that clicked like the dead girl's bones, and his car smelled of new car air freshener. He drove and drove, and eventually cow fields gave way to buildings and cars, both of which thickened exponentially each mile closer Jonathan drew to his wife.

In the white noise of the taxi, Jonathan ruminated on the events of the past several hours, and discovered he was a pretty good guy. Foremost among the things he'd never done was kill a woman and hide her remains on a piece of country property. But he'd also never cheated on his wife, or become a secret drunk, or drugged a woman just so he could work a job she wouldn't like. He'd never toted around a shrunken human ear dubiously obtained, or hung his personal hopes and dreams on a mite-sized boy too myopic to tote them. He'd never shot at people because they crushed his corn. He'd never taken on employees he couldn't support and then set them loose and hungry in the world as soon as the good times ended. And even as low as he'd fallen of late, he'd never taken a handout, and he'd never fucking begged.

Not that Jonathan considered himself infallible. Or even better than most of the people he knew. What he realized during his long taxi ride was that if you took any man other than Jesus Christ himself, any double-human man, and looked close, what you'd see is failure.

This understanding set up a softness in his chest.

Jonathan leaned between the two front seats. "What's the worst thing you've ever done?"

Most of the taxi driver's dreads were wrapped tall on his head in a length of printed cloth. "What are you implying?"

"Nothing. I just want to know. Me, the worst thing I've ever done is punch my kid in the face. Although once, I trashed my own house. Broke a window out, wrote on the walls, broke half the shit we owned."

"My country has a lot of violence. That's why I moved here."

"So have you killed somebody? I talked with a man this morning who killed somebody. A woman. Killed her so long ago she's nothing but bones. He hid her in a cornfield and I'm the one who dug her up. Total accident."

"You like music?" The taxi driver turned on the radio.

Jonathan raised his voice. "If I hadn't dug her up, I'd never feel all this love now. That's what's in my chest, man. Love. Tenderness. All that shit. 'Yea, though I walk through the valley of death.' I get it."

"Hold onto that." The taxi driver changed the radio station, found a Lynyrd Skynyrd song. He turned the radio up louder. "Here's a song guys like you like."

"The thing is," shouted Jonathan, "we're all going to die. There's no escaping it. I learned that from that girl I dug up. All of this stuff we do, it's not real. We have to keep our expectations low. We have to be grateful. All this softness right here." Jonathan used both palms to massage his chest. "That's what you have to keep. If you don't, you'll hit your kid in the face or trash your own home. Maybe kill somebody."

64

In the examining room, Lexie peered into a baby's eyes. "Conjunctivitis. Pink eye. Nothing to worry about."

The mother was young and Hispanic. "Pink eye?"

"*No es una problema.*" Lexie had been learning Spanish by CD at night.

The door opened. Todd, one of the other nurses, came in. "Juliette's on the phone. I can take over here."

Lexie patted the mother's arm and left the examining room. Juliette didn't call the office often, only if something big happened in her life during the course of the day—a great grade, a new friend. Nobody minded. The conversations were short and even Lexie could see that accommodations needed to be made for her family. Her children were so shy, so polite: yes ma'am; no sir. She saw how they smiled and agreed with strangers. And Lexie herself— she didn't get half of the jokes made around the office, and she felt acutely her own inability to jump into conversations. She felt sometimes as if she and her children were an immigrant family, new to America and trying to learn the local ways, though Georgia was their native state. She'd moved them only a few hours away.

Lexie smiled at Linda, the receptionist. Through the window the day looked impossibly hot, white sky, limp trees. She put the phone to her ear. "Hey, Jules. How was school?"

"Dad's here. He was on the front porch when we got home. Now we're all in the living room. Me and Thomas and Dad."

Jonathan's voice came on the phone. "Hey babe. It's great, all you've done. This house. Your job."

Lexie sat in a child-sized plastic chair. Everything felt loose— her arm where it connected to her body, her tongue where it rooted in her mouth, her eyes where they settled in her head. Nothing fit, everything was too big—her body, the world. She couldn't grow large enough to occupy the demands of this man. "Let me talk to Juliette."

"I'll take them for ice cream. They said you get home about 5:30. I'll take them for ice cream, and then when you get home we'll all go for dinner."

Lexie couldn't hear her children in the background. She imagined them bound, gagged. Reciprocal kidnapping. "Let me talk to Juliette."

"I've had a hell of a time, Lex. You can't imagine."

"Johnny, I'm going to call you back on my cell. Wait by the phone." Lexie hung up and turned to Linda. "I need to run home. There's an emergency."

"Is someone hurt?"

Should she ask Linda to call the police? That seemed the sort of request that might cost her job. Lexie smiled. "No. There's just something I need to sort out." She went to the break room at the end of the hall and got her purse from the cubby, pulled out her cellphone, dialed her home number.

Jonathan answered. "Baby?"

"Johnny. I need to speak to Juliette."

"First let me tell you a story. Last year, after I left you, I met this little preacher in the woods. Guy couldn't have been over five three, and he had this kid he wanted to be a Nascar racer." There were no sounds of television on the other end, no sounds of dishes slamming around, no sounds of squabbling. There was only the sound of Jonathan talking. Talking.

Lexie made it to the parking lot. She started her car. "Let me talk to Juliette."

"Now this little preacher, he was a secret drunk. But he also had this side business digging gemstones."

Lexie pulled into the road, started toward her house. She lived close, ten minutes with no traffic.

"Came a point where I had to choose between Faster and Powell, between amethysts and rock dust. Shouldn't be too hard to figure what I chose."

"Johnny! Let me talk to Juliette."

Jonathan didn't pause. "But here's the problem with digging those amethysts: there's things to be found underground besides rocks. A skeleton is what I dug up in Bird Marxton's cornfield. The skeleton of a woman he himself killed and hid."

None of the sounds that should've been behind Jonathan in the house were there. Here it was, the reason for the fear that had jerked her from sleep since before she left Flyshoals. Her husband had found her and he'd done something to the children. "Let me talk to Juliette."

Jonathan kept talking. He told her how crystals formed. He talked about go-karts and a fish-smelling trailer. He talked about bones and backhoes and birdshot. Nothing he said hung together. Nothing he said made any sense. No longer did he carry even the single narrative she'd come to expect from him: the tale of his desperate, obsessive need for her.

Lexie pulled into her driveway. Her front door was closed. Jonathan explained over the phone why the loss of their home wasn't important because no double-human man was anything but a failure when you got right down to it. He told her that he forgave her for pawning his tools. He talked so fast Lexie couldn't understand some of his words.

"Let me talk to Juliette."

"The only important thing in the world is a soft heart, and—if you're goddamn lucky enough, thank you, Jesus—someone to share your soft heart with. That's why I came here first, Lexie Swilley. To you, my wife. To give you the chance to share in this thing I've found."

Lexie took Johnny's pistol out of her glove compartment, switched off the safety and got out of her car. She walked across her yard with the gun at her side. She made no efforts to hide the pistol because she'd learned from Amanda that a woman must be decided when she pulls her weapon. Small women, like Lexie, were easily overpowered. An overpowered woman might have her weapon used against her. Or against her children. Into her phone, Lexie said words to keep Jonathan predictable: "I love you, too. I've missed you too. A family isn't a family without a father. Thank God you found us. We've been so lost."

Lexie clicked the hammer, rotating the chamber past the empty barrel to the waiting hollowpoint.

There was overpenetration to consider. She'd have to locate the children when she stepped through her door. She did not want to shoot through Jonathan and kill her kids.

At her door, she slipped her phone in her scrubs and turned the knob with her left hand. She stepped into her living room. Jonathan stood before her. He wore a dirty t-shirt and dirty jeans and his stench filled the room. One side of his unshaven face and one arm were red and scabbed, as if he'd scratched his own skin away. *Meth*, she thought.

She located her children—huddled together to her right, at the far end of the sofa. Not bound, not gagged, but terrified.

Jonathan was talking, talking, never fucking quiet. He came toward her, arms spread wide. "I don't have a weapon. You don't need one either, baby. It's all about reunion, celebration. Come here and let me hold you against my soft chest. I'm born again. I stand before you now as a man you haven't seen before."

Lexie inhaled as she raised her arm and cupped her right palm with her left; exhaled as she lowered her chin to sight along her arm; fired in the pause.

It was the second ring of the target she hit, upper right quadrant. The heart.

Jonathan's mouth opened, but he stopped speaking. The noise of his fall was loud, and then the only sound was a soft bubbling coming from somewhere deep in his body and the shushing of his arms and legs on the carpet as he tried, for a heartbeat, to crawl away from fate.

Lexie bent and set the gun at his feet. His eyes were open, but when she went to the couch where her children huddled, his gaze did not follow her. Thomas and Juliette pressed themselves against her. She could barely hold them for their shaking.

"Go and take showers," she told them. "Put on clean clothes and give me your things to wash." Everything was soiled. The whole house was ruined now and forever would be, no matter what was remodeled, no matter who lived here next.

The children continued to cling to her.

"Go now!" she said.

Thomas hugged the walls as he stumbled out of the living room, staying as far from his father's body as was possible. When he hit the hallway, he ran. He ran into the bathroom he shared with Juliette, slammed the door behind him.

"What are we going to do?" Juliette said to Lexie.

Lexie grabbed her daughter's face. "Not we. Me. I did this. Now go take a shower in my bedroom. I don't want to tell you again."

Juliette hugged the walls as Thomas had while she left the living room, but at the hallway she stopped. She turned and looked at her father's body for several long seconds. Then she walked to her mother's bedroom.

Once the bedroom door closed behind Juliette, Lexie went to Jonathan's body, knelt at his feet.

Blood seeped out from beneath him, though the wound and the stain on his front were small. His face looked startled.

She had to call the police.

Once she called the police, her children would no longer be her own.

Jonathan said, "You claim to do it all for the kids but what's going to happen to them now? Foster children. That's what you've raised. Orphans. Wards of the state." He spoke to her but his mouth did not move. "Don't worry. I won't let you go to prison by yourself, Lex. I'll follow you there. Get us a girlfriend. We can still grow old together. I'll never leave you. No matter what."

"Mom?" Juliette stood at the end of the hall wrapped in a towel, her hair dripping down her back. There was no way the girl had done more than stand in the water long enough to get wet. Lexie went to her, guided her into her bathroom, picked up a wide toothed comb and gently brushed out her tangles as she hadn't done in years. She brushed until the tangles were gone, and then she kept brushing, brushed until Juliette's hair was as straight as a roadway, brushed until the comb left furrows, brushed until Thomas joined them in the bathroom in his clean clothes and frightened eyes.

"Momma?" he said. "I took a shower."

Lexie had to place her children before she called the police. She pulled her cellphone from her scrubs.

Jonathan's corpse screamed from the living room. "You should've listened! I was talking to you about murder. About sin. About how to be a lesser failed human. I was telling you what you needed to know! You should've listened, Lex."

Lexie dialed her mother-in-law.

65

Doreen answered the unknown number from the unknown area code.

"Doreen, it's me. Johnny's here."

"I'm almost there. Ten minutes tops."

They hung up without further explanations, without good-byes. It felt normal to both of them for Lexie to call in need and for Doreen to be on her way, even after months of silence. This is the way their lives had happened.

"Jonathan got there first," Doreen said to Janice.

66

Janice parked her blue Monte Carlo in Lexie's driveway. Doreen looked through the windshield before she got out. The house was cuter in person that it had been on Google Earth, with a decent front porch and a protecting oak.

Janice met Doreen on the far side of the car and hooked an arm through hers. They walked together toward the front door as they once walked together toward church. It was noisier in this place where Lexie now lived than it was in Flyshoals. Traffic, hammering, a leaf blower, a child laughing. A police siren. Janice squeezed Doreen's arm.

Lexie had finally called, as she'd promised to do one day. Jonathan had forced her hand, but she'd done it. Doreen was ready to return the manila envelopes stuffed with Santa letters and report cards, silken infants' curls. She wanted to come every weekend to this little house and help her daughter-in-law with grocery shopping, with childcare. It wasn't easy being a young single mother—Doreen remembered that.

Arm in arm, Janice and Doreen mounted the porch. Though the world around them was loud—the hammering matched now by a nailgun, the wailing siren growing ever closer—there were no sounds coming from inside the house. No shouts, no tears. It seemed to Doreen as if here, on this welcome mat in front of Lexie's new front door, time gelled, became a substance that held her in gentle suspension.

A fragment of memory surfaced: Jonathan in her lap when he was a toddler.

If you, she read.

Run away! he shouted.

I will run after you, for you are my little bunny.

He'd so loved that book. The memory passed as quickly as it had come, and time lost its viscous quality, and the siren grew close enough to drown out all other sounds, and Doreen pressed the doorbell.

ACKNOWLEDGEMENTS

A big thank you to those who first helped me find my way into this novel: Lynne Sharon Schwartz, Askold Melnyczuk, Douglas Bauer, and Alice Mattison.

Dr. John Hiers and Joy Pope-Alandete, thank you for reading that tedious early draft and offering such helpful feedback.

Thank you to Stephen Corey and *The Georgia Review* for publishing a different version of chapter 56.

Carmen Toussaint, thank you for your friendship. Rivendell Writers' Colony lives on in my heart.

Rick Tilson, thank you for touring me through the concrete plant and sharing the details of the very worst thing you've ever had to do as part of your job.

Dr. Chester Karwoski, thank you for answering every question I had about digging for amethysts near Jackson Crossroads.

Travis Tallant, Eddie Tallant, and Rick Saxon, my go-to sources for all questions of construction and destruction, thank you for helping me get the details right.

Jody Owenby, thank you for talking to me for hours one evening about insurance.

Alice Mattison, an extra thank you for your continued faith and support. In particular, I appreciate you asking me about this book every year or two until I finished it. Those emails meant so much.

Thank you to Paula McLain, Brian Groh and AWP for this opportunity.

Thank you to Kimberly Kolbe and everyone at New Issues Poetry & Prose for all of the attention and love you showed to this book.

Endless gratitude to the wise and patient humans of my writing groups, past and present: Marilyn Zion, Jean Hey, Mary Carroll Moore, Jody Forrester, Reid Jensen, Anna Schachner, and Joshilyn Jackson. You're the ones who keep me going—and keep me honest.

Grant Eager, thank you for two decades plus of inspired field geology lessons.

Pi Eager, thank you for helping me laugh at myself.

Grant and Pi, if it's true that we come to this earth with a purpose, you two are mine.

After thanking so many experts in their fields, I must emphasize that all errors in this novel are wholly my own. Especially my failures to laugh at myself.

Photo by Nicole Tyler

Ginger Eager grew up in Snellville, Georgia in a hardworking family that valued kith and kin. Ginger's reviews, essays, and short stories have appeared in *The Chattahoochee Review, Bellevue Literary Review, The Georgia Review, West Branch* and elsewhere. She lives in Decatur, Georgia, with her husband and their college-aged son.

A portion of the proceeds of *The Nature of Remains* will be donated to Circle of Love, a shelter for victims of domestic abuse in Greensboro, Georgia.